THE LANGUAGE
OF BEES

Laurie R. King

BANTAM BOOKS

THE LANGUAGE OF BEES

A Mary Russell Novel

THE LANGUAGE OF BEES
A Bantam Book / May 2009

Published by
Bantam Dell
A Division of Random House, Inc.
New York, New York

Book design by Robert Bull
Map illustration by Jeffrey L. Ward

Bantam Books is a registered trademark of Random House, Inc., and the
colophon is a trademark of Random House, Inc.

Library of Congress Cataloging-in-Publication Data

King, Laurie R.
The language of bees : a Mary Russell novel / Laurie R. King.
p. cm.
ISBN 978-0-553-80454-6 — ISBN 978-0-553-90646-2 (ebook)
1. Russell, Mary (Fictitious character)—Fiction. 2. Women private
investigators—England—Fiction. 3. Holmes, Sherlock (Fictitious
character)—Fiction. I. Title.
PS3561.I4813L36 2009
813'.54—dc22
2009004039

Printed in the United States of America
Published simultaneously in Canada

www.bantamdell.com

BVG 10 9 8 7 6 5 4 3

For Lynn and Robert
on whose backs this book was written

Atlantic Ocean

North Sea

Orkney Islands

RING OF BRODGAR □ ● Kirkwall
STONES OF STENNESS

● Thurso

● Inverness

SCOTLAND

● Edinburgh

------- HADRIAN'S WALL

LONG MEG AND □
HER DAUGHTERS □— HIGH BRIDESTONES

York ●

IRELAND

ENGLAND

Oxford ● London ●
LONG MAN
STONEHENGE OF WILMINGTON
□
CERNE ABBAS GIANT □
Portsmouth ● ● Eastbourne
(Sussex)

English Channel

0 Miles   100   200
0 Kilometers   200

FRANCE

© 2009 Jeffrey L. Ward

ONE

SUSSEX

August 1924

Chapter One

*First Birth (1): The boy came into being on a night
of celestial alignment, when a comet travelled the
firmament and the sky threw forth a million
shooting stars to herald his arrival.*
Testimony, I:1

AS HOMECOMINGS GO, IT WAS NOT AUSPICIOUS.
The train was late.

Portsmouth sweltered under a fitful breeze.

Sherlock Holmes paced up and down, smoking one cigarette after another, his already bleak mood growing darker by the minute.

I sat, sinuses swollen with the dregs of a summer cold I'd picked up in New York, trying to ignore my partner's mood and my own headache.

Patrick, my farm manager, had come to meet the ship with the post, the day's newspapers, and a beaming face; in no time at all the smile was gone, the letters and papers hastily thrust into my hands, and he had vanished to, he claimed, see what the delay was about.

Welcome home.

Just as it seemed Holmes was about to fling his coat to the side and set off for home on foot, whistles blew, doors clattered, and the train roused itself from torpor. We boarded, flinging our compartment's windows as far open as they would go. Patrick cast a wary glance at Holmes and claimed an acquaintance in the third-class carriage. We removed as many of our outer garments as propriety would allow, and I tore away the first pages of the newspaper to construct a fan, cooling myself with the announcements and the agony column. Holmes slumped into the seat and reached for his cigarette case yet again.

I recognised the symptoms, although I was puzzled as to the cause. Granted, an uneventful week in New York followed by long days at sea—none of our fellow passengers having been thoughtful enough to bleed to death in the captain's cabin, drop down dead of a mysterious poison, or vanish over the rails—might cause a man like Holmes to chafe at inactivity, nonetheless, one might imagine that a sea voyage wouldn't be altogether a burden after seven hard-pressed months abroad.* And in any case, we were now headed for home, where his bees, his newspapers, and the home he had created twenty years before awaited him. One might expect a degree of satisfaction, even anticipation; instead, the man was all gloom and cigarettes.

I had been married to him for long enough that I did not even consider addressing the conundrum then and there, but said merely, "Holmes, if you don't slow down on that tobacco, your lungs will turn to leather. And mine. Would you prefer the papers, or the post?" I held out the newspaper, which I had already skimmed while we were waiting, and took the first item on the other stack, a picture post-card from Dr Watson showing a village square in Portugal. To my surprise, Holmes reached past the proffered newspaper and snatched the pile of letters from my lap.

Another oddity. In the normal course of events, Holmes was much attached to the daily news—several dailies, in fact, when he could get them. Over the previous months, he had found it so frustrating to be

* The events of those months may be found in *The Game, Locked Rooms,* and *The Art of Detection.*

days, even weeks in arrears of current events (current English events, that is) that one day in northern India, when confronted with a three-week-old *Times,* he had sworn in disgust and flung the thing onto the fire, declaring, "I scarcely leave England before the criminal classes swarm like cockroaches. I cannot bear to hear of their antics."

Since then he had stuck to local papers and refused all offers of those from London—or, on the rare occasions he had succumbed to their siren call, he had perused the headlines with the tight-screwed features of a man palpating a wound: fearing the worst but unable to keep his fingers from the injury. Frankly, I had been astonished back in Portsmouth when he hadn't ripped that day's *Times* out of Patrick's hand.

Now, he dug his way into the post like a tunnelling badger, tossing out behind him the occasional remark and snippet of information. Trying to prise conversation out of Sherlock Holmes when he had his teeth into a project would be akin to tapping said preoccupied badger on the shoulder, so I took out my handkerchief and used it, and addressed myself first to the uninspiring view, then to the unread sections of the papers.

Some minutes passed, then: "Mycroft has no news," my partner and husband grumbled, allowing the single sheet of his brother's ornate calligraphy to drift onto the upholstery beside him.

"Is he well?" I asked.

My only reply was the ripping open of the next envelope. On reflection, I decided that the letter would not say if its writer was well or not: True, Mycroft had been very ill the previous winter, but even if he were at death's door, the only reason he would mention the fact in a letter would be if some urgent piece of business made his impending demise a piece of information he thought we needed.

Holmes read; I read. He dropped the next letter, a considerably thicker one, on top of Mycroft's, and said in a high and irritated voice, "Mrs Hudson spends three pages lamenting that she will not be at home to greet us, two pages giving quite unnecessary details of her friend Mrs Turner's illness that requires her to remain in Surrey, two more pages reassuring us that her young assistant Lulu is more than capable, and then in the final paragraph deigns to mention that one of my hives is going mad."

" 'Going mad'? What does that mean?"

He gave an eloquent lift of the fingers to indicate that her information was as substantial as the air above, and returned to the post. Now, though, his interest sharpened. He studied the next envelope closely, then held it to his nose, drawing in a deep and appreciative breath.

Some wives might have cast a suspicious eye at the fond expression that came over his features. I went back to my newspapers.

The train rattled, hot wind blew in the window, voices rose and fell from the next compartment, but around us, the silence grew thick with the press of words unsaid and problems unfaced. The two surviving aeroplanes from the American world flight were still in Reykjavík, I noted. And a conference on German war reparations would begin in London during the week-end. There had been another raid on Bright Young Things (including some lesser royals) at a country house gathering where cocaine flowed. Ah—but here was an appropriate interruption to the heavy silence: I read aloud the latest turn in the Leopold and Loeb sentence hearing, two young men who had murdered a boy to alleviate tedium, and to prove they could.

Holmes turned a page.

A few minutes later, I tried again. "Here's a letter to *The Times* concerning a Druid suicide at Stonehenge—or, no, there was a suicide somewhere else, and a small riot at Stonehenge. Interesting: I hadn't realised the Druids had staged a return. I wonder what the Archbishop of Canterbury has to say on the matter?"

He might have been deaf.

I shot a glance at the letter that so engrossed him, but did not recognise either the cream stock or the pinched, antique writing.

I set down the newspaper long enough to read first Mrs Hudson's letter, which I had to admit was more tantalising than informative, then Mycroft's brief missive, but when I reached their end, Holmes was still frowning at the lengthy epistle from his unknown correspondent. Kicking myself for failing to bring a sufficient number of books from New York, I resumed *The Times* where, for lack of unread Druidical Letters to the Editor, or Dispatches from Reykjavík, or even News from Northumberland, I was driven to a survey of the adverts: Debenhams' sketches delivered the gloomy verdict that I would need my skirt lengths adjusted again; Thomas Cook offered me educational cruises to Egypt, Berlin, and an upcoming solar eclipse; the Morris Motors adverts reminded me that it was high time to think about a new motor-car; and the London Pavilion offered me a Technicolor cowboy adventure called *Wanderer in the Wasteland*.

"They are swarming," Holmes said.

I looked up from the newsprint to stare first at him, then at the thick document in his hand.

"Who— Ah," I said, struck by enlightenment, or at least, memory. "The bees."

He cocked an eyebrow at me. "You asked what it meant, that the hive had gone mad. It is swarming. The one beside the burial mound in the far field," he added.

"That letter is from your beekeeper friend," I suggested.

By way of response, he handed me the letter.

The cramped writing and the motion of the train combined with the arcane terminology to render the pages somewhat less illuminating than the personal adverts in the paper. Over the years I had become tolerably familiar with the language of keeping bees, and had even from time to time lent an extra pair of arms to some procedure or other, but this writer's interests, and expertise, were far beyond mine. And my nose was too stuffy to detect any odour of honey rising from the pages.

When I had reached its end, I asked, "How does swarming qualify as madness?"

"You read his letter," he said.

"I read the words."

"What did you not—"

"Holmes, just tell me."

"The hive is casting swarms, repeatedly. Under normal circumstances, a hive's swarming indicates prosperity, a sign that it can well afford to lose half its population, but in this case, the hive is hemorrhaging bees. He has cleared the nearby ground, checked for parasites and pests, added a super, even shifted the hive a short distance. The part where he talks about *'tinnitusque cie et Matris quate cymbala circum'*? He wanted to warn me that he's hung a couple of bells nearby, that being what Virgil recommends to induce swarms back into a hive."

"Desperate measures."

"He does sound a touch embarrassed. And I cannot picture him standing over the hive 'clashing Our Lady's cymbals,' which is Virgil's next prescription."

"You've had swarms before." When bees swarm—following a restless queen to freedom—it depletes the population of workers. As Holmes had said, this was no problem early in the season, since they left behind their honey and the next generation of pupae. However, I could see that doing so time and again would be another matter.

"The last swarm went due north, and ended up attempting to take over an active hive in the vicar's garden."

That, I had to agree, was peculiar: Outright theft was pathological behaviour among bees.

"The combination is extraordinary. Perhaps the colony has some sort of parasite, driving them to madness?" he mused.

"What can you do?" I asked, although I still thought it odd that he should find the behaviour of his insects more engrossing than dead Druids or the evil acts of spoilt young men. Even the drugs problem should have caught his attention—that seemed to have increased since the previous summer, I reflected: How long before Holmes was pulled into that problem once again?

"I may have to kill them," he declared, folding away the letter.

"Holmes, that seems a trifle extreme," I protested, and only when he gave me a curious look did I recall that we were talking about bees, not Young Things or religious crackpots.

"You could be right," he said, and went back to his reading.

I returned to *The Times,* my eye caught again by the farmer's letter demanding that a guard be mounted on Stonehenge at next year's solstice, so as to avoid either riots or the threat of a dramatic suicide. I shook my head and turned the page: When it came to communal behaviour, there were many kinds of madness.

Chapter Two

*First Birth (2): The boy's mother knew the meteor to be
an omen when, at the very height of her birth pangs, one
of the celestial celebrants plummeted to earth in a stripe of
flame that hit the pond with a crash and a billow of steam.
It was still hot, after hours in the water.*

Testimony, I:1

WE HAD LEFT OUR HOME ON THE SUSSEX COAST-
land one freezing, snow-clotted morning back in January,
to return on a high summer afternoon when the green-gold countryside was as full and fragrant as a ripe peach in the palm of one's
hand.

I was pleased that we had caught the Seaford train rather than the
one to Eastbourne. This meant that, instead of motoring through an
endless terrain of seaside villas and sunburnt holiday-makers, we
quickly shook off the town to cross the meandering tidal reaches of
the Cuckmere, then threw ourselves at the steep hill onto the Downs.

Sussex had always enchanted me, the mix of sea and pasture, open
downland giving way to dark forest, the placid face of beach resorts
cheek by jowl with the blood-drenched site of the Norman conquest.

Daily, one encountered history protruding into modern life like boulders from the soil: Any foundation dug here was apt to encounter a Bronze Age tool or a Neolithic skeleton; ancient monuments dotted the hillsides, requiring ploughs and road-builders to move around them; place-names and phrases in the local dialect bore Medieval, Norse, Roman, Saxon roots. In this land, in the hearts of its people, the past was the present: It did not take much imagination to envision a local shepherd in winter—bearded and cloaked beneath his wide hat, leaning on a crook—as Woden, the one-eyed Norse god who disguised himself as a wanderer.

The motor that had coughed and struggled its way up the hill now seemed to sigh as it entered the tree-lined downgrade towards East Dean. Holmes shifted and reached for his cigarette case, and the abrupt motion, coming when it did, suddenly brought the answer to Holmes' mood as clearly as if he had spoken aloud: He felt Sussex closing in over his head.

Sussex was his chosen retreat from the press of London, the rural home in which he could write and conduct experiments and meditate on his bees yet still venture out for the occasional investigation; now, after seven busy months in free flight across the globe, it had become small, dull, tedious, and claustrophobic.

Sussex was now a trap.

I had forgot for the moment that Mrs Hudson would not be there to greet us, but when Patrick pulled into the freshly gravelled circle in front of the house and shut off the engine, the front door remained closed.

Holmes climbed down from the car before its noise had died. He tossed his coat across the sun-dial and dropped his hat on top, then set off in shirt-sleeves and city shoes, heading in the direction of the far field near the burial mound.

Patrick was well used to my husband's eccentricities, and merely asked me if I wanted the trunks upstairs.

"Thank you," I told him.

The front door opened then, to reveal Mrs Hudson's helper Lulu, pink and bustling and spilling over with words.

"Ma'am, how good it is to see you, to be sure, Mrs Hudson will be so vexed that she couldn't be here, and I hope you don't mind, but yesterday night a gentleman—"

The sudden appearance of a person who was not the one I wished to see, and a sudden unwillingness to immerse myself in the busy turmoil of homecoming, had me adding my own coat and gloves to the impromptu hat-stand and following in Holmes' wake, out onto the rolling expanse of the South Downs.

Once clear of the flint wall around the gardens, I could see him ahead of me, striding fast. I did not hurry. It mattered not in the least if I caught up with him before he turned back for home, which he would do soon—even a hive infected with madness was bound to shut down with dusk. I merely walked, breathing in the air of the place that, for nine years, had been my home.

My headache faded, and before long my sinuses relaxed enough that I could smell the sea, half a mile away, mingling with rich traces of hay recently cut. I heard the raucous complaint of a gull, then the lowing of a cow—no doubt Daisy, belonging to the next farmer but one, prized because she bore a healthy calf every year like clockwork and gave the creamiest milk that a bowl of porridge had ever known. The rattle of a motor-cycle followed the roadway between Eastbourne and Seaford; five minutes later, the evening train from London whistled as it drew near Eastbourne.

I caught sight of a head of white clover being worked over by a late bee, and I watched until the busy creature flew off—in the direction of the orchard behind me, not towards the madness of the far field. I bent down to pick the flower, and as I walked, I plucked its tendrils, sucking out each infinitesimal trace of nectar.

It was a perfect summer's evening in the south of England, and I dawdled. I meandered. Had I not been wearing the formal skirts and stockings of travel, I might have flopped back onto the cropped grass and counted the wisps of cloud.

India was spectacular and Japan was exquisite and California was a part of my bones, but God, I loved this country.

I found Holmes squatting beside the hive, shirt-sleeves rolled to his elbows. At a distance I was concerned that he would come away with a thousand stings, but closer up, I could hear the absence of the deep, working hum of a summer hive. The white Langstroth box was silent, its landing-board empty, and when he lifted the top of the hive, no cloud of winged fury boiled up from within. The only sound was the light jingle of the bells his friend had hung there.

I hoisted myself onto the wall, taking care not to knock stones loose, and waited for him to finish. The nearby burial mound was small enough to have remained undisturbed for four millennia, escaping even the attentions of the ever-curious Victorians. It cast its late afternoon shadow along the ground to the base of the wall. Raising my gaze to the south, I could make out the line carved by six thousand years of feet treading the cliff-side chalk soil; beyond it, the Channel had gone grey with the lowering sun.

Suddenly, the odour of honey was heavy in the air as Holmes began to prise up the frames of the super. Each was laden with dark, neatly sealed hexagons of comb, representing hundreds of millions of trips flown to and from the hive from nectar-bearing flowers. Abandoned now, with not a bee in sight.

More than that, we could not see, although I knew that come morning, Holmes would be out here again, hunting for a clue to the hive's catastrophe. Now, he allowed the frames to fall back into place, and replaced the top.

As I have said, I care not overmuch for *Apis mellifera,* but even I held a moment of silent mourning over the desolate rectangular box.

"Dratted creatures," Holmes grumbled.

I had to laugh as I jumped down from my perch. "Oh, Holmes, admit it: You relish the mystery."

"I wonder if I can get a message to Miranker this evening?" he mused. "He might be able to come at first light." He shot the white box an irked glance, then turned back across the Downs towards home. I fell in beside him, grateful that the moody silence between us had loosed its hold a degree.

"Was that who wrote you the letter?" The signature had been less than precise.

"Glen Miranker, yes. He retired and moved here last summer. He's a valuable resource."

To tell the truth, I'd never been able to pin down why Holmes found bees so fascinating. Whenever I'd asked, he would say only that they had much to teach him. About what, other than a flagellant's acceptance of occasional pain and perpetual frustration, I did not know.

As we walked, he mused about bees—bees, with the sub-topic of death. Alexander the Great's honey-filled coffin, preserving the conqueror's body during the long journey back to Alexandria. The honey rituals of *The Iliad* and *The Rig Veda*. The Greek belief that bees communicated with the beings of the underworld. The use of honey in treating suppurating wounds and skin ulcers. An ancient folk custom called "telling the bees," when a dead beekeeper's family whispered to the hives of their master's death. The infamous poison honey that decimated Xenophon's army—

After a mile of this, I'd had enough of the macabre aspects of the golden substance, and decided to throw him a distraction. "I wonder if Brother Adam might not have some suggestion as to your hive?"

The reminder of the dotty German beekeeper of Dartmoor's Buckfast Abbey cheered Holmes somewhat, and we left behind the shadow-filled hive to speak of easier things. When we reached the walled orchard adjoining the house, the sun was settling itself against the horizon, a relief to our dazzled eyes. The hives here were reassuringly loud as a thousand wings laboured to expel the day's heat and moisture, taking the hoarded nectar a step closer to the consistency of honey.

I watched Holmes make a circuit of the boxes, bending an ear to each one before moving on. How many times over the years had I seen him do that?

The first time was on the day we had met. Holmes and I first encountered each other in the spring of 1915, when I was a raw, bitterly unhappy adolescent and he a frustrated, ageing detective with little aim in life. From this unlikely pairing had sprung an instant communication of kindred spirits. He brought me here that same day, making the rounds of his bees before settling me on the stone terrace and offering me a glass of honey wine. Offering, too, the precious gift of friendship.

Nine years later, I was a different person, and yet recent events in California had brought an uncomfortable resurgence of that prickly and uncertain younger self.

Time, I told myself: healing takes time.

When he returned to where I was standing, I took a breath and said, "Holmes, we don't have to remain in Sussex, if you would rather be elsewhere."

He lifted his chin to study the colours beginning to paint the sky. "Where would I rather be?" he said, but to my relief, there was no sharpness in his question, no bitter edge.

"I don't know. But simply because you have chosen to live here for the past twenty years doesn't require that we stay."

After a minute, I felt more than saw him nod.

Communication is such a complex mechanism, I reflected as we rounded the low terrace wall: A statement that, at another time or in a different intonation, would have set alight his smouldering ill temper had instead magically restored companionship. I was smiling as my feet sought out the steps—then I nearly toppled down them backwards after walking smack into Holmes.

He had stopped dead, staring at the figure that stood in the centre of our terrace, half-illuminated by the setting sun.

A tall, thin man in his thirties with a trimmed beard and long, unruly hair, dressed in worn corduroy trousers and a shapeless canvas jacket over a linen shirt and bright orange cravat: a Bohemian. I might have imagined a faint aroma of turpentine, but the colour beneath the fingernails playing along the gaudy silk defined him as a painter rather than one of Bohemia's poets, playwrights, or musicians. The ring on his finger, heavy worked gold, looked positively incongruous.

I felt a spasm of fury, that whatever this stranger wanted of us couldn't have waited until morning. He didn't even look like a client—why on earth had Lulu let him in?

I stepped up beside Holmes and prepared to blast this importunate artist off our terrace and, with luck, out of our lives. But as I cast a rueful glance at the man by my side, the expression on his face made my words die unsaid: a sudden bloom of wonder mingled with apprehension—unlikely on any face, extraordinary on his. My head whipped back to the source of this emotion, looking for what Holmes had seen that I had not.

Unlike many tall men—and this one was a fraction taller even than Holmes—the young man did not slump, and although his hands betrayed a degree of uncertainty, the set of his head and the resolute manner with which he met Holmes' gaze made one aware of the fierce intelligence in those grey eyes, and a degree of humour. One might even—

The shock of recognition knocked me breathless. I looked quickly down at the familiar shape of those fingers, then peered more closely at his features. If one peeled away all that hair and erased five years, two stone, and the bruise and scratch along the left temple . . .

I knew him. Rather, I had met him, although I should not have recognised him without Holmes' reaction to guide me. Five years earlier, the face before us had possessed a delicate, almost feminine beauty; with the beard, the weight, and the self-assurance, he could play a stage Lucifer.

The amusement grew on his features, until it began to look almost like triumph. The lips parted, and when he spoke, the timbre in his voice reminded one that his mother had been a famous contralto.

"Hello, Father," he said.

TWO

FRANCE

August 1919

Chapter Three

*First Birth (3): The boy's mother breathed her last
when the full moon lay open in the sky, a round and
luminous door to eternity.*
Testimony, I:1

I MET DAMIAN ADLER ON THE SAME DAY HIS FATHER
did, in August 1919. Damian was twenty-four then, I was nineteen, and Holmes at fifty-eight had only discovered a few days before
that he was a father. It was not a happy meeting. At the time, none of
us were happy people. None of us were whole people.

Apart from it bringing peace to the world at last, 1919 was not a
year one would like to repeat. Its opening had found us in ignomin-
ious flight from an unknown and diabolically cunning enemy—we
told ourselves we were merely regrouping, but we knew it was a rout.
Mycroft, who held some unnamed and powerful position in the
shadier recesses of His Majesty's Government, had offered us a choice
of retreats in which to catch our breath. For reasons I did not understand, Holmes gave the choice over to me. I chose Palestine. Within
the month, he was taken prisoner and tortured to the very edge of

breaking. On our return to England, Holmes' body was whole, but his spirit, and our bond, had been badly trampled.

When I looked at him that spring, all I could see was that my choice had put that haunted look into his eyes.

Then at the end of May, we finally met our enemy, and prevailed, but at the cost of a bullet through my shoulder and the blood of a woman I had loved on my hands.

When Holmes looked at me that summer, all he could see was that his past had put that drawn look of pain and sleepless nights on my face.

Thus, that August of 1919 found the two of us wounded, burdened by guilt, short-tempered, and—despite living under the same roof while my arm recovered—scarcely able to meet each other's eyes or bear the other's company. Certainly, we both knew that the intricate relationship we had constructed before our January flight from England lay in pieces at our feet; neither of us seemed to know how to build another.

Into this tense and volatile situation fell the revelation that Holmes had a son.

Mycroft had known, of course. Holmes might keep his finger on the pulse of every crime in London, but his brother's touch went far beyond England's shores. Mycroft had known for years, but he had let slip not a hint, until the day the young man was arrested for murder.

Two unrelated letters reached us towards the end of July 1919. The first was for Holmes; I did not see it arrive. The second followed a few days later, addressed to me, written by a child we had rescued the previous year. The simple affection and praise in her laboriously shaped words reduced me, at long last, to the catharsis of tears.

A door that had been tight shut opened, just a crack; Holmes did not hesitate.

"I need to go to France and Italy for six weeks," he told me. Then, before I could slam the door shut again, he added, "Would you care to come with me?"

Air seemed to reach my lungs for the first time in weeks. I looked at him, and saw that, in spite of everything, in Holmes' mind our partnership remained.

Later that evening, sitting on the terrace while the darkness fell, I had asked him when we were to leave.

"First thing in the morning," he replied.

"What?" I stood up, as if to go pack instantaneously, then winced and sat down again, rubbing my shoulder beneath its sling. "Why the rush?"

"Mycroft always needs things done yesterday," he said. Far too casually.

"This is another job for Mycroft?"

"More or less."

By this time, my antennae were quivering. An off-hand attitude invariably meant that Holmes was concealing something of which I would disapprove. However, as I watched him reach for the coffee pot to refill a near-full cup, it seemed to me his discomfort had a deeper source than a need to manipulate me into cooperation. He looked genuinely troubled.

A year before, I would have pressed and chivvied him until he gave it up, but after the events of recent months, I was not so eager to beat my mentor-turned-partner into submission. He would tell me in his good time.

"I'll write Patrick a note, to let him know I'm away," I said. Holmes hid his surprise well, simply nodding, but I could feel his eyes on me as I went into the house.

The next day, the train had been crowded with summer merrymakers; the boat across the Channel was so heavy-laden it wallowed; the train to Paris contained approximately half the population of Belgium—none of whom were stopping in Paris. No-one in his right mind stopped in Paris in August.

With this constant presence of witnesses, it wasn't until we stood in the hallway of our Paris hotel that Holmes slid his hand into his inner pocket and took out the envelope that had been teasing his fingers all day.

"Read this," he said abruptly, thrusting it at me. "I shall be in my room." He crossed the corridor and shut his door. I waited for the boy to deposit my cases and receive my coin, then closed my own.

I laid the letter on the desk, eyeing it as I unpinned my hat and stripped off my gloves. Mycroft's handwriting, the unadorned copperplate he used for solemn business. No postal franking, which meant that it had been delivered by messenger. The envelope had seen a lot of handling. I had an odd image of Holmes, taking it out of his pocket and reading it again and again.

I sat down on the hard little chair before the decorative, unusable French desk, and unfolded the letter. It bore a date six days before— the day, I suddenly realised, that he had disappeared for many hours, to return even more preoccupied than usual.

Dear Brother,

In the autumn of 1894, half a year after you made your dramatic return to the London scene, I received a visit from a French gentleman whom I had met, briefly, some years before. His purpose was to urge me to travel to a village named Ste Chapelle, thirty miles south of Paris. As you well know, I do not travel, and told the man as much. He, however, put before me certain information that convinced me such a trip was necessary.

At the other end of the journey was an American lady of your acquaintance, whose name I shall not put into writing, but with whom, as you had already informed me, you had a liaison. You were led to believe that she tired of your presence after some months, that she resolved to return alone to her native country.

In fact, she did not return to the United States. Although she had become a British citizen after she married Godfrey Norton, after your departure, she moved to the village near Paris. There she bore a child.

It was to Ste Chapelle that I went, there to meet her and the infant. A boy. She named him Damian, appending her own maiden surname. He appeared in lusty good health. Certainly, he sounded so.

The lady wished me to know of the child, on the chance that something happened to her. She also swore me to a promise that you were not to be told while she was alive, and thereafter not until such time as I deemed it necessary. Her concern was that you not be, to use her word, distracted.

The price of my agreement was that she accept a monthly stipend, that the boy might be raised without financial hardship. Reluctantly, she accepted.

I came near to telling you in 1912, when she died, but at the time you were involved in the Mattison case, and that was followed by the Singh affair, and by the time that was over, you were in America preparing a case against Von Bork and his spy ring. There seemed no time when you were immune from distraction.

I did keep a close eye on the young man following his mother's death. He was then eighteen, attending university in Paris. In 1914 he joined the French forces—he being more French than American—and served honourably, starting as a junior officer and ending up, in the autumn of 1917, a captain.

He was wounded in January 1918, blown up in a barrage. He received a head wound and a cracked pelvis, spent a week unconscious, and was eventually invalided out.

Unfortunately, he did not manage to get free of the drugs used to control the pain. Unfortunately, he fell into hard ways, and among evil people. And now, the reason I am forced to write to you in this manner: He has been arrested for murder.

Stark details, and with your current responsibilities, no way to soften this series of blows. I have begun enquiries into the case against him, but as yet do not know the details—as we both know, the evidence may be so grossly inadequate, all he requires is legal support; on the other hand, it may prove so strong that neither of us can help him. I have arranged for one of the better criminal *avocat*s to assume his case, but in any event, it is no longer my place to stand between you.

I hope you will forgive me, and her, for keeping Damian from you. By all accounts he was a promising young man before the War, and before the scourge of drugs befell him. I should mention that, to go by his photograph, there is little reason to deny that he is yours.

Tell me what I can do to assist you. He is being held in the gaol in Ste Chapelle, the town where he was born, thirty miles to the east of Paris.

If you speak to him, please convey an uncle's best wishes.

Mycroft

P.S. I forgot to say: Damian is an artist, a painter. Art in the blood . . .

Chapter Four

First Birth (4): The meteorite was the boy's first playththat, his constant companion, as it remains to this day, reshaped and resubmitted to the fires to better suit his needs.

Testimony, I:1

DISTRACTED. THAT WAS A HELL OF A WORD.

And why had Holmes waited nearly a week before setting off for France? I turned back to where Mycroft had written "with your current responsibilities." Did this mean me? Was it I that had kept Holmes from flying to the aid of his son?

It took me some time to work up the nerve to cross the hallway. When I did, I found my friend and teacher at the open window, smoking and staring down at the darkening streets. Not a breath stirred. I sat on the hard little chair before his useless, ornate desk, and arranged the letter in the centre of its gilt surface.

"Well," I said. "That must have made you feel . . ."

"Guilt-ridden?" His voice was high, and bitter.

Guilt, yes. But, to be honest, gratitude as well, that she had not forced him to re-shape his life, his career, around a child. And gratitude would have brought shame, and resentment, and righteous indignation, and anger. Then in the days since the news had reached him, no doubt curiosity and sadness, and a mourning of lost opportunities.

"It must have made you feel as if you'd been kicked in the stomach."

He did not respond. The traffic sounds that had beat at the window when we first arrived were fading, replaced by the voices of pedestrians on their way to theatre or restaurant. It was quiet enough that I heard the faint shift of ice in the silver bucket that had accompanied our arrival.

At the suggestion, I rose and went to fill a glass with ice, covering it with a generous dose of some amber alcohol from the decanter beside it. I carried it over to Holmes, who just looked at it.

"Russell, I've known about this for the better part of a week. The time for a good stiff drink is well past."

"But *I* didn't know until now, and I think you can use this better than I."

He did not argue with my roundabout logic, simply took my offering. I went back to the chair.

"This is Irene Adler's son that Mycroft is talking about?" I asked: facts first.

The ice rattled as he raised the glass against his teeth. I took the gesture as confirmation.

"It . . . happened during the three years you were away from London?" When all the world except his brother thought Holmes dead, although in fact he had travelled—to Mecca, to Lhasa, and to the south of France.

"After Reichenbach Falls," he agreed. "When I came down out of Tibet and was sailing for Europe, news reached me that Miss Adler— Mrs Norton—that Irene had been in a terrible accident, which took the life of her husband and caused her to retire from the stage. As I happened to be passing near Montpellier, I thought it . . . acceptable to call on her. I suppose I entertained the notion that, if grief had driven her to abandon her career, perhaps adding myself to the chorus of protest might make her reconsider. She had an extraordinary voice," he added. "It was a pity to lose it."

"But it wasn't grief?"

"No. She had sustained injuries, subtle, but definitive. When I found her, she was living on the fine edge of poverty, eking out a living as a voice coach. I was in no hurry to return to London, so I paused there for a time, helping her become more firmly established. I lent her sufficient funds to purchase a piano and a small studio, and amused myself doing odd jobs in the city, everything from research into some aspects of coal-tar to peeling carrots for a restaurant. During those months we became . . . friends."

I hastened to interrupt. "And it would seem that the news of the mysterious death of Ronald Adair in London reached you at about the time she . . ." *Threw you out? Tired of you?* In any case, discovered herself with child.

"—told me she planned to return home to America," he provided. "Alone. And as soon as I was back in London, the life of the metropolis closed over my head. Nine years passed. It seemed but the snap of a finger. Then I retired, and nine years turned into a chasm. Had she wished to communicate with me, she knew where I was. She had not. Thus, it seemed, the matter had been decided. One of the more foolish decisions of my life."

He stared into his glass, but he must have been thinking of the nine-year-olds he had known, if nothing else among the street urchins he'd dubbed his Irregulars. Had he ventured an overture, he might have met the boy then, on the edge of adolescence. Had he sought her out—and he would certainly have found her—he might have had another life. A life that did not include bees or a hermit's retreat on the Sussex Downs. Or an encounter with an orphan named Russell.

"She was—going by Watson's story—a highly gifted woman," I ventured.

"In both talent and brains. I was twenty-seven years old when the hereditary king of what Watson chose to call Bohemia came to me, demanding that I retrieve an incriminating photograph possessed by this vain and scheming prima donna from New Jersey. I saw myself a god among men. An easy case, I thought, a satisfying payment in both gold and glory: A dab of paint, a change of costume, a dash of human nature, toss in a smidgen of distraction and a childish smoke-bomb, and *voilà*—I would take back this adventuress's tool of blackmail.

"Except that she was not out for blackmail, merely self-preservation from her royal paramour. What is more, she was one step ahead of me all the way—including on my very doorstep, utilising my own tools of disguise. 'Good evening, Mr Holmes,' she said to me." He dropped his voice for her imitation of a man's speech, bringing an eerie trace of the woman into the room. "And even with the scent of her under my very nose, even as I put up my feet and crowed to Watson how clever I was, she was laying her own plans, carrying out her own solution." He turned from the window, searching me out in the dim room. "You know she used me as a witness in her marriage ceremony to Godfrey Norton?"

"I remember."

He laughed, a sound that contained amusement and rue in equal parts, and I saw his outline stir, heard the rustle of his clothing. Something small and shiny flew in my direction, and I snatched it from the air: a well-worn sovereign coin with a hole in it.

"She paid me for my witnessing with that," he said. "I assumed at the time that she had failed to recognise me, but later found that she well knew who I was, and was amused, despite the urgency of her distress. I carry it always, to remind me of my limitations. Here—I even had her autograph it for me."

He crossed the room and switched on the desk lamp. I held the coin under its beam, and there on the back side of it I saw the scratched initials *IAN*. Irene Adler Norton.

I rubbed at the smoothness of the coin, oddly pleased that it served as a reminder of professional inadequacies and not of a person. I handed it back to him. He turned it nimbly over in his fingers, then clipped it back onto his watch-chain and tucked it away.

"Let us go and eat," he said, sounding relieved that the worst of the self-revelation was over.

"Can we find a place out of doors?" I requested.

"Paris is not at her best in the summer," he agreed.

When I had freshened and changed my dress, we left the hotel and walked down the street until we found a likely bistro, one that spread its tables onto the pavement.

But after facts, and before relaxation, I required instruction. "Since the letter came," I asked, "have you found any more about the charges against . . . ?" I found it difficult to shape the phrase *your son.*

"Damian. As you read, Mycroft has arranged the assistance of one of France's more capable defence attorneys. I have an appointment with him in the morning, and we shall then go to Ste Chapelle and meet the lad."

Did *we* include, or exclude, me? If the latter, would he not have said *he and I?*

"But, Holmes, why didn't you set off immediately you received the letter?"

"I did, in fact, telephone to Mycroft to say that I would leave instantly, but he talked me out of it. He thought I might be more effective if I waited until we had some data with which to work, but beyond this, he pointed out that, if the boy was coming out from under the influence of drugs while in gaol, he would not thank me for seeing him for the first time in that condition. And although I am not accustomed to permitting the personal to influence my investigations, in the end, I had to agree that it might be better to wait until the boy had his wits about him."

Somewhat mollified, although not altogether convinced, I picked up my knife and began thoughtfully to cover a piece of bread with near-liquid butter.

"Does he know?" I asked. "The boy?"

"Hardly a boy," he pointed out. "He knows now."

"How long . . . ?"

"I have no idea when or even if his mother told him about me. Mycroft was forced to explain the situation to the *avocat.* He in turn told Damian, but apparently Damian showed no surprise at my name. Which could also be due to his mental state. Or, I suppose he may have never heard of Sherlock Holmes."

"If a tribe of desert nomads in Palestine knows the stories," I said—

which had been the case during our winter sojourn there—"the chances are good a young man in France has come across them."

"I fear you are right."

"So, has any progress been made in the intervening days?"

"It looks," he said, with a mingled air of apprehension and satisfaction, "as though the evidence against him rests largely on a single eye-witness."

I understood his ambiguity. The testimony of a witness, a person there to stretch out a finger in court and declare the defendant's guilt aloud, was a powerful tool for the prosecution. On the other hand, placing the entire weight of a murder trial on one human being could easily blow up in the prosecutor's face. All the defence had to do was find some flaw in the accuser himself—criminal history, financial interest, flawed eye-sight—and the case began to crack.

If the legal person Mycroft had found to represent Damian Adler was indeed capable, I suspected that the man would be more than experienced with the techniques of destroying testimony.

Relief, a trace of optimism, and a faint stir of air cheered our dinner, and we spoke no more that night about either Adler, *fils* or *mère*.

But as I laboriously, one-handedly, dressed for bed in my stifling room, that word *responsibilities* came back to nag me, and the real question finally percolated to the surface of my mind: Why tell me about Damian? Why hadn't Holmes simply announced that he would be away for a time? Or not even bothered with an announcement—just disappeared, with nothing but a brief note or a message left with Mrs Hudson? God knew, he'd never hesitated to do that before.

Although the thought of waking one morning to find him simply gone would not have been an easy one. Since the shooting, I had come to lean very heavily on his presence. While resenting it at the same time.

I cradled my arm, looking away from my reflection in the glass. Had his response when I asked about his delay been a glibly prepared speech, designed to conceal his worry? Did he believe that I was so fragile that I might not withstand abandonment? Had my admittedly precarious mental state left him with no choice but to bring me along?

Certainly, Mycroft's reference to "your current responsibilities" suggested that both Holmes brothers saw my need for comfort as equal to a prisoner's need for aid.

Which led to the conclusion that Holmes felt there was nothing for it but to reveal to me one of the most private and distressing episodes of his life. To lay out his most personal history, while it was still raw and unformed, to my eyes. To allow my presence to rub salt into the wounds of what he had to consider one of his most abject failures.

I should go home, immediately. I should pack and call a taxi, leaving a brief note to preserve my own self-respect, and to provide a bulwark for the shreds of Holmes' dignity.

And yet . . .

I could not shake the notion that there had been a degree of relief underlying his chagrin. Almost as if the humiliation was a thing to be borne for a greater cause, to be got through quickly. But for what?

I found myself considering the previous summer, the beginnings of the case involving the child whose letter had recently reduced me to tears. My arrival at Holmes' house that day had been unexpected: I found him in disguise and about to depart, intending to slip off before I could become enmeshed. But why had he not simply taken an earlier train? That case—so nearly missed entirely—became a cornerstone of our subsequent partnership, firm foundation for a tumultuous year.

Had Holmes, deliberately or unconsciously, lingered that afternoon so that I might find him?

Was his present uncharacteristic solicitude for my tender state a means of ensuring my presence here?

I did not feel all *that* precariously fragile. Granted, I was not at my best, but surely he could see that I was finding my feet again? That I was not about to fall to pieces if left alone?

I raised my gaze to the looking-glass before me. I was nineteen years old. During recent months, I had proven myself strong, adult, and capable, not only to myself, but to Holmes—my teacher, my mentor, my entire family since I stumbled across him on the Downs, four and a half years before.

During the winter, the balance of our relationship had begun to shift, from apprentice and master to something very close to partnership. Several times I had even wondered if some deeper link was not in the process of being forged between us.

Holmes was a master of avoiding undesirable situations. If he had seen my recovery, and chose to discount it, then it followed that he wanted me here. That this steely, invulnerable man, once mentor, now partner, still friend, had his own reasons for laying his vulnerability at my feet, as a man kneels to expose the nape of his neck to his sword-wielding sovereign.

Another memory came back to me then, bringing a wash of foreign air through the sultry room. It came from Palestine, in February, shortly after the Hazr brothers and I had ripped Holmes from the hands of his Turkish tormentor. As we parted ways, the elder Hazr, Mahmoud—silent, deadly, and himself bearing scars of torture—had been moved to make a rare incursion into personal speech: *Do not try to protect your Holmes, these next days. It will not help him to heal.*

I nodded, and finished my preparations for bed. As I lay down on the lavender-scented sheets, I reflected that Holmes and I seemed to have a habit of forcing unpalatable decisions on one another.

Chapter Five

The Tool (1): The scrap of other-worldly metal sent the boy was of the four Elements: the earthy stuff that gave it substance, the fire that twice shaped it, the water that twice received it, and the air through which it arrived.
Testimony, I:2

THE DAY WAS ALREADY HOT WHEN WE SET OFF for the *avocat*'s office the next morning, the city air close and unhealthy against us. The sling chafed at my neck; my light dress was soon damp, as was my hair beneath the summer hat. Things were no better inside the legal gentleman's office, where the stifling air was compounded by the man's unbounded energy. He put us in chairs and then strode up and down the carpet, gesticulating and thinking aloud in fluent if accented English until the heat he seemed to generate made me light-headed.

Fortunately, we had not much time before the train left. His secretary came in with his hat in her hand, and bundled us off into a taxicab to the station. Monsieur Cantelet talked the whole time, Holmes listening intently, ready to seize the scraps of information being tossed on the freshet of words.

Holmes had been following the case, albeit at a distance, for a week already, and his occasional phrase of explanation helped me piece together the central facts: Damian Adler had been arrested for the murder of a drugs seller; the man sold mostly morphine and hashish, and Damian was known to be one of his customers; the two men had an argument in a bar that ended in a fistfight, although there was some disagreement as to whether the fight had been over the man's wares or a girl. In any event, two days later, the man was found in an alleyway, unconscious and bleeding from a head wound. He died in hospital; the police asked questions; the answers led them to Damian.

The evidence against him included the presence of morphine and hashish in his room, signs of a fight on his face and hands, and the clear accusation of a witness.

M Cantelet ran through all this with a light-hearted enthusiasm, which seemed odd, if not inappropriate, until he began to tell us about the witness. "The gentleman's veracity has been questioned," the lawyer said happily in his musical accent. Said witness, it seemed—one Jules Filot—was known to his more jocular intimates as an habitual snitch and manufacturer of evidence on demand, which explained his nickname: "Monsieur Faux."

M Cantelet did not think that it would take a great effort to smash the case against Damian Adler. His private detective had spent the days since Mycroft's request for assistance had been received insinuating himself into the life of M Filot, and would make himself available to us at mid-day. In the mean-time, we were to be permitted an interview with the prisoner, at the gaol.

"By great good fortune, M Adler had the sense not to admit to the crime."

"He says he's innocent?" Holmes asked.

"The young man neither admits nor denies, merely says he does not remember. Ideal, for my purposes."

Ideal it might be, but less than wholly reassuring for us.

Ste Chapelle was a tiny village, which I had already determined that morning by the fact that it did not appear on any of the hotel's maps. The town gaol was down the street from the station and across from a tiny café. It was, in fact, the local *gendarme*'s front room, little more than a small bedroom with bars across the windows and a square of glass set into its stout wooden door. The *gendarme* made note of our names in a record-book, unbolted the door, handed us a couple of stools, and left us alone.

I did not want to be there, but I did not know how to absent myself. I took a deep breath, and followed M Cantelet inside.

The young man, who stood with his shoulder touching the window-bars, looked startlingly like Holmes in a masterful disguise: thin to emaciation and pale as the walls, but with the same beak nose, the same long fingers, the same sense of wiry strength.

There, the similarity ended: Holmes' uncanny gift for tidiness was replaced by perspiration stains and the stench of old sweat; where Holmes was controlled even when excited, this younger version was vibrating with tension. His eyes darted about the room, his fingers plucked incessantly at shirt buttons and fraying cuffs. He was either nervy to the edge of a break-down, or still emerging from prolonged drug use.

The *avocat*, shifting to an equally energetic French, marched across the cell with his hand outstretched. The young man put out his hand, but his blank stare suggested a lack of comprehension. Surely he was fluent in French?

After a time his grey eyes wandered away from the voluble *avocat* to rest on me. It was a shock, because these were Holmes' eyes—same shape, same colour, same height above mine—but dull, with pain or confusion or even—hard to imagine—a lack of intelligence. I found myself searching for a glimpse of mind beneath the flat gaze, but there was no flash of wit, merely the weary perseverance of an animal in distress.

Then the hooded grey eyes came to Holmes. The head tilted in concentration, a gesture eerily like his father, and sense came into them. Curiosity, yes, but also animosity. I stepped aside, and suddenly he flushed. With colour came an unexpected beauty, the darkness of his lashes and the delicacy of his features making him for the first time utterly unlike Holmes.

The *avocat* filled the silence nicely. "*Capitaine* Adler, it is not often that a man is given the opportunity to say this, but may I present your father? Monsieur Holmes, your son, *Capitaine* Damian Adler."

Neither man moved. The *avocat* cleared his throat. "Yes, well, I shall leave you two alone for a few minutes, while I speak with the *gendarme* about the case."

I made haste to follow him out of the cell.

M Cantelet and I sat outside for a long time, waiting in the shade of a linden tree as village life went on before us. When Holmes emerged, he said nothing of what had transpired in that cell.

He never did.

We removed to a tiny hotel near the train station, where we were joined by M Cantelet's private investigator, M Clémence. The investigator was, it seemed, dressed for his undercover rôle, with flashy clothes, pencil-thin moustache, and oil-slicked hair parted in the centre, but he gave his evidence succinctly and showed no signs of the too-common shortcomings of the breed, which are an inflated self-confidence and an impatience with humdrum detail. I could feel Holmes relax a notch.

The man told us what he had done, gave a brief outline of where he intended to go from there, answered Holmes' questions, and listened calmly to Holmes' suggestions. At no point did he demonstrate scorn for the amateur, merely a workman-like and not unimaginative approach to figuring things out.

Holmes found little to object to, when the man had left us.

Which did not mean he intended to take his hand off the investigation. He might have put off his involvement in the case until now, but he had no intention of delaying it further. The *avocat* caught the post-luncheon train back to Paris, but we remained in Ste Chapelle to prepare our campaign: Holmes proposed to infiltrate the group in which the witness Filot—"Monsieur Faux"—moved, while I addressed myself to the more mundane aspects of property, relationship, and inheritance: the local records office, where my bad arm would not be a liability. We made a start that afternoon, going our separate ways until nightfall.

But in the end, our preparations came to naught. The next morning early there came a message from M Cantelet to say he was coming down, and requested us to meet his train. Holmes grumbled at the delay, but we were there when the train pulled in.

I had thought the *avocat* effervescent the day before, but it was nothing to the bounce in his step and the rush of his words today.

His private investigator had broken the case. In conversation with M Faux's lady friend late the night before, it had transpired that the man had in fact been elsewhere on the night in question. Filot could not have seen Damian Adler commit murder, because he was twenty miles away, roaring drunk, and did not arrive back in Ste Chapelle until the following afternoon.

This, of course, did not prove that Damian had not killed the drugs seller, but it did reduce the prosecutor's foundations to sand. M Cantelet anticipated a successful argument, and I think was mildly disappointed when we arrived at the gaol and found Damian Adler already free. He stood outside of the gaol with the scowling *gendarme* and a stumpy, round-cheeked woman of about forty, who was wearing a dress and hat far too *à la mode* for a village like this.

Damian's eyes would not meet ours. They wove their way along the doorway, up the vine shrouding the front of the house, along the street outside, while his fingers picked restlessly at his clothing. In the bright light, the bald tracing of scars could be seen beneath his short-cropped hair, and it suddenly came to me that this was not merely a drug-addled derelict, nor some nightmare version of Holmes, but a soldier who had given his health and his spirit in the service of France. He was lost, as so many of his—my—generation were. It was our responsibility to help him find himself again.

The woman watched us approach, and as M Cantelet launched into speech with the *gendarme,* she touched Damian's arm and spoke briefly in his ear before stepping forward to intercept Holmes.

"Pardon me," she said in accented English, raising her voice against that of the *avocat.* "You are, I think, Damian's father?"

"The name is Holmes," my companion replied. "This is my . . . assistant, Mary Russell."

"I am Hélène Longchamps," she said. "An old friend of Damian's. I own a gallery in Paris. Come, you will buy me a coffee and we will talk. Damian, you sit here, we will have the boy bring you a croissant."

Mme Longchamps, it transpired, had known Damian Adler since before the War. She had sold a score of his paintings, for increasing amounts of money, and what was more, she had cared for him: bullied him into painting, fed him when he was hungry, gave him a bed and a studio in her country house. And threw him out whenever he showed signs of drug use.

"You understand," she told Holmes, "he changed after the War. Oh, we all changed, of course, but I am told that a head injury such as his often has profound effects on a person's mind. From what I could see, more than the injury, it was the drugs. They take hold of a man's mind as well as his body—certainly they did so with Damian. And now it takes only a moment's weakness, a brief *coup de tête* or a dose of unhappiness or *ennui* or simply a party with the wrong people, and it swallows him anew. And when that happens I become hard. I refuse him help. I say, 'You must go to your friends, if that is how you wish to live,' and I withhold any monies from his sales, and I wait. We have done this three times in the thirteen months since he came out of hospital and became a civilian. And three times he has returned to my door, laboriously cleaned himself of drugs, and begun to paint again."

"Why do you do this?" I had to agree with the suspicion in Holmes' voice: A well-dressed, older woman with a talented and beautiful young addict was not a comfortable picture.

But she laughed. "I am not after a pretty bed-warmer, sir. I knew his mother, before she died, and I knew Damian from when he was five or six years. I am the closest he has to an elder sister."

"I see. Well, madame, I thank you warmly for assisting the boy. I should like—"

She cut him off. "If you want to help the boy, you will leave him here."

"I beg your pardon?"

"M 'Olmes, I imagine you will propose to take Damian back to *l'Angleterre, n'est çe pas?*"

"I should think it would not be altogether a bad idea to remove him from the source of his temptations," Holmes said stiffly.

"But yes, it would be a bad idea, the worst of ideas. The boy *must* find his own way. I know him. You do not. You must believe me when I tell you that attempting to shape a future for him will guarantee failure. You will kill him."

She leant forward over the tiny table, quivering with the intensity of her belief. The effect was that of a small tabby facing down a greyhound, and it might have been laughable but for those last four words.

Holmes studied her. Even the *avocat* across the way fell silent, turning to see what both the *gendarme* and Damian were watching so intently.

Mme Longchamps sat, as implacable as any mother.

Holmes looked over at his son, and then he nodded. Mme Longchamps closed her eyes for a moment, then looked at me and gave me an almost shy smile in which relief was foremost.

Holmes walked back across the road to where his son sat. "Mme Longchamps suggests that I return to England and let you get on with it. Is this what you wish?"

Damian did not actually answer, not in words, but the look he gave the woman—grateful, apologetic, and determined—was a speech in itself. Holmes reached into his breast pocket and sorted out a card.

"When you feel like getting into contact, that is where to reach me," he said. "If I happen to be away, the address on the reverse is that of your uncle. He will always know where I am."

Damian put the card into his coat pocket without looking at it; something about the gesture said that he might as easily have dropped it on the ground. Holmes put out his hand, and said, with an attempt at warmth, "I am . . . gratified to have made your acquaintance. The revelations of this past week have been among the most extraordinary in an already full life. I look forward to renewing our conversation."

Damian stood and walked over to Mme Longchamps. Holmes' face was expressionless as his hand slowly fell, but Mme Longchamps would not have it. She put her hands on the boy's shoulders and forced him around.

"Say *au revoir* to your father," she ordered.

He looked at Holmes with an expression of hopelessness and regret, a look such as a ship-wrecked man might wear when, seeing that help would not arrive, he chose to let go of his spar. I was only nineteen and was well supplied with problems of my own, but that look on his face twisted my heart. *"Adieu,"* Damian said.

"I am very sorry," Holmes told him. "That your mother never told me of your existence."

Damian lifted his head and for the first time, the grey eyes came to life, haughty and furious as a bird of prey. "You should have known."

"Yes," answered Holmes. "I should have known."

He waited. For weeks. I went back to my studies, but whenever I came down from Oxford, I saw how closely Holmes watched the post, how any knock at the door brought his head sharply around.

In the end, it was Mme Longchamps who wrote, in early December, to say that she was desolated to tell him, but Damian had gone back to his ways, and that no-one had seen him for some weeks. She assured Holmes that Damian would find her waiting when he grew fatigued of the drugs, and that she would then urge him to write to his father.

It was the only letter Holmes had, from either of them. In March, when she had not replied to two letters, he began to make enquiries as to her whereabouts.

He found her in the Père Lachaise cemetery, a victim of the terrible influenza that followed on the Great War's heels.

M Cantelet's investigator was immediately dispatched to Ste Chapelle, but Damian was gone. Cantelet and others searched all of France, but the trail was cold: No gallery, no artist, no member of the Bohemian underworld had heard news of Damian Adler since January. Even Mycroft failed to locate his nephew.

Holmes' lovely, lost son vanished as abruptly as he had appeared.

Until one summer evening in August 1924, when he stood in the middle of our stone terrace and said hello to his father.

THREE

SUSSEX

August 1924

Chapter Six

The Tool (2): A Tool that is shaped and used assumes a Power of its own. This Testimony is a Tool, a history, and a guide, that its Power may work on others.
Testimony, I:2

MY HAND WAS STILL BRACED ON HOLMES' ARM, where I had steadied myself after walking into him, and I felt the shudder of effort run through him: Being controlled is nowhere near the same as being unfeeling.

But he could not control his voice, not entirely; when he spoke he was hoarse as a man roused from a long sleep. "God, boy. I thought you were dead."

"Yes," Damian said simply. "I'm sorry."

Holmes started towards him, his hand coming out; instead of taking it, Damian stepped forward and embraced him. After the briefest hesitation, Holmes returned the greeting, with a fervour that would have astonished all but a very few of his intimates. Indeed, one might have thought Holmes had instigated the gesture, with Damian its more reluctant participant.

I moved towards the house, so as to leave them to their greetings, but the two men broke apart and Damian turned in my direction.

"And, Step-Mama," he said, coming forward to plant a very French kiss on my cheek.

"Call me Mary," I said firmly.

"I've come from London," he said to his father, by way of explanation. "Uncle Mycroft caught me up on your news. When he told me you were *en route* from New York, I decided to come down last night and wait for you—he sent along a note to your helpful young housekeeper, so she wouldn't set the dogs on me."

I'd heard precisely five words out of him at our first meeting, but I found now that his accent was as charming as the easy flow of his words—there was French at its base, overlaid with American English and something more clipped: Chinese? His clothing was a similar mélange, the canvas jacket homespun and local whereas the shirt had travelled a long, hard way from its beginnings. His shoes were, I thought, Italian, although not bespoke.

The dogs were a figure of speech—Mycroft knew we had no dogs. The housekeeper, however, was not, and I thought the reason Damian mentioned her was that he had noticed her standing in the door to the house: Lulu had her strengths, but silence and discretion were not among them, and it would not take a long acquaintance with her to realise that it was best to watch one's tongue when she was near.

"Pardon the interruption," she said, "but I've fixed supper. Would you like to eat, or shall I put it into the ice-box?"

I spoke up, overriding Holmes' wave of dismissal. "Hello, Lulu, how are you? Dinner would be greatly appreciated, thank you. Shall we come now?"

"If you like," she said gratefully. And as the table had been laid and the food already in its serving bowls, it would clearly have been a vexation had we said, No, thank you.

Mrs Hudson would have marked our homecoming with Windsor soup, a roast, potatoes, gravy, three vegetables, and a heavy pudding; she would have been red of face, and waves of heat would have pulsed from the kitchen doorway. Lulu, on the other hand, began with an interesting cold Spanish soup of finely chopped tomatoes and cucumber, then set down paper-thin slices of cold roast beef dressed with mustard and horseradish, a bowl of Cos leaves tossed with a light vinaigrette, and a platter of beetroot slices drizzled with pureed herbs—Lulu's aunt ran the nearby Monk's Tun inn, and the aunt's teaching was why I, for one, was willing to put up with Lulu's tendency to gab.

The two men ate what was before them, although I doubt either could have described it later. I, however, took second helpings of most, winning a beatific look as Lulu passed through with another platter.

In the presence of food and servants, conversation went from the summer's weather to Mycroft's health and then London's art world. Of Mycroft, Damian knew little, apart from finding his uncle looking well, but it seemed that he had been in the city long enough to converse knowledgeably about the last.

As he sat at our table and held up his end of the small-talk, I began to sense that somewhere beneath his deliberate ease and charm lurked the edginess we had seen before. On reflection, this would hardly be surprising: Their first meeting had ended on a note of pure animosity, and if neither of them was about to bring it up, nor were they about to forget it.

I decided that what Damian was doing with his friendly shallow chatter was to illustrate that he had grown up, to show Holmes that the natural resentment of a boy whose father had failed him had been replaced by a man's mature willingness to forgive, and to start again. That it was being done deliberately did not necessarily mean it was insincere.

Thirty-five minutes of surface conversation was as much as Holmes could bear. When my fork had transferred the last morsel of salad to my tongue, he waited until he saw me swallow, then stood.

"We'll take our coffee on the terrace, Miss Whiteneck, then you may go home."

"And thank you for that fine supper, Lulu," I added.

"Er, quite." Holmes caught up three glasses and a decanter on his way out of the door.

I followed with a pair of silver candelabras that I set on the stones between the chairs; the air was so still, their flames scarcely moved. The summer odours of lavender and jasmine combined with the musk of honey from the candles and after a minute, with the sharp tang of coffee. Lulu set the tray on the table, then retreated to the kitchen to do the washing-up. By unspoken agreement, while she remained within earshot, we sat and drank and listened to the rumour of waves against the distant cliffs.

I watched our visitor out of the corner of my eye, as, I am sure, did Holmes. The years had brought substance to the man, while the beard, and the candle-light, transformed his fragile beauty into something sharp, almost dangerous. More than mere weight, however, he had gained assurance: Bohemian or no, this was a man that eyes would follow, both women's and men's.

Lucifer, I'd thought him earlier, and I sat now with my coffee and mused over the idea. Originally, Lucifer was the name of Venus at dawn (Vesper being the planet at dusk). The prophet Isaiah had used the morning star's transient brilliance as a metaphor for a magnificent and oppressive Babylonian king who, once the true sun rose across the land, would fade to insignificance. Jewish and Christian thought elaborated on Isaiah's passage, building up an entire mythology around the person of Lucifer, fallen prince of angels, beloved of God, brought low by pride. Lucifer is, one might say, a failed Christ: Where Jesus of Nazareth bowed willingly to Pilate's condemnation, accepting crucifixion as the will of God, Lucifer refused to submit: Subjecting himself to his inferiors, he declared, would be to deny the greatness of the God who made, loved, and chose him.

The story of Lucifer was, I reflected, a window on fathers and sons that Sigmund Freud might spend some time investigating.

The kitchen clatter had ceased. We now heard the sound of the front door opening, and closing; in response, Damian stood up and shrugged his coat onto the back of the chair, dropping his cravat over it and turning up his sleeves as he sat again. His left forearm bore a dragon tattoo, sinuous and in full colour. He hadn't had that when we had seen him before, I thought. He also hadn't had the muscle that rippled beneath it.

Holmes set his empty cup on the table. "You've been in the East," he said. "Hong Kong?"

"Shanghai. How . . . ?"

"The cut of your trousers, the silk of the cravat, the colour in that tattoo. How long have you been there?"

"Years." He took out an enamelled cigarette case and a box of vestas: If he was anything like his father, tobacco signalled a lengthy tale.

The match flared and was pulled into the tobacco, then he shook it out and dropped it in the saucer.

"You remember meeting Hélène?" he asked us.

"Mme Longchamps, yes. The gallery owner."

"She was a great deal more than that. She was my saviour. She died, just after Christmas 1919. I was . . . I had been going through a bad time. They ran in a kind of cycle, the bad times did, usually lasting two or three months before I grew sufficiently disgusted with myself to crawl back and let her nurse me to health. I no doubt contributed to her death—she was ill, with the influenza, but when I sent her a message to say I wanted to come home, she nonetheless got into a taxi and came to get me. A week later, I was sober and she was dead.

"I stayed for her funeral, and then I simply walked away. I knew that if I remained in Paris, I wouldn't last the year. And although a part of me felt that might be for the best, to remove my sorry self from the world, at the same time I felt I owed Hélène a life. So I saw her into the ground and then I turned and walked across town to the Gare de Lyon, and boarded a train for Marseilles.

"The sort of ship that will take on a man with neither suitcase nor identity papers is fairly primitive, but I found one, the *Bella Acqua,* and signed on to work my way across the globe. No drugs, no parties, no paints, nothing but hard work, bad food, sea air, and a drawing pad for entertainment.

"I grew brown, I grew muscle, and at night—you can't imagine the dreams I'd had, before, but under that regimen, I'd fall into my bunk and sleep like a baby. Do you know what a blessing sleep can be?"

"Yes," Holmes said.

Damian's question had been rhetorical, but at Holmes' answer he paused to squint at him through the smoke, then gave a thoughtful nod. "So, six months: across the Atlantic, working our way down the coast of Brazil, taking on rum and coir in one place, trading the rum for timber in another, buying hides farther down, transporting the odd passenger who might have needed to leave a town quickly and without notice—whatever took the Captain's fancy. We rounded the Horn and worked our way up Chile to Mexico and San Diego, then set off across the Pacific. The Hawaiis, Japan.

"Finally, we came to Shanghai. Have you been there?"

"Once, briefly."

"A seething mass of corruption and vice—I think you'd enjoy the straight-forward criminality of the place. I found it filled with temptation, which you'd have thought a poor choice for a man in my position, but I was hungry to join the world again.

"With nothing to spend my pay on, I'd accumulated enough to take a small room in a . . . well, I thought at first it was simply one of the compounds they have in the city—*lilong* houses, they're called, with a number of units set into a series of courtyards, and a single entrance from the street. Within a day or two I couldn't help noticing that there were rather a lot of young girls living there who had a series of older male visitors. The whole *lilong* was one pleasure-house compound. I eventually found out that my landlord had three such, and made a habit of installing one or two large young men in each to help keep the peace. He may have expected that I should eventually become a client myself, but in fact his girls were little more than children, and my taste has never run in that direction. I became a sort of brother to them, and they could practice their English and come to me with problems. I took a job in the afternoons, washing dishes in a noodle shop. It paid a pittance—I still had no identity papers, so my choice was limited—but it gave me two meals a day and mornings free.

"The mornings I needed for the light, because I'd started to paint again. Er, I think you knew, that . . . ?"

For the first time, the young man's self-assurance faltered, with the question of what his father had or had not known. Holmes rose and walked into the house; Damian gave me a sharp look that called to mind his father's hawk-like arrogance, but I could only shrug.

Holmes came back carrying a flat object a foot wide and eighteen inches tall. He set it on the stones, propping it upright against an unoccupied chair.

"That's his?" I exclaimed. "That's yours?"

The unsigned painting had hung for years on a wall of Holmes' laboratory upstairs, a puzzle to me, although I'd caught him studying it from time to time. Holmes owned little art, and had showed no interest, before or since, in a thing as jarringly modern—weird, even—as this one.

Damian picked it up to examine it by candle-light; his expression softened, although I could not tell what he thought of the painting, or of finding it here. "Yes, this is one of mine. From before the War."

"I was told 1913," Holmes agreed.

"I would have been nineteen. Imagine, being nineteen. It's not bad, considering. How do you come to have it?"

"It came on the market in March 1920."

Damian turned his hawk-gaze on Holmes. "It was one of Hélène's?"

"Yes."

Damian put the painting down again, and we all three studied it.

The canvas showed a bizarre dream-image of the sort that came to be called Surrealism. In technique it was masterful, closely worked and as detailed as a photograph. Its background was an English landscape: neat fields set inside hedgerows, a lane with a bicycle, a cow in the distance. On the horizon, white lines described the chalk cliffs where the South Downs fell into the Channel—not far from where we sat. In the foreground was a table, the weave of its spotless white cloth clearly shown, and on the cloth rested an object from a madman's nightmare: Its front half was an everyday English tea-pot, blue and white porcelain, but the back of it became a huge, distorted honeybee, every hair painted with precision, its wings set to quiver, its stinger exaggerated into a tea-pot's handle, throbbing with menace.

I'd thought it an oddity, but now it was a revelation: At nineteen, a year after his mother's death, Damian had definitely known who his father was. He had known of Holmes' beekeeping avocation in his so-called retirement. He had painted this as a portrait of the famous man who had, to his mind, coldly abandoned mother and child. He had painted it with the consummate skill of a man, impelled by the fury of a scorned adolescent.

Chapter Seven

The Father (1): The boy knew no earthly father. He was raised by the feminine, moon-lit side of his race. All men were his father, all women his mother.
Testimony, I:3

S O," SAID HOLMES. "SHANGHAI."

"Yes." Damian took a breath, either summoning his thoughts, or rousing his determination. "As I said, you might think the city was the very worst place for a man vulnerable to temptation, but after my long sobriety aboard the *Bella Acqua,* it was as if my body came to value its natural state, and my mind found the tight-rope act of daily life in Shanghai exhilarating. It was a challenge simply to walk down the street for a newspaper, passing two gin-joints, an opium den, and the Sikh who sold *bhang* from a tray.

"And there was another reason Shanghai felt right. Do you know André Breton?"

"I have heard of him," Holmes replied. "The self-appointed spokesman for the movement known as Surrealism."

"Now, yes. During the War, André worked at the hospital in Nantes, where he came to adapt certain psychological theories of Sigmund

Freud to treat victims of shell-shock. That was where I met him, after I . . . after I was injured.

"André's idea was that if one could break through the madness of shell-shock and regain access to the unconscious mind, the conscious and the unconscious might, as it were, join forces, and wholeness would be regained. He used what he calls automatism, a pure up-welling of dream-thought and dream-images, without the guidance of rational or even aesthetic concern, in various forms of art: writing, painting, sculpting, drama.

"Before long, it became clear that automatism was not merely a source of healing damaged minds, but a philosophy of life, a means of bringing together the separate realities of the human experience. Anyone who has spent time on the Front knows that, when one lifts his head from a barrage and finds dead people all around, there is a moment when life is immeasurably sweet and intensely real. In a similar way, the shock of the unexpected in a piece of art can forge a momentary link between light and dark, rationality and madness, matter-of-factness and absurdity, beauty and obscenity.

"As you see in that painting, I'd already been feeling my way in that direction before the War—the Dada movement, although Dadaism was intellectual and political compared to what André had in mind.

"Shanghai—and particularly, being a foreigner in Shanghai—might have been purposefully designed by André to illustrate and encourage the 'sur-realist' impulse. Every moment there possesses an air of peculiarity, every corner brings a new gem of crystal-clear absurdity. My landlord, it turned out, was a policeman with a side business of child prostitutes. One of his girls used to sit in the courtyard playing the guitar and telling me of her dream to become a Catholic nun, once she had finished putting her older brother through university. The head of the missionary school where I taught for a while spent his every lunch-hour with an opium pipe. One discovered purity in the gutters and filth in the glittering shop-windows, every hour of every day.

"I found Shanghai to be the very essence of Surrealist doctrine: If the world is mad, then the maddest man is the most sane.

"So: I became sane by embracing madness. I became intoxicated by sobriety. I moved from one job to another, earning just enough to keep me fed, sheltered, and in paint. I walked and walked, I learned the language, I opened my eyes in wonder. And the images simply poured out of me.

"What I painted were intensely realistic renderings of impossibility. As one of the catalogues put it, I was their 'Max Ernst of the East.'

"Yes, within two years, I was in a catalogue. Let me tell you how that came about."

Holmes stirred in his chair, betraying a trace of tension. I saw the non-committal look on his face, and realised, as surely as if he had murmured it into my ear, that Damian wasn't here by accident. I don't know why it took so long to put it together—Damian's almost dutiful embrace; the lengthy formal narrative in place of conversation; even his presence the moment we arrived—but I finally saw that Damian had come here to Sussex, not to establish contact with his family, but because he wanted something.

Whatever he was after, Holmes' slight motion confirmed that we were circling in towards it now.

"I'd been there less than a year, painting furiously all the while, when a friend gathered up half a dozen paintings and took them into the International Settlement. She'd asked around, you know, to find which of the Western art galleries might be interested in my sort of thing. When she came back, she brought more money than I'd seen in years.

"Before I knew it, I was popular. More than popular, I was a Sensation, the darling of Shanghai's international set, proof that one did not need to live in Paris or Berlin to be *avante-garde*. At the drop of a hat, I had money, I had a house, a studio, servants—and I had problems.

"I'd managed to balance myself against the temptations of the city while I was poor. But success proved a greater madness than I could manage. One night I was at a party and dope was going around, and I reached for it, the first time in three years.

"And again, Yolanda saved me. She physically slapped the stuff out of my hand and dragged me away from the party.

"However, I haven't told you about Yolanda. She's the reason . . . No, I should start at the beginning, so it all ties together." He took a deep draught from his glass and crushed out the half-smoked cigarette, then fiddled with the case; in another minute, his fingertips would begin to pluck at his buttons.

"I'd met Yolanda my first week in Shanghai. She worked in a bar down the street from my *lilong*, but I met her in the courtyard outside of my room. She was visiting one of my neighbours—one of my landlord's girls, who was ill. Yolanda is Chinese, and although she worked in a bar and hadn't much education, she spoke good English because her family was Christian and sent her to the missionary school until she was eleven.

"Then her father died, and when she was sixteen, she found herself out on the streets. She went through a period of what she called 'hating herself.' She drank, did any kind of dope offered her, and—well, suffice to say she lived a pretty wild life." He did not look at Holmes, who sat with his fingers steepled to his lips. Damian played with the catch of his enamelled case and pressed on.

"The self-hate period lasted for a year, until one day she woke up a little more sober than usual, and she knew that one morning she would not wake up at all, unless someone dragged her out of it. She didn't think she had the will to rescue herself, so she went to the missionaries, and told them they had to save her."

He must have caught something of my reaction, because he gave me a crooked smile. "You like the image? Little painted bar-girl standing at the door to the local Christian do-gooders, throwing herself at them as you would a glove in a challenge.

"And give them credit, they tried their best. She stayed with them for three months until their rules became too much for her—but then, instead of giving up, she walked down the road to the Buddhist temple. She lasted a month there. And then it was a Shinto shrine, followed by some stray Hindus, then American Spiritualists. One after another, she worked her way through half the religions of the world, only at some point, it became more a hobby than a necessity. She went back to her bar, but only to serve drinks, and during her free hours she continued to sample the rich buffet of temples and churches and meeting places Shanghai has to offer.

"Until one day she encountered an odd French-American-English painter in the run-down house where one of her childhood friends was dying of syphilis. He saw a tiny little thing dressed in a tartan skirt, a Chinese silk blouse, a moulting rabbit-fur jacket, and a French beret, with cropped hair and painted eyes. She saw a tall, thin foreigner reeking of turpentine and blinking as if he'd just come from a cave.

" 'You need to eat,' she said. 'Take me to lunch.'

"What could I do? I took her to lunch, took her for a walk along the riverfront, and before I knew it, she was in my life. It was Yolanda who loaded up a rickshaw with my paintings and took them to the gallery. And Yolanda who haggled over the prices of the next batch. Yolanda who suggested that I become known, professionally, as 'The Addler'—a sort of trademark. And as I said, Yolanda who kept me on something resembling the straight and narrow.

"In the end, it was Yolanda who suggested it was time to move closer to the centre of the art world, she who besieged the British Embassy until they told her how I might register as a citizen whose papers had been lost. I did not want to leave Shanghai, not really, but it was hard on her—there are many places where the Chinese are not welcome. I thought of Paris, which is as colour-blind as one can hope for, but she was afraid the pull of the old life would prove too strong for me. Plus, she had no wish to learn another language. In the end, we agreed on London, with my mother's adopted nationality to build on.

"Your brother helped me, as I understand he had helped Mother when I was born. And, as I later found that she had, I asked him not to inform you until I could do so myself."

He laid the cigarette case down and looked straight at Holmes, for the first time in several minutes. "Once we decided to leave Shanghai, I married Yolanda. Neither of us believes in the concept, but I doubt the government would have permitted her to come otherwise." He waited for a reaction from Holmes, disapproval perhaps, but when no response came, he continued; there were clearly more revelations to come.

"As it happened, we arrived in London less than a week after you'd left for India—we probably passed you somewhere off the coast of France. It didn't take long before we were wishing we'd stayed in Shanghai—winter is a terrible time to come here from the tropics, everything is bitter cold and grey and lifeless. Yolanda had never had chilblains before, and the cost of coal to heat the rooms was more than the rent itself. I hired a studio and rediscovered the challenge of painting with shivering hands. Every day we thought of leaving, but we didn't, quite.

"Then April came, and the sun appeared. Everything was brilliant, seductive, cheering—the poets are right, to make much of this country in the spring. Yolanda began to look for more permanent housing, and I sent my first London paintings to a gallery she'd located off Regent Street.

"As spring wore on, that was our life: We scraped together enough to buy a little house with a garden in Chelsea, two streets away from my studio. Yolanda began to explore the nearby parks and religious centres, and made some friends. And one day I was in town and I heard my name called—a fellow I'd met in Shanghai. An artist. He was surprised to see me, of course, but took me for a drink and introduced me to his friends, and life began to settle into a pleasant pace. . . ."

"Until?" Holmes prompted.

"Until the latter half of June." Damian ran fingers through his long hair, revealing a glimpse of the scars, and went through the business of lighting another cigarette. He pinched out the match. "You have to understand: I promised Yolanda before we married that I would support her in all ways. That I would never force myself or my opinions on her. That I would always recognise her complete right to make her own choices. Yolanda and I have a marriage of freedom. We love each other, and are honest with each other, but we have our own lives and our own interests. I may do things for her churches from time to time, and she may come to dinner with my artist friends, but neither of us expects the other to pretend to interests that aren't compatible." He looked from Holmes' face to mine, searching for sympathy, I expect. "Ours is a modern marriage," he insisted.

"Very well," Holmes said. "What happened in the latter half of June? And, the date?"

"The date? I don't know, it was a weekend—a Sunday. I'd been to the park and came home to find Yolanda . . . troubled. She was in the sitting room with the curtains drawn and the windows shut, although it was stifling. When I turned up the lights, she cried out as if she'd seen a snake in the room. She wouldn't tell me what was wrong, but the maid said she'd started the morning completely normally, then after breakfast suddenly retreated into the room, and stayed there all day.

"I coaxed her to eat and put her to bed. The next morning she seemed better. She laughed when I asked her what had happened, and said something odd about being unaccustomed to happiness.

"She wouldn't let me stay home, insisted she was fine, tried to pretend she was herself again. But she wasn't. I could see that something was eating at her, but I thought perhaps it was simply as she had said, that when one has spent one's life tensed against life's next blow, security and comfort can themselves seem untrustworthy. I vowed to myself that I would sustain her comfort, until she became convinced that it was real, and permanent.

"Since then, I've done my best to convince her of her worth. I took her to Brighton for a few days, to amuse her, bought her books, even went to her favourite church with her. And I thought I was succeeding. Her friends started to drop by again, she's been out a few times— generally with a mundane purpose, to shop or visit the lending library, but the haunted look seemed to leave her, and she spent less time behind closed curtains.

"Until she disappeared." Holmes sat back, one finger resting across his lips; I sat forward. "This was Friday. Three days ago. I'd been up late Thursday, working, and I fell asleep in the studio—I keep a bed there, so I don't disturb the household with my comings and goings.

I slept until noon, then went home. The maid, Sally, told me that Yolanda had gone out first thing that morning with a packed valise, saying she wasn't sure when she would return."

"Had she received a letter? A telegram?"

"Not that Sally knew, and the only time she'd been away from the house was when she went to the greengrocer's Thursday afternoon. I was more puzzled than alarmed—Yolanda does this sometimes, goes off for a day or two. She calls them her 'religious adventures.' Still, she always tells me when she's going to be away, and with her recent uneasiness in mind, I found myself distracted. Twice I left my painting to walk home and see if she had come back. She hadn't.

"So on Saturday I woke up early, and when there was still no sign of her, I sent Sally out to do the round of Yolanda's friends, to see if any of them knew where she was. While she was doing that, I went around Yolanda's favourite churches and temples and the like, but no-one had seen her in days. I didn't know what else to do, so I went back to the studio, but I couldn't settle to work."

"You didn't wish to notify the police?"

"No. Not until, well, considerably longer. And then when I returned to the house around tea-time, Sally gave me an envelope she'd found under my pillow, where Yolanda had put it before she left. It could have sat there for days, if I'd continued to sleep at the studio, but when Sally'd come in, she couldn't decide what to do with herself, not knowing if we were in for dinner and all, so she'd decided to strip the beds."

Holmes made a small gesture of impatience with his finger, and Damian abandoned the question of out-of-sorts maidservants.

"Anyway, this is what she found."

Damian reached around for his jacket and fished out not one, but two envelopes. He half-rose to hand the light blue one to Holmes. For a moment, the slip of blue linked two near-identical hands, then Holmes' long fingers were pulling at the contents, tipping the page so that I, too, could read the words. They were written in a precise, bold hand:

Dearest D,

I am going away for awhile, on what I suppose is one of
my religious adventures. This time I've taken E with me. I
must ask you to be patient, although I know that you always are.

Your loving Y

P.S. I don't think I've told you in awhile, that you are the
best thing that could have happened to me and to E.

"Who is—" Holmes started, then cut off as Damian stood up and
held out the second envelope. His clenched jaws declared that here, at
last, was what he had been working towards: There was resentment in
his face, and embarrassment—perhaps even shame—but also determination.

Holmes took the envelope; Damian retreated, not to his chair, but
to the low wall at the back of the terrace, where we could only see his
outline and the glow of his cigarette. Holmes' fingers pushed back the
flap, and eased out a photograph.

It was a snapshot, showing three people. Damian Adler stood in
the back, wearing a dark, formal frock coat and high collar: From his
overly dignified expression, the costume was a joke. In front of him,
the top of her head well below his shoulders, stood a tiny Oriental
woman. She wore Western dress, looking more comfortable in it than
many photographs of Orientals I had seen. Her ankles were shapely
under a slightly out-of-date dress, her glossy black hair was bobbed;
her dark eyes sparkled at the camera with the same sense of humour
as his.

It was the third person in the photograph that made Holmes go
very still and caused my breath to catch: a child around three years
old, held in the woman's arms. Damian's right hand was on the
woman's shoulder, but his left arm circled them both; his hand
looked massive beside the infant torso. The child's features had
blurred slightly as she swivelled to crane up at Damian, but the glossy
hair was every bit as black as the mother's.

"My wife, Yolanda," Damian said into the pregnant silence—and there seemed no trace of embarrassment in his voice, only affection and worry. "And our daughter, Estelle."

He came off of the wall, to look over Holmes' shoulder at the photograph.

"Estelle is missing, too," he said. "I need . . ." He cleared his throat, and frowned at the picture in his father's hand. "I need you to help me find them."

His embarrassment, I saw at last, was not over having married a woman of Shanghai, nor even that his wife had a dubious past. His shame was because he had been forced to come to Holmes for help.

Chapter Eight

*The Father (2): Some men remember their childhood
among women. These few may reach back and find the
shadows to their light, the receiving to their giving,
and bring the worlds together.
These men are called saints, or gods.*
Testimony, I:3

I LEFT HOLMES AND DAMIAN TO THEIR DISCUSSION A
short time later, both through tiredness—we were, after all, just
off an Atlantic crossing, and I never sleep well on the open seas—and
cowardice: I did not wish to be there when Holmes suggested to his already estranged son that hunting through London for an eccentric,
free-spirited daughter-in-law might not be the most productive use of
his time.

Also, I needed some time alone to grapple with the idea of Holmes—
of myself!—as a grandparent.

Lulu had unpacked my valise, although she knew me well enough
to leave the trunks untouched, so I had hair-brush and night things
to hand. I ran a hot bath, and felt my muscles relax for the first time
in many days.

As I walked down the hallway to the bedroom, I heard that the men had moved inside, and one of them had considerately shut the sitting room door so as not to disturb me. The lack of raised voices indicated an amicable discussion, which suggested that Holmes had very sensibly agreed to assist his son. I climbed into bed, leaving the curtains open to the light of the moon, three nights from full.

From where I lay, I could see the grey glow of the treetops in the walled garden, and beyond them the ghostly outlines of the Downs. Thanks to the extraordinary appearance of Damian Adler on our terrace, I had missed the sunset completely.

I was grateful beyond words that he had re-entered our lives, and not only because of the hole that their uncomfortable meeting had left in Holmes. The world is large, when a man wishes to disappear, and the tantalising possibility that he was still out there had gnawed silently at us both.

I was especially pleased that Damian had grown into a man with weight to his personality—it would have been hard, had he turned out charming (a shallow quality, charm, designed to deceive the unwary) or dull. Instead, he was intelligent (which one would expect) and madly egotistical (marching in and laying his life and problems before us, without so much as a by-your-leave—but again, what might one expect of the offspring of two divas?) and he possessed that animal magnetism born of intensity.

It was difficult, with the artistic personality in general and the Bohemian way of life in particular, to know how much of their eccentricity was cultivated and how much was true imbalance. Damian had been hiding a lot, both in fact and in emotion. I had sensed deceit woven throughout the fabric of his story, everywhere but in his declared love for wife and child. However, subterfuge was perhaps understandable in a man coming to ask a favour of the father he barely knew, the eminent and absent father whose hand he had refused to shake, five years before.

The complexity of the man was both a comfort and a concern. I could only hope that, now he was here, Holmes would take considerable care not to drive him away—but, no, I decided, there would be little chance of that, not after he had held that photograph of Damian's family. I looked forward to meeting Yolanda Adler, wherever she had taken herself off to.

If nothing else, I thought as I pulled up the bed-clothes, a renowned Surrealist with a missing Chinese wife and small daughter promised to fill nicely the anticipated tedium of Holmes' return.

I woke many hours later with birdsong and the first rays of sun coming through the open window.

The house was still: Lulu would not arrive until ten, and the two men had talked until the small hours. Holmes had not come to bed, but that was a common enough occurrence when he was up late and did not wish to disturb me.

However, he was not in the small bedroom next door, nor on the divan in his laboratory. He was not in the sitting room, or on the terrace, or in the kitchen, and there was no sign that he had made coffee, which he did whenever he was up and out before the rest of the house.

I walked down to the door of the guest suite, where Lulu would have installed Damian. It was closed. I pressed my ear to the wood, hoping it wouldn't suddenly open, dropping me at my step-son's feet, but I could hear no sound from within. I frowned in indecision. Perhaps they had talked all night, after which Holmes had been struck by the desire to see his devastated hive.

Without coffee?

I tightened the belt on my dressing gown and reached for the knob. It ticked slightly when the tongue slid back, but the hinges opened in silence. I put my head around the door.

Nothing. No sleeping Damian, no foreign hair-brush or pocket change on the dressing table, no reading matter on the bed-side table, no carpet slippers tucked beneath the wardrobe. The bed had not been slept in; the window was shut. Stepping inside, I confirmed that the room was bare of his possessions, although clearly he had been here: He'd left a few crumpled bits in the waste-basket, along with a clump of hair from a hair-brush.

Upstairs, a quick search revealed that Holmes had not packed a valise for himself—but then, a man who maintained half a dozen bolt-holes in London did not need to carry with him a change of shirt and a tooth-brush.

Especially if doing so risked waking me with the creaks of the old wooden staircase.

I went back through all the rooms in the house, ending in the sitting room, where ashes and the level in the cognac decanter told of a lengthy session. There was no note to suggest when or why they had left, or for how long.

I sighed, and went to the kitchen to make coffee.

Holmes' unplanned and unexplained absence was by no means sinister, or even suggestive. We were hardly the free-love Bohemians of Damian's circle, but neither did we live in one another's pockets, and often went our separate ways. If Holmes had gone off with his son in search of a wayward woman and child, he was not required to take me with him, or even to ask my permission.

He might, however, have written me a note. Even Damian's wife had done as much.

I drank my coffee on the terrace as the world awoke, and ate a breakfast of toast and fresh peaches. When Lulu came, chatting and curious, I retreated upstairs, put on some old, soft clothing that had once belonged to my father, and began the lengthy task of disassembling my travelling trunks.

I emptied one trunk, reducing it to piles for repair, storage, and new possessions. As I was sorting through the odds and ends of the past year—embroidered Kashmiri shawl from India, carved ivory chopstick from California, tiny figurine from Japan—I came upon an object brought from California in a transfer of authority, as it were: the *mezuzah* my mother had put on our front door there, which a friend had removed at her death and kept safe for my return.

I looked up at a tap at the half-open door.

"Good morning, Lulu," I said. "What can I do for you?"

"Mr Adler, ma'am. Is he coming back? It's just that his room looks empty, and if he's not going to be needing it—"

"No, I think he's left us for the time being."

"That's all right, then, I thought he'd finished, and with Mrs Hudson coming home on the week-end and all I wanted—"

"That's fine, Lulu."

"Are you nearly finished in here, because I could help if you—"

Lulu was an implacable force of nature; as Mrs Hudson had once remarked, if a person waited for Lulu to finish a sentence, the spiders would make webs on her hat. I abandoned the field of battle, and retreated downstairs to start in on the mail.

By noon I had written an answer to a letter from my old Oxford friend Veronica, admiring the photograph she had sent me of her infant son, and responded to a list of questions from my San Francisco lawyers concerning my property there. Another letter from an Oxford colleague was pinned to a paper he was due to present on the Filioque Clause, for which he wanted my comments. I dutifully waded into his detailed exegesis of this Fourth Century addendum to the Nicene Creed, but found the technical minutiae of the Latin trying and eventually bogged down in his attempted unravelling of the convoluted phraseology of Cyril of Alexandria. I let the manuscript fall shut, scribbled him a note suggesting that he have it looked over by someone whose expertise lay in the Greek rather than the Hebrew Testament, and stood up: I needed air, and exercise.

But first, I hunted down a book I'd thought of on Holmes' shelves, then followed thumps and rustles to their source in the upstairs hallway. Lulu looked up as my presence at the head of the stairs caught her eye.

"I'm going for a walk," I told her. "Don't bother to set out any luncheon, I shouldn't think either of them will be back. And when you've finished here, why don't you take off the rest of the day?"

"Are you certain, ma'am? Because I really don't mind—"

"I'll see you tomorrow, Lulu."

"Thank you, ma'am, and I'll make sure to lock up when I go, like you and Mr Holmes—"

I laced on a pair of lightweight boots I had not worn for the best part of a year, took a detour through the kitchen to raid the pantry for cheese, bread, and drink, and left the house.

I turned south and west, following the old paths and crossing the new roads towards where the Cuckmere valley opened to the sea. The tide was sufficiently out to make the small river loop lazily around the wash; three children were building a castle in the patch of sand that collected on the opposite bank. Even from this distance I could see the pink of their exposed shoulders, and I thought—the back of my neck well remembered—how sore they would be tonight, crying at the touch of bed-clothes on their inflamed skin.

Which image returned me to my thoughts before sleep the night before: the photograph, and the child. Her name was Estelle, Damian had told us, after the bright stars on the night she was born. An odd little girl, troubled by everyday things another child would not even notice—she would exhaust herself with tears over the sight of a feral cat in the rain, or a scratch on the leather of her mother's new shoes. But clever, reading already, chattering happily in three languages. She and her father were closer than might normally be the case, both because she was in and out of his studio all day, and because of Yolanda's periodic absences.

He wanted us to understand, Yolanda was not an irresponsible mother. The child was well looked after, and Yolanda never went away without ensuring Estelle's care. It was simply that she believed a child did best when the parents were satisfied with their lives, when their sense of excitement and exploration was allowed full expression. Self-sacrifice twisted a mother and damaged the child, Yolanda believed.

Or so Damian said.

Personally, I thought he seemed too willing to forgive his wife both her present whims and her past influences. Without meeting the woman, of course, I could not know, but the bare bones of the story could easily paint a far less romantic picture, beginning with the blunt fact that a young woman whose friends were prostitutes was not apt to be an innocent herself. And, running my mind back over Damian's tale, it occurred to me that he had taken great care to say nothing of what she had been doing between leaving the missionary school at eleven and being kicked onto the streets at sixteen.

Without a doubt, he had been besotted with her—even his gesture in the snapshot testified to that—but this was a man whose life's goal was to embrace light and dark, rationality and madness, obscenity and beauty.

One had to wonder if the affection was as powerfully mutual. One might as easily posit another scenario: Desperate young woman meets wide-eyed foreigner with considerable talent and an air of breeding; young woman flirts with the young foreigner and engages his sympathy along with his passion: Young woman encourages the man's art, nudges him into financial solvency, and finds herself pregnant by him. Marriage follows, and a British passport, and soon she is in London, free to live as she pleases, far from the brutal streets of Shanghai.

Without meeting her, I could not know. But I wished Holmes had stuck around long enough for us to talk it over. I wanted to ask how he felt about having his son marry a former prostitute.

I left the path at the old lighthouse, to sit overlooking the Channel, and took from my pockets the cheese roll, the bottle of lemonade, and the slim blue book I had found in the library between a monograph on systems of zip fastening and an enormous tome on poisonous plants of the Brazilian rain-forest.

I ran my fingertips across the gold letters on the front cover: *Practical Handbook of Bee Culture,* the title read, and underneath: *With some Observations upon the Segregation of the Queen.*

I had read Holmes' book—which he, only half in jest, referred to as his *magnum opus*—years before, but I remembered little of it, and then mostly that, for a self-proclaimed handbook, there seemed little instruction, and nothing to explain why its author had retired from the life of a consulting detective at the age of forty-two in order to raise bees on the Sussex Downs. Now, nine years and a lifetime after I'd first encountered it, I opened it anew and commenced to read my husband's reflections on the bee. He opened, I saw, with a piece of Shakespeare, as I remembered, *Henry V:*

The honey-bees,
creatures that by a rule in nature teach
the act of order to a peopled kingdom. . . .

Chief among the everyday miracles within the hive is
that of how the first bee discovered the means by which
watery nectar, vulnerable to spoilage, might be made to
keep the hive not only through the winter, but through a
score of winters. Can one conceive of an accidental discov-
ery, a happenstance that arranged for the hive sisters to be
arrayed *en masse* at the mouth of their hive, fanning their
wings so vigorously and for so long that the nectar they
had gathered evaporated in the draught, growing thick
and imperishable? And yet if not an accident, we are left
with two equally unsatisfactory explanations: a Creator's
design, or a hive intelligence.

Suddenly a tiny brown object flashed towards where I sat and began to snap and growl furiously at my boot-laces. I quelled the impulse to kick the beast over the cliff, and received the apologies of its
owner with little sympathy.

"If that dog gets in among the sheep," I told the girl, "don't be surprised if it feels the end of a shepherd's crook."

Her boy-friend began to object, then noticed that I was actually a
female and toned down his remarks somewhat.

I rose, and continued with my literary stroll.

The language of bees is one of the great mysteries left
us in this age, the means by which this genus communicate. For speak they do, to tell their hive-mates of food, to
warn of invasion, to exchange the password of identity, to
reassure that all is well. Speech among humans is a complex interaction between tongue and teeth, lungs and
larynx, driven by mind and a thousand generations of tradition.

But what if we humans had developed along another line than that of primate? What if, instead of manipulative digits and opposing thumbs, we were given only arms, teeth, and wings? If in place of fist and weapon we were given a defence that required us to lay down our own lives? If we lacked the lungs and trachea that gave rise to speech, how would we preserve the intelligence of our own community?

Humans convey meaning in a multitude of ways: the lift of a shoulder, the sideways slip of a gaze, the tensing of small muscles, or the quantity of air passing through the vocal cords. How much more must this be so in a complex hive-mind that lacks the brute communication of words?

One finds common sense and intelligence in the newest of hives and the rawest of virgin queens, a discernment that goes far past mere dumb survival. No beekeeper doubts that the creatures in his charge have their own language, as immediate and real as that which might be found in a village composed entirely of brothers and sisters. However, whether bees communicate by odour, by subtle emanations, by faint song, or by infinitesimal gestures we have yet to discover.

A loud voice greeted me from a few feet away, and I looked up, startled, to see a group of at least twenty young women determinedly equipped for mountain-climbing—all had hiking poles, all sweated under sturdy trousers and heavy Alpine boots. Their leader, a stout bespectacled woman of forty, had hailed me. I paused politely with the book closed over my finger.

"Do you know where we might take some refreshment?" she asked with a touch of desperation.

I looked to see where I was, then pointed towards the distant rise. "You see that tower there? Keep going past it and you'll come to an hotel. I'm sure they'll have ices and tea."

The entire group thanked me and marched away, their boots thudding on the bare path like so many cattle hooves. I shook my head and resumed my solitary way.

The massacre of the males is a yearly occurrence in the hive—"Delivering over to executioners pale the lazy yawning drone." When the days close in and the last nectar ceases, the workers cast their gaze upon the drones, whom they have willingly fed and cosseted all the year long, but who are now only a burden on the food reserves, a threat to the future of the hive. So the females rise against the useless males and exterminate them every one, viciously ripping their former charges to pieces and driving any survivors out into the cold.

The female is generally the more practical member of any species.

What might we say of the intelligence of bees? On the one hand, it beggars the imagination that an entire species would permit itself to be enslaved, penned up, pushed about, and systematically pillaged for the hard-fought product of a year's labours.

Yet is this so remarkably different from the majority of human workers? Are they not enslaved to the coal face or the office desk, told where to go and what to do by forces outside their control? Do not the government and those who control prices in the market-place systematically rob human workers of all but a thin measure of the year's earnings?

I laughed aloud at this last paragraph, only to be startled by yet another voice, this one nearly on top of me.

"Good day, madam."

I jolted to a stop and looked at the man who had addressed me, a dapper figure with pure white hair underneath the straw boater he was lifting in greeting.

"Hullo," I answered.

"I wonder if you might know the shortest path to the Tiger Inn, in East Dean? I am supposed—"

"There," I said, pointing repressively. This fashion for countryside rambles looked to have severe drawbacks, particularly at this time of year.

When the white-haired gentleman had left, I checked my position again and found that I had just about run out of cliff-side path: Below me lay Eastbourne with its frothy pier-top pleasure palace and sea-front hotels. Its long curve of shingle beach was thick with holiday-makers and umbrellas, the waves dark with splashing bodies large and small.

Less than five miles up the coast from that frivolous piece of archi-tecture, on a sunny September morning 858 years before, half a thou-sand ships had come to shore, carrying a king, a flag, and enough men and horses to seize England's future.

I glanced around me warily, and abandoned the public footpaths for the pastures of sheep and gorse, reading in solitary contentment until a shadow fell upon the page: My feet had brought me home. I let myself through the gate, to stand beneath trees heavy with summer fruit; the air was thick with fragrance, and with the throb of activity from the hives. Lulu's bicycle still leant on the wall near by the kitchen door, so I cleared away some rotting apples and settled down with my back against a tree.

Beekeeping would appear to be a hobby for the tin-pot god, the man who seeks to keep an entire race under his control. In point of fact, a mere human has little control over bees: He shelters them, he takes their honey, he drives away pests, but in the end, he merely hopes for the best.

A bee has no loyalty to the keeper, only to the hive; no

commitment to the place, only to the community. A queen has no conversation for her human counterpart, and she or any other bee will attack the human protector if he makes a gesture that can be read as threat.

Despite millennia of close history, in the end, the best a beekeeper can hope for is that he be ignored by his bees.

In the hive, there can be but one ruler. The queen (Virgil, here, got it wrong, and imagined a bee king) is permitted a sole outing in her long life, one brief foray into the blue heights. She chooses a day of singular warmth and clarity, and sings her anticipation, stirring the hive into a state of excitement before she finally launches herself into the sky, pulling the males after her like the tail of a comet. Only the fastest can catch the queen, with her long wings and great strength, which ensures the vigour of their future progeny.

Then she returns to her hive where, if the beekeeper has his way, she spends the remainder of her days, never to fly, never to use her wings, never to see the sky again.

When one watches that queen, dutifully planting her eggs in the cells prepared for them, surrounded at every moment by attentive workers, fed and cleaned and urged to ever greater production, one can only wonder: Does she remember? Does some part of that mind live forever in the soaring blue, inhabiting freedom in the way a prisoner will imagine a rich meal with such detail his mouth waters? Or does the endless song of the hive fill her mind, compensating for the drudgery of her lot?

Perhaps that freedom is why the queen is the hive's one true warrior, jealously guarding her position against her unborn rivals until the regal powers wane, her production falters.

But a queen does not die of old age. If she does not fall in royal battle, or of the cold, her daughters will eventually turn against her. They gather, hundreds of them, to surround her in a living mass, smothering her and crushing her. And when they have finished, they discard her lifeless body and begin the business of raising up another queen.

The queen is dead, long live the queen.

That is the way of the hive.

My attention was caught here by motion at the top of the book: a bee, come to explore the possibilities of the printed page. Or more likely, taking advantage of a temporary resting place, for her leg sacs bulged with pollen, a load that the most doughty of aeronauts might reconsider. She walked along the blue binding, as heedless of me as I was of the sky overhead; reaching the spine, she gathered herself and flashed off in the direction of the white Langstroth box thirty feet away, in the shade of Mrs Hudson's beloved Cox's Orange Pippin.

I pocketed the book and followed the bee.

Holmes had situated the hive to be warmed by the morning sun but shaded by the apple tree during the afternoon. I knelt nearby, avoiding a wasp that was working at a fallen apple, and watched the bees come and go.

The Langstroth hive was a wooden structure roughly twenty inches on a side. On the outside it was a stack of plain, whitewashed boxes, but within lay a technological marvel of precise measurements and moving parts, all of them aimed at providing the bees with such perfect surroundings, they would stay put and work. One hive could produce hundreds of pounds of honey, under the right conditions, from bees that would be just as pleased with a hollow tree.

At the bottom front of the box was a long entrance slit with a porch on which the workers landed. Or, as on this hot day, stood facing the outer world while whirring their wings enthusiastically—this was the draught that Holmes had written about, air pushed through the hive to exit, hotter and damper than it had entered, through vents at the upper back. The sound this made struck the neophyte as a warning of high danger, as if the hive was about to erupt in fury and search for a human target for its wrath.

I knew Holmes' bees well enough, however, to hear that this was merely the roar of a hard-working hive, putting away its wealth, one minuscule drop at a time—until the beekeeper ripped off the top of their universe and pillaged the community's resources for his own savage needs.

One queen; a handful of males who spent their lives in toil-free luxury awaiting a call to shoot skyward in a mating flight; and thousand upon thousand of hard-labouring females, who moved up the ranks from nursery attendants to nectar-gatherers before their brief lives were spent. An organic machine, entirely designed to provide for the next generation.

Which when one thinks about it, is pretty much what all creatures are designed for.

And now, yet again, my thoughts had circled around to Damian Adler and his young daughter. In irritation, I rose and brushed off my knees: At last, Lulu's bicycle had gone.

I used my key on the French doors from the terrace—as Lulu had noted, it was idiosyncratic for rural dwellers to lock a house with such care, but Holmes and I never knew when London would follow us home. In the kitchen, every surface gleamed. I put my empty bottle in the box under the sink and went to the sitting room to take off my boots.

It was very quiet. When was the last time I had been alone in this house? Unlike Lulu, Mrs Hudson lived here, so it would have been some rare occasion when she was away at market and Holmes was off doing whatever Holmes did. Years, probably, since I had been all by myself there for more than an hour or two.

Normally, one is only conscious of the room around one, but when no-one else is present, one's awareness is free to fill all the spaces. I stood for a time and listened to the heavy old flint walls around me: silent; quiescent; welcoming. Passing from room to room, I threw open all the doors and windows. In the laboratory, I located a screwdriver, and carried it and the *mezuzah* downstairs, to mount it on the front door-jamb. I touched it with my fingers, saying the prayer and welcoming it to its new home, then took myself out to a shaded corner of the terrace to read.

Bees feel joy, and outrage, and contentment. Bees play, tossing themselves in flight with no point but for the pleasure of the thing. And bees despair, when hopelessness and loss have become their lot.

A hive that loses its queen and has no other queen cells to raise up is dead, its future sterile. Workers may continue for a time, but soon listlessness and melancholy overcome them. Their sound changes, from the roar of energetic purpose to a note of anguish and loss. One of the workers may try to summon the energy of the hive and lay her own eggs, as if to conjure up the presence of royalty by enacting its rituals, but every member, drone to new-hatched worker, feels the end upon them.

For the bee, unlike the human, the future is all: The next generation is the singular purpose of their every motion, their every decision. Not for *Apis mellifera* the ethical struggles of individual versus community rights, the protest against oppression, the life-long dedication to perfecting an individual's nature and desire. For the hive, there is no individual, merely the all; no present, only the call of the future; no personal contribution, only the accumulated essence of great numbers.

The sun sloped behind the roof, shadows crept through the orchard, and finally, I closed the covers of Holmes' little book.

As I'd remembered, it was less "practical handbook" than philosophical treatise. As a girl of fifteen, it had meant little to me. Now, having known the man for nine years and been married to him for three, I found the document astonishing, so revealing of this proud, solitary man that I was amazed he had given it for publication.

I no longer wondered why he had retired at such an early age; rather, I was grateful that he had turned his back on his fellow man, instead of letting bitterness overcome him.

The night air moved up towards the Downs, washing over sea and orchard. I breathed it in, and thought that henceforth, loneliness would smell to me like fermenting apples.

I left the book on a desk in the library and went to find a bottle of last year's honey wine, a beverage not improved by longevity but containing nonetheless a breath of that summer.

The twelvemonth since Holmes bottled it had been an extraordinary one. The cases had pressed fast upon us, one after another, each with its singular cast of players: Miss Dorothy Ruskin, the mad archaeologist of Palestine, had come to our door a year ago less two days. No sooner had that investigation ended than we were pulled into a mystery on Dartmoor, and on that case's heels we had entered a Berkshire country house inhabited by Bedouins. Afterwards, we had scarcely drawn breath before Mycroft had sent us to India and a middle-aged version of Kipling's Kim; on our way homeward, after a foray into the affairs of the Emperor of Japan, we had landed in San Francisco, where lay the haunts of my own past.

One calendar year, filled with revelations, hardship, intense friendships, painful losses, and a view into my childhood that left me, three months later, shaken and unsure of myself. Another year like this one, and people would no longer comment on the age difference between my husband and myself.

I set the wine to cool while I closed up the house against the creatures of the night, then put together a plate of strong cheese, oat biscuits, and summer fruit. I spread some cushions and a travelling rug on the warm stones of the terrace and dined in solitary splendour while the colours came into the sky. I lay with the soft rug around me, watching the azure shift into indigo, and spotted the first meteors.

It was the annual Perseids shower. We'd seen their harbingers a few nights before when the sea mists lifted, silent lights darting across the heavens, as magical as anything in nature. Tonight the shower was at its height, and despite a near-full moon, their brightness and numbers lit the sky.

I fell asleep watching them, no doubt assisted by the better part of a bottle of wine.

Chapter Nine

*Darkness: When such a man comes of age,
there comes a period of darkness, when emptiness and
disgust lie all about and there is no beauty in the world.
The lump of meteor-metal the boy carried went cold
and empty of Power.*
Testimony, I:4

DAMIAN, ANY MORE ALCOHOL AND YOUR WITS WILL be the worse for it tomorrow."

"I'll be fine."

"You will be upright and conversing, but hardly at your peak."

"My wits were at a peak today, and what good did it do us?"

"I did warn you that a round of the hospitals and morgues would be pure slog with little hope of success. If you were to permit the police—"

"No police."

"I assure you I am capable of inventing a story to account for my enquiries into one Yolanda Adler."

"I came to you because I thought it might let me avoid the police. If you can't do it, say the word and I'll go."

"I am merely suggesting that using the established machinery of the official enquiry agents could save us time."

"No police. Yolanda and Estelle have just begun to settle in here. To start out life with a police enquiry and a scandal would be too much."

"I appreciate your concern. And I am willing to circumvent the police force in order to salvage your privacy. However, it will make things all the more difficult if I am saddled with a bleary-eyed and half-intoxicated partner on the morrow. I ask again, Damian, please stop."

"Yes, all right. There. Happy?"

"Thank you."

"It isn't as if you had never indulged."

"Yes, thanks to Watson, all the world knows my peccadilloes. Do you wish to bath first, or shall I?"

"You go ahead. Although I'd have thought we could afford something a bit grander than this hole with a shared bath down the hall."

"Inconvenience is the price of invisibility."

"Holy Christ, that was cold! Was the geyser working when you bathed?"

"I looked at the device and decided not to risk an explosion."

"Well, save your penny, it doesn't work anyway. Brrr. And shaving—cold water is why I grew a beard in the first place, when I couldn't afford hot water—they sell it in shops, in Shanghai—and I grew tired of savaging my jaw-line with a razor. It looks as if I'll now have a full beard rather than just the trimmings."

"One does indeed dread the pull of the blade against cold skin."

"I can't see you in a beard."

"I have worn one from time to time, when a case suggested it. I cultivated a goatee in America before the War, but the longest I had a full beard was when I travelled in the Himalayas. The sensation of its removal, in an open-air barber's in Delhi with half the street bearing witness, was exquisite."

"America, eh? Where did you go?"

"Chicago, for the most part."

"Do you think these bed-clothes have been laundered in the last month?"

"I should doubt it."

"Perhaps I'll sleep on top of them."

"The night is warm."

"And use my clothes as a pillow."

"Head lice can indeed be a nuisance."

"You sure you don't want a small night-cap, to help you sleep?"

"Damian, I—"

"Yes, yes, you're right. Clear-headed."

"Shall I get the lights?"

"No! Leave them. For a bit. If you don't mind."

"As you wish."

"So. Did you go to New Jersey? When you were in America?"

"I passed through on my way from New York, that is all."

"I went there once. With Mother. When I was nine."

"Which would have been 1903?"

"That's right. Why?"

"1903 was the year I left London for Sussex."

"And took up beekeeping."

"Yes."

"Did you truly not know?"

"About you?"

"About me, about her, about . . ."

"Your mother was a remarkably clever woman. Too clever, I fear, for the men in her life. What she told me, I believed."

"Wanted to believe."

"I did not *wish* to be sent away. I . . . was very fond of your mother. She was an extraordinary woman."

"She was lonely. A son can only do so much."

"I fear she may have been too clever for her own good, as well."

"Easy for you to say."

"Not so easy, no."

"In any case, good night."

"I shall turn off the—"

"Leave it! One of them, if you don't mind. The small one."

"As you like. Good night, Damian."

Chapter Ten

Wrestling with Angels (1): The boy born of the Elements
went up to the high mountains, and there
he stood before the waiting Angels and said,
"Take me, I am yours, do with me as you will."
Testimony, I:5

I WOKE WHEN THE TERRACE GREW LIGHT, GROANING with the aches brought by alcohol compounded by hard stones. Was it Hippocrates who declared that moonlight affected the moistures of the brain, and drove a person mad? Certainly, it did one's body no good.

I staggered to the kitchen to make strong coffee. At seven o'clock I picked up the telephone and asked to be connected with the Monk's Tun inn.

"Hello, is that Johanna? Oh, Rebecca, good morning, this is Mary Russell. Could you— What's that? Oh, thank you, it's good to be back. Could I ask you to take a message to Lulu? Tell her she needn't come out today—in fact, not to come out until she hears from me. Oh no, everything is fine, I'd just prefer she not come out for a few days. That's right, Mrs Hudson is due back Saturday, and I'm sure she'll want Lulu's help then. Thanks. Oh, and give my greetings to your aunt."

I spent the morning settling into the quiet, amiable house, and finished up the accumulated correspondence. Feeling virtuous, I dropped the letters on the table near the front door and went to don clothing similar to what I had worn the previous afternoon, digging out a small rucksack from the lumber room and tossing into it another impromptu picnic, a few tools, some paper, and a pencil.

If Holmes was off dealing with one mystery, there was no reason I couldn't turn my mind to the one left behind.

The empty hive was on a lonely southerly slope in the lee of a stone wall, as remote as any spot on the Downs. On the other side of the wall was the ancient burial mound; in the distance was a branch of the South Downs Way, one of the prehistoric foot-highways that weave across England and Wales. Towards the sea, figures moved along a rise in the ground: striking, how human beings tend to cluster together rather than spread themselves over stretches of emptiness such as this.

As I quenched my thirst with the bottle of water I had brought, I studied the empty hive. It was typical of those Holmes used, with three stacked segments, the two larger making up the hive body, and a shallower segment on top called the super. All three segments contained sliding frames on which the bees made their comb; when these were full, other supers would be added on top, to satisfy the bees' desire to build upwards. Somewhere between the segments there would be a queen excluder, to segregate the larger queen and her eggs from the comb to be harvested.

When the bottle was empty, I went down on my knees for a scrutiny of the hive's empty doorway.

No sign of mice, a common problem with hives. No litter of dead bees in the forecourt of the hive, and Holmes would have mentioned the presence of the destructive wax moth. So far as I knew, the paint was the same used on all the hives, and the construction was of a kind with at least two others. I prised off the top, set aside the tinkling bells, and began to examine the frames. The fragrance was dizzying.

Even though I was not particularly enamoured with honey, the temptation to rip into a segment and pop a wad of ambrosia into my mouth was powerful.

However, I did not want to tempt a neighbouring hive into a raid, introducing bad habits where there were none, so I left the comb whole.

It took some time to slide up each frame, and some muscle to wrestle aside the sections. I shone my torch around what remained. No moths, no death, just full comb and emptiness, as if the entire hive, queen to drones, had heard the Piper's flute and taken off into the blue. I put down my torch and reached for the bottom section's first frame, to return it to its place.

"Did you find anything?" enquired a voice.

I dropped the weighty frame onto my foot, stifled an oath, and swung around to glare at whatever holiday tripper had come to me for his entertainment.

He was a small, round man, clean-shaven and neatly dressed in worn tweeds and a soft hat. His arms were resting atop the dry wall, his chin propped on his fists. Clearly he had been watching me for some time while I had stood, top over tea-kettle with my head in the box.

Before I could send him on his way—the public footpath might be nearby, but this was decidedly not on it—he straightened. "Mrs Holmes, I presume?"

"More or less. Who—"

"Glen Miranker; at your service."

"Ah. The bee man."

"As you say. My housekeeper told me that you and your husband had returned. I rather expected to see him out here before this."

"He has been called away. But you're right, he came out to look at the hive immediately we got back on Monday evening."

"Did he have any thoughts?"

"Holmes generally does. But in this instance, he didn't share them with me."

"Am I right in believing that you are not familiar with the apiarist's art?"

"Merely an untrained assistant," I admitted. "However, I thought I might look at the hive and see if anything caught my eye. When we were here Monday, it was nearly dusk, and he only got as far down as the super."

I reached for the frame again, but as if my words had been an invitation, the man stretched out on the wall and then rolled over it, picking himself up stiffly from the ground and grabbing my torch. I waited as he conducted a close examination of the nooks and crannies, then I resumed sliding the laden frames into place.

"You have rather a lot of swarm cells here," he noted.

"As your letter to Holmes said, they swarmed," I noted dryly.

"But I checked the hive less than three weeks ago."

I glanced at his aged back, bent over the hive, and wondered how he had managed to unload the boxes by himself. Perhaps he didn't. Perhaps it had been more than three weeks ago.

When I shifted the boxes, he made no effort to help, confirming my suspicions that his back was not fully up to the task. Instead, he inspected, delivering all the while a lecture on the craft of beekeeping such as even Holmes had not inflicted on me. I heard about varieties of bee and methods of hive construction, chemical analysis of the wax and the nutritional composition of various sources of honey, several theories of communication—Holmes' "subtle emanations"—and how the temper of the hive reflected the personality not only of their queen, but of their keeper.

"Which is what makes this particular hive so very intriguing," the man said. By this time I had returned all three sections to their former setting, and he was prone with one cheek on the grass, examining the hive's foundations. I obediently struggled to tip the heavy box off of the ground. "Your husband's bees tend to be eight parts methodical, one part experimental, and one part equally divided between startling innovation and resounding failure."

"Er, you mean that his techniques are either innovative or failures?"

His head came around the side of the hive. "No, I mean the bees themselves. Reflecting his personality, don't you know?"

"I see."

He paused to stare off into the distance; my muscles began to quiver. "I recall him describing how he had introduced a peculiar herb out of the Caucasus Mountains that he'd heard had an invigorating effect on the honey. The bees took to it with great enthusiasm, made an effort to spread that herb's nectar evenly throughout the combs, became disconsolate when the flowers began to fade. Unfortunately, as it turned out, the taste of the honey itself was absolutely revolting. Rendered the year's entire production unpalatable." He shook his head and continued his minute examination.

"So, are you suggesting that this hive's madness is a reflection of some aspect of their keeper?"

He sat up, startled, and I gratefully allowed the hive to thump to the ground. "No. No, no, no, I shouldn't have said it has anything to do with him."

I laughed at the vehemence of his protest. "I'm only joking, Mr Miranker. I should say it's every bit as likely that the hive decided it didn't like the subtle emanations coming from the burial mound across the wall." That outrageous theory silenced him for a moment, and I gathered my things to leave.

But not before he contributed a final shot. "One is always rather concerned when a hive fails to thrive," he mused. "In Yorkshire and Cornwall they believe that when bees die, the farmer will soon leave his farm."

I shivered, and said sharply, "It's just as likely the bees deserted because nobody bothered to 'tell' them Holmes was away and would return. In any case, if a season is so bad the bees die, I should think it a sign that the farmer's crops were suffering as well. Good day to you, Mr Miranker," I told him, and made my escape.

Ridiculous, to feel a sharp frisson of disquiet because of this old man and his folk stories.

I spent the rest of the day walking: up to my own farm, where I looked from a distance and decided I did not wish to spend any more of the day in conversation, and then west towards the Cuckmere. I passed the Wilmington Giant—225 feet of enigmatic figure carved into the chalk hillside—and crossed the Cuckmere to Alfriston, to enjoy a restorative cup of tea and a scone nearly as good as Mrs Hudson's. When I had retraced my steps over the bridge, I turned south on the narrow track through Litlington and West Dean. Birds sang, despite the lateness of the season, and the lush countryside soothed my parched skin and my thin-stretched spirit.

I came home sunburnt, footsore, and at peace. What is more, since I had the forethought to stop at The Tiger on my way through the village, I was well fed.

I bathed and put on a silk robe I had bought in Japan, and while the kettle boiled, I went to the library in search of a congenial book. What I wanted was a novel, but there were few of those and none I had not read.

The room looked just as it had when we walked out of the house in January, since Mrs Hudson would not dare to disturb the arrangement of objects—which Holmes claimed was precise and deliberate. The only change was the small mountain of neatly stacked newspapers, which doubtless contained every *Times* and *Telegraph* issued since we had left: A sheet of foolscap stuck out every so often, counting down the months in Mrs Hudson's handwriting.

The sight reminded me that, with Lulu away, the newspapers would be accumulating in the box at the end of the drive. While my tea was steeping, I went out to retrieve the four papers—two afternoons, two mornings, all delivered by a boy from Eastbourne many hours after they hit the streets in London—and started to add them to the mountain, then changed my mind. Instead, I took them with the tea onto the terrace, to while away the day's last light.

Little appeared to have changed in the past eight months. Politics were fermenting, the coal unions gathering themselves for another attempt at a living wage. I was mildly disappointed to find no further letters concerning suicidal or riotous Druids, but perhaps my interests were too specialised.

However—the light was almost gone by the time I reached the small box at the bottom of the page and I nearly overlooked it—two men had been charged with conspiring to commit mayhem at Stonehenge on the solstice. That reminded me, I'd meant to hunt down the original articles about the riot, and the suicide in—had it been Dorset?

I found the paper that I had read on the train in the kitchen, waiting to receive the next batch of potato-peelings or coffee grounds. Fortunately, the Letters page was still intact:

Dear Sirs,

I write in urgent concern over the sequence of events, the near-riot between two opposing ideologies at Stonehenge following the desecration by suicide of one of our nation's most spectacular monuments, down in Dorset. When one reflects upon the popularity of peculiar religious rituals among today's young people, one can only expect that such shameful events will continue, growing ever more extreme, unless nipped in the bud. Need we wait until the Druids return human sacrifice to Stonehenge at midsummer's night, before we mount even casual guard upon the nation's prehistoric treasure sites?

A Wiltshire Farmer

Dorset. The only prehistoric site I knew there was the Cerne Abbas Giant, a rude version of my neighbouring Giant that I had passed that afternoon.

My curiosity roused, I went back to the library to heave the stack around until I unearthed the middle of June. I turned up the lights and started with the day after the solstice, 22 June.

The outraged farmer's "near-riot," it seemed, had been a loud argument culminating in a shoving match between six middle-aged people in sandals and hand-spun garments and a group (number not given) of earnest young people. The details were not exactly clear, but it would appear that the older traditionalists objected when the younger people proposed to stand in the light that fell through the standing stones, that they might absorb the sun's solstitial energies.

Their elders had been strongly protesting, ever since the two groups had gathered with their blankets (and, one suspected, warming drinks) the night before, that the light needed free access to its recipient stone. So two of the young men elected to force their interpretation of the ritual on their elders, and thus became the men being charged with mayhem.

Every bit as ridiculous as I had anticipated. And if the farmer had exaggerated the pushing contest into a riot, what of the "suicide" in Dorset?

He gave no date, but I thought a Druid would probably choose to commit self-sacrifice on the summer solstice—although granted, my only evidence of his religious inclinations was from the farmer. I paged through the papers of 23 June, then 24, and came across no mention of Dorset or Druids. I reached for the 25th, then put it down and went back to the days before the solstice—perhaps the body had lain there for some time?

20 June, 19 June: nothing. This seemed peculiar. I knew *The Times* treasured its quirky letter-writers, but surely they wouldn't have published one that made up its references out of whole cloth?

But there it was, on the afternoon of 18 June, under the headline, *Suicide at Giant*:

> Two visitors to the giant figure carved into the chalk at Cerne Abbas, Dorset, this morning were startled to discover a blood-soaked body at the figure's feet. The woman, who appeared to be in her forties, had blue eyes, steel spectacles, bobbed grey hair, and no wedding ring. Police said that she had died from a single wound from an Army revolver, found at the body, and that her clothing suggested she was a visitor to the area.

The brief article ended with a request that anyone who might know this person get into touch with their local police, but the description could have been one in ten women in England. A sad death, but hardly one worth sitting up over.

I folded the paper and switched off the desk lamp, curiosity satisfied: The solstice had nothing to do with any death, nor did Stonehenge. I made to rise, then stopped with my hands on the chair's arms. Had they identified this poor woman?

Sometimes, curiosity can be an irritating companion.

I turned the light back on and took up the one day during that entire week in June that I had not read. Of course, that was where it waited:

> The woman found at the Cerne Abbas Giant at dawn on 18 June has been identified as Miss Fiona Cartwright (42) of Poole. Miss Cartwright was last seen on 16 June when she told friends she was meeting a man who had need of a type-writer for his advertising business. Friends said Miss Cartwright had been despondent of late.

A solitary woman, out of employment, had to be one of the most melancholy persons imaginable.

I rather wished I'd stopped before the mystery had been solved. Why had I got so involved with a silly piece of news like this, anyway? Not boredom. How could this blessed solitude be thought a tedium? I dumped the armful of newspapers any which way on the stack: Holmes could sort them out himself.

Unless he had decided to follow the bees off into the blue.

For lack of other fiction, I reached for Holmes' copy of *Eminent Victorians,* and took myself to bed.

Chapter Eleven

Wrestling with Angels (2): In that moment of
submission, the heavens opened upon the boy and the
Light spilled in, filling him to overflowing.
And when the boy came down from the high mountain,
he found he had been marked by the Lights, and that he
bore on his body forevermore the stigmata of divinity.
Testimony, I:5

D AMIAN, I SHOULD THINK YOU'D HAD ENOUGH
pacing about during the day. Couldn't you sit down for a
few minutes?"

"Did you have to lodge us in a *less* comfortable place than the one
we were in last night?"

"This is absolutely safe."

"That depends on what you are guarding against. Suffocation
clearly isn't a concern with you."

"You dislike being enclosed?"

"I dislike risking asphyxiation."

"Your tension suggests claustrophobia. Which, now I consider it,
would also explain the degree of agitation you showed at the gaol in Ste

Chapelle. I thought at the time it was taking unduly long for the drugs to pass from your system; you might have told me before we came here."

"I'm not claustrophobic!"

"If you say so."

"I'm fine. Here, I'm sitting down. Now can we talk about something else?"

"I will admit, I had expected to have some results for our labours by now."

"It's hopeless, isn't it?"

"Certainly today's lack of results calls for a reconsideration of method for tomorrow."

"Maybe she got it in her mind to go to Paris. Or Rome. She once asked me about Rome."

"Recently?"

"A year, year and a half ago."

"It would help if you could estimate how much money she might have taken with her."

"I told you, I don't keep track of money, Yolanda does. It's how . . . it's one way I prove that I trust her. All I know is, she didn't take anything from the bank, but she may have hoarded any amount of cash. She likes cash."

"Or she could have had another bank account entirely."

"Yes, so? Look, I *do* trust her. I gave her my word when I married her, that she could live her life as she wished. She's my wife, and the mother of my child; if it makes her feel better to have her own bank account—her own life—it's her affair."

"Most generous of you."

"Damn it, I knew it would be a mistake to bring you into this."

"Damian—Damian! Sit down. Please."

"I want some air. I'll be back in an hour."

"Wait, I need to let you out."

"Better now?"

"Look, I'm sorry, I get . . . when I get upset it's best for everyone if I just take a walk. And it doesn't help that I'm not painting. Painting bleeds off a lot of steam."

"Or drinking."

"I'm not drunk."

"Do you 'get upset' often?"

"No more than any other man. Why do you ask?"

"How did you come to have contusions on your hands and a scratch across your face?"

"My hands are always bashed about, but a scratch—you mean this?"

"It was less than a day old when I saw you in Sussex Monday night."

"What are you saying? Are you accusing—"

"I am merely asking—"

"—me of doing something—"

"—how you came—"

"—to my wife? To—"

"—to bear signs—"

"—my *child*?"

"—of violence."

"How could you believe that I would harm either of them?"

"I did not say that I so believe. Damian, think: I do not know you. Circumstances have made us virtual strangers. Were you a stranger in fact, come to me saying that his wife and child had vanished yet he didn't want to go to the police, that is the first question that I should have to ask."

"Did I kill my wife, you mean?"

"Did you?"

"You think I would have come to you—you, of all men—for help, if I had done that myself? For God's sake, man, I'm a painter, not an actor!"

"You are the child of two performers, a man and a woman prac-ticed in easy deception and assumed faces. I put it to you again: Did you harm your wife?"

"No! No, no, no, for God's sake you have to believe me. I would not harm Yolanda, I would not touch a hair on Estelle's precious head, not if I was drunk or insane with drugs I would not. I would sooner— I'd sooner cut off the hand I paint with than use it to hurt either of them."

"Very well."

"You believe me?"

"I do not think I'm yet decrepit enough that I cannot hear truth in a man's vow."

"Thank God for that."

"So how did you come by the scratch on your face?"

"Your orchard wants grazing."

"I'm sorry?"

"The trees around your house. They would benefit from having a cow turned loose in there from time to time, to prune the lower branches. That was what Mother used to do in France, so they didn't poke one's ruddy eye out when one decided to take a stroll through the garden in the moonlight."

"I see. I apologise for my neglect, I have been away—what? Why are you laughing?"

"Oh, it's—it just hit me, how your audience would react if they could hear us talking about pruning apples."

"*My* audience? How do you think your admirers would react were I to photograph The Addler, master of Surrealism, sitting in an over-stuffed chair wearing a Victorian smoking-gown and puffing on one of his father's ancient clay pipes?"

"I should think they would find it the very definition of Surreal."

"Ah, Damian. Your laugh . . ."

"What about my laugh?"

"It reminds me of your mother."

"Do you wish the lights left on again?"

"Yes please."

"May I turn off the one overhead?"

"Here, let me. You don't mind?"

"They are electric, we won't suffocate."

"I shouldn't bet on that."

"If you can make it through the night, we shall go elsewhere to-morrow. A place with a window."

"I'll live."

"Damian?"

"Hmm?"

"I suggest that we part our ways tomorrow, temporarily."

"Why?"

"The places I need to go, it may be good if you do not have to see them. To have them linked in your mind with your wife . . .

"Damian? Are you asleep?"

"Why should I link these places with Yolanda? Simply because I was living in a bordello when I met her?"

"Damian, there is no such thing as a willing child prostitute."

"Huh. You guessed. About Yolanda."

"I do not guess. I hypothesise, I put forth a theory, and I receive confirmation. As, indeed, I have now done."

"Yes. Well. I'm sorry I didn't tell you."

"It is hardly astonishing, that a man would not care to reveal the darker details of his wife's past."

"It was ugly. It's left her more fragile, more vulnerable, than one would suspect. But you're right, I didn't want her past or her . . . sus-ceptibilities to be in front of your eyes, the first time you met her."

"Drugs?"

"Not in a long time."

"You are certain?"

"I would know."

"What else are you not telling me?"

"What do you mean?"

"You are concealing something about your wife."

"There's nothing."

"I don't believe that."

"Nothing you need to know. Nothing that would explain her dis-appearance."

"That is a conclusion you need to leave to me."

"I'm not telling you any more. You don't need to know."

"Damian—"

"No! God, I should have gone back to Shanghai months ago."

"Are you about to go storming out again tonight? Because I have to say, both concealing information and abandoning the investigation slow matters down considerably. Why don't you have a drink instead?"

"Are you always such a cold-hearted bastard? What did my mother ever see in you?"

"I often wondered that myself. Now, is that light sufficient?"

"Yes."

"I still think it best that you not accompany me tomorrow. You do not need to have those raw images before your own eyes the next time she stands in front of you."

"I'm beginning to wonder if we will find her."

"We will find her in the end."

"Christ, I almost believe you. But no, I will go with you."

"As you wish."

"Good night."

"Good night, Damian."

Chapter Twelve

The Trance: When the boy came down from the mountain, he lay stunned, filled with Light yet empty of knowledge, until he felt the clasp of a hand taking his: A teacher had found him.
Testimony, I:7

BY THURSDAY MORNING, MY SOLITUDE WAS MORE A fact than an unexpected gift. I cooked myself an egg, which turned out as leathery as the toast although not quite as comprehensively burnt, then spent half an hour chipping the débris from the fry-pan, wondering all the while that no laboratory experiment had ever blown up in my face in the way a simple meal did. Cooking was nothing but chemistry, wasn't it? Why could I not perform as efficiently over a cook-stove as I did a Bunsen burner?

The pan would not deceive Mrs Hudson, so I would have to take another pass at its surface before she returned, but at least the smoke had cleared. I latched the windows and put on my boots.

I had decided during the night that there was no reason I should leave the abandoned hive's honey to be raided by human or insect thieves, and that a day's hard labour would do me good. It was righteous good will, not boredom—how could I be bored, in this place?—that had me loading up the hand-cart and trundling it across the dewy grass to the far-off hive.

The laden frames had been heavy enough one at a time, but together, they weighed a young ton. Plus that, I had neglected to bring gloves, which meant that when I reached the garden shed again, hours later, my palms were raw and my back ached with fighting the cart over the uneven ground. I staggered to the house, gulping three glasses of cool water at the kitchen sink and letting the tap run across my hot face. I chipped off a hunk of ice from the block in the ice-box to cool a fourth glass, and took it outside to the shade of the apple tree. This time the busy bees were less companions than they were haughty reminders of a job ahead. I scowled at the workers.

"If Holmes isn't back to deal with you lot, you'll just have to keep packing the nectar in until the place bursts," I told them.

They answered not.

After a while, I returned to the house to fetch Holmes' strong magnifying glass. I could have waited until the cool of the evening, which on a day like this would still be plenty warm to encourage the flow of honey, but I wanted light to study the evidence in the comb. Before attacking each frame, I carried it into the sun to study with the glass, hoping for a clue to the hive's aberrant behaviour. I found none. The earlier frames were neatly filled, side to side; when I had finished examining each one, I took it back into the shed and ran the hot knife over its comb, setting it into place in Holmes' homemade, hand-cranked centrifuge.

The later frames were less perfect, and darker as the nectar changed colour with summer's ripening. In the frames to which the queen had been limited by the excluder frame, I could trace her progress: growing brood, ready for hatching; smaller pupae, still subsisting on their pollen store; then mere eggs, laid, supplied with food, and sealed into their wax wombs. After that, nothing.

I counted no fewer than twenty-one empty queen cells drooping around the bottom levels of the hive, their larger dimensions pushing the neat hexagons out of alignment. This seemed to me a rather high number, for each queen cell represented either a potential swarm, or a deadly battle between the reigning queen and the virgin upstart. Generally speaking, the queen ripped any royal larvae from their cells and murdered them. Holmes, or Mr Miranker, might be able to tell whether the infinitesimal marks in the wax of these cells had been made from without or within the cell, but I couldn't.

These frames, I put aside for Holmes.

Extracting the honey took me most of the day, and left me sweat-soaked and incredibly sticky, all my muscles burning, my skin, nostrils, and mouth permeated with the cloy of honey. All the while, bees plucked their way up and down the screens Holmes had installed on the shed's windows, teased by the aroma of riches ripe for plunder.

I finished about four o'clock: jars capped, machinery clean, frames set aside for the next use. There was one partial jar. I picked it up, stuck one grubby finger into the amber contents, and put the resulting glossy burden into my mouth.

The honey from mad bees tastes much like that of others.

I left the jar on the kitchen table and went upstairs to put on my bathing costume. I got out the bicycle, checked that the tyres were still inflated, and pedalled down the lane to the shore, where I found—as I'd hoped—that the day's holiday-makers were beginning to leave, trudging up the cliff-side steps as I went down. I crunched along the shingle towards the abandoned reaches, the round flints making a noise like a mouthful of wet marbles. Through some odd quirk of memory, the sound always called to mind my long-dead brother.

I laid my outer garments and spectacles on my folded bath-towel, then picked my way through the exposed low-tide pools to the water beyond. I paused, as I invariably did, to peer short-sightedly around me at the surface of the water. Years before I knew him, Holmes had encountered a poisonous jelly-fish in these waters, strayed here after unusual weather. Ever since he'd told me the story, I had been in the habit of watching out for another one—as if the creature might reveal itself by a fin above the water. Perhaps I should ask Dr Watson to write one of his tales about the event, I thought: It might reduce the crowds on this particular beach, if not the whole of Sussex.

Today I saw no tell-tale fin or translucent bubble, and I dived deep into the frigid water.

I swam along the cliffs until my skin was rubbery with cold and my fingers puckered, dragging myself out onto a beach all but deserted of umbrellas and children. I amused myself for a time by tossing pebbles into an abandoned tin mug from ever-greater distances, then dressed and climbed the cliff to wobble my bicycle back to the silent house. There I drew a hot bath and stepped into the water with a glass of wine to hand—after all, alcohol aids muscular relaxation. I may have fallen asleep for a few minutes, because the water seemed to cool abruptly. I got out and put on a thick towelling robe, then hurried downstairs to fill the ravenous gap within.

I was pleased to find a portion of meat pie in the back of the ice-box, stale but still smelling good, and ripe tomatoes from the garden outside the door, into which I chopped some onions and cheese. A bottle of cider from the pantry, a slice of stale bread and fresh butter, and I was content in my small and no doubt temporary island of tran-quillity. I ate at the scrubbed wood table in the kitchen, and left my dishes in the sink until morning.

Not bored, not lonely: content.

Although I will admit that several times during the day, I had pushed back the suspicion that my labour was an attempt to exorcise the spirit of the empty hive, to turn its unnatural emptiness into a more normal thing. And that several times during the day, I had found myself wondering where Holmes was.

I decided to read outside until the light failed, and went to fetch Strachey's *Victorians* from the table beside my bed upstairs. As I went past the library, my eye caught on Damian's painting of the bee tea-pot, which Holmes had left leaning against the low shelves near the door (being, no doubt, unwilling to chance waking me by returning it to the laboratory—and, where *was* Holmes, anyway?). I picked it up to take it upstairs.

Such a peculiar image, I reflected when the painting was back on its wall in the laboratory: The scrupulous rendering of an impossibly bizarre creation. On the surface, it appeared an intellectual jest, yet there was no denying the disturbing currents down below. An English tea-pot with a nasty sting. Was this the only one of its sort that he had done? Or was this his general style?

Odd, that Holmes had been satisfied with just the one piece.

No, not odd: impossible.

Finding Holmes' collection of Damian's art was easy, once I thought to look for it—although in a Purloined Letter sort of way that took me the better part of an hour, since it was right under my nose. I went through both safes, the shelves in Holmes' study, his records in the laboratory. I was on my knees, about to take out the drawers in his bedroom chest, when I thought about where I had found the painting: He had left it against a shelf that contained art-related titles, from monographs such as "Lead Poisoning in the Age of Rembrandt" and "Death-Masks of the Pharaohs" to *The Great Italian Forgers* and *Sotheby's Guide to the Renaissance.*

Sure enough, on the far side of that bottom shelf, all but invisible behind *Paintings of the Spanish Inquisition,* stood a slim, over-sized book with a brown leather cover. On its front cover was the name Damian Adler. I laid it on the desk under the strong light, and opened it.

It was less a book than a bound album containing small original drawings and photographic reproductions of larger pieces, perhaps fifty pages covering a period of nine years. The first piece was a startlingly life-like pen-and-ink portrait of a woman, hair upswept, chin haughty, eyes sparkling with laughter. There was love, too, in those eyes—love for the artist—but it might explain why Holmes had never shown me this album.

The woman was Irene Adler.

The date in the corner was 1910. Damian had been sixteen years old. She died two years later.

There followed a series of small sketches of French streets: a market, the Seine as it went through Paris, an old man snoozing on a park bench. Three of the five were dated, all of them before Irene Adler's death.

Then came the shock: With one turn of the page the viewer stepped from an empty street with interesting shadows to a front-line trench under fire. The trench walls loomed high and threatening, as if the pit were about to swallow the figures within; the moon high in the heavens seemed to taunt. At the centre, a man cowered, wrapping his body around his rifle like a terrified child embracing a doll; the man beside him gripped the brim of his helmet with both hands, as if trying to pull it down over himself; to the right of the drawing stood a young man, head thrown back and arms outstretched in a stance that could have been sexual passion or the agony of crucifixion. The paper the scene had been drawn on was grimy with dried mud and held together by gummed tape.

There were seven war-time drawings in all. Although none were dated, their order was easy to determine, because the style grew increasingly precise as time passed. The last one, a close study of the upper half of a naked skull emerging from the mud, possessed the finely shaded detail of a photograph.

In all of the war-time sketches, the perspective was odd, the objects to the sides tending either to loom up, or to curl in towards those in the centre, as if the artist saw the entire world as threatening to engulf him.

The page following the skull was startling in a different way, being in colour. It and the rest were all photographs, most of them coloured, of paintings, bearing dates between 1917 and 1919. The quality and uniformity of the photographs suggested that all had been made at the same time. Probably, I thought, either at the instruction of Mme Longchamps, or by another following her death.

I had thought the bee tea-pot unsettling: It was nothing compared to these images.

The thirty or so pages remaining in the album, a closer examination showed, were taken from only nine originals. Each sequence began with the complete painting, the size of which seemed to vary, followed by several closer-up parts of the whole.

Some of the paintings were violent, showing dismembered bodies and wide pools of blood, every glistening inch painted with loving detail. Others were nightmare horrors: a woman with full breasts, delicious skin, and an oozing sore for a mouth; a child clutching a human heart, its veins and arteries trailing to the ground. A painting done in June 1918 showed a room in what could only be the mental hospital where Damian had been treated: a study in pallor, white-grey beds, white-pink curtains, a man with white-brown skin wearing a white-blue dressing gown, a patch of white-yellow sun hitting the white-tan floor: The painting felt like the moments under ether when consciousness fades.

All the paintings felt tortured. All were disturbing. The earlier ones had more overt depictions of the macabre, the latter images felt as though a horror lay just outside the room, but each painting seemed to be holding its breath in dread.

The last painting was a family portrait: father, mother, child. The mother, in the centre, was Irene Adler. The child on her left was a thin boy with grey eyes. The man on her right was Holmes. The figures were posed as if for a conventional portrait, facing the artist, the father standing behind the seated mother, the boy leaning into her lap in a pose that resembled a *pietá*. The wallpaper behind them faded at the top, merging into a dark, starlit sky: Above the man's head was a tiny sun, weak with immeasurable distance; above the mother rode a gravid-looking moon; over the son flew a streaking comet. At the bottom, wallpaper met carpet, but when one studied the odd colouring and perspective, it suddenly became clear that all three figures had begun to melt into the carpet, the colours of their clothes bleeding into its weave, their shoes no longer even an outline against the pattern.

Its date was October 1919. Damian had painted this after meeting Holmes, and shortly before he had left France entirely.

A celestial family bleeding into the ground: In another hand, it would have been mere Surrealist trickery, but here, one received the clear impression that beneath the calm of their faces, each of the three could feel what was happening, and that the process was on the edge of excruciating.

I looked out of the window, and saw that the sun had long since set. I closed the book, put it on the shelf, shut the library door, and even rattled the knob, to make sure the latch had caught. If there had been a bar across the door, I would have dropped it into place as well.

The sitting room's dark corners seemed to crawl with unknown threat. I poured myself a glass of brandy—odd, how much I had drunk the past couple of days—and picked up a travelling rug on my way out to the terrace. The moon would be full tonight, and the sky was so clear, I could practically read a newspaper. I spread out the rug on the deck-chair, and lay back to watch the sky. Perhaps I would see the occasional meteor, trailing after Tuesday's height.

My mind was both empty and occupied, all of the thoughts buzzing far below the surface. So it was not for some time that I realised that I had come out onto a dark terrace, and that I could not see my feet at the other end of the deck-chair. It was remarkably dark, yet the stars shone. Where was the moon?

I looked to the east, expecting to see its great mass slowly pulling above the horizon, but it was not there. In its place was a slim crescent, perhaps two days old.

My brain felt like a motor slapped abruptly into reverse. But the moon was full. I'd slept on this very spot not two nights past, and it was big and growing bigger, all but perfectly round. How, then—?

It was in the east. A setting sun, with a new moon in the east?

I experienced a sharp pulse of panic, convinced that Damian's macabre paintings had affected my mind in some profound way. Then I shook myself, and cast around for an explanation that incorporated the customary workings of the universe.

An eclipse.

I had read something about an eclipse recently, but nothing had prepared me for one here. An advert, that had been, for a boat tour to the eclipse. Why would one take a boat tour when one could sit anywhere in the country and see the moon fade?

I stared up, open-mouthed, as the last of the moon was overcome, and all one could see was a faint circular object in the sky, as much an absence of stars as a presence of a celestial body. It stayed dark for a long, long time, nearly an hour, before a faint suggestion of curve appeared. Shortly after ten o'clock, the earth's satellite began to move out of the planet's shadow: a thin curve; a fatter slice; a bulging half-circle; finally, an hour later, it was glorious and round; an hour after that, it was fully brilliant.

As I had felt a primitive's fear at the moon's disappearance, so I felt the profound reassurance of its return. Once the moon was securely in the sky, I went inside, less troubled by the images behind the library door. I slept that night, long and deep.

Chapter Thirteen

*The Seeker (1): An artist grinds lapis to make blue,
lead to make white, giving colour and dimension to the
artifice on his canvas. How not to spend his entire career
inventing techniques known by the painters who
have gone before?*
Testimony, I:8

DAMIAN? DAMIAN, WAKE UP! DA—"

"Bloody bastard, watch out for the—oh, I'll bloody murder
you, you son of a—"

"Damian!"

"What? What is it?"

"The light burnt out, you were having a dream. A nightmare."

"Don't be an idiot. I don't have nightmares."

"Then you were locked in battle against invisible foes. Here, I've
turned on the other lamp. Are you all right?"

"Of course I'm all right. I just need some air."

"The window is open."

"I have to get out."

"Damian—"

"If you try and stop me, I'll hit you."

"I wasn't going to stop you. But tomorrow? We'll divide up."

"Now there's a pity."

"And, Damian? Take your coat. You're dripping with sweat."

Chapter Fourteen

*The Seeker (2): Every man, however god-like and gifted,
requires a Guide to set him upon the path, to show him
how other artists have achieved their results, to show how
other Seekers have found their answers.*
Testimony, I:8

FRIDAY MORNING, I SAT AT THE KITCHEN TABLE,
reading Thursday's papers, drinking strong coffee, and eating
slices of stale bread covered with butter and jam—I'd become somewhat tired of honey, and had decided that a more substantial breakfast was not worth the effort of clearing smoke and scraping pans.
Mrs Hudson would be back tomorrow, and life would return, at least
in part, to normality.

I stood at the door looking over the terrace and the Downs, and
thought about what to do with my last full day of solitude. There was
no telling where Holmes was or when he might appear, but when he
did so, it would be satisfying to have solved his mystery for him.

I put on my boots, locked up, and set off once more in the direction of the mad beehive.

Once there, I left my rucksack in the shade of the emptied

Langstroth box and walked due east, going nearly half a mile before turning back to where I had started. I walked slowly, searching the ground, the air, the surroundings in general, to see what was different about this particular hive.

Back and forth I went, my senses open to that one lonely patch of downland. I climbed over stone walls, poked about in holes looking for poison bait, wrote down the name of every plant in the vicinity, the presence of sheep, the lack of trees.

After three hours, the sun was scorching and I was thoroughly fed up with the entire puzzle. I drained my last drop of warm lemonade and tried to put my thoughts in order.

There was nothing I could see that set this hive apart from the others. Except that it was, in fact, apart, this being the furthest of Holmes' hives. As yesterday's blistered palms could well testify.

Plenty of food—the honey in the frames had told me that. A fertile queen—any number of fertile queens. So what was it? Why dislike this place? What had so infected the community with alarm and despondency that they had deserted their brood?

With a sigh of resignation at my own unwillingness to let go of the conundrum, I got down on my hands and knees at the front of the hive and picked through the grass with my fingertips.

There were dead bees there, of course—workers only live a few weeks, and a sentimental burial is not in the hive's interest. Still, I dutifully gathered up those that were not dried to a husk, taking care not to impale myself on the stingers, and folded them into a sheet of paper. Perhaps examination under a microscope would reveal a parasite.

When I was finished, I climbed onto the wall and gazed at the slopes running down to the Channel. The water was blue today beneath the summer's sun; I counted twenty-three vessels, from light sail-boat to heavy steamer, in the patch immediately before me.

Not so this piece of hillside. Even in August, this was away from the shoes of long-distance ramblers and day-tourists alike. The nearest house was almost a mile away, the grassland was broken by nothing larger than gorse bushes.

A small and tentative idea, born of the loneliness of the place and three days of my own solitude, crept into the side of my mind. I looked speculatively down at the packet of bees.

Then I hopped down from the wall and went back to the house. I spent some time with the more scientific manuals on bees, until I was certain that they were all workers, then went to the honey shed to retrieve one of the frames containing queen cells. I wrapped it with care, laid it in my bicycle basket, and set off for Jevington, where Mr Miranker's letter had come from.

A woman tossing grain to her chickens directed me to the beekeeper's house, on the far edge of the village. I spotted the man himself over the wall, gathering windfalls from beneath the apple tree. He looked up, unsurprised to see me.

"Good day, Mrs Holmes."

"Hello, Mr Miranker."

"I'm trying to pick up the apples before the wasps find them," he explained. "I don't like to encourage wasps to spend time in the vicinity of the bees."

"Quite," I answered, remembering belatedly, and with some guilt, that Holmes had once told me something of the sort. As if to make up for my own poor husbandry of the bees left to my keeping, I bent to help him clear his apples.

"Was there something I might do for you?" he asked after a while.

"Oh, yes," I said. I dropped my load of bruised and spoiling fruit in the barrow and fetched the frame from my bicycle. He led me to a sunlit potting bench and moved away the collection of clay pots and gravel. I dusted off the boards and laid out my frame.

"I wonder if you can tell me anything about these queen cells?"

"Apart from the fact that they are empty?"

"Can you tell if they were opened from inside, or from without?" I had brought the magnifying glass, but he did not take it.

He picked up the frame, tilting it back and forth to the sunlight, while I told him my speculations.

"The hive is all by itself on the hillside. The nearest hive is nearly a mile away. Here's what I was wondering." And I laid out for him the story I had built in my mind.

When a hive swarms, the reigning queen takes with her the better half of the hive, leaving behind the honey, an entire hive's worth of infant workers in their cells, and one or several potential queens. The workers who remain behind nurture the queen cells until the first one hatches, at which point she tries to slaughter her potential rivals. Generally, the hive prevents her from killing all of them until she has returned successfully from her mating flight, ready to take up her long life as the centre of the hive's future.

The hours that she is away is a time of enormous vulnerability for the hive. A hungry bird, a chill wind—and their future fails to return. And if her hive has permitted her to kill all potential rivals, they are doomed.

The summer had seen periods of wet, and wind was always a problem near the sea, but I wondered if the remoteness of the hive had driven the queen to take a longer nuptial flight than normal, before the drones from her own and other hives caught her up.

I was not going to go so far as to suggest that loneliness had killed them, but that was the underlying idea.

Mr Miranker listened to this, radiating doubt as he methodically went over the frame I had brought him.

I asked him, "How do the drones know that the new queen is taking off?"

"There is, literally, a hum of anticipation that builds throughout the hive. And the queen sings, quite loudly. Then, once she is in flight they simply see her—she generally chooses a clear day on which to fly. It is also possible that she 'speaks' by sounds inaudible to human ears, or by her motions, or even by emitting an entire language of smells."

"How far can a drone fly?"

"Bees can fly two or three miles."

"What would happen if something kept her own drones from reaching her?"

Miranker glanced sideways at me, realising that he was discussing the mechanics of apian sex with a woman young enough to be his granddaughter. He cleared his throat, and replied gamely, "Generally speaking, drones from hives all around respond to the call of a virgin queen. Hundreds, even thousands of them."

"And if there were no other hives nearby?"

"There are always other hives nearby."

"As far as I can see, the nearest bees to that hive are those in our orchard, more than a mile away."

Miranker stared at me. "Are you suggesting that the queen's flight went, er, unconsummated?"

"Is that possible?"

"It is more likely that she did not return at all. That is why the hive produces a number of queen cells, in anticipation of failure."

"But if she was too bloodthirsty for them? If they didn't stop her from killing her rivals?"

"Then it might well be too late for them to raise up another from the eggs left by the previous queen." But just as I was thinking that I had succeeded in solving Holmes' mystery, he said, "However. These cells have been opened from within."

"What, all of them?"

"The five I see here. How many were there in all?"

"Twenty-one. They all looked pretty much—"

"*Twenty-one?* All like this?"

"As far as I could see."

"I should say that all of these hatched."

"You mean, this hive has made twenty-one queens? Every one of them hatched, and fighting for primacy?" Absolute chaos, if that was the case.

"More likely, hatched and flying off into the blue. In some hives, the difference between a cell intended for swarming and one intended for supersedure—replacing the queen—is clear. Here, I would not be so certain."

"So, one after another, the queen cells hatched and led a swarm?"

"Yes. However, you see this frame here? The brood?"

"Unhatched bees?"

"And eggs?"

When he pointed them out to me, I could see them. "What does that mean?"

"It means the queen was active until quite recently. Certainly there was a queen in residence when I last checked the hive, three weeks ago."

"So all this happened in the last three weeks? Twenty-one swarms?"

"No, the swarms took place beforehand. And that is the peculiar thing. Your hive had an active queen, and yet continued to hatch virgin queens, time and again. And not only did she not kill them, she did not lead any of the swarms. Just kept laying while the hive swarmed around her."

"Did the workers keep her from killing them?" A hive madness, indeed.

"In their decreasing numbers? I should be surprised if they could."

"Then what happened?"

"It would appear as if your queen simply ignored the imperative to murder, and went about her business while the hive swarmed itself to death around her."

The hive died because the reigning queen and all twenty-one of her royal daughters were too soft-hearted for murder, and the hive could not summon sufficient numbers to maintain the brood.

This struck me as highly significant, although of what, precisely, I could not immediately think. Mr Miranker, however, had moved past the reasons.

"In any case, as I suggested to your husband, filling the hive with a new colony should be done soon. He could add a second hive-box, in the event that solitude has compounded the problem." He sounded dubious about my theory.

Mr Miranker was clearly more concerned with solution than theory. Holmes, I thought, would prefer to dig into the cause—but then I recalled his initial proposition of doing away with the entire hive. Perhaps even he would not permit philosophy to get in the way of agronomy.

In any event, replenishing the hive was a task I was happy to leave to the professionals, since moving several thousand live bees around the countryside was not a challenge I cared to meet. Mr Miranker promised me that he would be on the watch for stray swarms that might appreciate a new home, and I said I would have Holmes arrange for a second hive-box at first opportunity.

I bicycled the four miles home from Jevington, well pleased with my solution to The Case of the Mad Hive.

Later, I carried the album of Damian's work onto the terrace to re-examine it by light of day.

Were the macabre overtones of his later paintings figments of my imagination? Was my own solitude working to cloud my perception?

One after another, I turned the pages, chewing my thumbnail in thought.

No, I decided: I was not reading a nonexistent message. Damian Adler's paintings were truly mad—although whether they were the deliberately cultivated madness of Surrealism, or an internal madness rising of his own, I could not say.

Studying them in the warm afternoon sunshine, however, I realised something else: Holmes would have asked the same questions.

He would not have been satisfied with a mere catalogue of his son's artwork. He would have gone back to the source and investigated its roots, its influences, and its effects.

And if Holmes had mounted an investigation, then somewhere he would have a case file. It might be an actual file-box, or an envelope stuffed with notes, or a document case tied and sealed with ribbons, but to his eyes, it would constitute records of a case.

Unlike the album, I could not find anything resembling a case file.

I searched for hours: in the laboratory, in the pantry, out in the honey shed, under the carpets. I tapped stones until my knuckles ached, pulled apart all the beds, looked inside every art book on the shelves.

Near midnight, I eased my sore back and decided reluctantly that he had left it in a bolt-hole, or with Mycroft.

I curled up in bed and closed my eyes, trying not to picture the lively features of Irene Adler as drawn by her son. Irene Adler, who had managed to get the best of Holmes in an early, and important, case. Irene Adler, whom he had sought out in France some years later, and, all unknowing, left with child. Irene Adler, whose musical life meshed with that of Holmes, an area of my partner's life in which I could not share, since my tin ear and my dislike—

I sat bolt upright.

Music.

I trotted downstairs to the shelf in the sitting room where Holmes kept his gramophone records. Because I had no ear for music, it was a shelf I rarely went near, and anyone else, knowing Holmes' passion for these fragile objects, kept well clear of it, as well.

Two-thirds of the way along the shelf was an inch-thick cloth-covered box of Irene Adler's operatic recordings. Inside, nestled between the second and third disk, was a manila envelope containing perhaps thirty pages.

The first was a copy of Damian Adler's birth record. The second a Photostat copy of his enlistment in the Army. The third was an arrest form, dated 27 April 1918. The fourth recorded his admission to the mental asylum in Nantes, on 6 May 1918.

He'd killed a fellow officer, ten days before.

Chapter Fifteen

The Guide (1): A Guide is rarely a person whom society will invite to its garden parties. The boy's Guide appeared as a coarse bully with compelling eyes and the overweening pride of a man who has conquered mountains: It mattered not, for the Guide possessed both knowledge and wisdom.

Testimony, II:1

HOLMES HERE."

"Mycroft, have you heard anything from Damian?"

"Sherlock, good evening. Where are you?"

"Have you heard from Damian?"

"Not since Saturday. Have you lost him?"

"We came up to Town together on Tuesday, but he left the hotel early this morning, and had not returned when I came in tonight. I wondered perhaps if he had telephoned to you."

"No. Which hotel?"

"The place in Battersea run by the cousin of my old Irregular Billy."

"Perhaps that explains it."

"His absence may have more to do with our activities yesterday than with the quality of our lodgings. I took him on a round of houses of ill repute."

"Is this related to our last telephone conversation, when you requested that I look into the wife's background?"

"Precisely. Have you had any results?"

"It's been little more than forty-eight hours. Sherlock—"

"Mycroft, we must find her."

"I see that. And him."

"It is also possible that he received a message."

"You speak of the one in *The Times* agony column, couched as an advert for nerve tonic?"

"I should have known you'd notice it."

" 'Addled by your family? Rattled by uncertainty? Eros has ten morning tonics for you to try on Friday.' "

"That's the one, although one rather wonders that it was accepted, considering the double entendre. Damian appears to have met the man at the statue on Piccadilly Circus, at ten o'clock."

"Am I to understand, Sherlock, that you have spoken with the staff at the Café Royal?"

"Damian took breakfast there early this morning, when he was given an envelope left for him two days earlier. He was later seen walking up Regent Street in the company of a man the porter did not know, a man of average height, in his forties, with dark hair, good-quality clothes, no facial hair, and a scar near his left eye."

"What do you intend to do now?"

"I've left a message for Damian at the Battersea hotel. He may yet return there. I've been past his house twice today, but there are no signs of life. I am going there now—I'll break in and get some sleep, then search the place by daylight. I cannot think why it has proved so difficult to find any trace of a Chinese woman and her child."

"Do you wish me to summon Billy to assist you?"

"We may have to, if it goes on for much longer."

"I understand. If Damian rings or sends a message, where can I reach you?"

"At Damian's home, if you can manage to ring a code so I'll know it is you. After that, I'll telephone to you again tomorrow night—Saturday."

"Anything else you would like me to do?"

"Nothing. Except, if the boy gets into touch, tell him . . . I can't think what you could tell him."

"I will convey your fervent best wishes."

"Something along those lines. Thank you, Mycroft."

"Take care, Sherlock."

Chapter Sixteen

The Guide (2): See the steps, lit clear: The boy, tormented
in soul, wrestled with the Angels and took on their volatile
essence. Thus, when he met his Guide, he was set alight,
as a volatile substance lights at the mere touch of flame.
Testimony, II:1

I TRIED, SATURDAY MORNING, TO CONVINCE MYSELF
that two long-ago accusations of violence, against a man actively
engaged in combat, were no great sin. Damian had not even been
charged with the 1918 assault, in part because both men were drinking and witnesses disagreed over which man had started the fight. To
compound matters, not only was Damian still convalescing from his
wounds, he was a decorated hero (which I had not known) while the
other officer was both hale-bodied and whole, and known to be bel-
ligerent when drunk: hence the verdict of shell-shock and a quiet
placement in the mental hospital at Nantes, rather than a court mar-
tial. If Holmes was willing to discount Damian's past, if he was willing to agree that the officer's death had been an accident stemming
from self-defence, who was I to disagree?

I got up early from my sleepless bed and spent two hours resolutely finishing the job of emptying my trunks and hauling them to the lumber room. I made toast and attempted to settle to the newspapers, but my eye seemed constantly preoccupied with my discoveries of the night before, and kept catching on headlines concerning death and madness and adverts for honey. When my eye was caught by a personal notice that began with the word *ADDLED,* I shoved the paper away and went outside, wandering restlessly through the garden, feeling as if I had drunk several carafes of powerful coffee instead of a single cup.

Around ten o'clock, I found myself in Holmes' room studying his unopened trunks, and decided to make a start on them before Mrs Hudson got back that evening. Half an hour later, with every inch of the room buried under the débris of long travel, I looked at the knot of worn-through stockings in my hand and came to my right mind.

I was not Holmes' housekeeper; neither he nor Mrs Hudson would thank me for my labours.

The reason for my uncharacteristic housewifeliness was, I had to face it, uneasiness: When I had turned the page in Holmes' file and seen the photograph of the dead officer, all I could think of was that the man looked like Holmes.

Which was ridiculous. I was not worried, any more than I had been bored or lonely in my solitude. Clearly I needed something to occupy my time other than sorting socks. The best thing was to keep busy. I had intended to return to Oxford later in the week, to resume my life and my work there. Instead, I would go now.

Although I decided to stop first in London and have a little talk with Mycroft. It was, I told myself, the sensible thing to do.

Holmes' elder brother was looking remarkably well, for a man who had peered over the abyss into death the Christmas before. He'd dropped a tremendous amount of weight, and from the colour of his skin, actually spent some time out-of-doors.

He brushed aside my compliments, admitted to a loss of "three or four stone" although it had to have been nearly five, then grumbled that bodily exercise was a tedium beyond measure, and commented that he had heard I joined the short-haired league.

My hand went to my hair, removed when we were in India. "Yes, I needed to dress as a man. Holmes nearly passed out with the shock."

"I can imagine. Still, I never thought the Gibson Girl look suited you."

"Thank you. I guess. Were you going out?" I asked, taking in his brown lightweight suit.

"It is of no importance," he said. "After luncheon I have developed the habit of going for a turn around the park instead of taking a nap, as I used to do, but I shall happily delay that pleasure."

"No, no, I'm just off the train, I'd appreciate a breath of air."

With a grimace at the disappearance of an excuse for lethargy, Mycroft caught up his stick and straw hat and we descended onto Pall Mall, to turn in the direction of St James's Park.

"Have you seen your brother?" I asked.

"I have not seen him since January, although I spoke with him across the telephone twice, on Wednesday afternoon and again last night."

"Was he in London?"

"I believe so. In any case, Wednesday's call was from Paddington, although that can mean anything."

"Or nothing." Paddington Station sent trains in all directions north of London, but it was also a main connecting stop on the city's Underground. "What did he want?"

"The earlier call was to request my assistance with an overseas element of an investigation."

Mycroft's oddly unfamiliar face—it now had bones in it, and the skin had gone slack with the loss of padding—was held in an expression I nonetheless knew well: noncommittal innocence. The quick mind inside the slow body was waiting to see if I knew what Holmes was up to before he revealed any more.

"Let me guess: Shanghai."

Inside Britain, Holmes' sources of information were without peer, but once an investigation stretched past Europe or certain parts of

America, his web of knowledge developed gaps. Mycroft, however, had spent his life as a conduit of Intelligence that covered the globe: When Holmes had need of information beyond his ken, he turned to Mycroft.

Shanghai had not been a guess, and Mycroft saw that.

"Yes, I was given to understand that young Damian had come to Sussex."

"Damian was there when we got in on Monday, then both of them were gone when I woke up Tuesday. I don't know where they were going, but last night I found Holmes' file on Damian, and I was . . . concerned."

"Concerned," he mused, nodding at the ground.

"Damian killed a man in 1918," I blurted. "Not the same man he was accused of killing in 1919."

"In neither was he charged."

"You knew, about both of them?"

"I did."

"Why . . ." I stopped: He hadn't told Holmes for the same reason he hadn't told him of Damian's existence in the first place. "Have you seen his paintings—Damian's?"

"A few of them. I hear he has a small show at a gallery off Regent Street, I'd planned on going to that."

"He paints madness."

"I'd have thought that a common enough theme amongst modern artists."

"With more or less deliberation. But there's something profoundly unsettling about his work."

"Hmm," Mycroft said.

"What about last night's phone call?"

"My brother was enquiring whether or not I had seen Damian."

"He's lost him?"

"I don't know if 'lost' is the correct term, but Damian left the hotel where they were staying early on Friday morning, and as of eleven o'clock last night he had not returned. I believe Sherlock would have got a message to me, had the boy reappeared."

"I see. Well, in any case, I should talk with Holmes before I go up to Oxford, just to let him know where I am and see if he needs my assistance. Do you have any idea where he might be?"

Mycroft reached into his breast pocket and took out a business card, crisply engraved on a startling bright red stock with an address on one of the lanes that connected with Regent Street. On its reverse, in Mycroft's handwriting, was another address: 7 Burton Place, in Chelsea.

"I do not know where my brother is, but those are the addresses of Damian's gallery and his home. Either of those might be a good place to start."

I looked at him in surprise. "You've simply been carrying this around?"

"When I heard that you were not with my brother, I knew it would not be long before you came looking."

I grinned and gave him a quick kiss on the cheek, then reversed my direction.

"What shall I do with your valise?" he called after me.

I waved a hand in the air and broke into a trot.

To my surprise, the gallery that sold Damian Adler's paintings was not some narrow and dingy upper-storey hole several streets "off" Regent Street, but a prosperous, glass-fronted shop a stone's throw from the Royal Academy. A bell dinged at my entrance. Voices came from behind a partition at the back and a sleek woman in her early forties poked her head around the wall, giving me a brief but penetrating once-over. I did not think that I impressed her overmuch, since I had not intended to enact a patron of the arts when I left Sussex. "I shall be with you momentarily," she said in a French accent.

"I'm happy to look," I told her. She went back to her conversation, which had to do with the delivery of a painting.

The gallery had two rooms. The first displayed paintings, and a few small bronze sculptures, that would have been considered dangerously *avant-garde* before the War but were now just comfortably modern. I recognised an Augustus John portrait, and two of the bronzes were Epsteins. It was the next room that held the more demanding forms: one canvas made up of paint masses so thick, it could have been the artist's palette board mounted on the wall; three twisted sheets of brass that might be horses' heads or women's torsos, but in either case appeared to be writhing in pain; a gigantic, wide-brimmed cocktail glass tipped to pour its greenish contents into a puddle on the floor.

I spotted the first of Damian's paintings immediately I came into the room. It was an enormously tall, narrow canvas, twelve feet by two, and appeared at first glance to have been sliced from a larger, more complete image: branches and leaves at the top, giving way to a length of marvellously realistic bark and, at the bottom, the clipped grass out of which the tree was growing.

The centre of the image was a confusion of colours and shapes: a hand outstretched, a leg and foot dangling above the grass, and most troubling, a piece of a man's face with a staring, dead-looking eye. With a shock, I realised that I was looking at a strip, as it were, of a larger image, showing a man hanging from a tree—but if the eye was dead, that tensely extended hand was definitely not.

In a lesser craftsman, I would have thought he had painted the eye badly; in a lesser mind, I might have assumed the artist did not know how a dead hand would hang. But this was Damian Adler, so I looked at the card on which the title had been typed:

Woden in the World Tree

If I remembered my Norse mythology, the god Woden—or Odin—had hanged himself for nine days in the tree that supported the world, so as to gain knowledge. Woden was blind in one eye.

I nodded in appreciation, and moved to the next painting, that of a hand shaking itself in a mirror—clever, but nothing more. The one after that appeared to be a solid wall of leaves, meticulously detailed, until one noticed that the twin points of gleam to one side were eyes: The hidden image gradually resolved into the ancient pagan figure of the Green Man.

Next time I walked through the woods, the back of my neck was going to crawl.

The room's far wall at first glance seemed to have a window in it, but did not.

What it had was a *trompe-l'oeil* painting, with shadows falling naturally both on the inner sill and on the scene "outside." It showed an alleyway, such as might indeed be on the other side of the wall: an expanse of dirty red bricks topped by a slice of sky. At the upper edge of the canvas was a crescent moon, translucent in the bright daylight. A man strode towards the right-hand edge of the canvas, his hat tipped back on his head, his right hand swinging forward, grasping some object that was cut off by the edge of the canvas—although something about his posture made one think he was perhaps being pulled along by whatever was in his hand.

The painting reminded me of something: I walked forward to see if I could figure out what.

Up close, everything changed. The bricks began to glisten and take on the texture of living matter, as if skin had been flayed from a muscle wall. Closer still, the cracks and mortar grew alive with tiny creatures, squirming and baring sharp, minuscule teeth; the pale shape in the upper corner suggested less a daylit moon than it did a mouth, poised to open. Taking a step back felt like a natural response.

I was not surprised to see the signature in the corner: *The Addler.* Suddenly, I saw why it looked familiar: If the brick walls had been sandbags and the businessman replaced by three soldiers, I would be looking at his 1915 drawing of the trench under fire.

"Mesmerising, is it not?" came a French accent from behind me.

"Disturbing," I said.

"Great art often is."

I thought about that. Was it possible that time would declare Holmes' son great? That the peculiarity of Damian's work was less the sign of a troubled mind than the fearless exploration of an artistic vision? Many had thought Holmes himself unbalanced. "Great or not, I don't know that I'd want it in my sitting room."

It was the wrong thing to say: When I turned, the woman had

raised a polite and condescending face. "Surrealism expresses thought without reason, pure artistic impulse with no hindrance from rationality or aesthetics. Perhaps you should take a closer look at the other room. Vanessa Bell has just sent me a very nice portrait that would look good on a sitting room wall."

I hastened to get back into the woman's better graces. "Oh no, I like Damian's work enormously. I like him, for that matter. It's just that some of his paintings are, what? A little too compelling for comfort?"

The small woman tipped her perfect head at me, considering. She herself was an artifice—at any rate, a flawless appearance and a sympathy for Bohemian artists did not go hand-in-hand. In the end, she decided that I, too, was not what I appeared.

"You have met Mr Adler?"

"I've known him for years," I said, which was the literal, if not the complete, truth. "He came to dinner the other night. When I heard you were displaying his work, I thought I'd stop in. This is another of his, isn't it?"

The other painting, on the room's back wall, bore his characteristic hand: painful, nightmare images painted with such loving realism, one was tempted to reach out and touch the surface, just to reassure one's self that it was two dimensional.

The moon, again. Only this time, it was a pair of moons, two bright eyes in the night-time sky, staring down at the eerie blue-tinged outlines below. The shapes of the landscape were difficult to determine. At first I thought it was a group of bulky figures walking along an unlit street. Moving closer, I noticed that the shapes were nearly square: tall buildings in a modern city during an electrical outage? The painting occupied the room's darkest corner, which did not help any. But when I was nearly on top of it, the details became clear.

The painting showed a prehistoric site, a grouping of massive stones both upright and fallen, forming a rough circle on a moonlit hillside. The grass around them was composed of a million delicate black and blue-black brushstrokes, the texture of a cat's fur.

I lifted my gaze to the dual moons, and saw that the craters and patterns on their near-white surfaces had been re-arranged to suggest a retina and iris: Two great pale eyes gazed down from a sable sky.

Had I seen this painting earlier, I should never have fallen asleep on the moonlit terrace.

"The Addler is known for his moons," the Frenchwoman said.

"Lunacy," I muttered.

"Pardon?"

"Lunacy. From Luna, the moon. There's a long belief that madness is linked to the phases of the moon."

"Most interesting," she replied in a chill voice, "but The Addler is not mad."

"Isn't he?"

"No more than any artist," she protested, then gave an uncomfortable laugh, as if to acknowledge that we were both indulging in clever badinage.

"The madder the better, when it comes to art," I agreed. "Have you met his wife?"

"But of course. And the child, such a winsome thing."

I thought about that word: Either the woman didn't like children, or she didn't approve of this particular child.

While we spoke, I had been studying the two-moon painting, the shapes of the stones, the texture of the black-on-black hillside. The man had skill, no denying that, although producing an endless string of works that made the viewer uneasy might not guarantee commercial success.

I started to turn away, then stopped as a shape redefined itself in the corner of my eye.

What I had taken for a flat stone in the centre of the circle was not an even rectangle; under scrutiny, the faint reflections of moonlight off the myriad leaves of grass made the shape appear to have extremities. I removed my glasses; with lack of focus, it became clearer. The stone had the outline of a human, arms outstretched, as if bathing in the moonlight.

With my glasses on again, the suggestion of humanity faded, until I could not be certain it was there at all.

"How much is this one?" I asked.

She arched an eyebrow at my two-year-old skirt and unpolished shoes, and named a price approximately three times what I anticipated. Then she added, "I might be able to come down a little, since you are a friend of the artist."

"I'll take it. And I'll think about the others."

She frankly gaped at me, but I knew Holmes would like the piece—although I might ask him to hang it in one of the rooms I did not spend much time in.

I made the arrangements for shipping it to Sussex, and left, meditating on the idea of painting *thought without reason* and *pure artistic impulse*. If Damian had searched long and hard for a way to set himself in opposition to his rationalistic father, he could not have found a better style than that of Surrealism.

I rode the Piccadilly line down to South Kensington and walked towards Burton Place. After the prices the Frenchwoman had quoted me, Damian's home address became more understandable.

Bohemia was torn between a scorn for money and a basic human appreciation for comfort. Too much success in art was seen as a dubious achievement, if not outright treason to The Cause, proof that one had strayed onto the side of the bourgeois and middle-class. Money (be it earned or inherited) could be justified by sharing it with less fortunate members of the Bohemian fraternity, but from the image of Yolanda that I had begun to form, I rather doubted Damian's wife would be enthusiastic about hangers-on.

Number seven, Burton Place, proved to be on a quiet cul-de-sac, one street over from a park, in an area composed of similar neat, narrow, two- and three-storey houses. Indeed, as I strolled up and down the adjoining streets, I began to feel I was walking the human equivalent of honeycomb, identical compartments broken only by the occasional queen cell. Not the sort of neighbourhood one might expect to shelter a bearded painter of staring moons and bizarre city-scapes—

Chelsea was for the well-heeled, unlike the more working-class Fitzrovia where the true artists nobly starved.

There was no sign of life within the Adler house, but much coming and going from those nearby: Any break-in at this time of day would not go unnoticed.

So I did what any investigator would do on a pleasant Saturday afternoon, and went to talk to the neighbours.

Chapter Seventeen

*Reward (1): Mere weeks after he has been transformed,
the new-born man learns that this most ephemeral of
apprenticeships has preserved the mortal life of the Guide
from flames and the turmoil of an angry earth: a reward.*
Testimony, II:2

THE REACTIONS AT TWO HOUSES SUGGESTED,
and the third confirmed, that I was not convincing for my
rôle. A maid at the first and a man with a newspaper at the second
both got as far as my first dozen words—"Good evening, I'm a friend
of the Adlers at number seven and"—before their gaze strayed to my
nondescript shirtwaist and unremarkable skirt and their faces shifted
to polite disbelief.

The third time it happened, at number eleven, the person whose
suspicions I raised was a child of perhaps eight or nine. She opened to
my knock, and although I expected a parent to appear any moment,
the child faced me with all the aplomb of a householder. So I told her
who I was and what I wanted. She put her head to one side.

"You don't look like one."

"One what?" I asked. How did one talk to a child, anyway? I hadn't much experience with it.

"Like a friend of the Adlers."

"Why, what do they look like?"

"Not like you," she said helpfully.

I looked down at my skirt, and pulled a face. "I know. I had to visit my parents today and this is how they like to see me."

"You're too old to have to dress for your parents."

"One never grows too old for that."

Her shiny head tipped to the other side as she considered. "They give you an allowance, and you have to keep them happy?"

"Something like that." My parents had been dead nearly a decade, but that did not mean I had not, at times, changed my appearance to satisfy other figures in authority.

"That's dreadful," she stated, making it clear that I had just scotched her entire expectations for life as a free adult.

"True, but its merely on the surface. May I ask you—"

But our discussion on the merits of Bohemia was interrupted by the child's own figure of authority, as fingers wrapped around the door eighteen inches above hers and pulled it open. At last: the mother.

The girl craned her head upwards and said, "Mama, this lady is looking for 'Stella."

"Actually," I said, "I'm looking for Estelle's parents."

"Why, what did they do?"

An interesting assumption. "Nothing, as far as I know. I'm a friend of Damian's, in Town unexpectedly, and I was hoping he and Yolanda would be here. But no-one answers, and I wonder if you have any idea where they might have gone?"

The eyes did their downward glance. "Frankly, you don't look like one of the Adlers' friends."

I stifled a sigh, but the child cut in. "She's just come from visiting her parents and she's afraid of being cut off so she has to dress like that, just like us and Grandmama."

There was humour in the woman's face at that, the sort of humour that indicates a degree of wit.

"I haven't worn the skirt since last year, and I didn't have time to adjust the hem," I admitted. "But it's true, I've known Damian for years. I met him in France, just after the War."

The claim either sounded real or contained a fact that she knew to be true, because she looked down at her daughter and said, "You run along and pour the tea for your dollies, Virginia. I'll be there in a moment."

Reluctantly, the child withdrew to trudge, shoulders bent, for the stairway. When her feet were on the steps, her mother turned back to me.

"There was a gentleman here the other day, asking after Yolanda."

I could hear the accusation in her tone, and scrambled hastily to assemble a harmless explanation. "Tall, older man?"

"Yes. You know him?"

"My father. Or rather, step-father. When I knew I'd be coming up, I asked him to call by and tell Damian and Yolanda. They weren't answering their telephone, and she's a terrible correspondent. When he didn't find them, I hoped perhaps he'd just missed them."

"I see," she said, accepting both the explanation and the insider's comments about the Adlers. "Normally on a Saturday evening I'd say you could find Yolanda in church, but I haven't seen either of them for some days. They may be out of town."

"When did you last see them?"

"Let me think. You know, I don't believe I've seen *her* for quite a while, although I saw him more recently. Sunday, was it? Yes, he walked down the street with a valise as we were leaving for dinner at my mother's. He said hello to the children. But I haven't seen either Mrs Adler or the child since . . . oh, I know, we met in the park perhaps ten days ago, just after the rains stopped. Our daughters enjoy playing together." I thought it unlikely that the bright-eyed child I had just been speaking to would share too many interests with an infant less than half her age. More likely their "playing together" was a convenient pretext for their mothers to linger on a park bench, chatting.

"That would have been, what, Wednesday?"

"I think so."

"And Damian, you saw him Sunday afternoon?" With a valise—leaving for Sussex?

"That's right."

"You said Mrs Adler goes to church on Saturday night. Where is that?"

"Well, I don't know that it's church, exactly. It's one of those meeting hall places full of odd people."

"Is it nearby?"

"I think so—it's my husband who told me about it, let me ask him. Jim? Jim, could you come here for a moment, there's a lady looking for the Adlers in number seven. My husband, Jim," she said when a rotund man of forty came to the door, pointedly carrying a tea-cup. Distant voices indicated other children, under the supervision of a nanny. And the presence of an undistracted wife at the door at a time when cooking odours filled the house indicated a cook on the premises as well: no Bohemians, these.

"Mary Russell," I said, holding out my hand first to him, then to her.

"Jim, can you tell Miss Russell where that meeting hall was that you saw Mrs Adler going into, some weeks back?"

Jim was not the brains of the family, and had to hunt through his memories for the event in question. After a while, his round face cleared. "Ahr, yais. Peculiar types. Artistic, don't you know?"

"That sounds like the Adlers," I agreed merrily. "Do you remember where the hall was?"

He stirred his tea for a moment, then raised the cup to slurp absently: The act stirred memory. "It was coming back from the cinema one night. Harold Lloyd, it was. Wonderful funny man." I made encouraging noises, hoping I was not to hear the entire plot of whatever picture it was.

Fortunately, his wife intervened. "Which cinema house was it, Jim?"

"Up the Brompton," he answered promptly.

"Not the Old Brompton?"

"Nar, up near the V and A."

"Isn't that the Cromwell Road?" I asked.

"Thurloe, for a time," she corrected me.

"Not Thurloe," he insisted. "Below that." This, my mental map told me, did indeed put us onto the bit of the Brompton Road that jogged to join the Fulham Road. I did not know how a stranger ever found his way around this city, where a street could be called by five names in under a mile.

"So was the meeting hall along the Brompton Road?"

"Just this side." Between them, they narrowed it down for me, and although I knew the area well enough to be certain there was no true meeting hall in that street, there were any number of buildings that could have a large room above ground-floor shops, and his description of "atop the stationers' with the fancy pens in the window," was good enough to start with. I thanked them and wished them a good evening.

Jim left, but the wife stepped out of the door and lowered her voice. "You said you're a friend of his? Mr Adler's?"

"Originally his, yes," I said carefully.

"But you know her a little?"

"Not as well as I do him, but a little." One photograph and a husband's description might better be described as a *very* little, but the woman wished to tell me something, and I thought she was asking for encouragement.

"Is she . . . That is to say, is Mrs Adler dependable?"

An interesting word. "Dependable?"

She looked to be regretting the question, but she persisted. "I mean to say, Mr Adler seems a nice enough sort, for an artist, that is. Polite and so very good with the little girl, but the wife . . . well, she's a bit queer."

"Hmm," I said, desperate for a hint as to Yolanda's particular type of oddness. "She does strike one that way, it's true. Perhaps it's just that she's foreign."

"True. But you'd say that, deep down, she's a good wife and mother?"

Ah. "She loves the child a great deal," I said, with somewhat more assurance.

"Oh yes, no doubt about that. It's just, well, they've had three different nannies in the few months they've been here, and the agency—it's the agency I use, when I need anyone—they told me that word is getting out that it's not an easy post. Nice people, don't you know, but . . . foreign. They don't understand the proper way things are done. In any case, this means that Damian—Mr Adler—seems to care for the child on his own rather more than one might expect."

"Yolanda does go away from time to time," I offered.

"Exactly!" the non-Bohemian wife and mother said.

"Well," I said. "You know artists. They live differently from other people. I believe Damian rather enjoys being a . . . daddy."

She took no note of my hesitation, which was less at the idea of Damian's pleasure in fatherhood than it was a matter of the unfamiliar vocabulary: *Mummy, Daddy,* and the language of the nursery did not come easy to my tongue. Her face softened with relief. "That's very true, he loves little Estelle to death. So you'd say he takes her to the park because he enjoys it, not because his wife, well, abandons them?"

I did my best to assure her that Damian enjoyed nothing better than to spend his every daylight hour with the child while his wife flitted around doing God knew what, then I thanked her again and left her to supervise the dollies' tea-party.

As I walked down the steps, I reflected that a woman who did not think to offer her name to a visitor might not be the best judge of a woman whose interests lay outside of the home.

I found no help from the three remaining houses, and considered: Branch out through the adjoining streets, or head for the Brompton Road meeting hall?

I decided that a further canvass of the more distant houses held little hope of striking gold, so I re-traced Jim's steps, out of Chelsea along the Fulham Road and along the crooked tail of Brompton.

There I found a doorway next to a stationers. The shop was open, the door was not, although a hand-lettered sign tacked to its centre read:

Children of Lights meeting, 7:00 p.m. Saturdays

I let my gaze stray to the reflection in the stationers' glass. The young woman there did not resemble a potential child of light—lights, I corrected myself, although I had to wonder if the plural was an error. If I had anywhere near the right impression of Yolanda Adler, my dowdy skirt and sensible shoes would not serve to ingratiate myself into her circle. In any event, there was no doubt that I should have to do something about my appearance before entering the venue that would come after.

Some years before, I'd kept a flat in the city, but the married couple I'd hired to keep it up had since retired, and the bother of maintaining it outweighed its occasional usefulness. Now, on the rare occasions I was in Town without Holmes, I would either stay with his brother or in my women's club, the whimsically-named Vicissitude. Or, in a pinch, one of Holmes' bolt-holes.

It was the latter that held the wherewithal to transform me from drab chrysalis to full-blown butterfly; as it happened, there was one very close to hand.

I continued along the commercial streets until I came to the department store in which Holmes had built a concealed room. I let myself in by a hidden key and invisible latch. Of his various hidey-holes across the city, this was one of the more oppressive, as dim and airless as the wardrobe it resembled. But it was packed to the brim with costumes, and in minutes, I had an armful of likely garments to hold up before the looking-glass.

Or perhaps *unlikely* garments might better describe the raiment I wrapped myself in: a diaphanous skirt with a deliberately uneven hem-line, a gipsy-style blouse whose yoke was stiff with embroidery, a scarlet leather belt with a buckle fashioned from a chunk of turquoise, and a soft shawl that might have been attractive in a less garish shade of green. Everything on me apart from my spectacles and shoes was eye-catching, everything was bright, all the colours clashed.

I traced a line of kohl around my eyes and added a peacock-feather bandeau to my hair, then on second thought changed the half-dozen glass bangles on my right wrist for a silver chain to which were attached various tiny and esoteric shapes. As a piece of jewellery it was both ugly and uncomfortable, but on previous occasions I had found it to offer great opportunity for conversation. I studied the result in the glass, then checked the time on my lamentably mundane wristwatch.

Twenty minutes to seven. I could by-pass the Children of Light, or Lights, as may be, ignoring the wife's interests to plunge directly on the trail of Damian himself. On the other hand, this church of hers would appear to hold very limited hours, as the other place I was headed did not.

No, I decided: I would stop briefly at the meeting hall, then go on. I could only pray that, in neither place would I meet anyone who knew me.

Of course, I could always claim I was dressed for a costume ball.

Chapter Eighteen

Reward (2): Through his Guide's embrace,
the man found himself possessed of gifts both profound
and primitive, insights human and divine:
what men call clairvoyance.
Testimony, II:2

THE NARROW DOORWAY BESIDE THE STATIONERS'
was now attracting people. Three young women in very ordinary dress went in, causing me to question my costume, but then a
man in a dramatic black velvet cape that must have been roasting
stepped out of a cab and swept inside, the woman left behind to pay
the driver wearing garments only fractionally less outrageous than my
own, so I kept coming.

The doorway led to a narrow, unadorned stairway, with the sound
of a crowd coming from above. I climbed, and found a room twice the
size of the stationers' downstairs, half the chairs filled by fifty or sixty
or so professional Seekers, poetic undergraduates, bored young
women, and earnest spinsters. I was by no means the most colourful.

One of the Earnest Spinsters with bad skin and dyed-black hair
greeted me with a proprietary air coupled with an enthusiasm that

made me uneasy. She grasped my hand in both of hers, holding it while she told me her name (Millicent Dunworthy), asserted her long history as a Child of Lights (plural, I noted), and delivered her assurance that I, too, would find myself Enlightened by the Evening and sure to have any Questions from my Heart's True Heart answered (all capital letters clear in her pronouncement). I withdrew my hand with some difficulty, accepted the brochures she thrust at me, and backed away while she was still talking.

Fortunately, some others came in then and kept her from following me to a seat in the back between a woman with a nose like a tin-opener and a young man with sloping shoulders and damp-looking hands.

The only suggestion that the evening might include a religious element was that the chairs were arranged with an aisle down the middle, to permit a sort of procession. The room itself was made up of three nondescript wallpapered walls and a fourth of new-looking wooden storage cupboards. It was this wall towards which the seating had been arranged, which seemed an odd choice, particularly as the centre doors were held together by a large, utilitarian padlock. Heavy curtains sagged alongside the three windows overlooking the street, although they were drawn back and the windows open in a vain attempt to disperse the room's heat: If the evening's entertainment included photographic lantern-slides and a closing of the curtains, I would slip away.

Since the room itself told me nothing, and the congregants seemed to me the usual gathering of cranks and other gullible sorts, I turned to the pamphlets I had been given.

The "lights"—plural—in question, it seemed, were the sun, the moon, the planets, and the stars. And not necessarily in that order, I saw as I read the poorly printed but coherently written brochures. Like homeopathy, which declares dilute substances a more efficacious cure than powerful doses of the same substance, the influence of the far-distant stars was regarded as equal to that of the sun and the moon.

I sighed. Why were so many religions built upon such nonsensical foundations?

The sharp-nosed woman beside me heard my noise, and bristled. "Do you see something to disapprove of?" she demanded.

I lifted up a solemn and wide-eyed expression. "That was a sound of mourning, that I had gone for so many years without hearing this message."

The true believer looked suspicious. Fortunately, activity at the front of the room distracted her from further accusations.

A jolly-faced woman, brisk and tidy as a nurse despite the long white robe she wore and the large gold ring on her right hand (nurses tend to avoid rings) marched to the front of the now-full room to address the padlock on the double doors. She had problems, becoming more and more flustered until a man who might have been her brother, also dressed in a robe and wearing a ring, got up to help her. Between the two of them they wrestled the thing off and pushed back the doors.

My first surprise of the evening was the back-drop thus revealed: a painting by Damian Adler.

Not that it was immediately recognisable as such. In fact, it was not even instantly recognisable as a painting, merely an expanse of black broken by tiny white specks. From my seat at the back, I could see little more than velvet darkness and a sense of depth, but having spent the past two days with his work, I had no doubt that it was from the hand of The Addler.

The two acolytes had pulled a somewhat shaky-looking table before the open doors and were now draping it with a black cloth. The woman set up a pair of incense burners and held a match to the contents, which began to weep a thick smoke that made me glad for my seat at the back. The man drew a silver candelabrum from one of the cupboards, put it onto the cloth, and started working candles into it. The candles were black.

I perked up. Was I about to become a participant in a Black Mass?

I had spent enough time in theological studies to have come across various parodies of the Roman Catholic Mass, from Fools' Feast to orgy-on-the-altar. But surely nothing too extreme would take place here, in a public meeting hall that invited strangers off the street?

No: Neither the people nor their attitudes suggested that they were about to enact an orgy atop the flimsy table. Disappointing, perhaps, but then again, I had no wish to be arrested in a raid. Holmes' rivals in Scotland Yard would never let either of us live it down.

It took the flustered brother and sister a while to get the reluctant wicks lit, but when the light was growing at the end of each dark taper, they stood back and glanced at the audience. The entire congregation—some of us belatedly—rose to its feet, and those in the know gave a ragged chorus: "Light from darkness."

Half the lights in the room were turned down, a relief in temperature if nothing else, and with that, a figure in a startlingly white, hooded robe swept down the central aisle, a book carried reverently before her. It was Millicent Dunworthy, the woman with the badly dyed black hair who had welcomed me. She, too, had a gold band on her right hand, although I was certain she had not worn it earlier. And when I looked down at the hand of the woman beside me, I saw that she wore one as well, a large, roughly made band of bright yellow gold.

As Miss Dunworthy took her place at the front, a tremor ran through the audience: Feet shifted, people looked at their neighbours with raised eyebrows, a small murmur could be heard.

She laid the book on the impromptu altar and raised her face; her first words explained the reaction. "The Master couldn't be here tonight, and asked me to lead the worship. He sends his love, and hopes to return next week."

The congregation, reluctantly it seemed, settled into the chairs. With no further ado, she opened the book, revealing a brief glimpse of a simple design worked in gilt on the dark cover, and read in a voice of theatrical piety:

The Stars

The man was but a child when he began to hear the message of the stars, to grasp the precision of their meaning, to feel the tenuous link between their paths and those of human beings.

It is no secret that greatness and celestial motions go hand-in-hand. Throughout the ages, the heavens have recognised the births of notables, providing a hanging star for the sages to find the infant Jesus. And celestial bodies at times cooperate, sending a shooting star to convey heavenly approbation of a human endeavour, or even lending an assist to the actions of mere men: William the Conqueror moved to the throne with a comet in the night sky overhead; when Joshua needed more hours in which to complete his conquest, the sun lingered in the sky to lighten his way.

It was the usual religious nonsense that had flowered since the War's end, equal parts delusion, untidy thinking, and egomania. My own tradition of Judaism believes that there is nothing God loves more than a quick-witted argument; the words Millicent Dunworthy read were an excellent illustration of the need to teach Rabbinic debate in public schools. Her audience drank it in, educated and prosperous though they were, although it was clear many of them had heard the text before. One or two of those near me were even shaping the words under their breath as the woman read.

It went on, and on, personal revelation linked with Biblical references, world mythology, and historical events, all of which was designed (if one can use that term) to place "the man" (clearly, an autobiographical third person) firmly in the pantheon of holy men throughout the ages, and to link his ideas with those found in the world's great religions. The inclusion of Nordic deities brought a degree of innovation—most synthesisers drew on the Egyptian or Indian pantheon—but apart from Loki and Baldur where one might expect Thoth or Shiva, I heard nothing that would justify the violence done to rationality. The room was warm, the incense cloying, and it had been a long day; I kept from dozing off entirely by alternating the composition of a rude letter to Holmes with a running list of fallacies, errors, and lies.

The reading came to an end at last. The book was allowed to close, and the woman looked expectantly over our heads at the back of the room. Footsteps came down the aisle, the robed man and woman carrying, respectively, a carafe of clear liquid that looked as if it belonged on a bedside table, and a pair of ordinary drinking glasses. They placed the utensils in front of Millicent Dunworthy and stood to the side; for an instant, she looked like a woman in a night-gown getting herself a drink of water, and I choked back a laugh. The woman beside me shot me a look of glowering mistrust, and I hastily rearranged my face to solemnity.

"For those who thirst for the light, drink deep," Miss Dunworthy's voice declared. I was startled, for the words resembled those of another religious leader I had worked with some years before. However, I soon decided that this was not mysticism, but melodrama. The congregation rose and made their way to the front, where each took a worshipful swallow. Five more of them, four women and a man, wore matching gold bands on their right hands.

When all but I and one other had received their communion, the woman drank some herself, dashed the remaining drops on the floor, and declared, "Go your way in the love of The Master of Lights."

She tucked the book in her arm and swept down the aisle again. Her robe, I noticed, had a small crimson shape, an elongated triangle topped with a circle, embroidered over the heart—the design I had glimpsed on the cover of the book:

A keyhole? Or a spotlight, illustrating the church's name?

To my pleasure, the service was followed by tea and biscuits served by their equivalent of the Mothers' Union—stewed tea served in an attitude of sanctity was an ideal setting for the picking of brains. However, the congregants did not seem inclined to linger, either because of The Master's unexpected absence or simply the stuffiness of the room, so I should have to move quickly.

I turned to my neighbour, on the theory that the toughest nuts to crack (so to speak) hold the sweetest meat.

"What a most satisfying reading that was! And tell me, was that just water you were drinking?"

"You could have had some yourself," she said.

"Oh! I didn't know, I thought it was only for the initiated. What a pity. I shall make certain to go forward next week."

She relented a fraction. "You plan on coming back, then?"

"Of course! If nothing else I'd like to hear The Master—isn't that what you call him? I thought he was always here."

"He usually is, but there are times when his body is emptied of Self, and he cannot attend in his corporeal person. He was, no doubt, here in spirit."

"Oh!" I squeaked, as if a ghost stood at my shoulder. "Good, I so look forward to meeting him. Yolanda Adler told me about him. Do you know Yolanda?"

"Certainly, she's one of the—one of our regulars." I wondered what she had been about to say. One of the initiated? The Leading Lights, as it were?

"Oh, and would anyone mind if I went to look at the painting up front? It's by her husband, isn't it?"

She had begun to gather her things to leave. Now she paused to look at me more closely. "It is. Most people don't even notice it's a painting."

"Really? I'd have thought it was unmistakable." I stepped towards her, forcing her to give way and let me into the centre aisle. I thought she might follow, but I heard her say good night to some of the others, and she left.

The painting was nearly all black. Its texture came from hundreds of circles, ranging from tiny dots to those the size of a thumb-nail. All showed the same pattern of light: droplets on a window, reflecting a cloudless night sky. In each and every one, a long streak of light indicated the moon, distorted by the droplets' curve; around the streak a sprinkling of smaller spots were stars.

It was subtle, complex, and breathtaking.

I don't know how long I stood there, oblivious to the emptying room and the tidying away of the altar and candelabrum, but eventually Millicent Dunworthy, sans ring and robe now, came to shut the painting away behind its doors. I stepped back reluctantly, eyeing the feeble padlock and thinking that this was one Adler I should not mind having on my sitting room wall. . . .

But I was investigating, not planning an art theft. "Oh!" I exclaimed. (Such a useful sound, that, for indicating an empty head.) "It's like raindrops on a window!"

"Yes, it's lovely, isn't it?" She paused, and we both gazed at it. "Did you enjoy the service?"

I suppressed a degree of the empty-headed enthusiast, for this woman was more perceptive than the sharp-nosed woman I had stood beside. "Oh, it was ever so fascinating, all that about the light and the dark. It makes such sense, don't you think?"

Miss Dunworthy did think. "I'm glad you enjoyed yourself. Do come again, and bring your friends."

"Oh, I will, most definitely. In fact, it's because of a friend I'm here—Yolanda Adler, Damian's wife," I clarified, gesturing at the painting.

"You know the Adlers?"

"Her more than him, but yes. They've been coming here for a while, haven't they?"

"Well, Mrs Adler certainly. And him from time to time. Such a nice young man, he reminds me of my brother. Who was killed," she added sadly. "At Ypres."

"I'm sorry. But the Adlers weren't here tonight."

"No. Something may have come up."

"You haven't talked to her, then?"

"Not for the past week, no." There was an air of puzzlement in her voice, indicating that she not only had no idea where Yolanda Adler was, she was surprised not to have seen her.

"Such an interesting person, isn't she?" I gushed. "So exotic. Where was it she's from? Singapore?"

"I thought it was Shanghai?"

"You're right! I'm a bit of a fool when it comes to geography. But I just love her accent."

"It is charming, although it's so light, with your eyes shut you'd think she grew up in London."

"How long is it she's been coming here, anyway?" I asked it absently, my attention on the painting.

"She was here at the beginning. January, meetings began. Although I have to say, she's never seemed as thoroughly committed to The Master's work as some of us. Over the past months, she seems to have lost interest."

"Does she have any particular pals, among the Children? I was just wondering if she, too, found you because of a friend."

"I've never noticed her being especially close to any of the others. Apart from The Master, of course. In fact, I rather had the impression that she knew him before."

She reached for the doors then, to close Damian's painting away, so she didn't see my mouth hanging open.

"What, in Shanghai?" My question was a shade too sharp. She glanced at me over her shoulder, and I hastened to clarify. "I didn't know that the Children were an international organisation. Isn't that great!"

"As far as I know, this is the only centre. I merely meant that Mrs Adler knew him before we opened up."

"Ah, I see. When was that, do you know?"

"Meetings began in January, we moved into this space the following month. Now, was there anything else?"

"Just, do you know if 'The Master' will be here next week?"

"One never knows," she replied blandly, and bid me good night.

That blandness suggested that she knew more than she was saying, if not about Yolanda Adler, then about The Master. Perhaps I should know a little more about the competent, unattractive, and vulnerable Millicent Dunworthy as well.

I was waiting across the street when she left the meeting hall, the last one out and locking up behind her, a bit awkward around a white-wrapped parcel the size of the book and robe. She got the door locked, settled the bundle safely into her left arm, and marched away down the street, where the thick, petrol-scented air soon cleared the incense-induced headache from my skull.

Fortunately, the woman lived in walking distance of the hall—boarding a bus without her taking notice of me would have been tricky—and within a quarter hour she was vanishing behind the front door of a run-down apartment house. I waited until a light went on at the west side of the second storey, then I left.

It was now far too late to continue knocking up the Adlers' neighbours, even if I had been dressed for the deed, but nine-thirty would be just about perfect for the occupants of another district of Town.

However, I was having second thoughts about the garments I had chosen. They had been just right for the Children of Lights, but for an assault on the stronghold of London's *avant-garde*? Something less frivolous was required, more dramatic.

Fortunately, the bolt-hole was on my way.

Before tonight I had discovered that, by a judicious use of safety pins and sticky tape, I could transform a pair of Holmes' trousers into something that did not look like a child playing dress-up from her father's wardrobe. Tonight's victim of my tape assault was a beautifully cut evening suit that I'd thought he kept at Mycroft's, although this might have been an exact duplicate of that garment. In either case, I made short work of converting it to my frame, and put it on over a white shirt fresh from the laundry, adding a sumptuous embroidered waistcoat I found in the back of a cupboard. My blonde hair, cut above my ears back in February, still only came down to the lobes, so I slicked it with some pomade and painted my eyes a little, dropping a silk scarf around my neck.

I looked, surprisingly enough, like what I was: a woman in (mostly) man's clothing. I opened the safe and helped myself to various forms of cash, then drew an ivory cigarette holder from the bristle of pens and make-up pencils in a cup and slid it into my breast pocket. After another look at my reflection, I painted my lips a brilliant red, then nodded in satisfaction.

The clothing I had started the day in, back in Sussex, I folded into a black cloth bag, adding one or two things from the wardrobe, just in case. I let myself out, and put out a hand for a cab to take me to the capital of Bohemia.

Chapter Nineteen

Reward (3): The man was left knowing the path but without the Tools to explore it, sensing his divinity but lacking the means of bringing it to the fore.
Testimony, II:2

E VEN A PERSON WHO SPENDS HER LIFE ENGAGED in criminal investigations, preoccupied with academics, or out of the country entirely could not fail to locate the capital of Bohemia. Trace Regent Street to where it crooks its arm to embrace Eros; draw a line between the Royal Academy and the theatres of Shaftesbury Avenue, between Soho and St James; describe the intersection of finance with sensuality, where art crosses pens with drama, and there you will find the Café Royal.

It was nine-twenty on a Saturday night, and despite the scaffolding of its ongoing renovations, the Café Royal was turning over nicely. I waited until I saw a likely couple approaching its doors, then I fell in beside the woman to address her a remark about Dora Carrington. Our apparent conversation got me safely through the door—a single woman was still, even in these enlightened days, looked upon with suspicion by restaurant guard-dogs. I ostentatiously handed the porter a glittering tip to keep my black cloth bag (gold guineas were archaic, unspendable, and impressive as hell: Holmes kept a good supply of them in his bolt-holes for precisely that purpose) and swept inside.

When I had been here with Holmes, some years before, one had a choice between the Restaurant proper, the Grill Room, or the Brasserie downstairs—known to its habitués as the Domino Room for the constant click of the tiles to be heard there. The renovations looked to be sweeping away much of the Café's scruffy charm, but as I went down the stairs, I ceased to worry that its *clientele* would desert it altogether. A wall of noise awaited me amongst the gilded caryatids and rococo mirrors: Strident voices, piercing feminine laughter, and the ceaseless clatter of cutlery against plates emerged from a miasma of tobacco smoke and alcohol fumes that bore localised tints of blue, gilt, or scarlet from the walls and the plush banquettes.

The maître d' had that race's innate ability to make himself under-stood despite the handicaps, and I responded in type, by telling him that I was meeting a friend and holding up my wrist to check the time. He read the words on my lips, or perhaps merely the gesture, and although a few years before he might have hesitated, these were the Twenties. He stood aside while I looked about for my imaginary companion.

A woman of my height, in male clothing but with scarlet lips and flowered waistcoat, was noticed even in that place. I surveyed the room, allowing the room to survey me, before shaking my head at the man and telling him, "My friend isn't here yet, why don't I sit at that table over there and wait for her?"

Had the table not been small and awkwardly situated behind a par-ticularly raucous group, he might have had another suggestion, but in that mysterious osmosis that functions in a well-run café, in the thirty seconds I had stood there, the man had learnt of the coin I gave the porter, and merely bowed me forward. Either that or, as occurred to me much later, he recognised me as a one-time companion of Sherlock Holmes, and decided to give me leave.

I ordered a drink, drew out the ivory cigarette holder, frowned at the lack of a cigarette in my pockets, and leant over to borrow a smoke from one of the men at the raucous table. Less than three minutes after I had walked in, I had a cigarette in my hand and a chair at the crowded table; the waiter swept over in his floor-length white apron to place my cocktail before me, and twenty perfect strangers clasped me to their Bohemian chests.

I had chosen the difficult little table with care, for the noisy group was clearly assembled around a Great Man, their numbers swelled by sycophants edging up at the far end. I was halfway down the length of the table, close enough to catch his eye if not his ear, but it didn't take long to figure out who he was.

Augustus John was that most unlikely of creatures, a prosperous Bohemian—one who had even been invited into the Royal Academy. Perhaps his nonconformist ways had even contributed to his success, for in an artist of the Twentieth Century, outrageousness and *avant-garde* were to be desired—and a man who extolled the superiority of his friends the gipsies, who kept a household of two peasant-dressed wives and their assorted barefoot children while still collecting mistresses and befriending royalty, and who went around London looking like a Canadian trapper in a velvet cloak was the very definition of nonconformist.

He was also a fine painter, which helped matters considerably.

I let the conversation bounce around me for a while as I sat and smoked and nodded my response to opinions on politics and a scandal encompassing a print-maker and a violinist (this was a Bohemian scandal, and therefore involved money and bourgeois attitudes rather than money and sexual promiscuity) and the relative merits of Greece versus the south of France as cheap, warm spots conveniently strewn with decorative rustics where one might spend the winter painting.

When my glass was empty, I ordered drinks for half a dozen of my nearest table-mates. The noise level of the Café pounded like surf; the smoke grew so dense, the golden walls ceased to shine. The poet to my left fell asleep against my shoulder. I transferred his head to the table; the man across from us helped himself to the poet's half-empty glass. The two people beside him, who had been pretending their legs weren't brushing together under the table, could bear it no longer and left, five minutes apart and fooling no-one. A woman in a suit similar to the one I wore lingered at my shoulder for a time, trying to make conversation until it was clear I was not interested, when she went away in a huff. The Great Man at the head of the table spotted this little play, and caught my eyes after the lesbian had moved on. He winked; I shrugged; a few minutes later a scrap of folded paper began to circulate down the table. It had a sketch on the front of an angular young androgyne in spectacles that could only be me. I unfolded it, and read:

I could do something intriguing with a model like you. Interested?

Underneath, it gave an address. I looked up to see his eyes on me, and I'm afraid I blushed, just a little, before gamely raising my glass to him.

"*Sastimos!*" I called down the table, which made his bushy eyebrows rise.

"*Sastimos! Droboi tumay, Romalay.*" His return of my Romany greeting was perhaps a test, and I summoned a memory of Holmes' long-ago tutorials in the language.

"*Nais tukah,*" I replied politely.

"*Anday savay vitsah?*" he asked, which was a little more complicated, both the language and the question of what group of Roma I belonged to. But the noise and the crowd covered any errors I made, and before he could order me down the table to him I made a show of folding the paper and slipping it into my pocket, as if to say that we would continue the conversation at another time.

(I had, in fact, no intention of doing so, but as it turned out, I did go to see John at another time, and he did end up doing a small portrait. That is one piece that Holmes values without question.)

By ten-forty, the peak of the evening was reached, and the revellers began to move on to other late-night venues. A lavender-clad playwright stood up and announced that he thought he would go to a party he'd heard of in Brompton, and he departed with a woman on each arm. Two married couples across from me shook hands all around and then they, too, left, although it seemed to me that each went out of the door with the other's spouse. Eventually, Augustus John rose and made his way out, looking irritated at the half a dozen admirers who drifted after him. The sleeping poet snorted awake, dashed down the contents of the nearest glass, and staggered off in the direction of the entrance. When the waiter returned, I ordered another drink, although my glass was still half full, and asked the two people next to me if they'd like another. They would.

"That was Augustus John, wasn't it?" I asked the woman, a thin, brown creature with untidy fringes and mismatched clothing.

"You must be new in town, if you don't know him." She had an appealing voice, low and just beginning to roughen with the cigarettes she smoked.

"I've been away for a while, in America," I told her, although John had been a fixture in the Café Royal for years.

She asked me about America, I made up some stories about the art world there, about which I knew next to nothing, then asked about John again.

"I wonder if he might know where a friend of mine is, another artist. I should have asked him before he left."

"Who are you looking for?"

"Damian Adler."

"Sorry, don't know him."

"Yes, you do," piped up the man at her side. "Painter chap, French or something, his wife knows Crowley."

"Oh, right—him. I haven't seen him for a while, though."

"Aleister Crowley, do you mean?" I asked the man—a writer, as I recalled. Yet another writer.

"That's the chap."

The woman interrupted. "Except it wasn't Crowley, was it, Ronnie?"

"It was, though," he asserted.

"No, they were talking about him, but I don't think she knew him."

"But why should I—oh, you're right, it was Betty who was talking about him, to her."

I wasn't sure I was following this fairly drunken conversation. "You mean Mrs Adler was talking to someone else about Aleister Crowley?"

"Betty May. Crowley killed her husband."

"Betty May's husband?" This was sounding familiar, although not the name May.

"Raoul Loveday. Took a first at Oxford, fell into Crowley's circle, died of drugs or something down in Crowley's monastery in Italy or Greece or someplace."

"Sicily," I said automatically. I remembered this, from the newspapers a year or more ago. "So Yolanda Adler was talking to Betty Loveday, here?"

"Being lectured by her, more like," the woman said. "Poor Betty, she's terrified of Crowley, any time she comes across someone interested in him she feels she has to save them from him."

"And Yolanda was interested in Crowley?"

"Yes. Or maybe not Crowley directly." She blinked in owlish concentration.

"Someone like Crowley?" I persisted.

"Or was it that someone she knew was interested in Crowley, and she was looking into how much trouble he was? Sorry, I really don't remember, it was a while ago. I'm Alice Wright, by the way. And this is Ronnie Sutcliffe." I shook her hand—bashed, scraped, and calloused—and his, considerably softer.

"Mary Russell," I said, introducing myself to her for the second time that night. "You're a sculptress, aren't you?"

She beamed. "You've heard of me?"

I hadn't the heart to admit that her hands had told me her avocation. "Oh, yes. But forgive me, Ronnie, I can't place where—"

"Ronnie's a writer. He's going to change the face of literature in this century, taking it well past Lawrence."

"D. H.," Ronnie clarified, looking smug.

I nodded solemnly, and gave way to an unkind impulse. "Are you published yet?"

"The publishing world is run by Philistines and capitalists," he growled. "But I had several poems published while I was still up at Cambridge."

"I look forward to seeing your work," I assured him.

Alice remembered what we had been talking about. "Why are you looking for her, anyway?"

"For Yolanda? I'm more trying to find her husband, Damian. He's an old friend, known him for years, and as I said, I'm recently back in town. I was hoping to see him."

The arch smile Alice gave indicated that she had read all the wrong meaning into my desire to see Damian Adler, but I caught back the impulse to set her straight: If it made her think me a denizen of the artistic underworld, so much the better. I shrugged, as if to admit that she was right.

The Café was being tidied for the night, the chairs arranged around the marble tabletops, glasses polished and set back on the shelves. The remaining seven members of our party were one of three tables still occupied, and we would soon be politely expected to depart.

Fortunately, before I could come up with a reason to attach myself to them, my two new friends claimed me instead.

"Would you like to go on for a drink?" Alice asked.

"The Fitzroy?" Ronnie suggested.

"I'm running a little low on funds," I told them, "but I'd be happy to—"

"Why not pop on home?" Alice interrupted, before they could find themselves paying for the rest of the evening. "Someone left a couple of bottles there, and Bunny won't have finished them off."

Having encountered such a wide variety of human relations that evening, I should have been willing to bet that Bunny was not, in fact, a large rabbit. However, since there might be more information to be had from the two, I agreed readily.

Outside on the street, we all three blinked under the impact of fresh air. After a moment, a man came out of the Café and pressed an object into my hand—the bag containing the skirt and blouse that I had put on in Sussex many long hours before. I thanked him, but he

vanished before I could find a coin for him, and I joined my two companions as they turned up Regent Street, braced together against the
sway of the pavement. My own feet meandered uncertainly, but once
my ears stopped ringing and the stinging sensation in my eyes
cleared, I discovered that it was a very pleasant evening.

Alice talked at me over her shoulder, in tones that reached those in
the buildings around us as well. She was a modern sculptress, she
said, providing a woman's perspective to the most male bastion of all
the arts. Her main problem, apart from the disinclination of the art
world to treat women seriously, was finding a studio large enough to
contain her vision. When we reached their home and studio, half a
mile away in Soho, I saw what she meant.

The garret she worked in, four sagging flights up from street level,
was intended to house servants, not to support a ton and a half of
scrap iron. I started to follow the two inside, then spotted the object
in the middle of the floor and stopped dead. Surely it was my imagination that put such a dip to the floorboards?

"I call it 'Freedom,' " Alice told me with pride. The sculpture appeared to have some vague representational basis, but whether the
extremities were the arms of a number of women strewing chicken
feed, or the legs of war horses, I could not tell.

"It's autobiographical," Ronnie added. "Where's the corkscrew?"
Since he was pawing through a drawer at the question, I thought he
was not asking about a component of the sculpture.

"Bunny was using it this morning to score the pots before she put
them in the kiln."

Lord, a kiln as well? "Are there people underneath us?" I asked.

"Just Bunny, and she won't hear us," Alice assured me, which
hadn't at all been what I was asking.

"How . . ." I stopped, at a loss for words.

"How am I going to get it out? The back wall is merely brick and
tin, I'll invite a bunch of friends over to bash out a hole and help lower
it down." She seemed proud that she had already solved that problem.

"Honestly, are there people living below? Because I really don't
think the floorboards are sturdy enough to support your . . . vision."

This struck the two as funny, and they began to giggle. Ronnie set off across the room, aiming for a bottle that sat on a long, high worktable, only to have his orbit pulled towards the monumental piece of art—no, the dip in the boards had not been my imagination.

"We're the only ones here, us and Bunny," Alice finally answered. "She owns the building, in fact, although her father is taking her to court to force her to sell it to cover some bills. But if the old man succeeds, we've told him he'll have to knock it down with us inside."

It didn't look to me as if he'd have to wait for the end of a court case to see the demolition of the building, but I was relieved that there were no families sleeping beneath us.

"I'm not altogether certain I don't own the building," Ronnie said, addressing the bottle with whose cork he had begun to wrestle.

"The law is so patriarchal," Alice commented to me.

"Er," I said.

"The husband has rights to his wife's possessions," she explained.

"So, Ronnie is married to Bunny?"

"Bunny isn't her name, of course," Alice said blithely. "We called her that after she proved so enthusiastic about—"

"Alice!" Ronnie chided.

She giggled again, and finished the sentence. "—about reproducing. Three children in four years indicates a certain enthusiasm, don't you think? But yes, she and Ronnie and I are married. Does that shock you?"

I was not about to confess to any shock at the doctrines of free love, but I did go back to my initial concern with renewed urgency.

"Are the children living here?"

"Not at the moment. Bunny's mother wouldn't have it, and came to take them away."

I breathed more easily; at least I didn't have the safety of innocents on my hands.

Ronnie cursed at the bottle; Alice propped her elbows on the high table to observe his struggles. I followed gingerly, keeping to the very edges of the room. The cork had come apart, so Ronnie jammed the remnants inside with a carving tool, then picked up the nearest glass, which bore both lipstick and food around its rim. He splashed some wine and cork bits into the glass and set it down in front of me. I raised it gingerly to the vicinity of my lips—although, from the raw smell rising out of the glass, any contamination would be well and truly sterilised.

"When did you meet the Adlers?" I asked bluntly. It had been a long day, and I figured these two were in no condition to require subtlety.

"The winter sometime."

"It was at the Epsteins' Christmas party, remember?" Ronnie said.

"Jacob Epstein gave a *Christmas* party?" I asked.

"It wasn't so much a Christmas party as a party at Christmas," Alice explained helpfully. "His wife gave it to show that she wasn't still angry at Kathleen. You know Jacob's wife, Margaret? She took a shot at one of Jacob's lovers last year, when she found out Kathleen was pregnant, although she'd been perfectly willing to raise the little girl he had by someone else five or six years before. She's usually perfectly content to let Jacob's lovers live with them, but for some reason she took against Kathleen. Anyway, that's settled now."

Heavens, my life was dull. "So that was when you met Damian and Yolanda?"

"Yolanda wasn't there, was she, Ronnie?"

"Wasn't she?"

"No, I remember because Damian couldn't come out with us to the country after the party, he had to be home because Yolanda would murder him if she heard he'd left the child by itself. It must have been when they first got here—that's right, there was some nonsense about finding a nanny. Children are so tedious, aren't they? Why can't one just leave them to their own devices?"

"Was Yolanda away, then?"

"Something religious, wasn't it?" he said, remembering.

"Probably," she agreed.

"I do remember now. You wanted him to come along because you hoped you could get him into bed."

Alice laughed and shot me a glance; I braced myself for further naughtiness. "Really, it was Ronnie who wanted to have a fling with him, and was hoping I'd join in. I would have, too."

"I don't blame you," I said evenly. "Damian is very attractive."

"Have you—"

"No," I said, my response a shade too quick. "No, I have not. Nor with Yolanda," I added, to restore my Bohemian *bona fides*.

"Neither have we. He turned us down, first one, then the other. Not that I've given up on him—he has a dark side one can practically taste."

"Er, what do you mean by dark side, exactly?"

"Oh, Damian comes across as the wholesome boy, married to one woman, a daddy even, but when one comes to know him, the darker impulses are there. I mean to say, just look at his paintings."

I had to agree that *wholesome* was not the first word one would choose to describe The Addler's paintings, but I couldn't tell if Alice actually knew something about Damian's "dark" side, or if this was merely romantic twaddle from a spurned woman.

"He keeps his temper under control," I ventured.

"One would hardly know he has one, most of the time," she agreed, which exchange got me no further.

I had taken but a single sip from the glass in my hand, but either the alcohol was strong or the conversation itself was dizzying. I put the glass down, caught it as it tipped, and moved it to a flatter place on the edge of a sheet of gravy-smeared newspaper, the remains of someone's lunch. Perhaps several days' lunches. Ronnie stretched out a hand and absently broke off a bit of crust from a dried-up stub of beef pie, ignoring the mouse droppings scattered around it. I shuddered, and would have averted my eyes except they were caught by a word on the gravy-smeared newsprint: *Sussex.*

Alice asked if Ronnie had picked up the eggs and bread she'd asked him to get, and he declared that it wasn't his job, causing her to retort that she was hungry, and they fell to wrangling about whose responsibility it had been to stock the pantry. Since I had no intention of putting any morsel of this household's food into my mouth, I idly nudged the wad of crust to one side, the better to see what event in the nation's placid southland had caught the attention of the afternoon paper. I read:

MYSTERIOUS DEATH IN SUSSEX

The body of a young Oriental woman in city dress has been found at the feet of the Wilmington Giant on the South Downs, near the busy seaside resort of Eastbourne.

Although the Giant is a popular landmark for country ramblers, Police say that the woman was wearing a summer frock and light shoes, inadequate for the footpaths that lead into the prehistoric si

This is the second death to

following the suicide at Cerne A

The rest of the article was glued to obscurity by brown gravy.

I ripped the page from the table and held it out to my companions. They fell silent.

"I must go," I said. "May I have this?"

Alice looked at the torn, grease-spotted sheet in my hand and made a gesture to indicate I should help myself.

I turned for the door, felt as much as heard the beams creak from below, and hastily veered back to the walls. At the doorway I paused to look at the two, staring after me in bewilderment and, perhaps, disappointment.

"You really mustn't put any more weight onto those floorboards," I urged them. "It's an awfully long way to the ground."

Silence followed me all the way down the stairs.

Chapter Twenty

*The Spark (1): The ancients spoke of a divine spark
within every individual, no matter how mean, a spark
that might be nurtured, fed, and coaxed into open flame.*
Testimony, II:3

B Y DINT OF PLANTING MYSELF IN FRONT OF A PASS-
ing taxicab with another of Holmes' guinea coins gleaming in
my outstretched palm, I reached Victoria and was sprinting across the
platform—folding up the sagging waist of Holmes' trousers as I ran—
just as the last southbound train of the night was gathering itself for
departure. The conductor glared in disapproval, but I was hardly the
first dishevelled latecomer to crash through his doors on a Saturday
night, and since my lip colour had long since worn off, he no doubt
thought I was just another young man in fancy dress.

I subsided into my seat, plucking sadly at my costume, and remembered the parcel of nondescript ladies' wear in which I had begun this
extraordinarily long day. Would I ever see it again, I wondered, or
would it be buried under a mountain of rubble and brick? Or become
nesting material for the mice?

And with that profound thought, I fell asleep. However, twenty minutes later, I was wide awake again, staring out of the window as I considered the implications of this southward flight.

I was being absurd. I had no reason to think what I was thinking. On Friday night I had been visited by an irrational, groundless fear born of solitude and dark thoughts and—yes, admit it—envy. My husband's son, that handsome, magnetic, hugely talented, and utterly fascinating young man, had walked into our lives and effortlessly spirited Holmes away. I had read his dossier and pictured him as a killer; my mind was too ready to build a gallows out of smoke.

But this was Holmes, after all. Sherlock Holmes did not fall for the easy patter of a confidence man. He did not mistake plausibility for truth, loyalty for moral rectitude, or need for necessity. He would see that we had to question Damian, and we would do so, and when we had established that he had an acceptable alibi, we would proceed with the investigation.

Assuming, that is, that this dead woman at the Wilmington Giant proved to be Yolanda. Which no doubt it would not.

I stared at the passing countryside as the train covered the slow miles south, pausing at every small town before jerking back into life. I thought about getting off in Polegate, the station nearest the Giant, but there would be little benefit to shivering out the hours until dawn in the open instead of in my own bed. So I stayed on the train to its terminus of Eastbourne, where I was fortunate enough to find a taxi-cab with the driver snoring behind the wheel. Two other passengers and I looked at each other, and in the end, the driver looped through the suburban villas to drop them at their doors before turning for the Downs, and home.

I had him leave me at the end of the drive, not wanting to wake Mrs Hudson with the sound of wheels on gravel in the wee hours of the morning. I walked along the verge in the bright moonlight, listening to the engine noise fade and the ceaseless downland breeze rise to take its place.

The house was locked, as I expected. I used my key and stepped inside—then my head came up in surprise: The odour of tobacco was considerably fresher than five days old. A small creak of descending weight on the stairs confirmed it: Holmes was home.

He stood on the landing, his hands in the pockets of his dressing gown; the touch of his eyes, running with amusement across my person, was an almost physical thing.

"A pity," he remarked in a mild voice. "I was rather fond of that suit."

I gazed ruefully down at the sagging trousers with their well-scuffed hems. "I'll buy you another one. Holmes, where have you been?"

"I might ask the same of you."

"Is Damian with you?"

"I have not seen him since Friday. You've come from London?"

"The last train."

"I thought I recognised the sound of the motor. Harry Weller's cab, was it?"

"Yes, although his brother was driving tonight. Holmes, did you—"

He put up one hand, and came the rest of the way down the stairs. "I suggest you go up and draw a bath. I shall bring you tea and a slice of Mrs Hudson's unparalleled squab pie. We can talk afterwards."

I was abruptly aware of how simultaneously ravenous, parched, and filthy I was. "Holmes, you're a genius."

"So I have been told."

The water was hot and plentiful; the tea was the same; the pie, although it gave me a brief frisson of unease at its evocation of mouse-gnawed scraps on a newspaper, was of sufficient excellence to make the comparison fade away. Replete and cleansed if not exactly easy, I wrapped myself in a robe and went into the bedroom. There I found Holmes gazing out of the bedroom window, pipe in hand.

I walked over to lean against his shoulders.

"I see you fastened your mother's *mezuzah* on the door," he said.

"Yes."

"Good." He allowed his weight to push back, to the balance point where we held each other upright.

"You heard of the body at the Giant?" I asked after a while.

"I did."

"Have you seen it?"

"They took it to Lewes. When I rang there, it proved too late to reach the coroner's offices. Why do you ask?"

Why indeed?

If any question was heavy with unvoiced consequences, it was that one. On the surface, it was obvious why I should wonder if this particular dead Oriental woman might not be the missing Yolanda Adler. Below that, the responses waited to pour forth like the plagues from Pandora's box: Why should a dead Yolanda Adler be found virtually at our doorstep, if it weren't her husband who left her there? Why had Holmes not given me a full answer, but side-stepped the key detail of what time on Friday Damian had left him? And why had I not immediately asked him what time? Why was Holmes not treating the husband as suspect, unless that possibility was one he could not bear to consider?

I found that I had detached myself from his comforting shoulders; to cover my involuntary retreat, I went to the dressing-table and took up my brush, passing it through my damp hair, unwilling to voice my thoughts. What were my thoughts, anyway, other than the stark awareness that, if Holmes were able to give his son an alibi, it would have been the first words out of his mouth?

"The newspaper described the woman as 'Oriental,' " I began.

"Which is precisely why I intend to see her, at the earliest possible moment."

"When will that be?"

"I was told the coroner would make himself available at ten o'clock. It's Huxtable; I've met him once, was not hugely impressed."

"I'm sorry to hear that. Could we also look at where they found her? It's been a while since I last visited the Giant."

"Do you wish to take the motor-car?"

"It would be easiest."

"The quickest, certainly." Holmes had resigned himself to my driving, over the years, but he had never developed an affection for it.

"Good. Now tell me, what were you doing in London this past week?"

"Crawling through the sewers."

"Literally?"

"Figuratively," he answered, which was something of a relief. "Tuesday we searched the hospitals, morgues, and clinics, and started on her known friends. Wednesday we made the rounds of all the churches that Damian could recall her mentioning—an exhausting number, as it proved. Thursday . . . Thursday we visited bawdy houses."

"Bawdy—houses of prostitution, you mean?"

"Starting at the top and working our way down."

"Why should she have gone there?"

"Russell," he chided.

"Oh, yes, I realised from the start that she'd probably been a . . . professional herself, but I shouldn't have thought anyone would wish to return to that life once they got out."

"Not the life itself, but certain elements. Money—"

"But Damian was making money."

"—drugs."

"Yes," I said reluctantly. "But she had the child with her."

"That being precisely why I did not investigate those houses that specialise in children until Damian was no longer with me, on Friday."

"Oh, Holmes. You can't imagine . . ." I found myself unable to complete the sentence.

"At this point, I know so little about Yolanda Adler, I may as well be working blind."

"Holmes, no mother would—"

"Damian thought it possible that his wife had left the child with a friend while she went away, and although a woman would be mad to hand a small child over to a stranger while there was a loving father at home, I pretended to agree with him that it was a possible scenario. I don't think I need to tell you that mothers have been known to . . . act irresponsibly."

Of course they did. If Yolanda had grown tired of the child, or been led astray by a seducer, or tempted by money, or . . . My stomach went suddenly queasy around Mrs Hudson's cooking, and the air from the open window felt cold.

I pulled down the bed-clothes and climbed underneath them, propping the pillows behind my back. "Why did Damian leave you? Did he say?"

"He simply left, before dawn, after being wakened from a nightmare. He had left once before; this time, he did not return. He was last seen at ten o'clock Friday morning, walking up Regent Street with a man." He described the man, clearly searching his memory as he did so for any similarity to someone he knew, but equally clearly failing to make any connexion. "I believe he received a message to buy a copy of *The Times*, where he saw an agony notice with the instructions for the meeting."

"Addled," I exclaimed.

"You saw it?"

"I did, but I thought it a coincidence." Before he could scold me for dismissing a clue, I asked him about the man, and he told me about interviewing the Café Royal porter.

So: Holmes could not prove his son's whereabouts. My thoughts went back to the body lying in the nearby morgue. "Holmes, I find it difficult to reconcile a person who would . . . do as you suggest, with the Yolanda Adler I have heard described these past days. She may be colourful, and certainly has some decidedly odd religious beliefs, but even the neighbours who wondered if she was entirely reliable didn't actively claim that she was—is—a neglectful mother. I'd have said she was reformed from her ways."

"So Damian claimed. And the first two days, he seemed as much irritated as concerned. But for whatever reason, by Thursday night his mood darkened. He spoke of drugs and suggested that, since the end of June, something has been disturbing her."

"It's true, a dependence on drugs has a habit of going dormant rather than extinct."

"As we well know," he said in a dry voice, then continued briskly.

"His description of her actions to us the other night was, I venture to say, fairly conservative compared to the facts of the matter."

We sat quietly contemplating the mind of a young man who would knowingly marry a drug-addicted prostitute in a foreign country.

"Well," I said at last, "if she fell back, it must have been a fast journey. Ten days ago she was chatting with her neighbour in the park while their children played."

He rubbed tiredly at his eyes. "It has been some time since I have toured the depths of the city's depravity—two hot baths and I still feel unclean. I cannot say I hit upon every establishment in the city, but certainly most of them. Yolanda and her child are not there."

I firmly kept my mind's eye turned away from the picture. "What about outside of London? Couldn't she have gone to Birmingham, or even to Paris?"

"Indeed."

Or to Sussex, to die at the feet of a prehistoric hill-carving.

Tomorrow would tell.

"Have you any thoughts on where Damian went?"

"I believe messages were left for him in several places where he was apt to go. An envelope with his name on it was left at the Café Royal on Wednesday; the porter gave it to him when he appeared early on Friday. And when I broke into their house in Chelsea last night—"

"Ha!"

"Sorry?" he asked at the interruption.

"I was outside of the house earlier this evening, and decided to break in later and spend tomorrow—today—Sunday searching it by daylight."

"I shall save you the trouble, then, Russell, and say that the only thing to suggest where either of them might have gone was a typed message saying, 'Look at the Friday *Times* personal adverts.' By which time, I had already seen the 'Addled' notice. Too late. There may well be one at his studio as well—I'd intended to look there tonight."

"Instead, you heard about the body at the Wilmington Giant and caught an evening express, arriving here too late to investigate there, but early enough for Mrs Hudson to cook you a squab pie."

"A newsboy was calling the headline on Oxford Street at three o'clock. And in fact, Mrs Hudson and I walked in within a quarter hour of each other. She had been somewhat taken aback to find the house empty on her arrival."

"I left her a note!" I protested.

"I quote: 'Holmes and I have been called away, I'm not certain when we will return, I hope you are well.' She did not find this terribly informative."

"I gave her all the information I had," I snapped, "which was more than you did."

"True," he agreed, without a trace of apology. He pawed through the litter on the window-sill for something to tamp his pipe with, coming up with a large nail that he had once thought might be evidence in a case, but was not. "Your turn."

"I solved your bee mystery," I told him.

Such was the intensity of his concern over Damian that he looked blank for a full two seconds. "Ah. Yes?"

"I'll tell you about it later. But I also found your album of Damian's early work, and on Friday I finally uncovered your records of his history."

"Not until Friday?"

"I wasn't looking for it earlier," I retorted. "I was busy with your dratted bees. And I thought that if you wished my assistance with Damian's wife, you'd have asked me."

"What made you change your mind and go to London?"

"Perhaps it's because we've been moving forward for so many months, that sitting still felt peculiar. And I was uneasy, after reading his case file."

"Hardly a case file," he objected.

"Holmes, he killed a man."

My husband sighed, but he made no attempt to defend or justify his son's act. Perversely, this made me want to try.

"Although granted, he was—"

He cut me off. "You are correct. When a man kills in the heat of battle, he is a soldier. When he does so off the battlefield, he is a murderer. Damian's mind was unbalanced, but that does not excuse his actions. However, boredom or no, I shouldn't have thought you would immediately assume that because a man kills someone in a bar fight, six years later he is still dangerous."

"I didn't! It was more . . . Well, the officer who died, he looked more like you than Mycroft does. I was . . . uneasy."

He stared at me, then began to splutter with laughter. "Russell, Russell, we must ensure that you are never again subjected to inactivity, if it introduces such flights of fancy into your mind."

"What was I to think?" I demanded. "You vanish without a word, even Mycroft doesn't know what you're—"

He held up a placating hand. "Yes, very well, I see I was in the wrong, that my failure to communicate has cost you both time and mental distress. I apologise."

My outrage subsided, and died. Unexpected apologies were such disarming things. "My time wasn't entirely wasted, I think."

He moved to the window-sill to scrape out his cold pipe onto the shrubs below. "So tell me, apart from beehives, where did your investigations take you?"

"I started with Mycroft, who said you had asked him to make enquiries in Shanghai. Then I went to Damian's gallery to look at his art, and to Chelsea to talk with the neighbours. The gallery told me that he is an immensely talented painter who revels in disturbing images, his neighbours indicated that he has a surprisingly conventional home life, except for the occasional disappearances of his wife.

"I then went to visit Yolanda's church."

"Which one?"

"They call themselves the Children of Lights, with a mish-mash of a service run out of a meeting hall in the Brompton Road. It's new, started up in January, but there were over a hundred people there the other night, despite the heat. People with a certain amount of money, I'd say."

"On a Saturday. Are they Adventists?"

"Not exactly." I described the hall, the participants, the service. "The Children of Lights—plural—are led by a man who calls himself The Master, although he wasn't there that night. The woman who led the service did little more than read from a book, although she took care to keep me from looking at it too closely, afterwards. She thought that Yolanda might have known The Master before he started the London meetings—not necessarily in Shanghai, but still. And considering Yolanda's interest in spiritual matters, it seemed possible that either the book or this woman—Millicent Dunworthy is her name—might lead me to The Master, who in turn might know where Yolanda is. So I followed her home."

"Describe the book."

"It's an oversized volume with a design but no name on the cover. Privately printed, I'd say, judging from the ornate black and gold cov—"

"Yes," Holmes interrupted.

I wriggled upright from where I had been slumping against the soft pillows. "You've seen it?"

"The Adlers have one, among a surprisingly large collection of religious esoterica. That one caught my eye, the cover being, as you say, striking."

"You didn't look at it?"

"Not inside, no."

The faint edge of regret in his voice kept me from remonstration: Holmes' determined lack of interest in things theological had long been a bone of contention between us.

I took off my spectacles and laid them on the bed-side table, rubbing my eyes. It had been a long day, filled with bees and Bohemians, children scrubbed for bed and children in the most terrible distress. Troubling facts and distressing images chased each other around my fatigued mind, until I fell asleep thinking of the painting I had agreed to buy: a hillside of darkened cat's fur; standing stones circling a spread-eagled figure; a doubled moon looking on. In the confused jumble as fatigue overcame me, the thought occurred that the outstretched figure was not asleep, it was dead.

Chapter Twenty-one

*The Spark (2): In those willing to devote themselves,
the divine spark begins to smoulder. With greater effort,
with unbroken concentration, a tiny flame will appear,
reaching greedily for fuel to its Power:
Transformation is at hand.*
Testimony, II:3

I SLEPT FITFULLY, AWARE OF HOLMES IN THE WINDOW-seat, outlined by the brilliant moonlight. At half past four, he brought me coffee; we were dressed and in the motor before the eastern sky was more than faintly light.

The Giant is less than five miles from the house in a direct line, but by road nearly twice that. As we turned north beside the Cuckmere, I asked Holmes, "Do you want me to go into Wilmington?"

"The footpath near Lullington is the more commonly used. Let us look there first."

Half a mile past Lullington, I edged the car into the grass beside the road, hoping we could extract it when we were finished—and hoping, too, that no wide lorry or hay wagon would need to pass on this Sunday morning. While I was lacing on my walking shoes, Holmes examined the verges up and down the intersection of footpath and roadway. I could see that he found nothing of interest.

We left the motor and set off along the pathway to Windover Hill. This was a section of the prehistoric South Downs Way, the ridgeline path worn by six thousand years of travellers that crossed the chalk landscape from Winchester to Eastbourne, dotting the hills with villages, dykes, forts, burial mounds, and monuments such as the one we were approaching.

As with many archaeological artefacts in Britain, the age, purpose, and design of the Giant, or Long Man, engender vigorous debate. Fifth Century or Fifteenth? Does he represent a farmer, or a warrior? Had the original details been smudged with the centuries, or had he always been an unadorned drawing in the turf? Solar calendar? Religious site? Or an elaborate thumb of the nose to the priory that faced it?

Whatever his date and purpose, the Giant was now the stark outline of a big-headed figure, hands held out to grasp featureless lines as tall as he is. Whether these lines were originally farming implements, spears, or something else entirely only adds to the debate.

"You know Hughes' theory of the Long Man, in that Kipling book?" I called at Holmes' back as we walked, eyes on the ground.

"That it was carved by fairies?"

"Better than that. It's the sun god, Phol, holding back the gates of darkness."

Holmes glanced over his shoulder. "*Is* there a sun god Phol?"

"Well, there is a set of Medieval incantations that indicates Phol is another name for Baldur, and Baldur is sometimes depicted standing in the gates to the underworld. And don't forget, Polegate is just over the hill."

He did not dignify that with a response, merely saved his breath for climbing.

The air was rich with the mingled odours of fresh-cut hay and a dawn breeze off the sea. Birdsong rose up with the light, to join the bleats of sheep. The sky shifted from pale rose to cloudless blue, and the corduroy surface of Windover Hill, terraced by ten thousand generations of meandering hoof, turned to rich green: August had been wet, before we arrived.

The morning was perfectly beautiful, and I could have walked forever. In minutes, I rather wished we had.

It was clear where the dead woman had lain, both from the heavy traffic of many booted feet and from the marks that had gone before them.

"She was actually killed here," I said.

"One rather suspected as much," Holmes mused, hunkered down over the gruesome stain. "It's quite a trek with a dead weight slung across one's shoulders."

"Would you say her throat was cut?"

"They've trampled into invisibility everything but the main area of pooling, but assuming that mark over there is blood and not tomato sauce from some idiot constable's luncheon pail, then I should say yes, the distance indicates arterial blood."

"Did she struggle?"

"We will know when we see her, and her clothing. The ground here and along the path is too torn up to say."

I stepped away from the gore-soaked centre of his interest, and bent to study the surrounds, looking for anything that would suggest how, and why, a woman died—a stranger, yes, but very possibly one linked to me by her marriage and my own.

We quartered the ground around the Giant's feet for two hours, gathering bits of paper, cigarette ends, the odd stub of food from the lunch of hikers' picnics, anything that might have been left in recent days. Holmes, bent double with his strong magnifying glass, found some odd dark grey crumbs, a substance that puzzled him although I thought they looked like pebbles, or even gristle from someone's sandwich. Halfway between the figure's feet, a metre from the edge of the blood, he found an untrampled smear of ash, which he gathered assiduously. He spent a long time near a wide rock protruding from the ground a dozen feet from where the woman had died, measuring and sketching a pair of indentations in the ground below it that sug-

gested someone had sat there, and gathering two envelopes of material—a black thread and a few grains of sand, both of which seemed to
me as remarkable as lumps of coal in Newcastle or fish scales in
Billingsgate.

My own contribution to the evidence envelopes were: the wrapper
from a packet of Italian almond-and-oat biscuits, blown down the
hill; a delicate handkerchief embroidered with the letter *I*, or perhaps
J; and a dry, chewed-over thigh bone from a domestic chicken.

We continued along the footpath past the Giant to the village of
Folkington; there, finding nothing more suggestive than an assortment of cigarette stubs.

"Do you want to knock up the people who live along here?" I asked
him.

He studied the nearby buildings, then shook his head. "We need to
see the body first, then we can decide. In any event, I should think
that the police will have questioned them already."

Returning, we followed the ridge-top path above the Long Man, an
area littered with archaeological curiosities—an old flint mine, a couple of quarries, several barrow mounds, and traces of the Roman ridge
road. I sat down to remove a pebble from my shoe; Holmes settled beside me, scowling at the magnificent view that stretched out at our
feet: hillside, trees, the Cuckmere valley, the Weald beyond. Church-
bells drifted across the freshening air. Were it not for the thought of
what awaited us, I should have been ravenous.

"Did I give you the booklet by Alfred Watkins on British track-
ways?" he asked; before I could respond, he continued. "Developing
an earlier work by a madman named Black, theorising that Britain
has certain innate geometrical lines that connect prehistoric monuments and the later Roman roads. Ley lines, Watkins calls them, the
human landmarks reflecting the organisation of the land itself."

Aimless chatter like this, often nonsensical, was the way Holmes
distracted himself. I knew from what.

"You've found no sign of the child Estelle, here or in London?" I
asked. It was not really a question, but Holmes shook his head.

"It is lamentably easy to dispose of a small body," he said. "Add to that the inescapable human fact that the younger the child, the more attention it attracts. If this woman was Yolanda Adler, I think it unlikely that we shall find her daughter alive."

A spasm of pain ran through the beautiful morning, and I was grateful when Holmes launched himself straight down the near-vertical hill to the path near the Giant's feet.

It was near nine o'clock and the sun was well up in the sky. I craned my neck for a last look at the figure, then turned towards the lane where we had left the motor. Ten steps along the path, Holmes dropped to his knees and pulled out his glass.

It might have been a heel-mark, the dent left by a shoe "inadequate for the footpaths," as the newspaper had put it. It might also have been the mark left by a walking-stick or a sheep, but Holmes found several more of them, and traced the dimensions of the clearest one onto a piece of paper before resting a stone over it, in case he wanted a plaster cast.

"It would suggest that she came here willingly," I said to Holmes' bent back.

"It would suggest that she came under her own power," he corrected me. "That is quite another matter."

It was five minutes before ten when we located the office of the local coroner, which was in fact the doctor's surgery. The clamour of bells calling the faithful together faded around us. I ran a hasty comb through my wind-blown hair and checked the state of my hands and skirt before following Holmes to the door.

The man who answered was clearly intending to join a church service before too long—either that or he had a remarkably formal attitude towards his job. He introduced himself as Dr Huxtable, and shook Holmes' hand, then mine.

"Come in, come in, I was just making certain that all was ready for you. Come, here's my office, have a seat. Would you like tea? Coffee?"

The tramping had made me thirsty, and I slipped my grateful acceptance in before Holmes could turn him down. The doctor got up from behind his desk and went out of the room, which made Holmes grimace, but we heard a woman's voice, so he was not about to do the task himself. And indeed, he was back in a moment.

"My wife will bring the tea, the kettle's just boiled. And I have to say, it's an honour, sir, to have you in my surgery. My wife feels the same—she was, in fact, rather hoping to be permitted to meet you, when I told her that you were coming. So, you said you thought you might know this young lady. Is this to be one of your mysterious cases, to be written up in *The Strand*?" The doctor tried to hide his eagerness behind an air of worldly joviality, but without success.

"I could hardly reveal the details of a case, if in fact she is a part of one, could I?" Holmes said repressively.

"No, no, of course not, I certainly agree, it's not to be thought of. Perhaps I should point out, however, that I am a duly sworn servant of His Majesty, in my rôle of coroner, which may qualify me for, well . . ."

Holmes just looked at him.

The door opened, fortunately, and the doctor's wife came in, staring so avidly at Holmes that she nearly missed the edge of the desk with the tea tray. I caught the corner and shoved it back into balance, and she gave a startled laugh at the sudden rattle of cups. "Oh! My, how silly of me, I nearly had it all on the floor."

I regretted my craving for tea, and by way of compensation took a heavy lacing of milk and gulped the still-hot liquid. Holmes fielded inquisitive remarks like a tennis champion, and the moment my empty cup hit the saucer, he got to his feet.

"Shall we go and see what you have?"

The muscles of a corpse, a day and a half after death, have gone through rigor mortis and slackened again. Even with the relative coolness of the room's stone walls, the decomposition of summer had begun to change the shape of her face and taint her pale skin. Her eyes and mouth had been leached of colour, her black hair lay flat and damp against her head, and the sheet that covered her diminished the outlines further; nonetheless, there was no question.

This was Yolanda Adler.

Holmes reached out for the sheet at her chin; I turned sharply away to lift the other end and examine her feet.

They were tiny, neat, and nicely kept, although they bore signs of having spent much of their life bare or in ill-fitting shoes. In recent years they had fared better, and showed few of the calluses and bunions that many women suffer. However, she had recently walked some distance in ill-fitting shoes: Her toes and heels were blistered.

"May I see the clothes she wore?" I asked.

"Oh, we burnt those awful things."

We both turned to stare at him, speechless. Huxtable looked back and forth between Holmes' narrowed grey eyes and my widened blue ones, and spluttered his protest. "They were dreadfully blood-soaked, I couldn't have them around the place, really I couldn't. A nice frock, my wife has one very like it—didn't want her to think of it every time she went to put hers on. And she had some very pretty, you know, underthings, but—"

"You even burnt her under-garments?" Holmes demanded in outrage.

"Between the bloodstains and having to cut them off of her, there was nothing left, so I put them into the furnace rather—"

"Have you never heard the term *evidence*, man?"

"Yes, of course, but the police had taken their photographs, and they had the description of the garments, even a tag in the back of the frock—from Selfridges, like my wife's. I never thought to ask."

"What about her shoes?" I asked.

He turned from Holmes' frigid condemnation with gratitude. "Yes, oh certainly I have those, and her stockings as well, those were silk and not much stained at all, so I kept them, for when the body was claimed. And the hat, of course. Do you—"

"Yes. Please."

The doctor scurried into the next room and came back with a paper-wrapped parcel that he laid down on the generous margins of the autopsy table. I pulled open the twine and drew out a beautifully made shoe of light brown leather, and set its heel against the sheet of paper Holmes spread out with his sketch of the path-side indentations: an exact match. The shoes were so new they had not yet developed creases. The right one had a splash of dried blood on its toe. The soles and heels were clotted with damp chalk and grass, matching the boots I had left in the car outside.

I picked up the left shoe and slid it onto her foot; as I'd thought, there was room for two fingers behind her heel.

"The shoe is at least a size too large," I commented. Holmes grunted, and turned back to his close examination of her small, soft hands.

I tucked the cloth back over her naked feet, then took my time re-wrapping the shoes. I held the stockings up to the light, but all they told me was that she had fallen to her right knee on soft ground once, leaving a green stain and starting a small hole in the mesh that had not had time to unravel. The hat was a summer-weight straw cloche, as new as the shoes. Close examination showed one small fragment of grass adhering to the left side of the brim, with a smear of chalky soil beside it: The hat had fallen from her head and rolled on the ground.

With reluctance, I turned my attention farther up the table, to have my eye caught by a mark on her torso. I pulled the sheet down as far as her navel, and saw a dark red tattoo, an inch and a half long, in a shape that, had I not seen it elsewhere already, my eyes might have read as phallic:

It lay in the centre of her body, between the umbilicus and the rib-cage; its soft edges indicated that it had been there for years. I pointed it out to Holmes, who turned his attention away from the finger-nails of her left hand (where, I noticed, she had worn a wedding ring, no longer there).

Over the protest of the doctor, we pulled away the sheet entirely, and turned her over (the unnatural flop of her head made me very glad I had not eaten the cake on the wife's tea tray), but there were no other tattoos, and what marks she bore had been done long ago.

We turned her back and pulled the sheet up again. Before her head was covered, Holmes tipped her head slightly to show me the skin behind her left ear: A lock of hair had been snipped away, leaving a bare patch the diameter of a pencil. I nodded, and walked around to look at her right arm and hand. She had a bruise on the tender inside of her wrist, old enough to have begun to fade; one of her neatly manicured finger-nails was broken; there was a grey stain on her middle finger.

I pointed it out to Holmes. "Ink?"

He took her hand, splaying her child-like fingers so as to see more clearly. "Yes," he said. He returned her arm to her side, but his own hand lingered on hers. He studied her, this woman his son had loved. "I wonder what manner of voice she had?" he murmured.

Then he twitched the sheet up to cover her.

"When will you do the autopsy?" he asked Huxtable.

"I was scheduled to do it this afternoon, although—"

"I would appreciate it if you would send me a copy of your results. You have my address?"

"Yes, but—"

"Who is the officer in charge of the investigation?"

"Well, it would have been Detective Inspector Weller, but I understand it's been given to Scotland Yard because of the . . . unusual aspects of the case. Which is why, as I was about to say, the poor girl might be taken up to London for the autopsy. I was told I should hear one way or the other before Sunday dinner."

"I see. I shall ring you later today, then, and see where it stands. Good day, Dr Huxtable."

Our hasty departure took us as far as the doorway before Huxtable remembered why we had come in the first place.

"Er, sorry," he called, "the message said you might be able to identify—"

"No!" Holmes snapped. "We don't know who she is."

I stared at him, but he swept out of the door, leaving the doctor spluttering his confusion as to why we had shown such interest in a stranger.

At the car, I got behind the wheel and turned to ask Holmes why he had claimed ignorance, but one glance at the side of his face had me reaching for the starter and getting the motor-car on the road.

The expression that hardened his features and turned his eyes to flame was one I had rarely seen there.

Rage, pure and hot.

Chapter Twenty-two

Study (1): The next years were spent in a study of Transformation: How could the man control the process? What Tools might shape Transformation, what methods bring it about?
Testimony, II:5

HALFWAY TO POLEGATE, HOLMES FINALLY STIRRED, and reached for the cigarette case in his pocket. When the tobacco was going, he rubbed the match out between his fingers and let the breeze take it, then seemed to notice for the first time that we were on the move.

"Where are you going?"

"Home. If I pass through a second time without greeting Mrs Hudson, she might just go back to Surrey permanently. Apart from which, with that expression on your face, I figured you'd be wanting your revolver."

"This was my son's wife." His voice was like ice. "A young woman who had lifted herself from the gutter on the strength of her own wits. A person whose acquaintance I was looking forward to making. Instead of which, I find her laid out like a slaughtered farm-animal."

"Did you see anything under her finger-nails?"

"If she struggled, it did not include digging her fingers into the ground or scratching at an assailant."

I thought this as good a time as any to tell him what I had seen. "Those shoes were very new and not inexpensive, but a woman would never have bought that ill-fitting a pair for herself. They gave her blisters. And the stockings she wore were far too long for her. She'd had to hook the garters down into the stocking itself—one of them had already worn through."

"One might add the general unlikelihood of a Bohemian choosing to dress in silk stockings and a flowered summer frock. I saw no such garments in her wardrobe at home."

I thought of my conversation with the neighbour's child. "Perhaps she dressed that way to make a more staid impression on someone."

"But if, as you suggest, she chose neither the shoes nor the clothing herself, then either she assembled the garments from another woman's wardrobe, or she was given them to wear."

"By someone who didn't know her size very well," I said without thinking. To my consternation, Holmes did not react, even though my statement clearly suggested that Damian's knowledge of his wife's dress size was a factor to be taken into consideration. He simply smoked and looked daggers at the passing view, while I bent over the wheel and concentrated on not driving over any distracted church-goers or Sunday ramblers.

Greetings with Mrs Hudson cost me an hour, which Holmes spent shouting down the telephone and crashing about in his laboratory. I was saved from the enumeration of her Surrey friend's ills by Holmes' bellow from above that he wished to leave in a quarter hour. I tore myself away and hammered up the stairs, throwing an assortment of things into a bag and conversing with him as we went in and out of various rooms.

"—need to speak with the station masters in Eastbourne, Polegate, and Seaford, and show them her photograph."

"Do you have her photograph, then?"

"How else should I intend to show them it?"

"Sorry. Do you wish me to bring weapons?"

"Your knife might be wise."

I shuddered at the brief vision of a blade crossing the ivory throat of Yolanda Adler, but added my slim throwing knife and its scabbard to the heap on the bed. "I should like to see the Adler house for myself, Holmes. Might we spend the night there, so I can look at that book by light of day?"

"I would have stolen it for you, had I known you were interested." His voice was muffled by the door to the lumber room down the hallway, and I heard thumps and a crash.

I raised my voice, a trifle more than mere volume required. "I'm interested because she was. Both of them, come to that—Damian's art is infused with mystic symbols and traditions."

Holmes' voice answered two inches away from my ear, making me jerk and spray a handful of maps across the floor. "Religion can be a dangerous thing, it is true," he remarked darkly, and went out again.

I got down on my knees to fish the maps out from under the bed. "Did you find out who is in charge of her case, at Scotland Yard?"

"Your old friend and admirer, Lestrade."

"Really? I'd have thought him too high-ranking for an unidentified woman in a rural setting."

"I haven't spoken with the good Chief Inspector himself, but I am led to understand the newspapers are summoning outrage at the 'desecration of Britain's ancient holy places,' and to have this following a death in Cerne Abbas and an assault at Stonehenge means that Scotland Yard will be doing all it can to deter a *cause célèbre*."

I found myself smiling. "I can just imagine what Lestrade has to say about having to investigate suicidal Druids."

In a moment, his head appeared around the door frame. "Was the woman who killed herself at Cerne Abbas a Druid?"

"She was an unemployed secretary, according to the papers. It was a farmer's letter to the editor that mentioned Druids."

"Disappointing," he said, looking both at me and through me. "I don't know that I have ever before encountered Druidical suicides."

"It would be an original means of marking your return."

"The lunatics rejoice," he said, and nearly chuckled. Then he caught himself, and his eyes came into focus. "Are you ready Russell?"

But now it was my turn to look through him, as a thin idea stirred in the back of my mind. Lunatics and linked deaths; Holmes sitting in the moonlit window; a startling eclipse; full moons doubled above a cat's-fur hillside; a conversation: *Madness is linked to the moon.*

"Er, Holmes, I'm going to be a bit longer. Would you mind awfully taking a look at the orchard hives before we leave? It seemed to me that a couple of them were wanting the addition of a super, and it would be a pity if it drove them to swarm while we were away." I could see that he was torn between the urgency of the case and the call of his long-time charges, so I added, "Holmes, it's Sunday. How much do you imagine we'll be able to accomplish in London anyway?"

"One hour," he said, "no more."

I waited at the window until I saw him cross the orchard. Then I trotted downstairs to the library and looked up the phases of the moon in the 1924 almanac. Dry-mouthed, I pushed the almanac back into place and went upstairs again, glancing out of the window to make sure he was still occupied before I fetched the key to the lumber room.

The oversized storage cupboard that Holmes called his lumber room was where all the useless odds and ends of a lifetime waited to be dragged into light as evidence, exemplar, or key piece of arcane research. (Including an assortment of deadly poisons—hence the lock.) It took a while to find his collection of outdated almanacs, in one tea-chest amongst a dozen others. I was not certain that there would even be one for that war year of 1918, but there was, although undersized and on the cheapest of pulp paper.

I perched atop an African wood drum and cautiously turned the limp pages to the calendar showing phases of the moon.

In April 1918, the full moon came on the 26th.

The day before young Damian Adler had killed a man in a drunken brawl. My hands trembled as they reached for the next year's volume.

Full moon: 11 August 1919.

Four days later, Damian had been arrested in the death of a drugs seller, fifty miles from Paris—to be released, not through proving an alibi, but through disproving a witness.

Yolanda Adler had been killed on 15 August 1924, when the moon was still full in the sky.

And as I had found downstairs: Miss Fiona Cartwright of Poole died of a bullet wound on 17 June: the night of a full moon.

The hair on the nape of my neck stirred.

Damian Adler, a painter of moonscapes and madness.

A sound came from somewhere in the house, and my hand flung the almanac into the chest and slammed down the lid. With only a degree more deliberation, I locked up the lumber room and returned the key to its hook in the laboratory, then took a furious brush to the dust on my skirt.

Absurd. Damian was no lunatic.

What if I had it the wrong way around? In 1918, Damian Adler—convalescing, shell-shocked, and drunk—had hit a man. If the other officer had been sober, or younger, or stronger, Damian would have been guilty of nothing more than fisticuffs in a bar, not a killing. It had been the night of a full moon; the moon came to haunt the artist's work, not as a stimulus of death, but as a reminder?

And the other deaths? Were Fiona Cartwright and Yolanda Adler merely coincidences? I mistrusted coincidences as much as Holmes did, but in fact, they did occur. And Fiona Cartwright's death was a suicide. Wasn't it?

"Ready, Russell?"

The voice up the stairs startled me. I threw the clothes-brush onto the bed and began to stuff the waiting valise.

I would say nothing of my . . . I couldn't even call them suspicions. Morbid thoughts. This was Holmes' son. If there was evidence, Holmes would follow it, and Holmes would acknowledge it. I would say nothing, although the awareness of those dates was already eating into me like a drop of acid.

I caught up my bag and walked down the stairs.

"Here I am, Holmes. Let me just see if there's anything Mrs Hudson wishes from Town."

Chapter Twenty-three

Study (2): With Despair and hunger at his heels,
he followed the faint paths of those who had gone before.
After long years, he found the first keys:
the Elements and Sacrifice.
Testimony, II:5

AS I SETTLED IN BEHIND THE WHEEL OF THE MOTOR-
car, I noticed the red welts on my companion's hands, testimony to the disinclination of bees to be disturbed. "Are the hives well?" I asked him.

"All five needed an additional super," he replied.

"It'll make Mr Miranker happy that you've paid them attention."

"He has looked after them well, in my absence."

"I like him."

"You've met?"

"We met Wednesday, at the abandoned hive. I told you I solved that mystery—I should have said, he and I together did so." As I negotiated the light Sunday traffic into Eastbourne, I described my investigation of the missing colony of *Apis mellifera*. We broke off so I could park the motor at the station while he bought tickets and showed the staff Yolanda Adler's photograph, then met again in an empty compartment (the week-end flow of travellers back towards London still being occupied with eking out their final hours of sun).

"None of the men working today was on duty Friday," he grumbled, so I finished telling him about the bees, touching lightly upon my own suggestion concerning the remoteness of the hive and quickly going on to Mr Miranker's conclusion. The story went on for some time, since I thought he would like to know every small detail of the matter. At last I came to an end, and presented my conclusion. "The hive died because the queen was too soft-hearted, Holmes."

He snorted at my interpretation of the hive's failure; belatedly, I heard the echo of wistfulness in my voice, and glanced sideways at him.

It had been not a snort, but a snore: Following one night spent staring out at the moon over the Downs, and the night before prowling the city in search of a son, Holmes had fallen asleep.

An hour later, his voice broke into my thoughts. "I trust you did not tell Mr Miranker that you believed the hive succumbed to loneliness?"

"Not in so many words, no. Although he did agree that it was possible the lack of proximity to another hive might have contributed to its extinction."

"Loneliness alone does not drive a creature mad, Russell. However, I freely admit that an excess of royal benevolence is not a diagnosis that would have occurred to me. One can hope that Miranker's replacement queen proves sufficiently ruthless. Do you suppose Lestrade will be at the Yard today, or ought we to hunt him down at his home?"

"He might be at work, although you'd have to conceal your identity to have him admit it over the telephone."

"True, the cases which have brought me into his purview have tended to demand much of his time. The same, now that I think of it, might be said of his father before him."

The younger Lestrade had followed his father into the police, then New Scotland Yard, and thus inevitably into contact with Sherlock

Holmes. I had seen a considerable amount of Lestrade the previous summer, during a complicated and ultimately uncomfortable case involving an ancient manuscript and modern inheritances. I doubted he would relish the opportunity of working with either of us again this soon.

"Do you suppose they will look into the meaning of her blisters?" I asked him.

"I should doubt it."

"But you don't wish to tell them who she is?"

"I intend merely to say that this is a Sussex crime I have been asked to investigate by an anonymous party, no more."

"Holmes, if you—"

"I will not come to their aid in this matter," he snarled. "There is too much here I do not yet understand."

"Well," I said, "if I can find where the shoes came from, I might find who bought them for her."

"Is that a line of enquiry you can begin today?"

"I can start, but the shops themselves will not be open."

"Do what you can. In the meantime, I shall hunt down Lestrade and see what I can prise out of him."

"I'd also like a copy of that photograph you have."

He slid his hand into his breast pocket and drew out a note-case, handing me a freshly printed reproduction of the photograph Damian had given him. The facial details were not as crisp as the original, but would be sufficient for my purposes.

I studied it, as I hadn't before. Yolanda was not, in fact, as pretty as I had remembered. Her face was a touch too square, the eyes too small, but the face beneath the dowdy hat was alive and sparkling with intelligence, which made her far more attractive than any surface arrangement of features. The child in her arms was blurred and turning to the side, but the corner of her eye suggested an Asian fold, even though the child's glossy hair lacked the thick, straight texture of the mother's.

Beside them, Damian's right hand rested on Yolanda's shoulder, giving that half of his image the air of a Victorian paterfamilias; the other half with its encircling arm suggested a person more relaxed and modern. He looked happy, prosperous, proud, and amused at that incongruous frock suit.

Yolanda's skirt was not, I noted, flowered. Its cut and hem-line seemed out of date to me, although not as archaic as his coat. No doubt one should not expect the latest in fashion from a Bohemian matron—here in London, Bohemians tended to resemble gipsies or pipe-fitters. "I wonder why they chose such conventional dress and setting for a portrait? It's almost as if they were in disguise."

"Or fancy-dress," Holmes said.

"Yes. Especially when you look at the expressions on their faces." Perhaps Yolanda's face was sparkling with humour rather than intelligence. It made her more sympathetic, somehow.

I was about to put the photograph into my pocket, but Holmes took it from me, laid it face-to against the window, and folded the top down at the line of Damian's shoulders. He ran his thumb-nail hard against the fold; when he handed it back, Damian had been reduced to little more than a black back-drop and a hand on the child's torso. "If you're looking for her, his image will only confuse matters," he told me.

It was true, the eye focused on a lone woman more easily than with a bearded man looming above her. Still, I couldn't help being aware of the symbolic aspect of the fold as well: Holmes wanted Damian left out of this enquiry.

When we reached Victoria, Holmes, impatient to be about his business, set off on foot towards Westminster and Scotland Yard while I took my place in the taxi queue. I frowned at his back until it disappeared around the corner, then took out the photograph and studied it.

Was it conviction, or apprehension, that made him so determined to exclude Damian?

My club, the Vicissitude, was not an ideal beginning for a hunt into the world of fashion—one was more likely to find expertise on Attic

Greek or the missions of China than on expensive clothing—but as it happened, I drew a lucky straw, and some time later sat down to tea with a cousin of the sister-in-law of the Vicissitude's manager, a dangerously thin individual wearing a Chanel dress that was too large for her. She had, until her recent illness, supervised the millinery section of one of London's large department stores.

"I am trying to trace a pair of shoes. The woman who wore them is dead," I added, before she could suggest I ask their owner. I described the shoes closely—the shape, the quality of the leather, the tiny bow on the heel. "They didn't look like ready-made shoes, but if they were bespoke, they were for someone other than the woman wearing them. They didn't fit her."

The thin face made a moue of disapproval. "You would have mentioned if there were an identifying name in them," she said. I agreed, I would have. "The bow suggests a recent line of quality footwear out of Cardiff, of all places. Harrods carries them, in several styles and colours, although I believe Selfridges is trying one or two lines as well."

"The woman's frock was from Selfridges," I reflected.

"Then perhaps you should begin there."

"I shall, first thing in the morning." I took care, in shaking her hand, not to bear down with any enthusiasm, lest I crush the bird-like bones.

I came out onto the street to the sound of bells from nearby Westminster cathedral. To my surprise, considering all that had happened that day, it was not yet half past four. The streets were dead, but then, even Oxford and Regent streets would be echoing and empty. On a Sunday in London, one could walk, worship, or improve oneself.

I chose the last option, making my way down to the Tate to spend an hour meandering among paintings that might have looked modern had I not been recently introduced to the work of one Damian Adler.

When I was thrown out at closing, I found a tiny café that offered a meal it called dinner, and dawdled the dusk away, strolling down the river and through the by-ways into Chelsea, waiting until half past eight, when it would be nearly dark enough to break into the Adler house unseen.

Except that I ran into a slight problem.

The police were there first.

Chapter Twenty-four

*The Elements (1): A word (which is air) written on a
piece of paper (which is earth) and burnt (thus, fire) with
the ashes stirred into a glass of water, awaits the throat of a
man. But the glass does not hold the word's essence,
unless it has employed the keys of Time and Will.*

Testimony, II:6

I T WAS A SHOCK TO CROSS THE ENTRANCE TO BURTON
Place, expecting a quiet cul-de-sac with a dark house at its far
end, and to see the road crowded with onlookers and official motor-
cars, and every light in number seven burning. I drifted into the street,
coming to rest amidst a group of ogling neighbours, and primed the
gossip pump with a few innocuous questions.

The police, according to one of the children, had been in residence
for less than half an hour. They had brought a locksmith, a servant
volunteered, who worked on the door for a good ten minutes before it
had opened. The people in number eleven had 'phoned the police at
tea-time, another maid was eager to say, after some woman had come
asking about the Adlers the night before.

I watched for a few minutes, then faded away, to circle around the back of the house through the service alley. I stood on tip-toes to peer over the wall, seeing with disgust the signs of a house being thoroughly searched: constables framed by the sitting room window off to the left, more constables in an upstairs bedroom, the noise of loud constabulary voices and heavy constabulary shoes.

I decided to wait for a while, but before five minutes had passed, I heard the sound of running feet behind me. I ducked behind a bush, one with an unfortunate number of prickles in it, then noticed that the person fast approaching not only lacked a torch, but was trying to run quietly on the dirt surface. As he darted past, I saw his silhouette, and hissed loudly.

His feet stopped instantly although the rest of him did not, and he slid along the loose surface for several feet, arms flailing. He did not fall, but whirled and came back to where I stood.

"Well done, Holmes," I said in admiration. I was not at all sure that I could have performed the manoeuvre without going down.

"The police traced her," he whispered.

"My fault, I'm afraid. One of the neighbours I talked to last ni—"

"I thought to have more time," he cut in urgently. My own pulse quickened.

"Time for what?"

"There is an object I must remove from the house before the police find it."

"What is it?"

"Later, Russell. Come." He dragged me to the gate, raised his head to look over, then went up on his toes and stretched his arm down; I heard the click of a latch.

The house had two doors that opened onto the garden: one near the sitting room, the other to the kitchen at the right. The kitchen door stood open, light spilling out, but at the moment there was no constable outside of the house. We slipped into the garden, closing the gate, and Holmes pointed to the stairway one could see through a window above the kitchen.

"In five minutes, anyone in the upper storeys will come down those stairs. One minute afterwards, I will go up them; I will need no more than three minutes, then I will come down again. If anyone starts up the stairs while I am still inside, you must create a diversion. Any diversion at all, I don't care, just so you are not caught. An arrest would be disastrous."

"Holmes—"

"Russell, we have no time. I will meet you at Mycroft's later."

"Fine, a diversion. Go."

To my surprise, he headed not for the house, but back out of the gate into the alley-way. I patted through the soil at my feet and came up with soil, pebbles, some bits of bone, and a soft object that startled me until I decided it was a child's doll. Finally my fingers encountered a solid chunk of rock, then a fist-sized corner of brick. From next door came a faint sound of breaking glass, muffled perhaps by cloth. Two minutes after that, the sound of a telephone, ringing in the Adler house.

Two uniformed constables in the sitting room turned and looked across the room, but neither moved to answer the machine. It rang again, and another constable appeared. He said something, but the others hesitated. I was aware of movement off to my right, as of someone scrambling over a wall; at the same moment, I saw a figure in brown scurry across the half-landing window, fast descending the stairs. It was Lestrade, with two more constables at his heels; I caught a glimpse of the men as they went down the hallway behind the kitchen, then saw them enter the sitting room. Lestrade snatched up the telephone receiver, and in a flash, Holmes bounded up the kitchen steps and into the house, disappearing in the direction of the stairway. I began to count: at five, his form darted past the half-landing window and continued up the stairs.

Lestrade spoke into the telephone, frowned, spoke again, then reached down to rattle the hook: twenty-three seconds. After another sixty-four seconds, the exchange gave the Chief Inspector the information he needed. He dropped the instrument back on its rest, and stood for seven seconds, deep in thought.

He then spoke to one of the men in uniform: that took thirty seconds. The man left the room, no doubt heading for the empty house next door whence the call had come. Lestrade stayed where he was for another nineteen seconds, talking with the men, then went back to the door, and out.

I couldn't be certain he would return upstairs, but I moved onto the lawn, just in case. Sure enough, seconds later I saw a brown figure move past the doorway in the direction of the stairs—two and a half minutes were all Holmes was getting.

I trotted across the lawn, took aim, and heaved the rock through the exact centre of the sitting room window; an instant later, the brick punched a hole in the narrow window beside the garden door. Breaking glass makes a most satisfying noise, exploding through the night; the constables in the sitting room ducked down and I ran, out of the gate and down the service alley to the street beyond, where I dropped to a quick walk. I maintained the pace to the corner, then slowed to an amble until I was safely among the crowd in Burton Place.

When five minutes went by and Holmes was not dragged out in handcuffs, I rubbed my damp and shaking palms down the front of my skirt, and walked innocently away.

Had it not been a Sunday, I would have gone straight into the nearest public house and had a drink. Or two.

It being a Sunday, I had to wait until I reached Mycroft's flat. I went on foot, past the meeting hall where the Children of Lights had met (dark and locked up tonight) then up Knightsbridge and around the Palace to Pall Mall. I half expected Holmes to catch me up; he did not.

Mycroft made haste to provide both the drink and an explanation of Holmes' sudden appearance in Burton Place: He had been here when Lestrade telephoned.

"The Chief Inspector asked if I had seen my brother. I naturally said no."

"Naturally." Why should one co-operate with the police, after all?

"When Sherlock is working, I volunteer no information until I can see the ramifications. Lestrade had heard that Sherlock was at

Scotland Yard this afternoon, asking about the body of an Oriental woman found in Sussex, and he wanted to say that if Sherlock was endeavouring to discover the young woman's identity, not to worry, Scotland Yard had not only her name, but her address. Apparently one of the neighbours reported an entire family missing, among whom was a young Oriental woman. When Lestrade sent one of his men over with a morgue photograph, the neighbour confirmed that it was she. The Chief Inspector offered to let Sherlock see the files in the morning, if he was still interested."

"And instead, Holmes flew out of here as if the house were on fire."

"Faster than that, I should say."

I took a swallow from my glass, which emptied it. Without comment, Mycroft refilled it. I told him, "Holmes was there, behind Damian's house. He came running up, asked me to make a diversion, and went inside to get something. That's what he said, anyway."

"You doubt it was so?"

"Mycroft, I don't know what to think. He said he'd meet me here and explain it all. I left Chelsea a good hour ago. I expected him back before me."

"When did you last eat?"

"Eat? I don't know. I'm not hungry."

"Nonetheless." He got up—easily, without the grunt of effort he'd have given a year ago—and crossed the room to the telephone, to debate the options available with the invisible staff somewhere in the depths of the building.

While he was doing that, I decided to draw a bath—with Holmes, it was always best to be prepared for an instantaneous departure, and I felt grubby. I closeted myself in Mycroft's enormous bath-tub with a lot of hot, fragrant water; when I emerged, the food had come. Holmes had not.

I ate largely in silence. I wanted to dive into my brother-in-law and prise out every scrap of information he had regarding Damian, Irene Adler, Holmes' past—everything. But pressing Mycroft would put him in an awkward position: If Holmes wanted me to know these things, Holmes would tell me. It wasn't fair to Mycroft to ask.

Apart from which, as he'd said, he tended to volunteer no information—to the police, and perhaps to me. And I did not want his refusal to stand between us.

Better to fume in silence.

An hour later, Mycroft had retired for the night and I had reached that stage where concern and irritation were piling atop one another to create a volatile mix. However, when Holmes finally walked in, one look at him and my anger deflated.

He dropped a roughly-bound parcel on the table beside the door, tossed his hat in the direction of a chair, draped his overcoat on the nearest sofa-back, and sat. Silently, I handed him a large brandy. When he had drunk that, I exchanged it for a plate of cold meat and tired salad. I thought he would refuse it, as I had, but he forced himself to take one bite, and soon was head down over the plate, tearing at the stale rolls with his teeth.

I retreated into Mycroft's kitchen to make coffee, which took no little time since he'd got a new and highly elaborate machine for the purpose, a thing of glass and silver that looked as if it belonged in a laboratory. But I managed, without blowing anything up, and when I carried the tray out, Holmes looked less grey around the edges.

I gave him coffee, with brandy in it, and sat down with my own.

"When I was searching the house early Saturday," he told me, "I noticed a package addressed to me, on a shelf in Damian's dressing room. At the time, I had no reason to remove it: Damian could give it to me when he chose. However, if Lestrade had come across it—and he would have, within minutes—the link between Damian and me would have made things exceedingly complicated. Without it, Lestrade will have to follow his usual channels of enquiry."

"But he'll trace Damian Adler to Irene Adler eventually."

"Not if Mycroft interferes."

"Oh, Holmes. A formal intervention will be a red flag to a bull. If Lestrade finds out you blocked his investigation, he'll never speak with you again."

"If Lestrade finds that I have a personal interest in this case, he will not only cut me off, he will actively harass me and dog my every step. Worse, he will pour all his efforts into Damian, and dismiss outright any information or suspects we may uncover. An invisible intervention means that the name Adler may catch his eye, but what does that matter? Irene's married name was Norton, and Adler is a common enough surname. If Lestrade sees no link, then I appear to be merely looking into the death of a woman, and he will see no reason to hamper my investigation. No, it's best if the information simply ceases to exist."

I studied him. I had known Holmes to be unscrupulous, even cold-hearted when it came to manipulating others for the sake of an investigation, but this was personal. Frankly, I hadn't thought him capable of that.

Except, perhaps, to protect me.

And now, Damian.

I did not like it: Holmes had been known to act as judge, jury, and very nearly executioner, but never had he done so without cost to himself.

He put down his half-empty cup and examined it minutely. "He has nightmares. Damian. Night after night he wakes, drenched in sweat, shivering. He must have the lights on, needs the windows open wide, even in the winter. From his words, and from his art, I believe he dreams of trenches whose walls are crumbling in on him. Of being at the bottom of a well, looking up at a circle of stars. Of being in the hold of a ship and hearing the scrape of collision. Of being buried alive in a casket.

"The key element is enclosure. A horror of being closed in, locked up, kept from the sky. I believe it may be why he so often paints the sky." He sighed, and dry-scrubbed his face. "Russell, Damian Adler is a damaged man on a solid foundation. His wife's death will threaten everything he has built. If his daughter is gone as well, I do not know if he will recover. Locking him away would guarantee that he does not. If he is arrested, I fear for his sanity. And they will arrest him, if they find him. I must maintain open communication with Lestrade so I know what they are doing, and so I can find Yolanda's murderer for them. Because you know that Scotland Yard will not look beyond Damian."

I said nothing; he raised his eyes to mine. They were set with unwavering intent.

"Damian did not kill his wife," he said flatly.

"Holmes, you can't—"

"I must. He did not kill her. Yes, he is capable of killing—which of us is not?—but not this murder. Not a cold-blooded slaughtering of his wife and his child."

I looked into his grey eyes, and slowly nodded. "All right."

The tension seeped out of him, and he got up to retrieve the parcel he had left beside the door. As I watched him cross the room, I reflected that in any other man, the relaxation would have been from relief, that he had talked his wife into agreement.

I knew him too well to think that. Tension in Holmes was not the sign of a disagreement with others—even me—but with himself. *I must,* he'd said. He had to believe that his son did not do this dreadful thing, and I, for the moment, had to go along with that decision.

But that did not mean I had to believe it as well.

He put the flat package on the table in front of me. "I hadn't time to fetch the book you wanted. We'll go back, when the police are no longer in possession."

This, too, was a book, wrapped in brown paper and bound in twine. The twine had been cut and re-tied, the paper inattentively wrapped; faint indentations on the paper suggested that it had sat for weeks, if not months.

It was a beautiful volume, leather-bound and tooled with gilt with the name Damian Adler on the front.

When I opened the book and saw what it contained, I knew why it had taken Holmes so long to return to Mycroft's this evening.

"Did he tell you about this?" I asked.

"He never mentioned it. I expect he had it made some time ago, intending to send it to me when we returned."

"And he would hardly bring it with him to Sussex, considering why he came."

"No."

It was a book of Damian's sketches and watercolour paintings, mounted and magnificently bound. None was larger than eight inches by six; some were intricate pen-and-ink drawings, others leisurely pencil outlines. The watercolours had a wistful, autumnal air to them, even those clearly showing spring. None of the pieces had moons or trenches; none of them was done in the style he used now. One watercolour of Irene Adler in a garden chair was stunning.

"What is this cottage he's done several times, the one with the pond in the garden?"

"His mother's house, outside of Paris in Ste Chapelle."

"Where he was born."

"Yes. I went to see it that day, after we'd seen him in gaol."

I turned the page, and recognised the ivy-draped face of the Ste Chapelle gaol. A tall, thin, middle-aged Englishman filled the doorway, his face in the shadows.

I reached the end, and turned back to the first page, considering. On the surface, the book was a son's demonstration to his father of skill and personal history. But there was more to it than that.

Take this first drawing: a portrait of Irene Adler. Holmes' other album also began with her, as a woman beautiful and filled with life; here, she was still lovely, but it was the ethereal beauty of a woman ground down by troubles. She seemed to be contemplating a deep well of sadness within. Had that particular woman ever borne that expression? Had Irene Adler ever been ethereal?

The next sketch, showing a dark-haired little boy on a deserted beach, had a similar air of loneliness to it.

And, looking more closely, the man in the doorway of the gaol was unnaturally rigid, cold amidst the warmth of old stone and luxurious vines.

No: This was not a collection of work brought together to please a father. The paper was the same, beginning to end: Each piece had been done expressly for the purpose of this book.

For what? So that Damian could come home to lay his accomplishment at the feet of a father he hoped to know? Or so he could shove his hard life and his current success into his father's face? The overkill of the book, so ornate the binding nearly overshadowed the art within, made one aware of anger in its beauty.

The book had been designed to make Holmes wince.

I closed the cover and looked at Holmes. He was slumped into the chair, outstretched ankles crossed, eyes shut. This was not the moment to address the question of filial affection.

"Do you really—" I started, but he cut me off.

"He did not anticipate liking me," he said. "It galled him, to ask for my help, but he put his feelings aside because he loved his wife. Three days in my company changed him. I'm not certain he would have given me that book, in the end."

"Do you think you can keep Lestrade from finding out that Damian is your son?"

"All it requires is inefficiency and misfiled information. Mycroft can arrange that."

"I hope you know what you're doing, Holmes."

One grey eye came open. "My dear Russell," he said lightly, "I have been deceiving the official police since before you were born. At that art, I am the expert."

Chapter Twenty-five

The Elements (2): The man learned to manipulate
the Elements. As his Guide had taught him to control the
weak, now his inner Guide led him in turning the
Elements to his divine will.
Testimony, II:6

WE TOOK OUR INNOCENT FACES TO NEW SCOTLAND
Yard bright and early on Monday morning, and were only
kept cooling our heels for half an hour before Lestrade came to lead
us into his office.

The newspaper headlines that morning had read: *Third Outrage in
Prehistoric Monuments,* with details of Yolanda's death, but not yet her
name.

"Mr Holmes," Lestrade said, his joviality forced, but still a relief: He
did not suspect that there might be a link between our presence and
the young woman whose search for Yolanda Adler on Saturday had
led to his presence on Burton Place last night. "Sorry to have missed
you yesterday, I was told you had been by. Did you get the message I
left with your brother?"

"I did, although not until late. Has the dead woman in fact been identified?"

"Oh yes," he said over his shoulder, "there's no doubt. Her husband is missing, and their child."

"A child as well? How unfortunate. Do you expect to find all three dead?"

"I expect to find that he killed her and fled the country with the child. He's foreign, you know—or anyway, only English on paper."

"Of course, it is so often the husband, particularly with foreigners. I don't suppose you have such a thing as a motive?"

"He's an artist, Mr Holmes, a dyed-in-the-wool Bohemian. Probably a Bolshevik as well, most of them are."

"Yes, that certainly explains it. You are doing an autopsy?"

"Later today, yes, although there's little question as to the cause of death." We'd reached his office; he held the door.

"So I understand, however, the possibility of drugs . . . ?"

"Was she involved in drugs?"

"How should I know that?" Holmes said in surprise. "I don't even know who she is, merely that she was found near the Long Man."

"She doesn't look much like a drugs user."

"I was thinking more along the lines of sleeping-tablets."

Lestrade's suspicion faded. "But even if we find that she was up to her pretty eyebrows in cocaine, it makes no difference in the investigation."

"It might point you to suspects other than the husband," I interjected before Holmes could bristle.

"Ah, Mrs—er, Miss Russell, you're looking well. I see you have joined the smart set. The hair-cut," he explained.

"Chief Inspector Lestrade," I replied, holding out my hand.

"Er, do sit down. Now, Mr Holmes, explain again your interest in this woman?"

"In fact, it is the pattern I am investigating."

"Yes, I wondered if that might not be the case. The 'pattern' is a figment of a newsman's imagination. Evidence suggests that the suicide at Cerne Abbas was just that, and Stonehenge was random violence

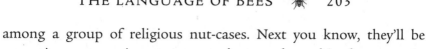

among a group of religious nut-cases. Next you know, they'll be mounting a campaign to set guards over that white horse up in Oxfordshire and along the length of Hadrian's Wall. Anything to sell papers."

"And yet I see you have the two files out on your desk. Shall I look them over, and let you know if anything in particular catches my eye?"

From Lestrade's expression, he was remembering Holmes' habit of taking over his investigations, if not his life. No doubt he would have preferred us to stay in America.

"I don't know that I should permit that," he began.

Holmes studied his finger-nails. "I can, if you wish, summon recommendations from your chief, or the Lord Mayor, or the Prime Minister, or even—"

The Chief Inspector gave a sigh of resignation. "That won't be necessary, Mr Holmes. I need not remind you not to remove anything from either of these files, and not to speak of the cases to others."

"Of course. But, may I ask, was there in fact a ram found, in Cumbria?"

We both stared at him. "A *ram*?" Lestrade demanded.

"Yes, there was a—"

"You think Scotland Yard investigates dead *livestock*?"

"Only if there is—"

"Mr Holmes, I have never lived outside of London, but even I know that sheep die sometimes, and that foxes and dogs eat them. No ram was slaughtered." Lestrade's chair squealed back. "Now, if you will excuse me, I have an investigation to run, and I'd like to keep one step ahead of the papers. Artists," he declared, shaking his head as he put on his hat. "Interviewing artists makes me bilious."

Rather to my surprise, he did not plant a uniformed constable over us, to ensure that we did no mischief to his office.

"How long before he suspects, do you suppose?" I asked Holmes in a low voice.

"That you and I were both looking for Yolanda Adler long before she died? He will know by the time he has interviewed the neighbours."

"What do you suggest we tell him then?"

"I suggest we keep out of his way until he is no longer interested in the question," he replied, and opened the older, thicker file. But first, I had to know:

"What was that about a ram, Holmes?"

"Found last spring, at a stone circle in Cumbria called Long Meg and her Daughters."

"Was that in the paper this morning? I didn't see it."

"You did not read the letters."

"Oh, Holmes, not another outraged farmer?"

He did not answer me. There were times I had some sympathy for Lestrade's opinion of Holmes' techniques. I pulled towards me the crisp, new folder labelled with the name of Yolanda Adler, and gingerly opened the cover.

I was grateful that it did not yet contain the details or photographs of the autopsy, although it did have a sheaf of photographs from the hillside where she had been found. Her frock was indeed beyond repair, and I supposed that if I were faced with that garment, I might be tempted to rid myself of its unfortunate juxtaposition of sprigged lawn and dried gore.

When I had finished with the thin offering, Holmes pushed across the section of the Fiona Cartwright file that he had read. I picked up the pages with interest.

Fiona Cartwright was a forty-two-year-old, unmarried secretary and type-writer, originally from Manchester. She had moved to Poole shortly after the War when her employer, Fast Shipping, opened a branch there. When the owner, Gordon Fast, died in 1921, the business was sold and Miss Cartwright was replaced by a younger woman.

Since then, she had worked at a series of secretarial jobs, and the previous summer had registered with an employment agency that had placed her in eight temporary positions during the autumn and winter months. The agency had arranged an appointment for Miss Cartwright with a new client, Mr Henry Smythe, on Monday, 16 June, but never heard back from Miss Cartwright to say whether or not she had taken the position.

Mr Smythe was a salesman travelling in paper goods, from "somewhere in the north" (according to the agency), who telephoned from an hotel in Poole requesting secretarial assistance for the two or three days he was in town, specifying (again, the agency) "a lady who was not too young and flighty."

Mr Smythe had not been heard from again: A note at the bottom, dated that morning, indicated that Lestrade had ordered an enquiry into Smythe's company and his whereabouts.

Miss Cartwright's brother, still living in Manchester, described his sister as "down" over the lack of permanent employment and "troubled" by her dull future, although very recently she'd written a rather odd letter home about the importance of heavenly influence on human life. "She liked funny old religious things," he said. "I thought she meant that the tides of fate were turning, and that she'd get a job soon."

Reading between the lines, even Fiona Cartwright's brother believed it was a suicide.

The description of the autopsy was cursory, spending less time on describing the path of the single bullet than it did the presence of the weapon beside her, and agreeing that the verdict should be suicide. Stomach contents were dismissed as "normal," whatever that meant, and the state of her epidermis was similarly categorised with the incongruous phrase "no signs of violence." There was, however, one oddity: She had a deep cut in the palm of her left hand, unbandaged and fresh.

Holmes flipped over the covers of Yolanda Adler's file.

"What do you make of that cut on Fiona Cartwright's hand?" I asked him.

"The coroner seems to think she received it in a fall climbing to the place where she died. With no photographs, no details of the scene, not even the question of whether her clothes were blood-stained from the cut, all we can conclude about her death is that the coroner is incompetent. Shall we go?"

I put the Cartwright file together, then glanced at my watch. "I'd like to see about the shoes Yolanda wore, before Lestrade gets around to it. The shop should be open."

"And I must compose an anonymous letter to Damian's lawyer in Paris, advising him that the police may call. Shall we meet back at my brother's?"

"How about the Café Royal instead?"

He raised his eyebrows. "We shall have our passports stamped for Bohemia. At one o'clock, then, Russell."

On foot and by sardine-tin omnibus, my steps took me out of Westminster and past the Palace to the Brompton Road again, although not as far down as the meeting room for the Children of Lights.

Harrods is a meeting place for another kind of worship, that of excess in all its glory. Under the stoutest of circumstances, I can tolerate twenty minutes inside its decorative doors before my fingers begin to twitch and my eyes scan the endless halls for an exit. But then, I am not a person who considers browsing through shops a recreational activity.

Even with a specific objective in mind—ladies' shoes—it did not prove simple. Did I wish walking shoes, riding boots, ballet flats, shoes for the hunt, shoes for tennis—ah, heeled dress shoes. Daytime, evening wear, or for Court?

I eventually tracked down the department featuring the Cardiff designer: There sat the shoe, glossy and unsullied by grass or bloodstains, the small, pointless bow at the back a bit of frippery that should have looked pathetic but instead struck me as oddly brave. One of the VAD nurses I knew during the War had painted her lips with care each morning before stepping onto the ward, to cheer up the boys, she said. This shoe in my hand had the same attitude.

"A lovely shoe, that," said a voice at my shoulder.

"Not, however, for me," I said.

"It is also available in a patent black."

I put the shoe down and turned to give the woman a smile. I could see from her encouraging expression that she had already glanced at my feet, and knew that the only way I could be wearing this shoe would be if I ordered a pair made to fit.

Although, this being Harrods, she could probably arrange that as well.

It would almost be worth it, to see Holmes' expression.

"Actually," I said, "I am trying to find a person who purchased just this shoe recently. Is there someone who would be able to help me?"

She reached out to shift the display model, rectifying my deliberately careless placement of the shoe against its mate. The proprietary gesture confirmed what I suspected: This woman *was* this department.

"I rather doubt that would be possible," she answered.

"Let me explain. My sister is two years older than I, and received all the family elegance and little of its common sense. This spring, while I was out of the country, she fell in with a man of dubious background. Very good looking, you understand, and enormously plausible, but not, shall we say, out for my sister's best interests. Lally—that's what we call her, her name's Yolanda—always wants to believe the best of a person, and I've always been around to keep her from doing anything too stupid, until now.

"I must speak with her, but this man denies that she is with him. I even managed to track them to an hotel in Paris this past week, but they had just left. No doubt they caught wind of my search. The only trace of them was a shoe under the edge of the bed, just one shoe. This shoe."

The woman had gone from mistrust to the edge of enthrallment—still uncertain, but wanting to believe, wanting the romance of one of her shoes in the midst of a tale of misplaced love and sororal fealty. One thing might bring her onto my side.

I stretched out a finger and touched the little bow. "However, I have to say, the shoe we found wasn't quite as pretty as this one. It looked as if Lally'd been made to walk through puddles in it."

"But she's only had the shoes for a week," she exclaimed.

I kept all trace of triumph from my face. "Yes, I thought they looked new. A week, you say?"

"Almost to the hour. Monday last, they were. One of my first sales of the day. I notice those early sales," she confided. "I find the weeks tend to continue as they begin."

"Did she come in herself, to buy them?"

"I'm afraid not," the woman answered, clearly much taken with the scenario of a foolish girl whose love led to near-imprisonment.

"Was it him, then? Tall, thin?"

But she was shaking her head before I started the second sentence—and with a jolt I realised that I felt relief at her denial, because my vague description could also be a specific description of Damian. "Those shoes were purchased by a woman."

"Yes? Not an Oriental woman, though?" I asked, holding my breath.

"No, an older woman. And, frankly," she added, lowering her voice lest a Harrods' authority might hear, "not the sort of person I'd have expected to be interested in those shoes."

Person, not *lady.* Interesting. "What did she look like? It might have been his secretary. Or his sister," I hastened to add, to cover both classes.

"Secretary, perhaps, although if so I trust the gentleman does not have much dealing with the public. She wore an unfortunate dress and would have benefited from face-powder," the saleswoman declared in sorrow. "As for the dye in her hair, it was as subtle as boot-black."

Millicent Dunworthy.

The second-storey flat of the stand-in leader of the Children of Lights services appeared to be empty—at least, there was no response to ringing the bell beside the name Dunworthy at the entrance. I put my laden shopping basket on the landing and squinted down at a piece of paper. A few minutes later, one of the residents came down the stairs and attempted to get out of the door.

"Oh! Sorry," I exclaimed, "I seem to be in the way. Here, let me just move that—no, it's fine, I was just rereading this in the light, silly of me not to think—" The door shut on my self-effacing apology, with me on the inside and the man going down the steps, shaking his head.

There is nothing so disarming as a basket of vegetables and an attitude of feminine disorganisation.

I put the sheet of paper—an advertisement from a hair-cutting salon—into my pocket and carried the basket (which held mostly lettuces, for their lightness) up the stairs. The hallway was empty; the stairway door squeaked as it drew itself shut. I listened, but heard nothing, so I walked down to the end where the light had gone on the other night, and knocked softly.

When there was no answer, I put the basket on a table in the corridor and got to work with my pick-locks.

Millicent Dunworthy's flat consisted of three rooms: The largest combined sitting room—worn upholstered chairs, a chipped deal desk, and a wireless set—with kitchen—little more than gas ring, cupboard, and a table scarcely large enough for two. A pair of doors broke the side wall: The one on the right led to a bedroom with a narrow single bed, a cheap white-painted dressing-table, and a wardrobe that was too large for the room, so that the door hit against it rather than opening all the way to the wall. The other door was to a small lavatory with a wash-basin. The bath-room must be a shared one down the hall.

I moved through the rooms, confirming that the occupant was not there, and confirming also that the only escape, should I be discovered, would be a sheer drop to the pavement, twenty-five feet below. Then I got to work, starting in the bedroom.

The wardrobe contained clothing as dull and worn as the chairs in the sitting area, showing a preference for flowered blouses and sack-like skirts, the one striking exception being the white robe she had worn in the meeting hall. The dressing-table held little of interest but a jewellery box that might have been a present for a child's thirteenth birthday. The scraps of adornment it held were commonplace and without monetary value, with one exception: the coarse gold band I had seen her wearing. My finger felt scratches on its inner surface; when I carried it near the window, I saw the same overlapping triangle and circle that had been embroidered on the robe and tattooed on Yolanda Adler's abdomen.

Other than that, the ring contained no inscription. I put it back as I had found it, and closed the childish box.

The wash-room contained nothing more sinister than mild medical nostrums—no drugs in the water-closet, no cipher-books among the bath-towels.

The desk in the sitting room, somewhat prosaically, was where Millicent Dunworthy kept her secrets. The desk-diary was not informative—one week looked much the same as its predecessor, with two blocks of time marked out, week after week, for the past several months: Every Saturday night since late January bore the notation *Children*: In March every Wednesday added the word *Circle*, both at eight o'clock. Interspersed were two appointments for "dentist," "lunch, mother" every other Sunday, and a morning meeting of "Children" on Saturday, the 30th. The only item of interest I saw in the last eight months was a notation on 14 May. There the usual Wednesday meeting had the large, proud addition: *Testimony and Ring: a Child of Lights.*

I wondered, as I flipped through the barren pages, why she bothered keeping a diary. Was she methodical, or was her life so empty that regular marks were themselves reassuring?

I arranged the diary as I had found it on the precise corner of the desk, and opened the first and shallower of the desk's two side drawers.

The drawer had been lined with black velvet—amateurishly done, the corners uneven, the tacks awkwardly spaced and poorly hammered. In the middle of the drawer was the book she had read from on Saturday night, with that same symbol on its cover. I reached for it, then hesitated, knowing that once I opened it, I should be lost to the desk's other contents. I closed that drawer for the moment and opened the lower one.

It held files. The first one contained Dunworthy's personal income and expenses, recorded in a 1924 ledger in the same fussy hand that had penned the notice on the meeting-room door. Rent, bills from the newsagent, the grocer, the butcher, small contributions to a savings account in the expenses columns; income in another, regular amounts for the past three months; before that, the sums varied in

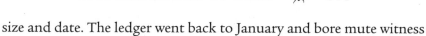

size and date. The ledger went back to January and bore mute witness to a life of considerable tedium.

The file behind it bore the notation: *Children of Lights*.

I opened it on the desk-top. It, too, had a ledger, with weekly amounts for tea, biscuits, hall rental, newspaper adverts, and the like. Every so often there would be small amounts for "supplies," the type unspecified. The earliest noted expense was for hall rental, paid on 1 February of this year. It was followed by a man's name with the notation *Builder*—for the fitted cabinets in the meeting-hall, no doubt.

No payment had been recorded to Damian Adler for the painting.

The back half of the ledger was a list of names, dates, and sums. About half the names repeated, some of them every week, with amounts ranging from £10 to £1,000. I raised my eyebrows, because by rough tally, the Children of Lights had brought in just under £12,000 in seven months. I copied the names of everyone who had donated more than £100; the list came to forty-seven names.

Behind the ledger was an ordinary mailing envelope containing assorted bits of paper, including the receipt for a pair of shoes from Harrods on 11 August. It was pinned to a sales receipt for a frock from Selfridges, another sales receipt for a pair of stockings, also from Selfridges, and a straw hat from a shop just a few doors down from Selfridges on Oxford Street.

Also in the envelope were a piece of note-paper with a list of sums, although no indication of what they might be for; a scrap of lined paper with several times written on it, again with no explanation; a chemist's receipt for "The Mixture"; and a piece of different note-paper on which was written:

two first class return tickets, Victoria to Eastbourne
1 picnic basket Fortnum & Mason, to be called for

I read the lines, and wondered darkly if a child of three required her own ticket.

I copied the information concerning chemists, picnic baskets, and sums, and returned the envelope to the file and the file to the drawer. A glance at the other files showed nothing of interest, so I closed the drawer and returned to the top one, this time drawing out the book. It was a thing of beauty: hand bound, heavy paper that was a pleasure to touch, and again the symbol. I turned to the title page, half expecting it to be called *The Book of Lights,* but instead saw only the word *Testimony* in the precise centre of the page. Below the word was the symbol, this time with a number beside it, hand-written in brownish ink:

There was no publishing information, which did not surprise me; what interested me more was the lack of an author's name. I turned to the beginning of the print, and ran my eyes over the text:

First Birth

The boy came into being on a night of celestial alignment, when a comet travelled the firmament and the sky threw forth a million shooting stars to herald his arrival.

Birth is a nexus, a time in which the Elements come together to form a new thing. Earth and air, fire and water, mingle and transform, to create a living being with the potential to become a vessel, glowing and pulsating with True Spirit.

The boy's mother lay on her birth-bed and saw the meteor shower, and knew it to be an omen. She felt no surprise when, at the very height of her birth pangs, one of the celestial celebrants plummeted to earth in the pond at the foot of the house—stripe of flame roaring through the air to hit the water with a crash and a billow of steam— and once she had given the new life suck, she rose from her bloody sheets to oversee the rescue of the precious scrap of metal. It was still hot, even after hours in the water.

Three lines down the second page, sudden voices jolted through me, shockingly near. The stairway door squeaked shut as the voices approached. I flung the book into the drawer, risking a split second to arrange it back to the centre, then snatched up my notes, shoved the chair back into place, and leapt for the bedroom.

"Well, I shall certainly have a word with Mr Wilberham about those pipes, the hammering is simply unbearable, and if you—oh look, Millicent, is this your shopping basket?"

Millicent did not answer, not that I heard, but while the other voice was puzzling loudly over the unclaimed basket of lettuces, perched on the hallway table like some idiosyncratic flower arrangement, the basket's owner was ducking behind an unclosable bedroom door, her heart pounding. An instant later, the key hit the lock.

The door to the flat opened to the other woman's ongoing debate over the ownership of these wilting vegetables. Millicent Dunworthy came inside, and I heard the other woman say, "I do hope you're feeling better, dear, these things can be such a shock, I—"

The door closed; the voice trailed off. I strained to hear, but the only sounds were the clump, clump of heavy shoes retreating down the hallway. A distant door slammed. I frowned: Why was Millicent Dunworthy just standing there? Had she somehow perceived that her home had been invaded?

To my relief, sound came at last: a small sigh or stifled cry, then by the soft slap of a newspaper hitting a table, followed by keys and some other object. Her feet clacked over the floorboards, crossed the carpet, then clacked again on linoleum. Water ran into a kettle. I wrapped my fingers around the knob that brushed my hip, lest the door drift open.

She set the kettle onto its ring and flame popped into life. Her heels rapped again: Lino, carpet, boards, then she passed by me, a foot away on the other side of a flimsy door. I stood tensely, my nose against the wood, scarcely breathing.

The wardrobe door rattled open, causing its yellowing side to shift against my left shoulder. Hangers scraped; the door clicked shut; she walked past me again, her footsteps turning immediately to the right. I heard the snap of a light-switch.

I drew a slow breath, then let it spill. Counting to twenty, I opened my fingers on the knob to let the door drift open, then took a step around it into the bedroom. Sounds from the lavatory assured me that Millicent Dunworthy was occupied for the next half minute or so. I pressed myself to the narrow swath of wall separating the two doors, and craned my neck forward a fraction of an inch—then smiled in relief: Millicent was the sort of lady who automatically closed the lavatory door even when she was all alone. It was not completely shut, and if she happened to be staring directly at the gap, she would see motion, but short of stretching out beneath her bed and hoping I didn't sneeze before she left for work the next morning, this was my best chance for escape.

I stepped briskly on my crepe-soled shoes to the door, then paused. The tinkling sounds had ceased, but over the rising burble from the tea-kettle was something else. Crying. Millicent Dunworthy was weeping softly. I scowled downward as I listened, and my gaze slowly came to focus on the folded newspaper she had laid on the table along with her keys and hand-bag. Here was the explanation of her tears:

ARTIST'S WIFE SLAIN AT LONG MAN
"THE ADDLER" AND SMALL DAUGHTER MISSING

The front door-knob rattled slightly under my hand; if the apartment behind me had been completely still, she would have heard the door coming open, but it was not, and she did not.

I left the shopping basket where it was and hurried down the stairs, my usual light-hearted relief at a successful burglary diminished considerably by that headline: Newsmen baying at our heels were not going to simplify matters one bit.

Outside, the growing heat and the enervating stink and humidity brought my spirits down another peg. My ransacking of Miss Dunworthy's flat had been, in truth, only partly successful. I wanted that book so badly I had even considered snatching it from the desk and stealing it outright. Had I no alternative, I might have risked it.

But I had an alternative—although not during daylight hours.

Which reminded me of Holmes. I walked to the corner and whistled up a cab to take me to the Café Royal.

I arrived a quarter hour late, and found Holmes well on his way to a conquest of Bohemia.

Chapter Twenty-six

The Sacrifice of Submission: Be clear: Sacrifice is whole-hearted, or it is nothing. It must cost dearly: Abraham offering his son; Woden hanging himself in a tree; the Son of Man accepting an agonising death. The greater the cost, the greater the energies freed for Transformation.

Sacrifice is the flame that sets quiescent Power alight, and consumes the world in a crash and a billow of smoke, and then in a whisper.
Testimony, II:8

DOMINOES MIGHT NO LONGER BE A FIXTURE IN the Café Royal, but Holmes had summoned a set, and was playing against a man I recognised as one of the foremost bookmakers in London; Holmes was winning. I looked with care around the other tables, not wishing to run into Alice or her Ronnie, but fortunately they were absent.

There was no doubt the Café community knew that Yolanda Adler was dead and Damian was being, as they say, sought for questioning. From the thrilled tones on all sides, it was the foremost topic of conversation.

The same gentleman who had ushered me in on Saturday night now escorted me to where Holmes sat, murmuring my name under his breath as he left. I looked after him in surprise.

"I *thought* I recognised him the other night," I said to Holmes, "but he gave no indication that he knew me."

"Of course not," Holmes said. "The staff of the Café Royal are nothing if not discreet."

I ordered something non-alcoholic and waited with little patience for Holmes to finish beating the bookie at dominoes. An importunate newsman made it to the first tables before being pounced upon and thrown out. Finally, Holmes accepted two pounds from the loser, then handed them back with instructions to place them on something called Queen Bea to win the next time she ran. The two men shook hands, the tout taking his beer and his loud check suit away to a table of similarly dressed individuals across the room.

I leant forward over my glass and started in. "I just had a few minutes in Miss Dunworthy's flat," I began, only to notice that his attention was clearly elsewhere. He put down his glass and rose with a look of mingled resignation and mild amusement.

I swivelled on the red plush seat and saw a small, well-made woman approaching, dressed in gipsy-bright garments, dark eyes sparkling in olive skin. She had the panache of a Cockney, and I was not in the least surprised when she marched up and pumped Holmes' hand; an onlooker might have thought them old friends.

"Mrs Loveday," Holmes said. "Good to see you again. This is my wife, Mary Russell. Russell, this is Betty Loveday, also known as Betty May."

I caught myself before I could say, "I've heard of you," since the knowledge that one has been discussed is never a comfortable one. However, the little thing grinned as if I had voiced my admission, and I thought that she was, in fact, well accustomed to being a topic of conversation.

Holmes gave her a chair, ordered her a drink, and lit her cigarette before turning to me. "Mrs Loveday was in earlier, when I was talking to a mutual friend about Damian Adler. She seems to think that Mrs

Adler might have been murdered because of her interest in things spiritual."

The small face and dark eyes fixed on me. "Do you know Aleister Crowley?"

"The spiritual ch—" I caught myself, and changed charlatan to "—leader? I've never met him personal—"

"Never, never go near him! He is a demon in human guise. I am risking my sanity merely entering this place, where he sometimes comes to gloat and to hunt for fresh victims."

I looked at Holmes, startled, but he was busying himself with to-bacco.

"Er," I said.

"The Mystic killed my dear, loving husband Raoul. He tempted Raoul and hypnotised him and then led him into hell in Sicily," she declared.

It was, judging by the tempo of her storytelling, a well-worn tale, and I wasn't at all sure why Holmes had inflicted it on me. He smoked and drank and after a while caught the waiter's eye and ordered three meals, as our Bohemian Ancient Mariner churned on with a recital of drugs and ill health and the terrible knowledge that her beautiful young undergraduate was being degraded and trampled into the mud of morality by the detestable Crowley.

Our meal arrived, and I gladly dug into it, nodding attentively as she wound through a detailed account of the Crowley monastery in Sicily, where sex and drugs were central to worship, and the only God was Crowley. There is little new under the sun, when it comes to religion—the only truly distasteful part of it was the presence of children, although it sounded as if they were kept away from the drugs and the orgies.

Short of walking out on her in mid-sentence, I could not think of a way to stop her. I concentrated on my meal, listening with half an ear to her sad and unsavoury story, until I felt a sharp tap of another shoe against my own. Looking up, I saw Holmes watching me; I obediently returned my attention to the woman.

"He hypnotised my Raoul, and took away his inner strength by drugs, until Raoul had not enough will left to resist when The Mystic told him to commit murder."

"Murder?" I repeated, startled.

"Yes, of a cat. She was a small and harmless cat, but she scratched The Mystic one day when he frightened her, and so he told Raoul that she was an evil spirit and had to be sacrificed. And Raoul had to do it."

"Good heavens."

"Yes! Raoul! Who wouldn't hurt a fly, but would catch it and put it outside. They all had to gather around in their robes and chant and then Raoul had to take the knife, and they . . . they had to drink the blood, and my poor Raoul got sick and died from it, from drinking the poor cat's blood."

I just gaped at her, my meal, the surroundings, even Holmes forgotten. Gratified by my response, she continued the story, telling of the nightmare of having her husband die in her arms, of his burial, of her awful trip home . . .

My intention of questioning the Café's habitués about Damian Adler shrivelled and died. I laid down my utensils, and told Holmes, "I believe I've heard all I need. I'll wait for you outside."

The heat bouncing off the pavement washed over me. For an instant, the image of the slaughtered cat merged in my mind with Yolanda, making me so queasy, I thought I might disgrace myself there on the street, but soon I felt the first buoying effects of anger, first at the woman May, for polluting the Café with her disgusting tale and spoiling a perfectly good meal, and then at Crowley, that such a man was allowed the freedom of England. When Holmes came out of the Café doors, I turned sharply on my heel and marched away in the direction of Oxford Circus. Soon, he was beside me, and before long my hand had gone through his arm.

"How soon before we can go back there?" I asked.

"Oh, she's liable to be in residence for hours. Still, I'm glad you heard her story."

"Why on earth would you want me to hear that dreadful tale?"

"I admit, I hadn't considered its effects when delivered over a dining table. However, I thought it a worthy illumination of the extremes to be found in modern belief."

"Crowley's been called the wickedest man in England."

"By himself, certainly."

"You think it an act?"

"Not entirely. He's like a petulant boy who searches out the most offensive phrases and ideas he can find, to prove his cleverness and his superiority. You know that his so-called church takes its motto from the Hellfire Club."

"*Fait ce que vouldras,*" I murmured. "Do as you like. Which, if you are rich enough, covers any sin and perversion you can invent."

"Crowley is not wealthy, but he manages very well, in part because he is deeply charismatic, with eyes some find compelling. No doubt he has brains, and ability—he was at one time a highly competent mountaineer. At seventeen, he climbed Beachy Head to the Coast Guard outpost in under ten minutes. If one can believe his claim."

"Have you any reason to think that Yolanda was involved with this Crowley nonsense?"

"Were he in the country, I should wish to take a closer look at him, but he has not been here for some time. I shouldn't think Crowley is your group's 'Master.' "

I resolutely turned my mind from the image of slaughtered cats. "Did you discover anything of interest before I came?"

"Damian has not been seen there since he passed by on Friday morning."

"Where can he be?" I wondered aloud.

"And you: Have you found anything?" he asked, ignoring my plaintive remark.

"Yes, a great deal."

As we threaded our way along the once-noble colonnades of Regent Street, surrounded by the irritable shouts and klaxons of a city in summer, I told him what I had found in Miss Dunworthy's flat: the ledger for the Children of Lights; the receipts for the clothing Yolanda Adler had worn to her death; the overheard weeping.

"However, Holmes," I said at the end of it, "I cannot envision the woman with a knife at Yolanda's throat."

"She lacks the independent spirit?"

"I should have said, she lacks that degree of madness."

"It amounts to the same thing," he said. "She is a follower."

"Definitely. And of a man, not a woman."

"The spinster true-believer is a species I have met before, generally in the rôle of victim. They beg to be fleeced of all they possess."

"I shouldn't say Miss Dunworthy possesses much."

"Her wits, her energy, her palpable innocence and good will."

"Those, yes. But, Holmes, about that book, *Testimony*. She had a copy, in a drawer she's lined with velvet as a sort of shrine. I didn't get much of a chance to look at it."

"You wish to return to Damian's house."

"I need to see that book. You don't suppose Lestrade took it?"

"I shouldn't have thought so, although he will have left a presence there, on the chance Damian returns."

"Several constables, do you think?"

"Unlikely. Shall we toss a coin for who creates the distraction this time?"

"You know—" I stopped, reconsidering what I was about to say. "You know where the book is, so it would make sense for you to fetch it. On the other hand, I should be interested to see what else the Adlers own in their collection."

"Religion being your field, not mine," Holmes noted.

"Not if you consider Crowley's practise a religion. My expertise is about twenty-five hundred years out of date. But still, you're right, I'm better suited than you."

"Then I shall endeavour to draw the constable's fire while you burgle the household of its exotic religious artefacts."

"I shouldn't think the constable on duty will be armed, Holmes."

"Only with righteous indignation and a large stick."

"Mycroft will stand bail, and I'll bring dressings and arnica for your bruises," I assured him.

At eleven-fifteen, we were in our positions on either side of the Adler house.

I was in the back. My soft soles made no noise going along the alley. I laid a hand on the gate latch, but found my first hitch: The gate was now padlocked from within.

I had, however, come armed for burglary, with a narrow-beamed torch, dark clothing, and a makeshift stile for climbing fences. I jammed the bottom edge of my length of timber into the soil, propping its upper end against the bricks of the wall. I got one foot onto the step this made, and hoisted myself onto the wall.

I sat there for a moment, grateful that some past owner hadn't seen fit to set broken glass along the top, and surveyed the house. Much of it was dark, but one upstairs window had a dim glow, and the downstairs sitting room lights burned low behind drapes and around the boards nailed over its broken windows. The kitchen alone was brightly lit. I retrieved my stile by the length of rope tied around its middle, then dropped down into the garden, setting the board against the wall again, in case of a hasty departure.

The lawn behind the house was dry with the heat, and crackled underfoot; the rucksack on my back and the clothing I wore rustled with every step; neither would be heard from the house, but they were enough to grate on my nerves. Breaking into a middle-aged woman's flat was not the same proposition as invading a house guarded by a police constable.

The next hitch came when I saw that said constable had taken up residence in the kitchen, ten feet from the back door through which I intended to go. He was sitting on a kitchen chair with his collar loose and his feet up on another chair, reading a detective novel. A tea-pot, milk bottle, and mug sat to hand. Shelves behind him held cooking implements unusual for a British household: the wide, curved pan called a *wok*; a stack of bamboo steamers; a row of small tea-cups without handles.

Holmes and I had agreed to a delay of a quarter hour for me to work on the locks before he created his distraction; now, there was little I could do for that quarter hour but watch the constable turn his pages and drink his tea.

A young eternity later, the bell rang, and rang, and rang again. At the first sound, the man in the chair dropped his book in surprise and swore an oath. His feet hit the floor the same instant the second ring rattled the night, and on the third he was passing through the doorway, hands going to his collar-buttons.

I jumped for the door and slid my picks into the mechanism.

Holmes had promised me a bare minimum of four minutes of freedom on this first disturbance. At five minutes, sweating and swearing, the lock gave way. I turned the knob; to my intense relief, the bolt inside had not been pushed to.

I closed the door gently and heard the front door slam. I scurried for the stairs and reached the first floor before the PC's chair squawked from below.

Safe in the darkness, I bent over with my hands on my knees, breathing in the foreign odours of the house—sandalwood and ginger where most of the neighbours' would smell of cabbage and strong soap—while my racing heart returned to something under a hundred beats per minute.

Eight minutes until Holmes' second disturbance.

I reached the study with a minimum of creaking floorboards. Once there, I unlatched the window and raised it a crack (to make sure it opened, if I was interrupted) before placing a rug at the bottom of the door and a chair under its handle. I switched on the torch, its narrow beam all but invisible outside of the room.

I found the book straight away: *Testimony*. Here again, the title page had just the name, with no author, no publisher, no date—although despite the book's beauty and expense, it looked as if a child had been permitted to lick a chocolate ice over the title page, leaving behind a narrow smear that could not quite be wiped away. I turned a couple of pages, and saw the first illustration: a small, tiled roof beneath a night sky whirling with streaks of light. The drawing was not signed, but there was no question as to the artist.

I paged through until I found another finely worked drawing, then a third before I made myself stop. I slid the book into the rucksack, and went on searching—for what, exactly, I was not certain. I found a *planchette,* for the consultation of spirits, and several small statues of Asian gods, including a superb ivory carving from China covered with scenes from the life of the Buddha. There were several paintings on the wall, none of them by Damian, all of them either overtly or vaguely religious. The shelves were not heavily laden, either because the Adlers were not great readers or because they had only arrived here a few months before, but I saw among the volumes the most recent collection of Conan Doyle stories, and beside it a magazine. I was not surprised to find it was *The Strand,* from January, which as I recalled had Dr Watson's rather feeble episode concerning the so-called Sussex vampire.

Two shelves were filled with religious esoterica. Some of the titles were familiar, others I took down to glance at, putting them away again when they confirmed my expectations. Two volumes suggested a closer look; they went into the rucksack with *Testimony.* A book by Crowley I left where it was.

The desk was little used, although some notes and a list of book titles confirmed that the letter Damian showed us in Sussex had been written by Yolanda.

The sound of Holmes' second interruption broke the stillness of the house: the clanging of the brass bell; constabulary footsteps; two minutes of raised voices as he sent this persistent drunk on his way; the PC's footsteps returning.

Holmes would watch for the signal that I was outside and safe; when it did not come, he would wait twenty minutes, then ring a third time. Past that, he risked arrest for disturbing the peace of the irritated PC: If I wasn't out by then, we had agreed, I should be on my own.

A narrow cupboard beside the bookshelf that held religious works revealed a white robe with the Children of Lights emblem embroidered on the left breast. I measured the garment's length with my eyes: It might come to my own shins, which suggested that, unless Damian wore it short like an undergraduate's gown, this belonged to Yolanda. There was no gold ring, but there was one oddity: a small, very shadowy painting of an old man in a cloak and a wide-brimmed hat dipped low over his left eye: Damian's work. Woden again? Why hang it inside of the cupboard? I lifted it from its hook to check the back, but could see nothing unusual about it. Perhaps Yolanda had liked it but Damian considered it a muddy failure, and did not want it displayed in the open? A puzzle.

I gently closed the cupboard door and slid the rucksack onto my shoulders, then disassembled the blockade on the door and eased it open.

No glowering PC awaited me.

Moving along the edge of the hallway to lessen the chance of squeaks underfoot, I explored the other doors, putting my head inside each room and giving a brief shot from the torch to tell me what it contained. The Adlers' bedroom was the room whose dim light I had seen from the garden, from a fixture high on a wall that looked as if it stayed on all of the time. They had a single wide bed, a table on either side with reading lights. Her bed-side table had a drawer with several hand-lotions and nail files. His table held a framed photograph of Yolanda in a traditional high-necked Chinese dress, looking less at home than she had in the Western dress of the other photo.

Next door was Yolanda's dressing room, with a variety of colourful, fashionable clothing. Not a flower in sight, I noticed: Yolanda had died wearing Millicent Dunworthy's taste.

Damian's wardrobe was not quite what I had expected, for it showed an awareness of style not reflected by what he had worn to Sussex. I wondered if he had chosen those scruffy clothes to underscore his Bohemian identity, or as a statement that he didn't care what Holmes saw him in.

Between the dressing rooms were a sumptuous bath and a modern lavatory, with a medicine cabinet that contained a number of packets with Chinese labels, some corked bottles containing unlabelled herbs, and a few modern nostrums that suggested Damian had suffered from a chest cold and Yolanda occasionally required a pill against female aches. Then another bedroom, this one fitted out as a nursery.

Dolls, books—a lot of books—and a basket of brightly coloured toys. A diminutive enamel-ware tray with a miniature tea-set for four, missing one cup but otherwise perfect, and perfectly exquisite. A neatly made bed, a diminutive wardrobe. But the walls were the reason the room pulled me in: Damian had painted them.

Even under the fitful gaze of my torch, the walls were incredible. The room seemed to be atop a hill, with a blue sky broken by the occasional puffy cloud overhead, a changing landscape stretching out in all directions, and a green carpet underfoot to remind one of grass: One half expected a fresh breeze on one's face. To the north stood a city on a bay, its boats suggesting a location considerably farther east than London: Shanghai, perhaps? Then came a tropical beach, with coconut palms and birds too exotic even for Nature. Farmland came to the south, more French than English, with a small, Tuscan-looking hill town in the distance. That gave way to jungle, with monkeys and a sharp-eyed parrot watching over the child's cot. Everything there looked real enough to walk to.

It must have taken him weeks.

I would happily have stood there for an hour—would very happily have curled up to sleep in that tiny bed—had I not heard the third and final ring of the doorbell. Reluctantly, I pulled myself out of the room and padded down the hallway to the sound of loud constabulary curses from downstairs.

I waited until he had yanked open the front door and was shouting at Holmes before I trotted down the stairs and through the kitchen. Holmes was apologising loudly, sounding for all the world like a sobering drunk. "The wife says I should bring you these, she baked them this afternoon, and tell you I'm sorry to disturb you. She's right, I don't know what I was thinking, I ought to know my own front door and this surely isn't it."

In the face of open apology accompanied by a tray of biscuits (brought for the purpose, freshly baked by Mycroft's invisible kitchen) the constable's righteous anger deflated. I passed out of the kitchen door and let the latch lock behind me, scaling the wall and dropping the block of rope-bound wood into the nearest ash can before the PC had dunked his first biscuit.

Holmes was waiting at the agreed-to spot; the tension left his shoulders when I rounded the corner.

"The constable was in the kitchen when I got there," I explained. "I didn't think it a good idea to pick the lock with him drinking tea ten feet away."

"I should have expected that he would settle there," he said.

"In any case, I have the book, and a couple of others. And I found a white robe like the one Miss Dunworthy wore the other night, far too short for Damian. But—when you were there, did you see the child's room?"

"Briefly."

"Extraordinary, isn't it?"

"My . . . son." He hesitated; this was the second time, in all these years, that I had heard him say that phrase. Now he repeated it, saying quietly, "My son loves his daughter."

Chapter Twenty-seven

Second Birth: Many go through life born but once,
scarcely aware of good and evil. Those who are born
anew—spiritual birth—take their first step outside
of the Garden when they perceive the difference
between good and evil.

Testimony, III:1

HALFWAY THROUGH TUESDAY AFTERNOON, I LOOKED up from the final page of *Testimony* and noticed how very empty Mycroft's flat was. I had slept late and came out of the guest room to find both Holmes and Mycroft away, Mycroft to the office where he had worked for most of his life, and Holmes, as a terse note on the dining table informed me, "Gone to Cerne Abbas." Mycroft's housekeeper, Mrs Cowper (whose odd hours I never could predict), made me breakfast and then left me to my work. Since one or the other of the men had taken with them the list of forty-seven names from Millicent Dunworthy's ledger, my work consisted of the book I had stolen the night before.

My formal training, the field in which I had spent much of the past seven years, was in the analysis of theological texts. Thus I ap-

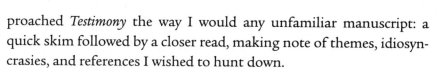

proached *Testimony* the way I would any unfamiliar manuscript: a quick skim followed by a closer read, making note of themes, idiosyncrasies, and references I wished to hunt down.

Six hours and a whole lot of words later, I closed the cover and my attempt at scholarly detachment faltered. I looked at the symbol on the book's cover, and saw a tattoo on a dead woman's belly. I went to make myself a cup of tea, and thought I heard something move in the back of the apartment. When I looked into Mycroft's study to see, I then thought I heard the front door open and close. I checked that it was locked, and started to go through the entire flat. When I caught myself stooping to look under a bed, I loudly said a rude word and left, taking with me nothing but the key.

I marched along Pall Mall and through Cleveland Row to Green Park, turning up the Queen's Walk and continuing down the other two sides. Then it dawned on me that I had just described a triangle, the shape that figured so prominently in everything to do with the Children of Lights. Impatiently, I crossed over to St James's, making myself slow down and pay attention to my surroundings: up the Mall, down Horse Guards Road, then back along the Birdcage Walk—where it struck me that not only was St James's Park laid out as a sort of triangle itself, it even had a circle—the Victoria memorial—at its peak.

I abandoned the parks entirely, and made for the Embankment.

Testimony was nonsensical, even silly in places—I had found myself chuckling aloud at the thought of Millicent Dunworthy declaiming some of its fairly blatant sexual imagery, all about energies bursting forth and enveloping. Much of the writing employed tired heresies and re-worked exotica, leavened by the occasional flash of imagination and insight, and I had found the author overly fond of ornate language and self-aggrandisement.

So why had it left me feeling as if I had read someone's pornographic journal?

As soon as I asked myself the question, my inner eye provided the answer: Yolanda Adler, dressed in new clothing, sacrificed at the foot of an ancient monument, probably with the weapon the author called the Tool.

I walked, and walked. Eventually, I burnt off the worst of the crawling sensation along my spine, and made my way to a nearby reading library to track down some of the Norse and Hindu references. At half past five, I walked back to Pall Mall and let myself into Mycroft's flat. He came in as I was pouring myself a cup of tea.

"Good afternoon, Mary."

"Hello, Mycroft. Do you know if Holmes planned to return tonight?"

"I believe he anticipated having to stay the night in Poole."

"He's going to talk to Fiona Cartwright's employment agency?"

"Depending on what he found in Cerne Abbas. He borrowed my small camera, although I do not know what he expects to record with it."

"He doubts it was suicide?"

"My brother accepts nothing he has not judged with his own eyes."

True: An unexplained cut on the hand of a gun-death was enough to make him question the official verdict. "Was it you who took the list of names from the table?"

"I put a man on it. He should have a complete report tomorrow."

"What about Shanghai; anything from there?"

"It is not yet a week since I wired," he protested gently.

"It's been a busy week," I said, by way of apology, although I was thinking, How long does it take someone to hunt down a few records anyway? "Here, have a cup of tea, Mrs Cowper's made plenty."

"I was thinking to change for my afternoon perambulation."

"Shall I keep you company?"

"I should be very glad to have you join me on my self-imposed penance to the gods of excess," he pronounced, and went to trade his black City suit for something more appropriate to a stroll through the park.

In light-weight and light-grey suiting, whose gathered waist-band emphasised its elephantine wrinkles, he took up a straw hat and held the door for me.

Neither of us spoke much as we passed by the open windows along Pall Mall, but once we were among trees, he asked, "Have you learnt anything from the book you purloined?"

"It's left a very nasty taste in my mouth."

"I see."

"Anyone who capitalises that many English nouns should be shot."

"The author's diction offends you?"

"The author's arrogance and assumptions offend me. His dedication to the idea that all happenstance is fate offends me. His imprecision offends me. His images are both pretentious and disturbing. The sense of underlying threat and purpose are . . ." I heard myself speaking in the erudite shorthand the Holmes brothers used, and I cut it short. "He scares me silly."

"Tell me how," Mycroft said, equally capable of brevity. I walked for a bit, ordering my thoughts, before I went on.

"The book concerns the spiritual development of a man—one assumes the writer, although it is in the third person—from a boy born under signs and portents, through his dark night of the soul, to his guided enlightenment. It has four sections with eight topics each—eight is a number significant in many traditions, although it could mean nothing, here—and a concluding section that acts as a coda. What begins as standard nuttiness darkens in the middle. The fourth section—Part the Fourth, he terms it—concerns his 'Great Work,' which appears to be a mix of alchemy and, well, human sacrifice. Only two of his thirty-two topic headings are repeated: 'Sacrifice,' which is divided into its submissive and its transformative aspects, and 'Tool.' I'm not certain, but thinking about it, I wonder if the Tool could be a knife forged from meteor metal."

"A sacrificial knife," he said.

One who did not know Mycroft Holmes would have heard the phrase as a simple intellectual conclusion: I could hear not only the distaste, but the pain underlying that: He, too, had Yolanda Adler before his eyes.

"He doesn't say it in so many words," I told him. "And when he mentions primitives cutting out and eating the hearts of their enemies, it sounded as if he took that as metaphorical, not literal. Everything in *Testimony* is couched in these pseudo-mythic terms; the author is deliberately crafting a holy scripture."

"Megalomaniacs I have known," he mused. "I believe you are familiar with Aleister Crowley?"

"His name has come up a number of times in the past few days."

"So I would imagine, if that text of yours is representative of this circle's interests."

"Holmes thinks that Crowley's manifesto is in large part artifice, stemming from and feeding into an overweening egotism. If Crowley is God—or Satan, which for him amounts to the same thing—then how can his followers deny him his wishes, whether those be sex, or money, or just admiration of his poetry? If his desires are unreasonable, that's because he's a god; if he's a god, then his desires are reasonable."

"A convenient doctrine," Mycroft agreed.

"However, I should say that the author of *Testimony* may actually believe in his rigmarole. If Crowley is dangerous because shocking and scandalous behaviour is a way of convincing the gullible of his divinity, then this man would be dangerous because he actually believes he *is* divine."

"May I assume that your presence here indicates an uncertainty as to the author's identity?"

"There are bits of evidence scattered throughout the thing, but I'm not sure how dependable even those are—he seems very willing to adopt a flexible chronology, even when it goes against good sense. For example, he claims a small meteorite fell into a pond outside the house as he was being born, and that his mother personally supervised its retrieval, but he then says the thing didn't cool for hours. Of course, most religious texts find symbolic truth more important than literal, just as *kairos*-time—when things are ripe—is more real than *chronos*-time, which is a mere record of events."

"Perhaps you might assemble a list of those items with evidentiary potential, so we could reflect on those?"

"Er . . ."

"You have done so? Very well, proceed." He clasped his hands behind his back, the cane dangling behind him like an elephant's tail, and listened.

"He draws from the Old and New Testaments, Gnosticism, Buddhism, Hinduism, Zoroastrianism, alchemy, and a variety of mythologies, with an especial interest in the Norse. I'd say he's read a number of works on mysticism, from Jung's psychological theories to William James's Gifford Lectures on *The Varieties of Religious Experience*. The sorts of books I saw in Damian's house. The author claims, as I said, that he was born during a meteor shower, but there was also a comet in the sky—which could be actual fact, or a sacrifice of accuracy in favour of mythic significance. And come to think of it," I mused, "that design they use, which I took for a spot-light, could be a stylised comet.

"He has travelled—he mentions France and Italy, the Far East, and the Pacific. He honours and, I think, finds inspiration in the mixed heritage of Britain. In two or three places, he employs artistic metaphors. And, I, well . . ." I exhaled. "There are eight drawings by Damian in the book."

We navigated the crossing of Piccadilly and Park Lane and were well into Hyde Park before Mycroft spoke. What sounded like a tangent went in fact directly to the heart of what I had been telling him.

"My brother permits few people inside his guard. Four people in his first sixty-three years, I should say: myself, Dr Watson, Irene Adler, and you. For those inside his affections, Sherlock's loyalty is absolute. In another man, one might call it blind. Any one of us four could commit cold-blooded murder, in Trafalgar Square, in broad daylight, and he would devote every iota of his energy and wit to proving the act justified."

"And now there are five."

"I have not seen my brother and my nephew together, but I should not be surprised to find Damian added to the fold."

We paced in silence for a time, until I responded with an apparent tangent of my own.

"Has Holmes told you what happened in San Francisco this past spring?"

"He mentioned that you had received unexpected and disconcerting information concerning your past."

"I doubt he couched it that mildly. I discovered that pretty much everything I thought I knew about my childhood was wrong. That after my family died, I shut my life behind a door and forgot it. Literally. 'Disconcerting' isn't the word—I felt as if the ground beneath me had turned to quick-sand. It has left me doubting my own judgment. Doubting whether or not to trust anyone else."

"Including Sherlock."

"Him I trust, if anyone. And yet, I can't help thinking that Damian's mother deftly outflanked him. Twice."

"Yes, although when Sherlock met her, he assumed her to be a villain, when in fact she was not. That is quite a different thing from falling for the schemes of a villain one believes innocent."

"You think he could not be deceived by Damian?"

Another lengthy silence, then he sighed. "You think Damian wrote this book?"

"Do you know his birthday?"

"The ninth of September, 1894."

The Perseid meteors would have been finished; I should have to find if there were any comets that year. "What about his mother? Did she die on a full moon?"

"She died in June 1912, but I do not know the precise day. This is in the book?"

"To answer your question, I *hope* Damian had nothing to do with *Testimony* beyond the drawings. But if I can't trust my instincts, I have to use my head. And my head tells me that there are points I cannot ignore."

"Perhaps you had better list them."

"The moon, to begin with: It's in nearly all his paintings, two men near him died around the full moon, and now his wife. The house where he was born had a pond—I've seen a drawing. The author of *Testimony* had no father and was raised by women; as an adult he was badly injured, went into some sort of a coma, and came out with what he calls 'the eternal stigmata of divinity.' Damian was raised without a father, he was injured in the trenches, and the scars on his head might be considered Christ-like. The man in *Testimony* then went through a period of darkness before finding a 'guide,' who took his hand and showed him the way ahead. After Damian killed his fellow officer, he was sent to the mental hospital in Nantes; there he met André Breton, who introduced him to automatism. Damian's paintings and *Testimony* are both permeated with mythological elements, particularly the Norse god Woden. And, he has a self-portrait showing Holmes, Irene Adler, and himself with a sun, a moon, and a comet over their heads.

"Damian explains his art by saying that he became sane by embracing madness, finding beauty in obscenity. The book is both mad and obscene.

"Finally, there is the child's name. He and Yolanda named her Estelle, or star. *Testimony* makes much of stellar influence."

"Possibly. On the other hand, Estelle was also the name of my mother. Our mother."

I turned to stare at him. "Really? I never knew that. Would Damian have known?"

"One should have to ask Sherlock."

And asking Sherlock would mean opening up this entire can of worms and setting it in front of him with a fork. Neither of us wished to do that without some kind of actual evidence.

We had crossed the Serpentine, where the good cheer of the crowd at the tea house made a mockery of what we were saying.

"What of evidence to the contrary?"

He was not about to admit that my damning list of links between Damian and the book was in any way evidence, certainly not for any court of law. Nonetheless, damning it was.

"First and foremost, it's nonsense. Intellectual trash. I can't think Damian's mind works that way."

"Unless," Mycroft said, playing devil's advocate, "the nonsensical nature of the writing is a deliberate choice, aimed at catching the imagination of a certain audience."

"It's not just intellectual snobbery speaking when I say that it's deeply troubling, and frightening, to think that Holmes' son could produce such a thing."

"So say the families of any of the world's spectacular murderers."

"All right, what about this: Holmes has considered the possibility that Damian killed Yolanda, and rejected it." Mycroft was silent, which constituted an agreement that this was a heavy weight on the side of innocence. "There is also the clothing Yolanda was wearing—an ugly frock, and shoes and silk stockings far too large for her. They were purchased by Millicent Dunworthy, under orders from someone, but there is no indication that she was making the purchase for Damian. In any case, he would have known the size of his wife's feet and the length of her legs."

"Unless the clothing was intended to deflect suspicion, as well as raise a challenge to his father's intellect."

There was no arguing with that.

He added, "There is also the possibility that Damian's involvement is secondary. That he plays a peripheral rôle in . . . whatever this is we are looking at."

Nor with that.

"The author of that book," I answered at last, "whoever he might be, is either a dangerous charlatan, or an even more dangerous psychopath."

Mycroft said nothing: He was going to make me speak my thoughts to the end.

I went on. "In either case, he would strike one as both plausible and engaging."

No response, which was the same as agreement. I took a deep breath.

"The question is, could Holmes be duped by such a person?"

"Any man may be duped, if he wishes to believe."

This time, even a stranger would have heard the pain in his voice. I shook my head, more in denial than in disagreement.

"Yes," he insisted. "Even my brother. The key to deceit is to find the weak point in one's target."

"I've only spent a couple of hours in Damian's company, but I have to say, if he is the author of that book, I should look to madness, not duplicity. However—" I had to clear my throat before I could give voice to the end point of this line of thought. "The author of that book is almost certainly responsible for . . ."

"Where is the child Estelle?" Mycroft said, his voice soft.

Again, I shook my head; this time the gesture was one of despair.

Mycroft drifted to a halt, leaning on his stick to stare unseeing at Kensington Palace. "The one faint ray of light in all this is that, assuming it is tied to the influence of the full moon, we have twenty-three days until the next one. Surely we can lay hands on the young man, given three weeks."

He is Holmes' son, I thought but did not say aloud. I did not need to, not to Holmes' brother.

Holmes' brother was now, I noticed, staring at me.

"What is it?" I asked.

"Have you eaten today?"

"Yes. I think so. I don't remember."

"I thought not. You have that stretched look I have seen you wear, when you have not eaten. Surely we can remedy that, at the least."

And so saying he raised a hand and conjured a taxi.

The brothers Holmes have an irritating habit of being right, and so it proved now with Mycroft and food. Not that a meal rendered the world rosy, but an unstarved brain permitted my near-panic to take a small step away, that I might assemble my thoughts and come up with a plan.

Perhaps my attachment to Holmes made me too ready to condemn the son he had so eagerly clasped to his breast. My suspicions of Damian, though justified, were compounded by my burden of emotions, namely the residual resentments that I had lived with since the 1919 revelation that Holmes had a life from which I was precluded. It was unlikely that I should have a child: That Holmes had one already opened a separation between us.

But it was not merely the bitter edge of envy that set me in opposition to Damian Adler. Holmes had adopted Damian's cause with a whole-sale enthusiasm I would not have expected. Under less dire circumstances, I might almost be entertained by the chance to prove Holmes fallible; on the other hand, both experience and loyalty demanded that I throw myself over to Holmes' stance and labour to prove his son's innocence. But Damian's fate rendered the first option repugnant, and Yolanda's death made the second impossible: Were I to join in declaring Damian's innocence, the dead would have no voice.

Scotland Yard, it appeared, were positioned on one side; Holmes and Damian occupied the other: The equation needed a balancing point, a mind committed to cold facts, a heart given only to impartiality.

It was left to me to pursue the middle course of truth: me, and Mycroft.

Holmes had always freely bowed to his brother's superiority when it came to pure observational ability, declaring that his brother's ability to store and retrieve facts was matched by no living man. Mycroft had never come near to Holmes as an investigator, being severely limited by his disinclination to stir beyond his small circuit of rooms, club, and office. However, what I needed now was not an investigator, but a pure retrieval mechanism. It could save me days of tedium amongst the back-issues.

If the moon was at all significant, its meaning might have begun to manifest before the Cerne Abbas possible-suicide in June. When Mycroft was seated in his chair again, glass to hand and fragrant cigar in its ash-tray, I asked him.

"What," he said, "other murders around the time of full moons? There were none—none worthy of note."

"Not necessarily murders, but events. For example, Holmes mentioned a dead ram in Cumbria, although it was only another letter by an outraged gentleman-farmer to *The Times*."

His light grey eyes fixed on me, slowly losing their habitual vagueness. After a minute, he sat back, laced his fingers across his waistcoat, and let his eyelids drift half closed. I picked up my pen and the block of paper.

"March the twenty-first," he began, "was a Friday. London saw a death on the Thursday night, a sixty-nine-year-old woman in Stepney run down by a lorry. The lorry driver stopped and was detained, then released because the woman was nearly blind and deaf. On the following day, a man was found dead in an alley off the Old Bethnal Green Road, no signs of foul play, being drunk and it being a wet night. No bodies on the Saturday, although a house in Finsbury that was used as an informal Hindu temple had a rude word scratched on its door."

He paused, reaching for the next pigeon-hole of his orderly brain, then resumed. "In Manchester during those three days, there were no deaths, no crimes of a religious nature, but several arrests were made following a talk at a vegetarian restaurant concerning Madame Blavatsky. In York . . ."

This was going to be a long night.

Chapter Twenty-eight

*Blood: Blood and pain are companions of birth, no less for
the second-born, torn from the womb of ignorance to
stand naked before the storms of the world. A second-born
man is doubly vulnerable: This is the mystery of birth.*
Testimony, III:2

WEDNESDAY MORNING, MYCROFT SEEMED NONE
the worse for wear from his prodigious feat of memory of
the night before, but I was still fatigued as I read through my ever
more incoherent notes. There seemed a stupendous number of crimes
on my pages, and I wondered how the figures a week on either side of
the full-moon dates would compare—then winced at the thought of
having to go through that experience a second time.

In March, a man named Danielson had been knifed in a fishing village in Cornwall, his body found the morning after the full moon, his
assailant not identified. In April, a shepherd's death was probably exposure, but then on 18 May there was an interesting item: Blood was
seen near the entrance of a large chambered tomb in the Orkney
Islands. When the farmer went to see, he found a sheep dead inside
the chamber, its throat savaged by a dog.

Right, I thought, I can just see asking Lestrade to look into that. That reminded me: "What about Holmes' dead ram? It's not on this list."

Mycroft blinked. "Might he have been making a jest with Lestrade?"

"It didn't sound like it."

Mycroft's gaze focused on the coffee pot in the centre of the table, as he slipped effortlessly back into the retrieval state. Twenty minutes later, as I was myself eyeing the pot and wondering if it would shatter his concentration were I to pour myself another cup, he stirred and picked up his cold cup.

"The only dead sheep that received mention in the news or in my dispatches was the one in Cumbria, although it happened the first week of May, not during the full moon. I shall make enquiries with my colleagues in Agriculture." He sounded mildly embarrassed, as if admitting to failure, and I hastened to re-assure him.

"I shouldn't think it matters, just that if we're looking at odd deaths during full moons, especially if there is some link to Neolithic sites, then Holmes is right, we ought to take livestock into account."

He nodded, still looking abashed, and finished his breakfast. When he left, he had *Testimony* under his arm.

I studied the long list he had dictated.

Each date began with events in and around London, then dropped down into the southland before working its way north—indicating that Mycroft's mind had put the facts into order, rather than eidetically regurgitating the various newspaper articles. Although that would have been incredible enough.

I began to work my way down the pages, putting an *X* beside anything I thought worth a closer look, particularly those near ancient monuments.

Near the March full moon, three sheep had been found dead in a field in Oxfordshire, less than a mile from the Rollright Stones; the Cornish fisherman Danielson was killed, and although there was no mention of standing stones or what have you, Cornwall was so littered with prehistoric monuments, it was hardly worth noting; an old woman was discovered in a pew in a tiny village church near

Maidstone, after the Sunday morning service: Her fellow parishioners had not disturbed her, thinking she was praying, or sleeping, but it turned out she had been peacefully dead since the Friday.

In April, a shepherd in Yorkshire died from exposure, with no mention of burial mounds or ancient Druidic altars.

In May came the ewe in the chambered tomb in Orkney, and although it was mildly interesting that two sheep had died near Neolithic monuments in the same month, I anticipated that any report from Mycroft's agricultural colleague would give me a few dozen more: Sheep and standing stones both tend to be found in desolate stretches of land, for similar reasons: Valuable farmland would have been put under the plough already, with any inconvenient stones broken down and carted off for the farmer's use.

June saw the death of Fiona Cartwright at Cerne Abbas, a full moon, but the moon was a week past full when the summer solstice clash of opposing beliefs erupted at Stonehenge.

July was noteworthy for the largest number of events, possibly because with the long days and a stretch of warm weather, more people were out and about. There were no fewer than three injuries along Hadrian's Wall at the full moon, because (according to Mycroft) one of the local tourist agencies had decided to sponsor night rambles along the wall, with catastrophic results. None of the walkers had died, but one was still in hospital with a head injury, and it was not yet known whether he had fallen or been attacked. On the morning of 17 July, blood was found spattered across the altar of the Kirkwall cathedral in the Orkneys, although when no body showed up to go with the blood, it was decided that a cat had brought its prey inside for a sacrilegious meal. I noted that this was the second mention of the Orkney Islands, but what I found more interesting was the idea of an Orkney cathedral in the first place: a grandiose image for a remote dot of land.

August was noteworthy for the death of Yolanda Adler at the Wilmington Giant; there had been other incidents scattered across the country, but the only likely fatality had taken place the Tuesday before the full moon, a man who celebrated the loss of his job by going up to a remote site in the Yorkshire moors to slit his wrists. I made note of this one, to find details not contained in Mycroft's newspapers.

While I was pushing the multitude of incidents around in my mind and wondering how best to investigate any links, the telephone rang. The housekeeper picked it up, then I heard her say my name.

It was Holmes, and although his voice was all but incomprehensible with distance, my heart jumped with the reassurance that he was safe.

"Russell, is that you? Thank goodness, it's taken me an hour to convince the operator that I did in fact require a trunk call. Is there any word of Damian?"

"None, although the morning papers are baying after him."

"I've seen. I'm on my way to Stonehenge, and then—"

"Holmes, before we're cut off, let me tell you what Mycroft and I have been looking at." I gave him a quick outline of sixteen of what I deemed the most likely incidents, from the three sheep at the Rollright Stones to the Yorkshire suicide.

At the end of it, the line crackled for several seconds, alarming me that he had not heard most of my recitation, but then his voice came into my ear.

"Thank you, Russell, I shall see how many of those I can investigate over the next days, beginning with Stonehenge. I've been to see the agency in Poole, which is a fairly low-end affair, and will post their description of—"

The ear-piece went dead. I lingered at the table, shuffling papers and reading the newspaper, but eventually I gave up and asked Mrs Cowper to call me from the bath if he came through again. When I had dressed, I took my hat and bag and went to tell her that if Holmes rang, she should simply write down what he told her.

"Very well, ma'am," she said. "Did you want me to tell him about the letter?"

"What letter is that?"

It had come while I was in the bath, thin paper and a post office pen, sent first to Sussex, then re-addressed to London in Mrs

Hudson's writing. The franking showed it had been processed in London on Saturday morning. There was no return address and I did not recognise the hand, but I tore it open and read:

Friday evening, 15th

Dear Father,

I have received a message from Yolanda to say that she and Estelle are with friends in the country, and that she hopes I will join them there. I apologise for getting the wind up so and hauling you from your needed rest in Sussex. I ought to have known that it was merely Yolanda being her sweet and maddening self. I can only hope this reaches you before you have spent too much more energy on the paper chase I've laid you.

I will not apologise, however, for having got to know you somewhat during the past days, even under such trying circumstances. I had anticipated—this will be no surprise to you—that matters between us might be less congenial than in fact they turned out to be. When things settle somewhat, I shall be back into touch and we can begin afresh, with a proper meeting and introductions all around. I can only trust that the manner in which you "met" Yolanda will not overly influence your future relations with her.

D

P.S. You were right about my mother. She was an extraordinary woman, and she had a lovely laugh.

I sat down, and read it again.

Then I took off my hat, and read the letter a third time, slowly.

Written Friday, picked up from a letter box Saturday, arrived in Sussex late on Monday, back into the post there on Tuesday, and thus to London.

At last, I told myself, a piece of evidence supporting Damian's innocence.

Or, was it? Could this letter be the work of a very clever villain, laying a false trail?

Cold facts and impartiality pointed out the two possibilities: One, on Friday afternoon Damian Adler was in London, writing a graceful apology to his father before reuniting with his wife and child. Or two, on Friday afternoon, an associate of Damian Adler's had posted a previously written letter to lay the groundwork for an alibi.

If this letter was the work of a villain, then he was not only immensely clever (and Damian was certainly that) but highly practiced: Holmes himself could not have composed a more disarming note.

No, this proved nothing.

I looked at the silent telephone, cursing the poor timing of this missive's arrival, then thought of how it might change my plans for the day.

Today was Wednesday, with its regular evening meeting marching through the weeks of Millicent Dunworthy's desk-diary. If the police had not already shown Yolanda's photograph to the railway personnel in Eastbourne, Polegate, and Seaford, asking if she had passed through on Friday, and with whom, then this letter made it ever more urgent that I do so.

However, travelling to three towns in Sussex would put me back in London too late to follow Miss Dunworthy to her meeting. I could not go south today.

It was on the edge of my tongue to add to my message for Holmes, but the letter was not the sort of thing I wished to convey through the offices of Mrs Cowper—neither the message that his son had written to say he was safe, nor the equally likely message that his son was in danger.

Instead, I put the letter back in its envelope, put my hat back on my head, and went out to hunt down a maid, a chemist, and a provider of high-class picnics.

The Adlers' maid, Sally Blalock, told me little about the Adlers that I could not have guessed (were guessing permissible in the vicinity of Holmes). Yolanda was a woman of whims and peculiar habits

("The things that family eats!" Sally declared. "Garlic, in everything! And Missus Adler doesn't touch meat, can you imagine? How can a person survive on nuts and such?") and even more peculiar interests, fond of the child but not permitting child-care to interfere with the important matters of her life. Nannies came and nannies went—three of them inside six months, lost through odd foods and peculiar attitudes concerning discipline and education—and only her husband's firm insistence prevented Mrs Adler from dragging Estelle to Spiritualist meetings, interminable lectures from the Vedanta Society, and week-end spiritual courses in Yoga or Numerology or Egyptian Meditation, whatever that might be.

Not that her husband kept her from her interests—far from it. He encouraged her, merely requiring her to arrange for some appropriate care for Estelle before Yolanda went off to Cambridge or Surrey. For short meetings, that was generally the maid; for longer absences, it was often Damian himself.

"He doesn't mind, I don't mean to say that, he doesn't at all, it's just that he's an artist, you know? An Important Artist, and how can a man be expected to make his paintings with a child underfoot? And 'Stella's a lovely child, I don't mean to say she isn't, bright and usually friendly, but that little girl does have a mind of her own, and if she doesn't want to sit quietly and play with her dollies, she will not be jollied along, which means that he doesn't get too much work done when his wife's away, as you might guess."

Husband and wife seemed to be on friendly terms ("I don't mean to say otherwise, if you see what I mean?"), although there was the occasional disagreement and some shouting, and from time to time the missus would pick something up and throw it at the wall—or at Damian—but he'd never respond in type. She'd never seen Damian hit or even threaten his wife, he just would look tired—"resigned, like, you know what I mean?"—and return to his studio.

Judging by how the young woman talked about her employers, Yolanda was unaccustomed to servants, and thus alternated between overbearing and over-solicitous. Damian was more natural—"ever so nice, like"—but drew clear lines, not permitting Sally to set foot into his studio, for example, and remonstrating with her when she became distracted by a gentleman friend in the park one day, and let Estelle wander. Another man would have fired her outright, and she and I both knew it.

She had spoken with the police, and told me what she had already told them, which was essentially the same tale Damian had given us: Friday's missing wife and Saturday's discovered letter. Sally had not been to the house since the police had taken possession on Sunday, so she could not say if her employers had returned.

When I left, she asked if I thought she should be looking for another position. I could only say that I did not know.

The chemist was less forthcoming. He did not think he ought to talk about prescriptions he had filled for others, not without their permission. So I took out the letter I'd written that morning, in a hand that resembled the writing in Millicent Dunworthy's desk, and repeated my tale: Aunt Millicent's accident, upending the "Mixture" into a basin of soapy water; her need for the prescription before she left with the church group to Bognor tomorrow, but her inability to get free from work; hence the letter.

If he had her telephone number at work, I should have to make a quick escape, but he did not, and clearly, he did not know her handwriting well enough to tell it from mine.

Grumbling, he filled and labelled a bottle, took my money, and declared that this would not be permitted again.

Nodding meekly, I committed a criminal act in his ledger and left. On the street, I took the box of cachets from the brown paper wrapper: Veronal, a powerful barbiturate. There had been none in her medicine cabinet; however, ten or fifteen grains of this would be just the thing to knock out a woman, preparatory to murder.

The hardest challenge would be Fortnum and Mason, where the customer is king and information is never freely bandied. If I could not prise what I needed out of them, I should have to pass the task to a certain friend, whose title would have the staff scraping the floor in their eagerness to serve. I wanted to avoid bringing him in, if I could manage on my own—the fewer who knew of the tie between Holmes and The Addler, the better, and this particular amateur sleuth would put the whole picture together in a flash.

So I presented myself before the desk where picnic baskets might be ordered, and began talking in my most breathless and aristocratic manner.

"There's this garden party, early next month, you see? And we could have the usual fizz and caviar, but really, where's the fun in that?" I blinked my wide blue eyes, and the gentleman could only agree. "So a friend, well, I suppose the secretary of a friend, but what does that matter? This friend's secretary—her name is Millicent, Millicent Dunworthy, isn't that extraordinary—she happened to order a picnic basket and then the two people it was originally intended for, something came up, who knows, and so she had the basket out on the desk, you see, for people to help themselves, because why let good food spoil? And I'd been out all night with Poppy—you know Poppy, you help with all her parties—and we stopped off to see my friend on the way home, and here was this open basket and I was famished, absolutely raving famished, so I had this little crusty thingmabob that was really quite, quite nice, and later when I was thinking about this garden party I'm doing I said to myself, Ivy—that's my name, you see— Ivy, that crusty whatsit would be just the thing. So I doddled along to talk to you about the chance of finding out what that thingmabob was, and can we maybe order two hundred or so of them? And the rest of the baskets, of course, one for each. And if you could put some nice things like peaches and a really good fizz and perhaps quails' eggs or something?"

I blinked, waiting for him to pick his way through the fusillade of words, but he caught the idea of two hundred very expensive picnic baskets the moment it flew past him, and he smiled.

He brought out the order book, located the name Dunworthy on the Monday previous, and produced a brochure which would tell me precisely what had been in the basket: *The Vegetarian Epicure*, it was called.

My eye ran down the description, searching for anything that might qualify as the desired morsel, when near the bottom it caught on an item that made me blink.

"Good heavens," I said involuntarily.

"Pardon?"

"Oh, nothing, I just . . ." I pulled myself together and manufactured a frown. "You know, it wasn't Monday I saw the basket and tasted the crusty widgets, I'm sure it wasn't."

"No, madam, it was probably on Friday. The order was made on the Monday, but the lady specified that it would be picked up by her brother on the Friday."

I looked up, startled. "Her brother?"

"Well, I assumed so. The name was Dunworthy. Perhaps I was mistaken. I thought she was considerably older than he, but then of course—"

"Oh, her brother, yes. Tall young fellow, long hair—an artistic type?"

"No," he said slowly. "He was in his early forties, with ordinary hair. Not at all what I should call 'artistic.' He had a scar near his eye," he volunteered, laying a finger next to his left eye.

"Oh, *him*," I said. "Her *other* brother. I always forget about him, I've only met him the once. Did he have his wife with him? Pretty little Chinese woman?"

"I didn't see anyone answering that description. Might I—"

But before he could ask me why I was so interested in the brothers of a friend's secretary, I said, "But if they had *that* basket, then *what* could it have been I tasted?"

He perused the list of contents before asking tentatively if it might not have been the strawberry tartlets, although clearly he'd been looking for something rather more exotic that had attracted my palate.

"Oh, exactly! You clever man, it must have been those! Thank you for reading my mind, you have *saved* my entire party from the touch of the bourgeois. Shall I have my secretary telephone to you with the details? Yes, that's what I'll do, she's so much better than I, and now that I know what it was that put you in mind . . ." To his confusion, I was still talking as I went out of the door, the brochure firmly in hand.

He might have been even more confused had he seen me come to a halt on the street outside, to look again at the brochure. Yes, I had read it aright: Included with the nut pâté and three flavours of cheese for afters was a packet of almond-and-oat biscuits, from Italy.

A biscuit packet that currently lay on the work-table in Holmes' laboratory in Sussex, awaiting his attentions.

So: A clean-cut man in his forties, with a scar beside his left eye, whose name was almost certainly not Dunworthy. Not only did this description in no way fit Damian Adler, it sounded like the man seen walking with Damian up Regent Street, the last time Damian was seen.

Some day, I reflected, we should have to invent a means of actually locating a person based on a finger-print, as photographs were circulated to police departments now. Until that day, the prints a villain left behind were useful primarily in court, a nail of absolute proof in his coffin.

The biscuit wrapper would have to wait in Sussex, until we had a print to compare to it.

Chapter Twenty-nine

The Gods (1): Man teaches by story, the distillation of
his wisdom and knowledge. The earliest stories are about
the Gods, beings of inhuman strength and morality,
yet also stupid, gullible, and greedy. The extremes of the
Gods are where the lessons lie, whether it be
Greek heroism or Norse trickery.
Testimony, III:3

BEFORE LEAVING MYCROFT'S FLAT THAT MORNING, I
had assembled a burglar's kit ranging from sandwiches to
steel jemmy, wrapping the tools inside a dark shirt and trousers and
tucking in a pair of head-scarfs—one bright red-and-white checked
cotton, the other the sheerest silk in a subdued blue-green design—
then placing the whole in an ordinary shopping bag. I had deposited
the bag with the Left Luggage office at Paddington, knowing that
dragging it around all day would tempt me to jettison some if not all
of its weight.

I went to Paddington now to retrieve it, then crossed town on the Underground to the accountants' office that had filled the "income" column of Millicent Dunworthy's personal ledger during recent months.

It was a street that had, once upon a time, been a high street, in a building that began its life, three centuries earlier, as a coaching inn.

The income listed in the ledger indicated a full working week. Since she had taken off most of the previous week's Monday to buy a frock, shoes, and picnic basket for Yolanda's rendezvous with death, I thought it unlikely that she would miss another day this soon.

And I was right, she was there, her desk clearly visible from the front window. I found a café and had a coffee, then went into the booksellers' next door and spent some time with the new fiction at the front window. A book called *A Passage to India* so caught my attention that I nearly missed Miss Dunworthy's exit from the office across the way; when I looked up from the page, she was down the street and walking fast. I dropped the book and hurried after her, the checked scarf wrapped prominently around the brim of my hat.

But she was merely going to the nearest bus stop. I slowed to a more casual gait and followed, head averted, trying to decide if she was the sort of woman who would climb to the upper level of the bus. If so, it would be difficult to hide from her. If not, I might manage to duck quickly up the stairs without her seeing me.

And then what—leap from an upper window, when I saw her get off?

Yes, if it came to that.

Or I could engage a taxi now, and manufacture some story that justified following a city bus as it made its halting way through the town.

A bus approached, its number identifying it as a route that meandered far out into the suburbs. Millicent Dunworthy stepped forward, and I pressed closer in her direction, slumping to reduce my height beneath the level of the gentlemen's hats and taking care to keep a lamp-post between us.

She got on, and moved towards the front. I wormed my way into the queue, bought my ticket, and trotted up the stairs.

It took several stops before I could claim a window seat with a view of the disembarking passengers, but by employing sharp elbows and a winsome smile, I beat an old woman out of her choice. Ignoring her glare, I removed the bright scarf from my hat and pushed it into the shopping bag on my lap.

We travelled through endless London suburbs, with scores of stops and a constant flux of passengers, and still Miss Dunworthy did not appear below. I started to wonder if perhaps she had removed her hat—or changed her garments entirely, as I was equipped to do? Had she spotted me, and slipped past when I was trapped away from the windows?

The bus churned on, with ever fewer passengers. Solid terraces gave way to groups of houses, then individual semi-detached dwellings. The first field appeared, and another cluster of houses, and finally, when I was the only person on the top of the bus, we stopped again, and Millicent Dunworthy climbed down. She turned to exchange a greeting with the conductor—they sounded like old friends—and I ducked down. Had she seen my head so quickly vanish from sight? When the bus started up again, I risked a glance: To my relief, she was not staring after us in puzzlement, but had set off in the other direction, beside a high brick wall with heavy vegetation inside. The wall was not a perfect rectangle, but left the road at odd angles to encircle an isolated country house that had no-one overlooking it.

Just what I should want, were I up to no good.

I wound down the stairs and told the conductor that I would get off at his next stop, which proved to be the village centre, half a mile down the road. I strode up the row of shops as if certain of my destination, but in fact trying to decide: linger here until dusk and risk missing something at the house, or go back and chance being seen?

A sign on the other side of the high street decided me: *Estate Agent*, it offered; *Properties to Let*.

The office was about to close, it being ten minutes to six, but I slipped in, unobtrusively deposited my bag on a chair near the doorway, and walked up to the man behind the desk, my hand already out.

"I'm sorry, miss—" he began, but he got no further.

Really, what could he do, faced with an enthusiastic young lady who pumped his hand and declared that he was just what she'd been looking for, she was the secretary to Lady Radston-Pompffrey who was looking for a large house to let for her American niece and family, who for some odd Colonial reason wished a place that felt as if it were in the country whilst at the same time they could be in Town without bother, and this appeared to be precisely the sort of area Lady R-P would approve.

At the thought of what finding a large house for me could do to his monthly income, the gentleman settled back into his chair, apologised that he couldn't offer me a cup of tea but his assistant had already gone home, and took out his pencil to note the details of what the good Lady wanted for her American niece.

Interestingly enough, what this fictional aristocrat wished matched quite closely what I had seen of the house behind the tall brick walls. His face fell.

"Ah, well, I'm sorry you didn't come in last summer, we could have helped you there. Yes, I know the house you mean, and in point of fact, I acted as agent for it—the house is now under a two-year lease, not due to expire until November of 'twenty-five. However, I'm sure we can find—"

"November, you say? Do you suppose the tenants might have tired of it by now? Perhaps I should pop in and ask them."

"No. I mean to say, I wouldn't recommend that, they made it quite clear that they were looking for privacy."

"Ooh, how mysterious. Local folk?"

"A gentleman from overseas, I understand, although his agent was local. They hold meetings there, I think it's one of these new-fangled religious groups."

"Or perhaps they're Naturists, you know, prancing about the garden in the nude." That served to distract him. "Have you met the man? I wonder if I know him? Lady R-P dabbles in Tarot and Spiritualism," I confided.

"Er, sorry? Met him, no—saw him once, nice-looking fellow, but I shouldn't think . . ."

"Do you have his agent's name?" I asked, thinking, *Please don't make me break in and go through your books.*

"Gunderson," he answered absently. "Shady character, that one.

Look, I've noticed ladies going into the property from time to time. You don't actually suppose they—"

"I can certainly find out for you, through Lady R-P's friends. Gunderson, you say?"

"That's right. I can't remember his first name, offhand. . . ."

"Perhaps there's a file?" I suggested.

He instantly stood up and went to his cabinets, coming back with a thin file that he opened on the desk—the poor man did not at all care for the idea of nude orgies taking place on a property for which he was responsible.

"There, Marcus Gunderson, although the address he had is that of an hotel."

I looked over the paper. "You didn't ask for any personal recommendations?"

"He said his employer was from overseas, and didn't want to wait for an exchange of letters. But the bank draught he gave me for the first year's hire cleared with no problem, and the house had stood empty far too long, the furnishings were suffering. So I let him have it."

"It was furnished, then?"

"Completely. Well, such as it was. The old lady who owned it died and there's a question about inheritance, so I was ordered to find a tenant until they can settle things legally."

I wrote down the names and the details of hotel and bank, but there was little to go on.

Not expecting anything more, I said, "Can you tell me anything about the man you think might be behind this Gunderson chap? For Lady R-P's friends, that is—perhaps they'll know what he's up to."

"As I said, I never met him properly, but I've seen him driving through the village once or twice with Mr Gunderson. He's a tidy-looking gentleman of perhaps forty, dark hair, clean shaven."

"Well, thank—"

"Oh, and he may have a scar on his face."

I looked at him, then raised my left hand and drew a line down from the outer corner of my eye. "Here?"

"That's right—so you do know him?"

"Not yet," I said.

"But you know of him—so tell me, is there anything—"

"Absolutely not," I said. The last thing I needed was for this earnest estate agent to thrust his nose into things. "He's absolutely straight, but as you know, very private, extremely shy, in fact. He's a—an inventor, and you can imagine how they are—he's been known to move out of a house overnight if strangers poke into his business."

The relieved estate agent, not questioning that my aristocratic employer should know a reclusive inventor, hastened to assure me that he wouldn't dream of disturbing the gentleman.

I thanked him and said that, if he wanted to put together a list of appropriate residences, I should be by in a day or two to look at them. I retrieved my bag of burglary tools, and left.

It was just after six; the brick wall around the house was too exposed for me to risk lurking there by daylight, with bare fields on three sides and a house with brutally manicured hedges across the way.

I walked up the high street to a likely-looking inn, where I ate a surprisingly interesting meal while staring out of the tiny leaded windows facing the street. Four cars entered the gates through the brick wall, just before eight o'clock, followed by a group of three women on foot who disembarked at the bus stop. I paid and asked the way to the inn's facilities, where I changed into the dark clothing I had brought.

When dusk was drawing in, I walked through the field alongside the wall. When I was certain no eyes followed, I clambered over it, to drop down silently into the garden beyond.

As I let go, I was struck by the oddest feeling, that Holmes, somewhere, was doing precisely the same thing.

Chapter Thirty

The Gods (2): The Power of a story lies in the extremes: Hero Odysseus can be cruel and low-handed; the cowardly cheat Loki is brother to Woden and brings Thor the great hammer. The lessons of myths are not on the surface, but there for those willing to sit at the Gods' feet and learn. Thus this Testimony of one man's voyage to Power.

Testimony, III:3

THE GARDEN WAS AS UNTENDED AS IT HAD AP-peared from without, an unremitting tangle of decades-old rhododendrons against the near-dark sky. I listened, for guards or dogs, then cautiously pressed forward: As I did so, I recalled the eyes of the Green Man glittering from Damian's canvas, and had to push away the sensation that crept down the back of my neck.

Eventually, the wall of branches parted, opening onto what had once been the lawns. Still no dogs or protesting shouts, so I walked in the direction of the lights.

The walls might have described an idiosyncratic shape across the countryside, but the house they contained was one of those sturdy boxes beloved of the Victorian nouveau-riche, wanting an impressive lump of brick in which to display their large paintings and simpering daughters to others in their class. The windows in what I supposed was the drawing room, on the ground floor near the front door, were brightly lit, and I could hear a low murmur of voices. The room above it was not only lit, the windows were open. They were the up-and-down, double-hung sort, rather than shutter-style, which might halve the sound that could pass through, but I should have to take care to walk softly, and not step into the light cast below.

Forty feet from the house, my shoes touched gravel; off to the left I caught the reflection off polished metal and window-glass: Several motor-cars were parked there. I circled the house in the other direction until the grass resumed underfoot, allowing me to get close to its walls.

The drawing room windows, also open to the night but behind curtains, had been well off the ground. I took a detour into the out-houses in the yard at the back, and found what I had hoped in the sec-ond one: a large bucket with sturdy sides, although its bottom was a bit dubious.

Bucket in hand, I walked soft-footed back up the neglected garden-beds to the lighted rooms at the front. Long before I came near, I could hear voices, overlapping chatter from a mixed group of men and women. I settled the bucket top into the baked earth, let my kit slide to the ground beside it, and cautiously balanced myself on the metal rims.

If I went onto my toes, I could see a narrow slice of the room through a space in the centre of curtains so old, their lining showed cracks and tears. What I saw amounted to little more than movement and sparkle: the back of a head here, a hand with a glass half-full of greenish liquid there. It was not worth the leg-strain, so I lowered my-self back to the rims and listened to what sounded like a group of ten or twelve, more than half of them women. The murmur I heard earlier had begun to pick up, in volume and in speed.

I bent my head, concentrating on the sounds. With an effort I could unpick the threads of conversation to reveal that they were talk-ing about a person:

"—think she would have known that—"

"—charming, really, but I always wondered about—"

"—can't have had anything to do with it, can he?"

"—know artists, there's no telling—"

They were talking about Yolanda's death, and Damian's involvement. Considering that they had all been here by eight o'clock and it was now half past, they were past the first stage of discussing their shock and sadness and well into the I-told-you-so and she-brought-it-on-herself stage. It was, I decided, a process furthered by the liquid in their glasses, which was not the fruit punch it looked like—or if it was, then someone had spiked it. Laughter rose, was cut off, and then started again a few minutes later; this time it was not stifled. Soon, the talk had left Yolanda entirely and was about handbags, school tuition, a sister's baby, and horse-racing; soon, twelve people were sounding like twice that number.

Nine o'clock approached; the voices grew ever merrier; my ankles grew ever tireder. I stepped down from the bucket to ease the strain of the unnatural pose, and rested my shoulders against the brick under the window, hearing not one thing of any interest.

Then the village clock struck nine, and in moments, the noise from within grew to a crescendo that I feared meant they were about to take their leave, until I realised that to the contrary, they were greeting a newcomer.

No-one had come down the gravel drive, on foot or wheel, which meant that the new arrival had entered from the house itself. I craned to peer through the slit, but the man who belonged to the voice that was now dominating the room had his back to me. All I could see were three individuals with identical rapt expressions.

I bent to my bag and took out the sheer silk mottled scarf, tying it loosely around my entire head. With the danger of reflection off my spectacles thus lessened, I patted around until I found a twig, then climbed back up on the bucket and stretched out as far as I could reach. The twig caught in the soft lining, allowing me to cautiously ease the curtain a fraction of an inch to one side.

There were now nearly two inches of crack between the fabric, and the speaker's back came into view.

Or, partly into view. He was a stocky man with a few grey threads in his dark hair, wearing an expensively cut black suit. When he turned to the right a little, I caught a glimpse of English skin darkened by the tropics. His voice was low and compelling, a perfect blend of friendship and authority. He was from the north originally, a touch of Scots buried under English and overlaid by a stronger version of the clipped tones I had heard in Damian's voice.

Who are you? I asked. *And what are you doing in Damian Adler's life?*

I had no doubt at all: This was The Master.

He greeted his followers, thanked them for their work during the past weeks, and apologised for his recent absences. He singled out "our sister Millicent," for her especial efforts, and I stretched around until she came into view, pink and pleased. He then spoke about Yolanda, another "sister," expressing his grief over her death and his hope that the Circle, and the Children as a whole, would only be strengthened by having known her.

He sounded insincere to me, but then, I was prepared for insincerity: Religion has proved the refuge of so many scoundrels, one begins by doubting, and waits to be proven wrong.

The Master spoke for ten or twelve minutes, most of it touching lightly on phrases and images from *Testimony,* causing his admirers to nod their heads in appreciation.

Nothing that he said could be in the least construed as information. All his ideas, and many of his phrases, reflected the book that I could see lying open on an altar between two candelabra set with black candles. It might as well have been Millicent Dunworthy reading aloud, but for his compelling presence.

Even that, I found hard to understand. Perhaps I was simply outside his gaze and immune to the timbre of his voice, but the people in the room were not. They hung on every syllable, their pupils dark as if aroused, smiling obediently at any faint touch of cleverness or humour in his words. From my perch, I watched his effects on five congregants: Millicent Dunworthy was one, wearing a dull green linen dress that did nothing for her complexion, and with her two women in their fifties, one thin, one stout, both in flowered frocks—the stout one, I realised, was the woman whom I'd imagined as a nurse, who with her brother had set up the altar on Saturday night. Slightly apart from them stood the sharp-nosed woman I had spoken with, wearing a skirt and tailored blouse, her hair waved in a fashion that had been popular ten years earlier. Beside her was a stout, red-faced man in his fifties wearing a suit and waistcoat far too warm for the room. Millicent, the nurse, and the sharp-nosed woman all wore the gold rings on their right hands.

I wondered if any of them also had tattoos on their stomachs.

Then I saw a sixth listener, in the dim back corner, and wondered that I had taken so long to pick him out—this man did not belong in the same room as the others. He was big all over in a grey summer-weight suit that was slightly loose in the body but snug over his wide shoulders and heavy thighs; his face would have looked more at home above a convict's checks.

He may have imagined that his thoughts were invisible, hidden from the believers behind a straight face. But one did not need a bright light to know that there would be scorn in his eyes and a curl to his lips as he surveyed the backs of these people worshipping the man in the black suit. His very stance, leaning against the glass-fronted bookshelves, shouted his superiority and contempt. He looked like the bodyguard of a mobster; he looked the very definition of *shady character*.

Marcus Gunderson?

My leg muscles were quivering, and now the meeting began to break up—or no, merely changing. The group deposited their empty glasses on nearby tables, then moved towards the chairs that had been set up to face the altar. The black back walked away, but I stretched a fraction higher, because in a moment, he would turn to face them, and me.

"YAPYAPYAP!" exploded through the night, and my heart leapt along with my body. My shoes lost their precarious hold on the bucket rims and I fell, onto the shrubs with one foot inside the rotten bucket. My fall set off an even louder volley of yelps from somewhere in the vicinity of my heels.

"Bubbles!" came a woman's cry from within. I ripped the bucket from my foot and kicked soil over its tell-tale imprint, then snatched up bucket and bag and sprinted for the back of the house, Bubbles roaring hysterically along behind me.

At the out-houses, I kicked open the shed door, grabbed the madly shrieking handful of fur, and tossed it in, drawing the door shut behind it. With luck they would think that Bubbles had been chasing a rat and been trapped inside.

Then I disappeared into the night, moving at a fast limp.

Some investigator: routed by a lap-dog named Bubbles.

My ankle felt as if I'd stepped into a bear trap, but a thorough feel around my nearly-dry trouser leg reassured me that I might die of tetanus, but not from blood loss.

From deep in the rhododendrons, I watched people begin to stream out of the door and around the house. The stout woman in the flowered dress pressed to the fore, attracted by the sounds of distress from the back; eventually a light went on over the yard; the barking stopped. They were back there for some time, no doubt debating the puzzle, before returning to the house.

I was not surprised when a short time later, three people came out of the front door, including the woman, her dog Bubbles, and the man who looked like her brother. They climbed into a car and drove away, veering onto the grassy verge and over-correcting again. Others followed, two and three at a time.

I stayed where I was. Sure enough, when everyone else had gone, two men, The Master and his muscle, came out with a torch to examine the ground under the window. My brief kick was not enough to cover the signs completely by daylight, although I hoped the torch might not pick them out, and indeed, there seemed no consensus of opinion that there had been a spy outside.

They went in the house. I sat down beside my bag, to see what developed.

Nothing happened for some time, except that the upstairs room drew its curtains against the night. I wanted badly to creep back up to the house, but something about the big man's attitude suggested that he was not misled by a scatter of kicked soil, and that he would be expecting a second approach.

So until the lights went out and stayed out for a long time, I would stay where I was.

The village church bells ceased ringing at ten o'clock. Half an hour later, with no warning, light spilt out of the front door and three men came down the steps, carrying luggage.

Except that one of them, a tall, slim man with a full beard who had not been with the others earlier, turned, as if to cast a last look at a beloved home. He faced the house and its light for five long seconds, plenty of time for me to identify him, and to see that what he held to his chest was not a suit-case, but a sleeping child. Plenty of time to change everything.

Before I could react, the man in the black suit spoke, and Damian climbed into the car; The Master got behind the wheel.

I was on my feet, the shout in my throat strangling as I noticed the stance of the man in the grey suit: The reason his suit-coat had been cut loosely was because it concealed a hand-gun.

I waited until he, too, got inside the motor, and then I sprinted along the grass towards the drive to intercept them. The engine turned over and caught, and the driver put it into gear, spewing gravel behind him with the speed of his start. I ran, but reached the drive too late to catch anything but the last two digits of his number plate.

With no motor-car, not even so much as a bicycle, there was little point in charging after them. Instead, I turned back to the house, used my pick-locks, and slipped inside. Then, I listened.

How is one convinced that a house is empty? From the lack of sound, or vibration? Smell, perhaps, that most subtle of the senses? How is one convinced of a man's innocence—against all fact and rationality—from a man's arms around his child, and five seconds of his face turned to the lamp-light?

The language of bees is not the only great mystery of communication.

Certainly this house felt empty: I caught no vibration of motion, and the only noise was my own heart. I found the telephone, and rang

Mycroft: If any man in England could instigate a hunt for a car, it would be he.

I gave him the numbers, description, the information that the man in the front passenger seat had a pistol, and a quick synopsis of what I had discovered that day; then I went to search the house.

A quick survey downstairs confirmed the emptiness of the rooms, all of which except the drawing room were filled with dull, dusty furniture that looked as if no-one had used it for years. The kitchen had a new-looking ice-box and food on its shelves, with the sorts of biscuits and juices that men might stock when catering for a small child.

Upstairs, I went directly to the corner room with the open windows, and stood looking in at where Damian Adler had been hidden for the past five days: two iron bedsteads, wardrobe with a time-speckled mirror, a chest of drawers missing several handles, and an armchair draped with a throw-rug. The carpet on the floor was so worn, one could no longer discern its original pattern, or even colour. Out of place amidst the ancient furniture was a work-table fashioned from a door on trestles, now littered with personal items and art supplies. I recognised Damian's cravat, tossed over the back of an old dining-room chair, and there could be no doubt whose tumble of new brushes and nearly full paint-tubes those were, or who had done those drawings—although some were by the hand of a child, in bright wax crayon. The same child who had been taken from that smaller, still-rumpled bed, whose new-looking teddy bear lay abandoned among the bed-clothes, whose bright red Chinese slipper lay beside my foot—fallen off as she was carried through the door by her fleeing father.

I bent to pick up the slipper, then froze.

Air had brushed my skin, the briefest of touches. The air currents in the house had altered, just for an instant; had I not been standing in the doorway with an open window across from me, I should not have noticed it.

I strained to hear movement from below. Nothing: four minutes, five—and then a faint creak from the direction of the old, dry staircase, instantly stifled.

I eased the knife from my boot scabbard and straightened slowly; he and I both waited for the other to betray ourselves.

I cast a glance at the window: How many creaks in the fifteen feet of floorboard between me and it? How long would it take the big man to sprint up the stairs—or, back down the hallway and out of the front door—and take aim at my fleeing back?

The knife hilt grew warm in my hand, then damp. I moved it briefly to my right hand to wipe my palm, then took it back, my fingers kneading it nervously.

It is such an easy thing, to become prey. Especially for a woman, for whom biology and nurture conspire to encourage a sense of victimhood. When terror sweeps through the veins, we become rabbits, cowering in a corner with our eyes closed, hoping for invisibility. And a large man with a gun is a truly terrifying thing. I regretted coming, berated myself for not bringing someone with me; stood helpless, waiting for my death to come up the stairs. Bad judgment yet again, to face a gun with nothing but a sweaty-handled throwing knife.

I felt a ghostly slap on the back of my head, and Holmes' voice exhorting me, *Use your brain, Russell, it's the only weapon that counts.*

With a lurch, my mind dragged itself out of the spin into panic, my eyes casting about wildly for alternatives to a bullet.

Knife, yes, but this was an entire house full of deadly objects, from that neck-tie across the back of the chair to the electric lamp to the sharp pencil by my foot, and all manner of heavy objects with which to pound, pummel, and gouge a nice large target like my stalker. Heavens, if I could get him down, I could smother him with the teddy bear.

A pencil. I looked at the light-switch on the wall beside me, and stooped for the drawing implement, sliding the knife almost absently into its scabbard.

The switch was one of those with double push-plugs, currently in the ON position. I shifted around to face it (thankfully, the floor made no remark) and put my right thumb on the OFF button. Resting the pencil-point in the space between the button and its casing, I took a breath, and in one quick motion pushed the switch and snapped the lead point off in the space, effectively locking it down. The light from the hallway streamed through the door onto the window opposite.

The clamour of pounding feet—up the stairs, not down—covered my own swift steps into the lee of the chest of drawers. The doorway darkened, filled with angry man, who cursed as he fumbled and failed to work the switch. I wrapped my hand around the hair-brush I had grabbed from the chest-top, then tossed it underhand against the meeting-place of the curtains.

He heard the sound and half-saw the motion of the fabric, and leapt across the room to rip away the curtains and thrust his head and shoulders out of the window, gun aimed at the ground below.

I was already in motion, knife in one hand, snatching up Damian's cravat with the other. He heard me coming and nearly managed to extricate himself from the window before I slammed into him, knocking him half out of the room, then jerking the upper window down hard across his spine. He bellowed and shoved back hard. Glass and wood crackled, then went abruptly silent as he became aware of the tip of my knife, pressing into an exquisitely sensitive, and currently exquisitely vulnerable, part of his anatomy.

"Drop the gun," I said loudly. When he failed to respond, I twitched the knife, and his squeak was followed by a thud from the flower bed below. "Now show me your right hand."

His body tensed to brace himself against falling, and his right hand waved briefly on the other side of the cracked pane. Good enough. I wound the cravat around his ankles and snugged it into a messy but effective one-handed knot.

It took some doing to get the weight of him out from the window without permitting him freedom of motion, and he nearly had me twice, but finally, with his belt, three neck-ties, and the rope-tie from a dressing gown, I had him trussed. Bleeding, enraged, and trussed.

I walked on uncertain feet over to the light-switch, and managed to unscrew the face-plate and prise out the sliver of lead. I could hear him all the while, struggling against the various bonds.

By the time I got the lights on, the worst of my reaction had subsided, and I was faced with a conundrum—not, What to do with him? because I knew what I was going to do with him, but—How do I get him to talk?

I'd seen enough of this type of man to know that he would absorb a lot of damage before opening his mouth. If I were Holmes, or Lestrade, this man would spit on my questions. I could threaten him further with the knife, but it would take a lot to convince him that a mere girl would carry out the threats.

He'd be right, too: I might be willing to damage a thug to save Holmes, but for Damian and his daughter?

The man on the floor lay still now; I could feel his eyes on my back. I circled the room slowly, letting him think about his situation. That he was neither cursing nor demanding to know who I was told me that he had more brains than his overdeveloped muscles suggested.

I looked down at the trestle table and its litter of paint and drawings, and became aware that I was looking at myself.

Not myself, as in a mirror, but a simple, flowing continuous line of ink on paper, elegant as a Japanese master. It was not a sketch, it was a finished piece, done on a sheet of dense and expensive paper. At the lower left was its title: *My Father's Wife*. It was signed Adler.

I deliberately pushed it out of my mind, and reached for one of the tubes of paint, juggling with it for a moment before laying it back on the table. I put the knife down beside it, and returned to my captive. His eyes held mixed fury and contempt, which was fine. What I needed to see there was fear.

I grabbed the lapels of his coat. He smirked, expecting me to tug and struggle against his weight, but the secretions of the adrenal gland can be turned to strength as well as fear, and I hauled him in two great backwards strides to the corner of the worn carpet, and let his head thump down against the bare boards.

"Hey! What the hell is going on here, sister?"

I went around the room, methodically piling up the furniture until the carpet was free of encumbrance.

Then I rolled him up in it.

He was cursing now, an astonishingly vicious torrent, ever more breathless. Still silent, I walked back to the table for the knife, then knelt on the floorboards beside his head. I held up the stained blade for him to study. He looked at it—he couldn't stop himself, a thin, shiny blade edged with scarlet—but he did not believe I would use it.

I didn't. Instead, my eyes watching his face, I put it to my mouth, and slowly, appreciatively, licked it clean.

It was not blood, of course, it was bright red paint from one of Damian's tubes, but it was far more effective than mere blood. I took out a handkerchief and patted my lips delicately, then slid the blade away into its scabbard.

The unexpected can be frightening. His eyes no longer held contempt.

"You shouldn't have cursed," I told him.

I could see him wrestling with the unlikeliness of that opening statement. "What?"

"If you'd held a deep breath instead, you'd have more room now. As it is, your lungs are constricted. You'll probably pass out after a while."

"Lady, you're in deep trouble."

"When is he coming back for you?"

"Any minute." I had been watching his face, and saw the lie.

"I don't think so."

"He's coming up the drive now."

"I don't think he's coming at all. Certainly not in time to save you."

"You're not going to use that knife on me."

"Of course not. I don't have to. Tell me, how's your breathing? Getting any easier? You think you'll manage until your boss comes back for you?"

The first shadow of uneasiness passed through his eyes, telling me what I needed to know.

"I don't think he's coming. And next Wednesday, when those nice people come for their meeting. Do you think they'll persist until they get into the house, or will they just knock politely and, when no-one answers, go away?"

His breathing quickly grew more laboured.

"You see? I don't need a knife. I don't need to do anything, just walk away and lock the front door behind me."

"What do you want?" He said it with more obscenity, but I overlooked the words and spoke to the question.

"Where can I find the man who just drove off and left you here?"

He told me what I could do with my question.

I sighed, and stood up. At the motion, the uneasiness returned.

"Oy," he said. "Honest, I don't know. I know what he says his name is and I know generally where he lives, but he never told me what he was doing, and he never had me go to his house."

"You've worked for him since last autumn."

"Yeah, but it's just that, working for him. I drive him around, I do things for him. He never asks me what I think or tells me anything more than what I need to know."

I moved away, and he cried out, "Wait, don't"—I was only fetching a cushion from the chair. He eyed it warily, and looked relieved when I dropped it on the boards and settled onto it.

"Tell me what you do know about him."

"And if I do?"

"I'll see to it that you don't die here. If you don't talk, I'll go away and you can take your chances that someone will hear you shouting. Oh, and I'll strap a belt around your legs first. You won't be able to roll out of the carpet."

He didn't believe that I would use the knife, but he did believe this. He talked.

His name was indeed Marcus Gunderson, and he called his boss The Reverend, a name that was half disdain and half deference. The Reverend had called himself Thomas Brothers, and all the people at his church knew him by that name, but Gunderson had helped him set up that identity back in November.

"What's his real name?"

"Dunno. Honest, I don't know."

"How did he find you?" I asked.

"There's a group run by some of the churches, helps men when they come out of nick. Find jobs and that, you know?"

"And you were freshly out of prison?"

"Four years in The Scrubs."

Wormwood Scrubs prison was aptly named for the bitterness of one's experience there. "So this Brothers presented himself as a fellow churchman willing to give a convict a second chance."

" 'S right."

"Instead of which, he gave you a second career. Did you drive a young woman down to Sussex last Friday?"

"Friday? No, he gave me the day off Friday, and the week-end."

I watched him closely, and although I could see that he was concealing some knowledge, I did not think he was lying outright.

"And tonight? He's not coming back for you, is he?"

"No."

"Then how will you catch them up?"

"I won't."

"What, he's just driving off and leaving you here?"

"If he wants me, he knows where to find me."

"I don't believe you," I said, although I thought I might.

"He's his own man. I work for him, I'm not his partner. There's a lot he doesn't tell me, there's a lot he does without me."

I couldn't see that line of questioning taking me any further— either he was lying and he would continue to lie, or he was telling me the truth. I decided to leave it, and asked him about his background; about The Reverend and his scar, and *Testimony*; about what he knew, and didn't know, and guessed. After twenty minutes or so, his answers were coming shorter, his eyes wilder as he struggled for breath.

"You got to let me out of this," he said.

"I can't do that, Marcus."

"I'll die in here, and then it'll be you that's up for murder."

"If you just relax and breathe slowly, you'll be fine."

"I can't breathe, I tell you!"

"You're probably thirsty, though, from all that dust. How about a drink?"

"Christ!"

"Tea? Beer?"

"You are a piece of work, lady!"

"Thank you."

Before I left the room, I strapped a belt around his legs, so he couldn't reverse the roll of the carpet. I wasn't gone for more than five minutes, but when I got back, he was sweating with the fear that I had abandoned him.

The string of curses he gave at my entrance was weaker than his earlier efforts. I blithely shoved the carpet tube a quarter-turn over with my foot, then held the glass of beer to his mouth. The curses stopped, and although the floor under his face was puddled with the spillage, most of the contents of the glass went down his throat.

We talked for another ten minutes, until I was satisfied both that I had as much from him as I could get, and that he was not going anywhere for a while. I undid the belt, gently kicked him along the floor until he lay limply on top of the carpet, and then went downstairs to make another phone call to Mycroft.

"I'm sorry to wake you a second time," I said, and gave him the address of the house, and the request that he find someone at Scotland Yard who could rouse Lestrade and send him here to pick up Marcus Gunderson.

"He should be unconscious for another couple of hours," I said. "I located the Veronal that Brothers probably used on Yolanda. And turnabout's fair play—it works a treat on large men, too."

Chapter Thirty-one

Magic (1): The world is an alembic writ large, where forces may be brought to bear on Elements. Elements are Power, pure and simple. The greater the Elements, the greater the Power summoned, that the man of knowledge may free and take into himself.

Testimony, III:5

L ESTRADE RANG ASKING IF YOU WERE HERE," MYCROFT greeted me the next morning. He was beheading his second egg; I had not wakened him when I got in the night before—or rather, earlier that morning. I squinted at the clock.

"Already?"

"He seemed quite determined."

"You told him I wasn't here, I trust?"

"I rarely tell direct lies to the police," he replied, then to my relief added, "I merely said that I had not seen you for some time."

"You'd think he would know, after all these years, how to listen to a Holmes."

"Oh, you may find he does. In any case, I don't think the Chief Inspector entirely believed me." He tipped his head at the window; I took a swig of the coffee Mrs Cowper had poured for me, and took up a position behind the curtains to study the street: In thirty seconds, I had him. "Damn. He's already got a man down there. I'll have to borrow Mrs Cowper's dress to get out of here."

"Disguise will not be necessary," Mycroft said. "After the last time, I thought it expedient to arrange a back door. I now have not one, but two concealed exits—one onto St James's Square, the other into Angel Court."

"Don't tell me—the entrance is behind a moving bookshelf in the study?"

"I admit, I could not resist."

I laughed, but at his next remark, my amusement died.

"I'm afraid Lestrade has also loosed the dogs on Damian." Mycroft pushed the morning paper over to me: front and centre, Damian's face. The article that went with the photograph made quite clear that The Addler was wanted for arrest, not just questioning, and should be considered dangerous.

"Dangerous?" I exclaimed. "Didn't Lestrade see the walled house last night? Didn't he question Gunderson?"

"The police saw that Damian had been there, but was no longer. And they haven't been able to question Gunderson yet; he keeps falling asleep."

"Hell," I said. The only faint hope was that the newspaper's image of Damian showed a man with freshly cut hair and a beard, trimmed back to the jaw-line; when I'd seen him last night, his hair was to the collar and his beard full.

"Am I to understand that you now entertain the possibility of Damian's innocence?" Mycroft asked.

"There were no newspapers," I blurted. He raised an eyebrow, and I realised that I needed to be methodical about this. I began by retrieving the things I'd taken from the walled house; when I returned, Mrs Cowper laid my breakfast in front of me. When she was in the kitchen again, I went on.

"Last night was indeed a meeting of the Children of Lights' inner circle. Hmm," I said, distracted by a thought: *Circle.* Was that in some manner related to that shape they used? I shook my head and set be-fore Mycroft a sturdy capped glass jar filled with a bilious green liquid in which floated an assortment of objects that looked a bit like shoe-leather. "This is what the Circle were drinking. I found several of these bottles in the pantry—whatever those things are, the liquid they're steeping in is honey wine, despite the colour. Judging by their reac-tion, it's considerably stronger than mead. Can you have the contents analysed?"

He eased off the cork and held the bottle under his nose. "An un-conventional choice of beverage."

"Yes, but I don't know that it has any relationship with Holmes."

He set it aside; I went on.

"The man they call The Master was there—and yes, Gunderson and the estate agent agreed that he has a scar beside his eye, and yes, Gunderson was under the impression that this is the author of *Testimony*. He even helped transport the copies of *Testimony* from the printers. Unfortunately, I only caught glimpses of The Master, mostly from the back. Brothers, or whatever his name is, talked to them for a few minutes, but before he could start their services, a dog belonging to one of the Circle found me." No need to tell him that the creature would have fit into the pocket of his overcoat.

"I managed to get away from the animal, but the Circle left, and then Gunderson, Brothers, and Damian got into a car and drove away—that was the number plate I gave you. Damian was carrying a child with black hair."

"Ah, that is a relief."

"Yes. I went into the house and saw where they had been staying, but then Gunderson came back and I had to deal with him.

"But three things happened to . . . not 'change my mind,' because my mind was not made up, but let us say, shift my point of view. First, when Damian came out of the house with the child, he deliberately stood with his face to the light, as if he knew someone might be watching, and wanted to reassure us that he was fine. Second, this." I slid over the ink drawing I had found—I had gone through that room to remove anything that might link Damian to Holmes, but this particular drawing I would have taken in any event.

Mycroft brushed the crumbs from his fingers and took the heavy paper by one corner, appraising the black lines of my portrait as if analysing a finger-print.

"What does it tell you?" I asked.

He considered the question, and his answer, then laid the drawing back on the table before he replied. "This is not a drawing Damian Adler would have done even a month ago."

"Exactly!" I said, pleased that we were in agreement. It was an exquisite thing, a stirring use of delicate lines to depict strength in the subject: I did not for a moment think that I looked like the drawing, but I was very happy that Damian had imagined me so. "Holmes thought his son's mistrust of him had begun to fade, following the days they spent together. I should say this drawing indicates that Damian had a profound change of heart: If he accepts his father's wife to that degree, there could be little doubt that he accepts his father."

"It is hard to imagine that even a fine artist could feign affection so thoroughly," Mycroft agreed.

"And third, the newspapers. Damian had been in that house for days—perhaps since Friday, but certainly for long enough to ask for paints and a work-table. However, the only newspaper I found in the entire house was from Saturday. Since Monday morning the papers have been full of Yolanda's death, but if Damian has been in hiding since then, and if he has not seen a paper, he may still not know."

Mycroft's eyes went out of focus as he reviewed everything we knew, taking pieces of the case out of their pigeon-holes and comparing them. Finally, he nodded. "I am not sure I agree unreservedly, but I can see that you would be willing to move your attentions off of Damian."

Huge relief, that Mycroft saw firm foundations beneath my judgment. "However, I don't entirely understand the link between Brothers and Damian. Brothers hired Gunderson in October and started setting up the Children of Lights soon afterwards. Brothers is British—I heard him speak—but Gunderson thinks he was recently arrived, that he knew London a little but hadn't been here for some long time, certainly not since the War.

"Millicent Dunworthy was hired in December, to do a few hours of secretarial work—I didn't know that because her ledger only went back to January, and she seems to have become a convert to the Children by then. With both her and Gunderson, I should say their chief job was to function as Brothers' face. He hid behind one or the other of them for most of his transactions, from constructing a false identity to hiring a meeting hall."

"Purchasing clothing for Yolanda Adler," Mycroft suggested.

"Yes—someone will have to question Millicent Dunworthy. Now, Damian didn't get here until January, when—"

"December. They were here before Christmas."

"Really? He claimed they passed us off the coast of France."

"He told me that as well, but in fact, their ship docked on the twentieth of December. I check such things, as a matter of course."

"You knew he was lying from the beginning?"

"A man may have any number of reasons for telling a lie. In this case, I assumed it took him some time to muster his courage and approach his father. Later, when it turned out he had delayed too long, he was embarrassed to admit it."

"I suppose so." I drank more coffee, and realised that although the morning was overcast, my mood was sunny. The relief of thinking that Holmes was right and Damian was an innocent made for a rising bubble of optimism.

"Do you not wish to talk to Lestrade about this?" Mycroft asked me.

I sighed. "What do you think Holmes would want?"

"My brother would give nothing to Scotland Yard until he felt his case to be safe from their meddling."

"I was afraid you'd say that."

"However, in his absence—"

"No, we'll go along with that until he deigns to raise his head. In which case, I think I had better change my plan for today and go to Sussex."

"Is there something I can do for you here, Mary?"

"Well, we need to find Brothers' home. He didn't live in that mausoleum of a place behind walls. He and Gunderson used to meet on Chalton Street, between Euston and Phoenix roads."

He gave me a look.

"I know," I said. "Three train stations and six lines of the Underground to be had in five minutes' walk. Still—"

"—it has to be done," he finished my sentence. "I shall put a man on it."

"He has to be discreet."

"Yes."

"Sorry, of course you know that. Thank you. Tell Mrs Cowper I'm not sure if I'll make it back in time for dinner."

When I was ready, Mycroft let me out through the pivoting bookcase in his study, showed me where the candles and matches were, and told me how to work the locking mechanism from the other end. The odour of honey from the bees-wax carried me through a dim, narrow labyrinth; I came out well clear of any of Lestrade's men.

Many long hours later, I extinguished the candles and stepped back through the bookcase into the study. Mycroft spoke when I entered the sitting room, although he sat with his back to me.

"I should think you need a glass of wine. I opened one of Sherlock's bottles, if that appeals."

"No," I said, then modified the sharp response to, "I feel I've had a surfeit of honey, between one thing and another."

"A nice Bordeaux, then," he said mildly and handed me a full glass. I dropped the parcel I carried onto the table, and looked without enthusiasm at the plate he set in front of me: Mrs Cowper's cooking was not improved by two hours in a warming oven.

"Not just now, thanks," I told him. "But, in case Lestrade decides to

raid your flat looking for me, perhaps you should lock up that envelope. It contains everything I could find at home that might suggest a
link between Holmes and Damian."

When I'd got to Sussex that morning, I found that the police had
been to our house, and been stoutly repelled by Mrs Hudson.
However, if this went on for much longer, they would return, this
time with the authority to conduct a search. Now, they were welcome
to do so.

Mycroft picked up the parcel to take it away, but I said, "There is a
biscuit wrapper in there. It might be best to give that to a laboratory,
for the finger-prints."

Mycroft nodded, and took the evidence to his study, coming back
empty-handed.

"Anything from Holmes?"

He scooped up a letter from the side-board as he passed. It was addressed to him, in Holmes' writing, but opened without salutation
and in an almost telegraphic brevity.

> Wednesday, 21st
> The death of Fiona Cartwright at Cerne Abbas was
> murder, not suicide. Details when I see you.
>
> Poole employment agency describes Smythe as a middle-
> aged man wearing a good suit, dark hair and eyes, well
> spoken, a scar beside his left eye. No record of the com-
> pany he claimed to represent.
>
> Tourist charabanc to Salisbury and Stonehenge leaves
> in two minutes, I have bribed the conductor to begin with
> the latter. Have already been informed twice that I look
> like Sherlock Holmes. Kindly pray I do not have to ask you
> to stand me bail for murdering a visitor to Olde England.
>
> S

When I had finished laughing, Mycroft handed me an actual
telegram:

TO CUMBRIA AFTER DEAD RAM STOP WILL NEED
INFORMATION REGARDING ALBERT SEAFORTH OF
YORK FOUND DEAD THURSDAY LAST STOP

"How does Holmes intend to get this information from us?" I wondered.

"I took the otherwise unnecessary 'will' in the telegram to indicate that he would need it at some point, although not immediately."

"You're probably right. Still, it would be nice to let him know that Lestrade's on the war-path, so he can keep his head down."

"Sherlock tends to keep his head down in any event. I was pleased to find that you made it through the day without having hand-cuffs dropped around your wrists. Lestrade has telephoned twice more today. He sounded increasingly vexed."

"I'll ring him from a public box tomorrow, and see if I can placate him. I take it your man didn't locate Brothers, or Smythe, or whoever he is?"

"Several shop-keepers and residents thought the description sounded familiar, but without a photograph, or even a drawing, there is little to trigger memory. He will continue tomorrow, further afield."

"I had no better luck today."

I had gone immediately home, where I had offended Mrs Hudson for a third time by being unwilling to settle to a conversation or take a meal. I got what I needed and left, but no taxi driver or railway employee recognised either my photograph of Yolanda Adler or the vague description of a black-haired man with a scar next to his eye.

"However, I'm interpreting the lack of response as a positive negative: If Yolanda Adler took a train to Sussex last week, someone would have remembered her," I told Mycroft. "And Gunderson said his boss had driven the motor some time between Thursday night and Monday morning. He didn't notice the mileage, but he said it was nothing unusual for The Reverend to drive himself. I wonder if Lestrade has got any more out of him than I did?"

"The ears I have within Scotland Yard tell me no, that Gunderson is just a hireling. If he knew where Brothers and Damian had gone, he would give them up in hopes of winning some points for himself."

"They're not letting Gunderson go, are they?"

"Indications are that they will hold him, if for nothing else than the gun. Scotland Yard does not approve of felons with guns. I imagine, however, that he will have given Lestrade an adequate description of the Amazon who trussed him and poked holes in his epidermis."

"Lestrade will be steaming," I said with regret. "Apart from the search for Brothers' house, have you had any results?"

He had, clearly, been waiting for me to ask: He had been busy that day, and between what his "ears" at Scotland Yard had passed on, and what his own operative had been set to find, he had quite a bit. Reverend Thomas Brothers, newly born in November 1923, had a British passport under that name, issued four weeks later, and a sizeable bank account. His man was tracing the deposits and cheques written, but the preliminary report was that Brothers was inordinately fond of cash, even when it came to large amounts. Brothers either had a laden safe, or another account that received systematic deposits of bank notes.

However, as Gunderson had intimated, there was no record of a man named Thomas Brothers entering the country—or purchasing a house, or buying a motor-car. Mycroft had set into motion a close search through the records, looking at any middle-aged male who had come into Britain during the two months before Gunderson was hired, but that would take many days.

"I also," Mycroft told me, "took a look at our file for Aleister Crowley. Not, as you have said, that Crowley is directly related to this case, but I hoped it might suggest other avenues of investigation.

"There are certain points of similarity to *Testimony,* but I imagine those would exist between any two belief systems built around individuals who think themselves gods. One thing did come to my attention: Crowley was in Shanghai for a brief time, in 1906. He tells a story concerning a delay there that kept him from arriving in San Francisco, in April of that year."

I looked up, startled. "The earthquake and fire?"

"He claimed that but for the Shanghai delay, he would have been there at the time."

"You're suggesting that when *Testimony* says the narrator 'preserved the mortal life of the Guide from flames and the turmoil of an angry earth,' he is talking about Crowley and San Francisco?"

"It is one possibility. The other item of interest concerns the man's claim of a simultaneous meteor and comet. My informant at the Royal Astronomical Society suggests that, if we are looking for the birth date of a middle-aged man, the closest one may come is August and September of 1882. The Perseids were over by the time the Great September Comet was noticed on the first of September, but it reached its maximum brightness so quickly, it requires no great stretch of the imagination to claim that it was in the sky earlier."

"So we could be looking for an Englishman of forty-two, who was in Shanghai in 1906. Perhaps you could—"

"—ask my colleagues in Shanghai to factor that description into their search."

I was on the edge of asking when we might expect to hear from them, but bit back the question: Mycroft would be as attentive as I to the problem.

"One thing more," he said. "Damian's finger-prints are not on the biscuit packet."

"You had them? To compare?"

"Enough of them. If he touched it, he wiped it thoroughly before it was handled by at least three others. I am having the workers at Fortnum and Mason volunteer their prints, for comparison. One of the hands was small; I suggest it will match Yolanda's when we receive those prints. I will also see if I can get the prints from the walled house, for comparison."

"Not Damian's," I said. "Thank God for small blessings."

I hugged to me that minor confirmation of innocence as I went to bed that night, and it helped me to sleep.

Chapter Thirty-two

Magic (2): What does this mean, to summon, free, and take into one's self? When a word is spoken, writ, burnt, and stirred into water, this is simple Power, a child's magic. But it contains a grain of the Truth.

Testimony, III:5

FRIDAY OPENED WITH A TELEPHONE CALL FROM Lestrade. Mycroft answered the ring at a quarter to seven in the morning, and I knew instantly who it was when his eyes sought mine. I went back to his study, and eased up the earpiece of the second instrument.

"—not believe that you have no idea where your brother and his wife are, Mr Holmes."

"Chief Inspector, I am shocked that you would accuse me of lying to you."

"I'll just bet you are. I want to know what Miss Russell was doing rolling a villain like Gunderson up in a carpet, and then running off before we got there. I want to know what connexion your brother has with Yolanda Adler. And I'd really like to ask how he knew we'd find grains of Veronal in Yolanda Adler's stomach?"

"Did you?"

"We did. Along with some nut pâté and biscuits washed down by wine."

"Clever you. Have you had any luck in finding the men who left the house before Gunderson?"

"They abandoned their car in—wait a minute, how do you know about them if your brother isn't there telling you?"

"I have not seen my brother since Tuesday, Chief Inspector. I merely speak from what is already general knowledge."

"I don't think so. Maybe I ought to bring you in for questioning."

"Do you seriously think you have the authority to do that, Chief Inspector?" Mycroft sounded more amused than threatened.

Lestrade was silent, no doubt reflecting on the possibility of asserting any kind of authority over Mycroft Holmes. However, it is not always a good idea to point out a man's limitations.

"I may not. But I'm putting out a warrant for the arrest of your brother and his wife. They're concealing vital information, and I won't have it."

He banged down the phone. When I went back into Mycroft's sitting room, he was looking at the telephone, abashed.

"A new experience for me," I remarked, "being wanted by the police."

"I'm sorry, Mary. I should have known that remark would tip him into spite."

"I'm not sure it will make a lot of difference; he was looking for us already."

"If Sherlock is arrested on his way home, I shall have some explaining to do."

"Holmes will manage."

"If he does not manage to evade them, I shall have the dogs of the press on my door-step."

My first stop that morning was at the Save the Soul Prison Reform group, to look at their list of would-be reformed criminals. The police had not been there yet, which made my job easier, even as it convinced me that they were interested only in Damian Adler. The group's director was a thin, pale man with trembling hands and a wide clerical collar; I gave him a description of the black-haired man with the scar.

"Oh yes," he fluttered. "Reverend Smythe, I remember him well, he was so eager to help, made a most generous contribution, and met with a number of our former prisoners with an eye to employing one of them."

"And did he?"

"I believe so. Yes, I recall, it was Gunderson. Not the first time we've seen that poor man through here," he confided sadly, then brightened. "But then I haven't seen him since then, so perhaps he has found his way at last into the light of reason, pray God."

I didn't have the heart to tell him.

Nor did I let him know that there was no record of a Reverend Smythe on the books of any British church body.

Friday afternoon, a positive storm of information battered the door of Mycroft's flat.

Albert Seaforth, subject of Holmes' telegram, turned out to be an unemployed schoolteacher from York, fired in late May when one of his students told her parents that her Latin teacher had made advances. He had been found the previous Thursday morning, sitting upright against a standing stone, looking out over a desolate portion of the Yorkshire moors. His wrists had been slit; the knife was still in his hand.

"When did he die?" I asked Mycroft, who rang me from his office with the information.

"Approximately a day before."

"He'd been there for a day and no-one noticed?"

"The only neighbours are sheep."

I looked at the notes I had made while on the telephone: Seaforth. Fired 19 May. Knife in hand. If this man was another victim, it confirmed a pattern of marginally employed individuals.

An hour later, Mycroft rang again to say that his pet laboratory had analysed the mixture that the Circle had been drinking: mead, spices, Chartreuse (hence the colour), hashish (which I had expected), and mushrooms (which I had not).

"Mushrooms. As in toadstools?"

"As you know, the distinction is imprecise, and the samples deteriorated. The mycologist is continuing to work on it."

When I had rung off, I scratched my head for a bit and then gathered my things to leave, nearly overlooking, in my distraction, the danger of going out of the front door. I caught myself and changed direction, emerging five minutes later in St James's Square. This time I aimed my research enquiries at the Reading Room of the British Museum. I had a moment's qualm as I handed my ticket to the guard at the door, but either Lestrade hadn't thought to notify them, or they were above the fray, because the man waved me in without hesitation.

I found what I needed before closing time, although I nearly walked into the arms of one of Lestrade's men on Jermyn Street as I made my way to the Angel Court entrance. Fortunately, I saw him first, and made haste to evade him.

Mycroft was walking down his hallway, just returned from his walk, when I emerged from the odour of burning honey.

"Ah, Mary," he said, unsurprised at my appearance. "I have something for you."

"And I you."

We met in the sitting room over drinks, and exchanged our papers: I sat and read the results of the agricultural colleague's report, giving minute details of six months of dead livestock, while he frowned over my scribbled notes on the meal eaten by the dead warriors of Valhalla, preparatory to working themselves into their Berserker frenzy: mead and toadstools.

I set his report aside, all thirty pages of it, until I had pencil in hand and the other list of full-moon events beside it.

"Sherlock came through on the telephone this afternoon," he said. "Shockingly bad connexion, from Newcastle upon Tyne, but I managed to convey the need to keep his head down around the police."

"What is he doing?"

"He'd only got as far as telling me that he was headed to the Yorkshire Moors when we were cut off."

"Well, at least there's a chance you won't have to stand bail for him in Newcastle or some equally remote place."

"There is that."

After we ate, I took over the dining table and began to make my way laboriously through the livestock report.

As I had anticipated, there were dozens of animal deaths, from one end of the country to the next, and not one of them an obvious ritual sacrifice. Perhaps our man had a purpose other than bloody religion, I speculated with the half of my mind not taken up by dead cows. (Three had died in Cornwall during April, fallen one after another into an abandoned tin mine.) Maybe it was personal: He had a grudge against women—and this suicide in Yorkshire was unrelated. (An entire flock of laying hens had vanished in a night—but no, they were later found in a neighbour's henhouse.) Or perhaps Fiona Cartwright and Albert Seaforth were the two who were related, linked by an affair, or inheritance, or a place of employment. (A bull had been struck by a lorry, which fled the scene, although it didn't make it far since a bull is large enough to reduce an engine block to dead weight.) Or if "Smythe" had actually wanted a secretary and found Fiona lacking, then tried a male secretary at his next stop—but don't be ridiculous, Russell (A pig was killed by a Wiltshire farmer in June after it broke into his house and wouldn't leave.), there is no Smythe, your brain is fatigued, go to bed.

I looked up. But there were jobs. And Seaforth was out of work just as Fiona Cartwright had been—and Marcus Gunderson. I dropped my pencil. "I'm going to York," I announced. "Now. I'll telephone when I know where I'm staying—see if you can talk someone there into letting me read the police file on Seaforth's death. And maybe not arrest me, either."

"Take a room at the Station Hotel, I'll leave any message for you there."

I managed to catch a good train, and reached York while there was still life in the Station Hotel. They had a room, and a message:

Inspector Kursall, central station, 11 a.m.

I slept very little, ate early, and at nine o'clock stepped into the first on my list of York employment agencies. The question I had come here for was, if Cartwright, Seaforth, Gunderson, and Dunworthy were all jobless when he found them, did Brothers habitually use employment agencies?

At half past ten, I found the right one: small, run-down, and specialising, apparently, in the chronically unemployable.

"Yais, I dew recall him." The thin, pallid, buck-toothed man adjusted a pair of worn steel spectacles on his narrow nose. "Mr Seaforth encountered some difficulties at his last place of employment."

"He was fired for making unwelcome advances," I said bluntly.

"Well, yais. I suggested that his expectations of finding another school willing to take him on might be overly optimistic. Unless he were to leave York, of course. The last possibility I sent him out on was the tutoring of a fourteen-year-old boy who had been expelled for setting fire to his rooms at school."

In other words, Seaforth had been scraping the bottom of his profession's barrel.

"You're not surprised he killed himself, then."

"Not ectually, no."

"Did you meet this boy?"

"Oh no. Just the father."

"Can you tell me what he looked like?"

"Why should you—"

"Please, I'll go away and stop bothering you if you just tell me."

Why that should convince him to talk to me, I don't know, but I thought it might, and so it did.

"A pleasant man in his early forties, dark hair and eyes, a good suit. Seemed quite fond of his son, truly puzzled by the lad's behaviour."

"Did he have a scar?"

"A scar? Yes, I believe he did. Like the splash of a burn, going back from his eye. I recall thinking that he'd been lucky not to lose his sight."

"Back from his eye—not down?"

"Not really, no. A dark triangle extending towards the hair-line, wider at the back. My own dear mother had a scar on her cheek," he explained, "from a pan of burning fat. I might not have noticed it, other."

"I see." I did not know why it mattered, although it was helpful to have a description as accurate as possible, and if the scar ran one way rather than the other, it might jog the memory of a witness. "Did this gentleman give you a name, or any way to get into contact with him?"

"His name was Smythe. He is new to this area, still looking at houses, but he was particularly concerned with his son's welfare. He took the names I suggested and told me he would be back into touch when he had chosen a man for the position."

"How many names were there?"

"Er, only the one."

"Right. And do you know how Smythe found you?"

"I suppose he saw my sign from the street. I don't advertise any-where, and as for word of mouth, he was new to the area, and—well, to be frank he didn't look like my usual client."

It made sense, that a man searching for the most downtrodden of the unemployed, men and women of whom suicide would not be un-expected, should troll the streets for a store-front like this one, dingy and dispiriting.

I thanked the man, shook his thin, damp hand, and left the musty office.

On the street, it hit me: An eye with a long triangle of scar beside it might resemble that symbol on the books, in the rings, and tattooed on Yolanda Adler's body.

But what did it mean?

I got to my appointment early, but Inspector Kursall was waiting. He welcomed me into his office and handed me a thin file. "Not much there," he said.

But they had done an autopsy, and determined that Albert Seaforth had died late Tuesday or early Wednesday, 12 or 13 August, of exsanguination from wounds to his wrists. His cause of death was of secondary importance, however, for the *in situ* photograph of his hand with the knife beside it told me all I needed to know: The blade was covered with blood; the fingers were all but clean.

The pathologist had been thorough, both in his examination and in writing it up: middle-aged male, lack of muscle tone, no scars, mole on left shoulder, no wounds save those to his wrists, and so on. Then, in the third paragraph, it caught my eye: one-half-inch patch behind left ear where the hair was cut away. Had Fiona Cartwright's autopsy report been less perfunctory, I was certain that we would have seen a similar notation there.

I handed the file back to Kursall. "You need to talk to Chief Inspector Lestrade at Scotland Yard. Read him the third paragraph."

It was the least I could do, for a man who hadn't arrested me on sight.

I caught a train that would get me back into London by early evening, and spent the whole journey thinking about the full moon and murder.

The sky grew darker as we travelled south, and when we reached our terminus in King's Cross, the close, restless atmosphere presaged a storm's approach. I flung myself and my valise into a taxi and offered him double if he would get me to Angel Court in half his usual time. The man tried his hardest, and I was inside Mycroft's flat before the first raindrops hit the window.

My brother-in-law looked up, surprised, at my hurried entrance.

"I'm going to the Children of Lights services," I explained as I passed through the room. "I don't suppose you'd care to join me?"

I glanced back to see one raised eyebrow: Habits die hard, and apart from the self-imposed discipline of walking Hyde Park, his lifelong disinclination to bestir himself was not about to change.

"Anything from Holmes?" I called.

"Not yet. The prints on the biscuit wrapper do not include any of those found thus far in the walled house. And your suspicions concerning the mushrooms found in the drink were justified: *Amanita,* not *Agaricus.*"

"Hallucinogenic, then."

"If a person consumed several glasses of the drink you found, yes, mildly so."

"More to underscore the hashish, you would say?"

"Indeed. And you—were you successful?"

"Brothers definitely uses employment agencies to locate his victims," I said, and threw snatches of my findings at him as I rummaged through the wardrobe for suitable clothing—something more orthodox than last week's costume, but still idiosyncratic. Despite the weather, I ended up with a shirtwaist topped with a bright, hand-woven belt from South America, an equally bright neck-scarf from India, and an almost-matching ribbon around the summer-weight cloche hat.

Mycroft had long ceased to comment on the clothing I wore in and out of his flat, no doubt determining that I was incessantly in one disguise or another. This evening he merely glanced at the garish accessories, without so much as a remark at the clashing colours, and wished me a good hunt.

Chapter Thirty-three

Power (1): If all things are joined, if God has linked all creatures by ethereal threads, then Power is there to be absorbed. Primitive peoples see the shadow of this idea, when they eat the hearts of conquered enemies.
Testimony, III:7

I STOOD ACROSS THE ROAD FROM THE MEETING HALL until I was certain there was no police watch on the entrance. The rain was light, a harbinger of autumn and endings, but it was still enough to dampen me in the time it took to scurry across the evening traffic.

At the door, I again hesitated, and climbed the stairs with all my senses tuned for a figure at the top. The vestibule was deserted, but for the table of pamphlets, and I eased the door open a crack to see within.

The service was nearly over, and nearly empty: Last week's 120 attendees were three times that of tonight's. I did not think that due to the rain.

Millicent Dunworthy was reading again, in her white robe between two black candles. Her text described a sin-soaked yet peculiarly free city in the East where the author had come into his knowledge of the interrelatedness of Light and Dark and the Truth That Lies Between Them, but I thought she was paying little attention to the meaning of the words. She read fast, the words tumbling out with no attempt at meaning, and she stopped occasionally as if her throat had closed. She was bent over the book, not looking up, her hands gripping hard.

She was frightened, or angry. Or both.

When the chapter ended, her eyes came up for the first time, a quick hot glance at a large figure in the back, hunched in a pale overcoat. I looked more closely, noticed the empty chairs all around him, and let the door ease shut: Lestrade had sent a presence. And the Children knew who he was.

The hallway leading to the meeting room also continued in the other direction. I loosened the furthest light-bulb, and sat on some steps, waiting for the service to end. Before long, the doors opened and people made immediately for the stairs: no chatter, and no tea and biscuits. After a pause, the plainclothes policeman came out, followed a few minutes later by the brother and sister of the Inner Circle.

When the hallway was empty, I walked down to the meeting room and found Millicent Dunworthy, packing the pamphlets into their boxes with sharp motions. She looked up, startled, when I came near.

"I'm sorry, I missed the service," I told her.

"There was no service. There may never be," she said, and slapped some cards on top of the pamphlets.

"I heard. About Yolanda, I mean. I know it must be very disturbing."

"That's the least of it. No," she said, "I don't mean that, it's terrible, of course, but the police have been all over, asking questions, insinuating—"

She broke off, and picked up the box to carry it to the storage cabinet. I followed with the folding table. When we had the doors shut and the padlocks on, she turned to me.

"What do you want?"

"I'd like to talk about the Children," I said.

"You and everyone else!"

"I'm not with the police. Or the newspapers. I'm just a friend."

"Not of mine."

"I could be. Look," I said reasonably. "I noticed a café next door but one. We could have a bowl of soup, or a coffee, maybe?"

She hesitated, but just then the heavens contributed their opinion, and a growl of thunder accompanied by a thrust of drops against the window warned her how wet she would be if she walked home now. She agreed, grudgingly, and we scurried through the rain to the café. I moved with my arm across my face, holding my hat against the wind, but the police watcher appeared to have waited only to be certain that Brothers did not appear, then gone home.

Millicent—we soon graduated to the intimacy of first names—unblushingly ordered cocoa; I did so as well, although I had not downed a cup of the cloying liquid since my undergraduate days, and frankly I would have preferred strong drink for both of us. And when I pressed upon her the necessity for keeping her energy up, she added a request for a slice of sponge cake, "although I shouldn't."

"Make that two," I told the waitress, joining Millicent in her naughtiness. When the tired woman had taken herself away to fetch our drinks, I said, "Oh, I haven't had a slice of Victoria Sponge in yonks."

"It has rather passed out of popularity, hasn't it?"

I pounced, before she could redirect the conversation. "Even the name Victoria has gone out of fashion. What does that remind me of? Oh, I know—I've been thinking about the Adler child, Estelle, this week, another uncommon name. So sad, isn't it? And what do you imagine has become of Damian?"

She picked at the bundle that contained her robe and shook her head, not trusting herself to speak.

"I can't believe he had anything to do with her death, as the newspapers would have us think," I persisted. "I mean to say, he's odd, but not like that."

She sat up straight. "I think it's very possible. He's a very peculiar young man, is Damian Adler. The sooner they find him and take the child into safe keeping, the better."

"Really? Well, you know him better than I do. But it must be making a lot of trouble for you, in the Children, I mean. To have Yolanda a member and Damian missing. Plus that, your leader—The Master, don't you call him? It can't be easy to have him gone, too."

"The Master is here when we need him," she snapped. She might have stormed out but the waitress appeared at that moment. When the cocoa and sponge had been arranged before us, I turned the questions in another direction.

"I greatly look forward to meeting him, once this uproar is passed. Tell me, is there some kind of a study group, in addition to the services, where one might read more of the book you use?"

"We had been discussing that need, before . . . Perhaps in a few weeks we can find the time to arrange one. There is a weekly meeting of advanced students of the Lights, but the need is, as you say, for beginners. The Master is preparing an introductory text, the *Text of Lights,* with the message of *Testimony* but in a form that is more easily understood."

"Oh good," I enthused.

"This is very nice," she said, chewing on her cake.

In truth, the sponge was stale and the cocoa so hot it had cooked into a skin: As a memory of undergraduate days, it was a bit too realistic. But Millicent enjoyed it.

"You seem terribly knowledgeable about *Testimony,*" I said. "How long have you been studying it?"

"I received my copy in May, although I had been hearing it for some months before that. It is a book that rewards close study."

"Tell me about The Master. He must be an attractive person, to bring together such an interesting group of people."

She blushed. "It is an honour to serve the Children."

"That book, *Testimony*—is by him?"

It was the wrong thing to say. "It is not 'by' any man, no more than the New Testament is by any man. Portions of it were transmitted through The Master."

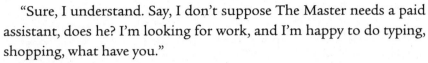

"Sure, I understand. Say, I don't suppose The Master needs a paid assistant, does he? I'm looking for work, and I'm happy to do typing, shopping, what have you."

"What he needs, I do."

"Oh, I see—you work for him as well. That's fine, but if you need help, keep me in mind." I swallowed some more of the drink, now gone tepid, and wondered if there was anything else to be had from her. Although come to think of it, there was one question she had sidestepped rather markedly.

"Do you think it's possible The Master will be here for next week's service?"

"The needs of the Lights may keep him away for another week, but he should return after that."

She pushed away her cup, making it clear that we had reached the end of our refreshment and our conversation. I called for the bill and looked towards the front windows, to see if it was still raining. A small man in a dark rain-coat was standing at the window, looking in; drops were coming from the brim of his hat, but not in a stream: Millicent would not drown on her walk home.

We chatted until the bill arrived, and I paid it. She thanked me, I told her I looked forward immensely to seeing her again, and we climbed back into our damp outer garments. At the door, I suddenly remembered a personal need in the back.

"But don't you wait for me, the rain's let up for the moment and you may be able to make it home before it starts again."

She peered at the sky, opened her umbrella, and scurried off. My original thought had been to share a taxi and accompany her home, but the face at the window had put an end to that idea. I waited until she was securely across the street, then stepped out to greet the man in the hat.

"You were looking for me?" I asked him. Had he been more obviously a policeman, I should have left through a back door.

"Mr Mycroft Holmes sent me to find you."

"And the skinny little bureaucrat wants to drag me clear across town?" I responded.

The man looked at me oddly, then realised what I was doing. He reached up to tip his hat in acknowledgment. "I'd hardly call Mr Holmes skinny, even now," he replied, "and Pall Mall is no distance at all."

He knew Mycroft; it was safe to climb into the car with him.

I glanced down the street, found Millicent Dunworthy gone, and got into the passenger seat of the car belonging to Mycroft's operative.

Chapter Thirty-four

*Power (2): It takes a practiced mind and a purified heart
to discern the subtle patterns of the heavens, freeing
sources of Power to fuel the divine spark.
The manipulation of the Elements is a life-time's work.*
Testimony, III:7

"WHAT DOES HE WANT?" I ASKED.

"Mr Holmes is not in the habit of sharing that sort of information with his employees," the man said, putting the motor into gear. "However, it may have to do with an arrival from Shanghai."

At last!

We were on the street near Mycroft's back door in no time at all. I got out, then looked back at the driver. "You're not coming in?"

"I was only sent to find you. Good evening, Miss Russell."

"Good night, Mr . . . ?"

"Jones."

"Another Jones brother," I noted. "Good night then, Mr Jones."

———

As way of proof that watched plots never come to a boil, my absence from Mycroft's home had opened the way for furious activity. For one thing, Holmes was back, looking sunburnt, footsore, and stiff, no doubt from sleeping on the ground. Also hungry, to judge by the ravaged platter of sandwiches on the table before him. He'd been there long enough to bath, and therefore long enough to be brought up to date by Mycroft—the files and papers relating to the investigation had been moved; Damian's redirected letter lay on the top.

I greeted him, with more reticence than I might have were Mycroft our only witness to affection. He nodded at me and returned his attention to the fourth person in the room.

Apart from his lack of sunburn, the newcomer looked even more worn than Holmes. The small man's now-damp linen suit was as wrinkled as a centenarian's face, and bore signs of any number of meals and at least one close acquaintance with oily machinery. He had not only slept in his clothing, he had lived in them for days, and for many, many miles.

The arrival from Shanghai was not a document.

"You have been in Shanghai, I perceive," I blurted idiotically.

The three men stared at me as if I had pronounced on the state of cheese in the moon, so I smiled weakly and stepped forward, my hand out. The small man started to rise.

"Don't stand," I ordered. "Mary Russell."

He subsided obediently, clutching his plate with one hand; the other one took mine with a dapper formality that sat oddly with his state of disrepair.

"This is Mr Nicholas Lofte," Mycroft said. "Recently, as you say, of Shanghai."

"Pleased to meet you," he said smoothly, with an accent as much American as his native Swiss.

One whiff of the air in his vicinity explained why Mycroft had left a space between himself and Lofte; it also meant that I retreated to Holmes' side rather than take the chair between them.

Mycroft circled the table with a bottle, playing host to the wine in the glasses as he told me, "From time to time, Mr Lofte takes commissions for me in the Eastern countries. He happened to be on hand in Shanghai, so my request for information was passed to him."

Which did not explain why Mr Lofte himself occupied a chair in Mycroft's sitting room: Was the information he had compiled too inflammatory to be committed to print? As if I had voiced the speculation aloud, Mycroft said, "His dossier of information was rather lengthy for telegrams, and writing it up and presenting it to the Royal Mail would have delayed its arrival until the middle of the week."

"As I had my passport in my pocket, I merely presented myself at the air field instead and, as it were, affixed the stamp to my own forehead," the man said. "Sat among the mail sacks across Asia and Europe, which doesn't leave one fresh as a daisy, if you'll forgive me, ma'am."

My distaste had not passed him by, but he seemed more amused than offended by it, his eyes betraying a thread of humour that, in a man less stretched by exhaustion, might have been a twinkle.

"No need for apology, Mr Lofte, I have been in similar circumstances myself."

"So I understand," he said, which rather surprised me. Before I could ask him how he knew, he had turned back to Mycroft. "It cost me a few hours to get free of my prior commitments after I'd got your orders, but Shanghai's a small town for its size, if you get my meaning. It didn't take me long to find your man."

He paused to add in the direction of Holmes and me, "My brief was to find what I could about an Englishman named Damian Adler, and about his wife Yolanda, previous name unknown. Adler's name came with a physical description and a date and place of birth, his mother's name, and the fact that he might be a painter. And that was all.

"I got lucky early, because he'd been in and out of the British Embassy a number of times last year, first to replace his lost passport, then to add his wife and young daughter to it. You hadn't said anything about a daughter, but I figured it had to be he, so I started from there.

"Before I go any further, do you want this in the order of how I came upon the information, or re-arranged chronologically? They're more or less reversed."

Mycroft answered before Holmes could. "You've had time to consider your findings; feel free to tell it as you wish."

Holmes shot him a glance, having no doubt been on the edge of demanding the bare facts as Lofte dug them out, and leaving the synthesis to his audience. But Mycroft knew his man, and the Swiss mind was more comfortable with an ordered sequence of events. Lofte picked up another sandwich, downed another swallow of wine, and began.

"Very well. My sources were the Embassy, several police departments, and the Adlers' circle of friends and business acquaintances. I wanted to speak with Mrs Adler's family, but their home was a day's travel away, and I judged that time was of greater import than complete thoroughness.

"The earliest sign of Damian Adler in Shanghai was June 1920. One man I spoke with thought Adler had been there for several weeks before that, but June was the time he took up rooms in a bro—er," he said, shooting me a glance, "in a pleasure house. The owner of the house had got in the habit of having one or two large and relatively sober young men living on the premises, at a low rent, to help keep the guests in line. I asked him if this wasn't like putting a fat boy in charge of a chocolate shop, and he told me that yes, there was a certain tendency to, er, indulge in the goods at first, but he had found that having one or two dependable neighbours gave the girls a sense of family, and someone to go to if a client became rowdy."

I did not look at Holmes to see how this version of Damian's tale was hitting him, but I had felt him wince at the phrase, "indulge in the goods." His only overt reaction was to take a rather deeper swallow from his glass.

"Yolanda Chin—the future Mrs Adler—was not a resident of the house at the time Mr Adler moved in, although it would appear that she had been some years before. According to the madam, the girl came in 1905 or 1906, when she was thirteen or fourteen years of age.

As, I fear, a prostitute," he told us, just to be clear. He glanced at our stony faces, and took a prim sip of wine as he arranged his thoughts.

"When she married in late 1912—"

"*What?*" Holmes exclaimed, an instant before Mycroft or I could.

Lofte looked at him in surprise. "But yes."

"You are certain?"

In answer, he reached down for a valise I had not noticed and withdrew a manila envelope. Unlooping its tie, he thumbed inside until he came up with the paper he sought. "This gives her age as sixteen, although her birth registration makes her three years older." He slid the page down the table to Holmes; I looked past Holmes' shoulder.

A marriage certificate, dated 21 November 1912, between Yolanda Chin, sixteen, and Reverend James Harmony Hayden, age thirty, a British subject.

This time, the exclamation was mine.

"Born in 1882—do you know what Hayden looks like?"

Lofte went back to his envelope and took out a square of newsprint, commemorating some kind of donation or prize-giving: The quality was as poor as might be expected, but it showed two men shaking hands and facing the camera, the man on the left clothed in formal black and silk hat, the grinning man on the right in light suit, soft hat, and clerical collar.

"The one on the right is Reverend Hayden. The occasion is the opening of a school for poor children for which his church helped raise funds."

Apart from the grinning teeth, all one could tell about James Hayden was that he was Caucasian, and that his eyes were dark. A shadow next to the left eye might have been wear in the page or a flaw in the printing, but I was pretty sure it was not.

"He has a scar next to his eye," I said.

"That's what it says in his description," Lofte agreed. "I haven't seen him, but I understand that he was in an accident in late 1905, a building collapse with live electrical wires. He was badly hurt. It was the following year that he set up shop as a reverend."

"He's not ordained?" Holmes asked.

"He may be. There are many religions in Shanghai."

"It's him," I said ungrammatically, my eyes fixed on the clipping. I had not seen his face, could not testify to the colour of his eyes or the shape of his hair-line, but I had no doubt.

"I agree," said Holmes.

Lofte waited for us to explain, and when we did not, he went on.

"He hired a small space on the fringes of the city's International Settlement, and began to hold services, a mixture of the familiar and the exotic, from Jesus as guru to the health benefits of Yoga. Mind-reading, I understand, was a regular feature. He claimed to have received personal messages from the shade of Madame Blavatsky, the Theosophist. Before long, he bought the building outright, thanks to the bored and wealthy wives and daughters of the English-speaking community, who just lapped him up."

"Mixing Hinduism, Yoga, mysticism, that sort of thing?"

"And Tantra," he added, then quickly moved on before I could ask for details—but I had no need to ask. Tantra employed sexuality as a means to mystic union: a true discipline in its original home, a means of exploitation by unscrupulous charlatans in the West. I should not be surprised to find among its devotees a man who would marry a child he thought to be sixteen.

Lofte dipped back into the envelope for another sheet. He handed it to Mycroft, who read it then laid it atop the first. "They were divorced in 1920. She cited abandonment for her and their child."

Holmes cleared his throat. "Child?"

"Yes. According to a woman who had remained friends with Yolanda after she left the—the pleasure house, she had a child in 1913." He went back to his envelope, this time for a telegraph flimsy. "I had to leave a number of elements in this investigation to others, you understand, since time was a priority. This was waiting for me in Cairo."

YOLANDA CHIN BORN 1893 FUNG SHIAN DISTRICT
STOP CHILD DOROTHY HAYDEN BORN 1913 LUAN

DISTRICT LIVING WITH GRANDPARENTS FUNG
SHIAN STOP

Holmes, reading this, made a tiny noise that might have been a
sigh, or a whimper.

Lofte continued. "It would appear that she and Hayden did not live
together, as he had a house in the International Settlement, where
Chinese were not made welcome. Certainly they were separated by
March 1917, when she began work as a barmaid two streets down
from the . . . house where she had lived. There is, I will mention, no
evidence of a child during this time. Giving a child over to one's
grandparents to be raised is a common practise for . . . among girls
who live in the city.

"Then in 1920, Damian Adler arrived in Shanghai. As I said, he
found rooms in—I shouldn't perhaps call it a house, it is a compound
of many dwellings, an arrangement that fosters close, almost familial
ties—the girls who were there at the time remember Mr Adler with re-
spect and affection. He went through periods of heavy drinking, and
was arrested twice in the waning months of 1920."

By now, Holmes did not even blink.

"The first arrest was for being so drunk the wagon that picked him
up thought he was dead."

"Well," I murmured, "he only claimed that he was free from drugs
use."

Holmes paid my comment no mind. "And the second?"

"Ah, well, that was a month later, and more serious. Mr Adler was
in a brawl in November 1920, and beat a man up. He was arrested, but
when the man came out of hospital three days later, he refused to
press charges. Adler was let go with a warning."

Lofte was watching Holmes in a manner that suggested anticipation. Holmes studied him, then obediently asked, "Do we know who
the victim was?"

A tiny smile flickered over the Swiss man's mouth, and he went
back to his envelope. This time the document was two pieces of paper

pinned together in the corner; it took Mycroft a full minute to read and pass on this one, a police report recording the injuries of one John Haycock: Concussion, broken collar bone, cracked humerus, contusions, broken tooth—fairly standard stuff for a bar brawl. Holmes flipped over to the second page, and there was a photograph of our human punching bag, his features so swollen and bruised, his mother would not have known him.

"John Haycock, eh?" Holmes mused.

"The address he gave the hospital was false," Lofte said.

The man's hair was dark, but there was no telling if he had a scar beside his eye.

Holmes was studying the photograph, then shook his head. "It's a pity—"

He stopped, his eyes darting to Lofte's fingers on the near-flat envelope. "You don't?"

In answer, the man in the worn suit drew out a glossy photograph and half-stood to lay it with great deliberation on the table before Holmes. He sat back, on his face a look of tired contentment. "This was put into my hands by a reporter of one of the Shanghai dailies, ninety-five minutes before—" He shot a glance at Mycroft. "Shall we say, I happened to know that a military 'plane was about to leave, and I thought that might be my best chance to get this photograph to London."

"What day was this?" I asked. Mycroft had wired his request for information ten days earlier; Lofte must have assembled all this information in a matter of hours.

"Sunday."

Two of us frankly stared at him; Mycroft studied his glass, but one side of his mouth had a small curl of satisfaction.

"Six days to cross two entire continents?" I marvelled. "Impossible!"

"Not if one is given *carte blanche* with requisitioning aeroplanes and rescheduling trains. I employed nine aeroplanes, three trains, eighteen motor-cars, two motor-cycles, one bicycle, and a rickshaw."

Mycroft spoke up. "My department has an ongoing interest in

what one might call practical experiments in rapid travel. Mr Lofte now holds the record."

"Won a tenner, too," our Twentieth-Century Mercury murmured. "Harrison bet me I couldn't do it in under eight days. My partner in Shanghai," he explained.

Holmes resumed the photograph, tilting it for me when I looked over his arm.

"My reporter friend became interested in Hayden a year ago when he heard a rumour that the good Reverend was quietly selling up church holdings—several buildings, in good parts of town, a lot of stocks and valuables that members had donated for charitable works which somehow didn't come to fruition. There were also rumours of darker doings, several deaths among his congregation. The photo was taken the tenth of September last year; the next day, the Reverend was on a boat for England. The reporter reckons various officials were paid off, not to notice. Hayden won't be prosecuted, but on the other hand, he won't be welcomed back."

Hayden's image was quite clear, despite having been taken across a busy street. The man, strong in body and haughty in manner, was dressed in a beautifully cut summer-weight suit and a shirt with an ordinary soft collar and neck-tie. He had his straw hat in his hand as he prepared to climb into a car waiting at the kerb. Something must have caught his attention, because he was turned slightly, face-on to the camera. He looked vaguely familiar, although I had only seen the back of his head, so far as I knew. His eyes were dark and compelling, his mouth full, his hair sleek and black. And his left eye was elongated by a stripe of darker skin, a scar like the tail of a comet. Like the re-appearing shape of the Children of Lights.

Holmes passed it over to Mycroft. "We need copies."

"Certainly. Lofte, did you have anything else for us?"

"A few clippings about the church, but that's it."

I shifted, and three pairs of eyes turned to me. Not that I wished to be greedy, however: "The Adlers have a child. Estelle. Did you come upon any birth record for her?"

Lofte's tired face sagged with remorse. "I was told to investigate the background of Damian Adler's wife, Yolanda, at all haste. I interpreted that to mean her background before their marriage. I did not pursue copies of their marriage certificate, or their current bank accounts, or the child's papers. I can get that information in a day, if you need it."

"The only urgent piece of information we need is, did she have another child, after Dorothy Hayden in 1913 but before she married Damian?"

"I was working at speed and may have missed some details. To be honest, I don't know if I would have caught sight of another child, had there been one."

"That's all right. Thank you."

Mycroft rose. "We shall turn you free to sleep the sleep of the righteous. You have a room?"

"The Travellers' will have one." He stood, a trifle stiffly, and shook hands all around. Mycroft led him to the door, but Holmes interrupted.

"Lofte?" The man turned to look back. "Altogether, a most impressive feat."

The younger man's face was transformed by a sudden grin. "It was, wasn't it?" he said, and left.

When Mycroft came back, he was not carrying the photograph.

Chapter Thirty-five

Third Birth: A man born once lives unaware of good and evil. A man born twice sees good and evil, within and without. Very few achieve a third birth: birth into divinity, knowing that good and evil are not opposing forces, but intertwining gifts that together make the burning heart of Power. A third-born man is little less than the angels. A third-born man is the image of God.

Testimony, III:8

MYCROFT CLEARED AWAY THE EMPTY PLATTER and the glasses, and returned with an antique-looking bottle and smaller glasses. Having cocoa and red wine already arguing in my stomach, I turned down his offer.

"I've been saving this for you to try," Mycroft told his brother. "I'd have brought it out for Mr Lofte, but I judged that in his condition, strong drink might render him unconscious." The two men sipped and made appreciative noises and traded opinions on districts and pre-war (pre–Boer war) vintages before my ostentatious glance at my wrist-watch returned us to the task at hand.

"I had two more telephone calls from Lestrade today," Mycroft said. "On the first, he informed me that he had, in fact, put out arrest warrants for both of you. On the second, he asked if you had fled the country with Damian Adler."

"*Has* Damian fled the country?" I asked.

"So far as I could determine, Lestrade's evidence consists of Scotland Yard's inability to find him. So, Sherlock, what have you found for us amongst the primitive monuments?"

Holmes pulled a travel-stained rucksack out from under his chair, undoing the buckle and upending its contents onto the low table: three large and lumpy manila envelopes, their ties securely fastened.

Mycroft went to his desk for a stack of white paper, while Holmes picked up the first envelope and undid the tie, pulling out six sealed standard-sized envelopes of varying lumpiness.

One by one he slit the ends, shaking the contents of each onto a fresh sheet of paper: sandy soil in one; a coin in the next; two burnt matches; a handful of leaves and blades of grass, each stained with what could only be blood; four tiny, dark lumps that looked like pebbles; two different shoe-prints on butcher's paper, from a woman's heeled shoe and a larger man's boot, taken from the plaster casts Holmes had made, inked, and abandoned at the site—plaster casts make for a considerable weight to carry about the countryside.

When the six sheets were displaying their wares, he waited for us to look at them more closely, then began to return the objects to their envelopes. I picked up one of the pebbles, and found it softer than rock. Wax, perhaps. Or—gristle from a picnic lunch? Yes, I had seen their like before.

The second large envelope used four sheets of paper: one for grass with the same stains, one for a piece of cotton cording not more than half an inch long, and a third for a pinch of bi-coloured sand, light and dark brown. The fourth appeared to have nothing on it, except I had watched Holmes upend the envelope with great care. He handed me his powerful magnifying glass; I got to my knees for a closer look, and saw two tiny objects approximately the colour of the paper, little larger than thick eye-lashes. Like finger-nail clippings, without the curve.

With care, I slid the paper across the table to Mycroft and gave him the glass. When we had finished, Holmes packed this manila envelope away, and reached for the third.

This was the thickest, and its contents were similar to that of the others: spattered grass; twists of paper containing three different samples of soil, one of them pure sand; four identical wooden matches; a chewing-gum wrapper; six cigarette ends, none of them the same and two with lipstick stains, pink-red in one case and slightly orange in the other; half a dozen of the soft pebbles; a boot-print that apppeared identical to that in the first envelope; one white thread and the twig that had caught and pulled it; and a final object that Holmes had wrapped first in cotton wool, then in Friday's *Times*, rolled to make a stiff tube. He snipped the string holding the protective layers, revealing a dirty plaster shape approximately six inches long and curving to a wicked point: a plaster of Paris knife blade. I picked it up, lifting an eyebrow at Holmes.

"This is from a remote site in the Yorkshire Moors, a stone circle known as the High Bridestones. Albert Seaforth chose it as a place to commit suicide. I found it interesting that, after slitting his wrists, he drove the blade into the soil to clean it."

"He was found with a knife in his hand," I said. "The blade was bloody, his fingers were not. The blade was not this shape."

Holmes said, "The hilt left an oval impression on the ground, with the slit in the centre. You can see where the plaster picked up the blood-stains."

He packed away the envelope, and said, "We'll need the evidence from the Sussex site."

"It's in my safe," Mycroft said. "I'll get it."

"I brought everything up when I heard Lestrade was out for our scalps," I told Holmes. "I was afraid to leave it for him to find. There were finger-prints, on—"

"On the biscuit wrapper, so Mycroft said."

"I was glad. Holmes, I am *so* glad I was wrong about Damian."

"Not half so glad as I," he replied.

"What were you doing at eight-thirty Wednesday night?" I asked abruptly.

"Wednesday? I would have been climbing over a church wall in Penrith to get away from a dog. Why do you ask?"

But Mycroft came back with the packet, and I just smiled and shook my head.

Holmes went through the same ritual of envelopes and paper: vegetation, sand, cigarette ends, a black thread, two wooden matches, three of the soft pebbles, and one of the tiny odd fragments that resembled finger-nails. Although in this case, one of those was easier to see against the white sheet, being lined in fading red-brown.

"What *are* those things?" I finally said.

"Mycroft?" Holmes asked of his brother.

"I haven't seen any for years, but they look to me like the trimmings of a quill pen." Mycroft's slow voice vibrated with meaning, but it took me a moment to follow.

When I did, I snapped away from the tiny brown scrap, a cold finger trickling down my spine. "A pen? My God, do you mean he . . ."

I couldn't finish the sentence, so Holmes did. "Dipped a quill pen in his victim's blood and wrote with it? So it would appear."

"Extraordinary," Mycroft rumbled.

"But . . . I mean to say, I can understand—intellectually, I suppose, although not . . . I can just understand that a mad-man might want to write a message with a victim's blood, but then and there? Trimming his pen while the body lies at his feet, blood still . . ."

I gulped, unable to finish the sentence.

"Blood remains liquid but a short time," Holmes said. "I ought to have known six days ago: Sand on chalk soil means something."

"What, it meant that someone had been to the beach before visiting the Giant?"

"This is not beach sand, Russell. It is blotting sand."

"Oh," I said. "God." I stared in disgust at the minuscule scraps of quill until Holmes had replaced them in their concealing paper, then I picked up his glass and tossed back a dose of brandy. It made me cough and caused my eyes to water, but Mycroft did not even rebuke me for my ill treatment of his precious liquid.

"Where are these from?" he asked, gesturing at the envelopes.

"The first, with the two foot-prints, was from Cerne Abbas. The second comes from a large stone circle in Cumbria called Long Meg and her Daughters; the farmer heard his dog barking on the first of May, and when he looked out, he saw what appeared to be a candle burning in the field where the circle was. Going to investigate, he found a ram belonging to the next neighbour but one, lying on the centre-stone with its throat cut. The third envelope, that with all the cigarettes, is from High Bridestones—the site, unfortunately, was the focal point of a motor-coach full of lady water-colourists, two days before Albert Seaforth died there. And the fourth, as you know, was from the Wilmington Giant."

"Same boots, same matches," I said.

"Identical candle-wax," he added.

"Is that what those soft pebbles are? Dirty wax?"

"Not dirty: dark."

"Dark? You mean black? Like those used by the Children of Lights. Or in a Black Mass."

"Is there actually such a thing as a Black Mass?" Mycroft asked. "One has heard about it, of course, but it always seemed to me one of those tales the righteous build to convince themselves of their enemies' depravity."

"Crowley practices it," Holmes told him. "Don't you remember, last year, the death of young Loveday?"

"Raoul Loveday died of an infection down at Crowley's villa in Italy, although his wife claimed Crowley's magic killed him."

"Yes, but he died after a Black Mass at which they drank the blood of a sacrificed cat," I said. "We met Loveday's wife, and although it wouldn't surprise me if she'd shared in the drugs side of the experience, what she has to say about the ceremony seemed real enough." A still more awful thought struck me. "Holmes, there's a line in *Testimony* about primitive people eating their enemies' hearts. You don't suppose that Brothers. . . ."

"Drank his victims' blood as well?" Holmes considered for a

moment, then shook his head. "I saw nothing to indicate that, no place where, for example, smears suggested a cup wiped clean. And if the blood was meant as a communal partaking, would he have done so when he worked alone?"

I hoped not. I truly hoped not.

I went to our room a short time later. As I was brushing my teeth, Holmes came in, looking for his pipe.

"You're staying up?" I asked, unnecessarily: The pipe meant meditation.

"I need to read *Testimony.*"

"What did you make of Lofte's information?"

"Which part of it?"

Very well; if Holmes was going to be obtuse, I could be blunt. "The part of it where Damian's wife was married to a murder suspect, Holmes. Did Damian know that she was married before? That she had a child by Hayden? That she's been attending his church? That the illustrations were for the man's book?"

"I believe he knew, yes."

"But why would he go along with it? And why not tell you?"

"I should imagine that he did not tell me for the same reason he attempted to conceal his wife's unsavoury past: He feared that if I knew who she had been, I should assume her to be a gold-digger of the worst stripe and wash my hands promptly of the business. It is, after all, more or less what I assumed when I first encountered Damian's mother."

"But isn't that precisely what this woman is—was?"

"You do not admit to the possibility of reform?"

I started to retort, then closed my mouth. Yolanda Chin had been a child when she was forced into a life of prostitution; she was not yet an adult when she married a middle-aged Englishman, who turned out to be a crook, and perhaps much worse. Did I have any reason to think that Yolanda herself was a criminal? I did not. Did I have any reason to believe she was betraying Damian, in any way but attending her first husband's church? I did not.

Holmes saw the internal debate on my face. "It is easier to picture the boy as a victim of an unscrupulous adventuress, but I see no evidence of that, Russell. He loved her. Still does, if you are correct and he does not know she is dead. My son loves his wife," he said simply. "That is the point at which I must begin."

"And yet you think he knows. About her continuing attachment to Brothers?"

"He knows. One must remember, the Bohemian way of life is not a surface dressing with Damian."

I thought about that, and about the denizens of the Café Royal: two couples, leaving arm in arm with the other's spouse; Alice, Ronnie, and their Bunny; the Epstein household of husband, wife, husband's lovers, and their various children; the manifold permutations of the Bloomsbury Group, with lovers, husbands, wives' lovers become husbands' lovers and vice-versa; all of it determinedly natural and open, all of it aimed at a greater definition of humanity.

Yes, Damian could well know, and knowing, permit—even approve of—his wife's continued liaison with a man to whom she had once been married.

I had to laugh, a little sadly. "I'm a twenty-four-year-old prude."

"And thank God for it."

"Still," I said, "I'd have thought that if Damian knew about Yolanda's links to Brothers, he'd have looked to Brothers when she disappeared."

"Yes, well, I believe he may have done so. On the Wednesday night, he left the hotel for a time. It appeared to be an attack of claustrophobia."

"He's claustrophobic?" I pictured the room Damian and Estelle had shared at the walled house, its two large windows wide open to the night. "Did he leave for long enough to get up to the walled house and back?"

"By taxi, yes."

———

I woke early the following morning, saw the vague pre-dawn shape of Mycroft's guest room, and turned over again. Then I noticed how quiet it was. In London.

Drat: Sunday again.

I was on my third cup of coffee when first Holmes, then his brother emerged. Mycroft was cheerful, or at least, as cheerful as Mycroft got, but Holmes shot a dark look at the windows in just the way I had earlier.

Sundays were most inconvenient, when it came to investigation.

Still, it was not a total loss. For one thing, at ten after eight, interrupting our toast and marmalade, a set of discreet knuckles brushed at the door. I went to answer, and found "Mr Jones," a thick packet in his hand. He peered around me to check that Mycroft was in before he handed it over.

I took it to Mycroft. He tore it open, removing a note; as he read it, his face went enigmatic, and I braced myself for bad news.

"The pathologists for Fiona Cartwright and Albert Seaforth report that there was no indication of Veronal grains in the stomachs of the two victims."

"They missed it," I declared.

"Perhaps with Miss Cartwright, but the Seaforth examination appears to have been quite thorough. He was not given powdered Veronal to render him unconscious."

He handed me the reports, which indicated that Fiona Cartwright had drunk a cup of tea at some point before she shot herself, and Albert Seaforth had taken a quantity of beer. I had to agree, if powdered Veronal had been there, the pathologist would have found it. Which meant that as far as the drugs Brother used, we were back to square one.

"Still," I said, "he must have drugged Seaforth in some manner. I can't see a man this size just sitting down and permitting his wrists to be slit."

"Veronal comes in liquid form as well," Holmes commented. "I imagine he required the powdered form for Yolanda because he could stir it before-hand into the nut pâté. It would be a simple matter to dribble some from a bottle into a cup of tea in a busy café or a pint in a pub, but it would require sleight-of-hand to do so on an open hill-side."

A truly macabre image: a man casually handing a pâté-laden biscuit and glass of wine to the woman who had once been his wife, sitting on the grass with a picnic basket at their feet, the Long Man at their backs, and a waiting knife on his person.

Mycroft handed the remaining contents of the envelope to Holmes. They were photographs, both the reproductions of the Shanghai newsman's shot of "Reverend Hayden," and two rolls of film that Holmes had taken at the murder sites. He divided them into four piles, one for each site, removing those that showed the great monoliths of Stonehenge. We pored over them, separately and together, but other than illustrating some very attractive pieces of English countryside, they told us little.

"Lonely places to die, all of them," I remarked.

"One supposes they were chosen, in part, for that reason," Holmes replied.

"Well, if he'd wanted to commit his acts in a prehistoric site surrounded by people, he'd have been hard put to find one. Most of those that survive are in remote areas—central England may once have had as many standing stones and dolmens and such as Cornwall and Wales still do, but central England has more people needing stones for houses and walls."

"Certainly I found these sites most inconveniently located."

I did not mention that I had heard his sigh of relief when settling into bed the night before, hours after I'd gone to sleep.

I swallowed my last bite of toast and picked up one of the Shanghai reproductions, which still looked familiar, but still did not tell me why. "I'm going up to Oxford, I shall be back before dinner. Holmes, promise me you won't vanish again, please?"

"I shall endeavour to be here by six o'clock tonight," he announced, adding, "Not that I shall have much luck in the daylight hours."

"You're hunting down where our man got the other sedative?" It was not so much a shrewd guess as the voice of experience, for when it came to London's underbelly, Holmes grasped any excuse to keep me clear of it.

"Drugs sellers tend not to take a Sunday holiday," he said.

"I shall take your word for it. And, Mycroft, are you—"

"I shall begin enquiries as to the history and whereabouts of Reverend Brothers. But you, Mary, what are you doing in Oxford?"

I put on my hat and picked up my handbag. "It's going to be a perfectly lovely day on the river. Perhaps I shall take a friend punting."

I left my bemused menfolk staring at my back and wondering if I, too, had not gone just a bit mad.

Chapter Thirty-six

Great Work (1): The once-born seeks simple life.
The twice-born seeks true understanding.
The thrice-born, divine-man seeks to shape the world,
and set volatile Spirit alight.
Testimony, IV:1

IN FACT, A BOAT ON THE RIVER WAS PRECISELY WHAT
I had in mind, although it was more means than end.

My academic interests (sadly neglected over the past year) were in those areas of theological enquiry codified before the beginning of the Common Era—what is generally called the Old Testament, what those of us whose religious affiliations stretch back before Jesus of Nazareth know more precisely as the Hebrew Bible.

However, if my own interests are early, that does not mean I am unaware of the more contemporary, even futuristic branches of theology. I have friends who are experts in the Medieval Church; I have attended lectures on Nineteenth Century Religious Movements; I know people whose fingers are on the pulse of the wilder reaches of modern religion—some of those very wild indeed.

So when a question arose about Black Masses, I knew just where to go.

Clarissa Ledger was a Huxley—cousin of some sort to Thomas Henry, "Darwin's Bulldog," whose grandson Aldous looked to be the literary world's latest *enfant terrible*. Clarissa Ledger was also C. H. Ledger, M.D., D. Phil, one-time Warden of St Hilda's, author of fourteen books on religious topics ranging from Chinese Taoism to the Sufis of the Arabian peninsula, a woman of enormous curiosity, determination, physical courage (I had seen her initiation scars from a two-year sojourn in the mountains of East Africa), and mental agility, all of which persisted into her eighty-seventh year. To her immense irritation, her body's infirmities meant that now, the world must come to her.

I found her at home, as usual on a Sunday, returned, fed, and rested after attending early Communion at one or another of the rich array of Oxford churches. This morning it had been St. Michael's, which she pronounced "deliciously gloomy," and delivered a wickedly perceptive and academically precise flaying of the rector's homily, making me snort with unkind laughter. Her attendant granddaughter shook her head in disapproval, and served us cups of weak tea and tasteless biscuits before leaving us to our talk.

Professor Ledger gazed mournfully down at the liquid in her cup. "One of the medicine men pronounced on the evils of strong drink, which caused my family to unite against me and deny me coffee. I think they are hoping it may have a calming effect on my tongue as well."

"I remember your coffee. Perhaps they are merely hoping to preserve the china from dissolving altogether."

"I threatened to move bag and baggage back to the desert, but they did not take the threat seriously." She looked up from her cup, and fixed me with a beady blue gaze. "If you receive a wire from me demanding assistance, know to bring your passport with you."

I laughed—slightly uncomfortably, I admit, since it was exactly the sort of thing this old lady would do. "Or, I could bring you coffee from time to time."

"That might be better, Mary. I'm not sure how my bones would care for sleeping on the ground now."

We talked for a while about adventures, and I told her about my time in India earlier that year, and about the spring in Japan. I thought she might disapprove of the interference such investigations had on my academic career, but she saw past that to the riches of experience. Eventually, she asked me what brought me to see her.

"I need to know about the Black Mass."

"Not here," she said immediately. "If you want to talk about that, we need to be in the sunshine."

I found myself smiling at her. "How would you feel about punting?"

Her wizened face lit up. "So long as I am not in charge of the pole, I should love it."

So in the end, I did spend the day messing about in a boat. Her granddaughter and I trundled Professor Ledger around to St Hilda's in a Bath chair, chatting all the while about northern India. Once there, it was no effort at all to transfer her slight weight onto one of the college's boats, which had been draped with cushions and rugs to rival Cleopatra's barge. The granddaughter added food and drink sufficient to an Arctic expedition, a large umbrella, and a parcel of smelling salts and aspirins. I stepped onto the stern, rolled up my sleeves, and pushed away upstream, the granddaughter's voice still calling instructions from the bank.

A punt is twenty-four feet of low, blunt-ended boat propelled by dropping the end of a young tree into the river bottom, leaning on it with precision, then snapping the dripping pole up, hand over hand, until all sixteen feet of it are clear of the water. Several hundred of these repetitions go into a day's entertainment. It is a skill that, once learnt, comes back naturally, although after a long hiatus, disused muscles protest.

We dawdled around the cricket grounds, past the Sunday throng sunning themselves at the Botanic Gardens, dodging amateur boatsmen and the seal-like heads of boys swimming in the high, mud-coloured water. The sun-dappled contrast to last night's rainy preoccupation with a series-murderer made me feel as if I were emerging from an opium dream into fresh air. From time to time, my elderly companion would engage the occupants of other boats—once when she sweetly but inexorably exchanged our six bottles of picnic lemonade for one bottle of champagne belonging to a group of Balliol students (they had several more) and later absently to stuff that now-empty bottle into the throat of an adjoining row-boat's blaring gramophone—but for the most part, she talked. The subject matter caused nearby boats to linger for a moment, uncertain that they had overheard correctly, then hastily paddle or shove away when they had confirmed that yes, that extraordinary old lady had in fact just said such a thing.

"The Black Mass is, essentially, magic," she began. "One might, of course, make the same accusation of the Church's own ritual Mass, depending on how seriously one interprets the idea of Transubstantiation and the transformation of the communicants who partake of Christ's body." A pimpled boy at the oars ten feet away dropped his jaw at this statement, staring at Professor Ledger until the shouts of his passengers drew his attention to the upcoming collision. She went blithely on.

"No doubt, a high percentage of communicants over the centuries have taken the symbol as actual, and indeed, the Church itself encourages the belief that the Host is literally transformed from wheat flour into the body of Christ, and that when we take of His flesh, we are ourselves transformed into His flesh. Cannibals the world around would instantly agree, that eating a person imbues one with his essence. Speaking of which, did my granddaughter pack along those little meat pies I asked her for? Ah yes, there they are. Would you like one?"

I permitted the punt pole to drift behind us in the water, steering but not propelling, while I accepted one of the professor's diminutive game pies. I took a bite.

"Grouse?" I asked.

"One of my grandsons takes a house in Scotland for the Twelfth every year," she said.

"Very nice." Also very small. I took the glass I had propped among the boards at my feet, washed the pie down with champagne, and resumed the pole.

Professor Ledger jammed a clean handkerchief into the neck of the bottle and tied a piece of string around it, then dropped it over the side to keep it cool but unsullied in the river water—a very practiced move, indeed. She then held up a morsel of the pie in her gnarled fingers, eyeing it with scientific detachment. "One must wonder, if one partakes of the essence of grouse, how does it manifest? Does one explode into violent flight, or begin to make odd noises, or start to reproduce spectacularly?" This time a courting couple on the bank overheard her; as we drifted past, they craned after us so far, I expected to hear two large splashes.

"In any event, if one insists on a magical element to religion, one cannot then be surprised when magic is taken seriously. The Black Mass developed originally from the Feast of Fools, when idiots ruled the day and strong drink and carnality flowed unchecked. Harmless parody helps relieve pressure, and by keeping it under the auspices of the Church, one might say that licentiousness was kept licensed.

"However, with a work of magic at its core, the Mass was vulnerable to the most crass of interpretations: that the Host itself was where the power lay. If it all comes down to the Host, then equally it all flows back from that same place, so that, by using that scrap of unleavened bread as the point of the wedge, the authority of the Mass, and of the Church, and of God himself, could be turned on its head.

"The Black Mass was originally intended to profane the Host so as to turn its power to profane uses. From that beginning, the Black Mass grew like lichen on a rock, until one finds, say, the mass performed by Étienne Guibourg in the Seventeenth Century, in which the mistress of Louis Quatorze was stretched out on the altar with the chalice between her bare breasts"—a bespectacled undergraduate walking the path along Christchurch meadow dropped his book of poetry, bent to pick it up while looking over his shoulder at us, and fell on his face—"while the priest chanted his Latin to the devil.

"Sexuality, of course, is the central element in many of these Black celebrations, doubtless because the Church has aligned itself so definitively against free sexual expression. You've read the Marquis de Sade?"

"Er," I replied. I felt a bit like the bespectacled undergraduate.

"Well, then you'll remember how often his corrupt sexuality contains reference to elements of the Church—the Host, the Mass, monks, priests."

"What about blood?" I asked, a bit desperately.

Professor Ledger's bright eyes came to rest on my face. "My dear, why don't you tell me what you're after? Is this academic? Or one of your little investigations?"

I took the boat to the side opposite the footpath and worked the pole into the muck below, trapping us against the tree-lined bank. Once secure, I stepped over to the centre and settled onto cushions, retrieving the champagne and topping up our glasses.

"It's a case," I answered, and told her about it, my voice just loud enough for her aged ears. I did not tell her all: not Holmes' personal stake in it, nor the identity of the dead woman found ten miles from my home. I think she guessed that I was leaving out a large part of it, but she did not comment.

"So," I concluded some quarter hour later, "when there were objects that resemble quill trimmings at the murder sites, stained by what appears to be dried blood, and bits of black candle-wax as well, we had to wonder."

"Necromancy," she pronounced, her old voice quivering with distaste. "From *nekros* and *manteid*: 'dead divination.' Blood spells and invocations. Sealing a covenant. The darkest of the dark arts. And to use fresh blood, *in situ* . . ." She shook her head. "You must stop this person, Mary."

I forbore to make reference to her deprecating "little investigations" comment, but dug the rucksack I had brought from London out from under half a dozen rugs, and handed her the Adlers' copy of *Testimony.* "It might help, if you were to look at this and tell me what you see."

"Of course," she said, although her hand hesitated, just a moment, before closing on the book's cover.

"I have to take it back to London with me," I said in apology.

She patted her pockets until she found a pair of reading glasses, and opened the book.

I extricated the pole from the sucking mud without swamping the boat, and continued idly downstream to the Isis proper, then looped back up the Cherwell. We passed under Magdalen Bridge and were nearly to Mesopotamia when the aged academic closed the book and removed her spectacles.

I continued to punt in silence, though my muscles burned and my back ached.

"He writes as if in conversation with himself," she mused. "No explanation, no attempt at a reasoned argument, no *discursus* at all, except to enjoy the sound of his own voice. And yes, it is a he, most definitely."

"Yet this is not a journal, it is a printed book, of which there are at least two in existence," I said.

"If there are two, there will be more. This is an esoteric document to be presented only to True Believers. I should imagine he may have another, either in existence or in preparation, to set his beliefs before the outer world."

"The *Text of Lights*," I said. "That was what one of his disciples called it."

"Light indeed seems to be the basis of his cosmology—or rather, as you say, lights of various sorts: sun, moon, comets. Which reminds me, which comet do you imagine he was born under?"

"We think that of September 1882. There were no meteors then, as far as I can find, but he seems more than a little flexible when it comes to chronology. And to astronomy and geography, for that matter."

"Hare-brained thinking at its best," she said in disapproval.

"Madness being no excuse for sloppy ratiocination?" I asked, half joking.

She was not amused. "When one encounters a mystical system based upon the physical universe, it is generally manifested by a tight, even obsessive internal logic."

"However," I replied, "internal logic is not the same as rationality. 'The desperation to support an untenable position to which one is nonetheless committed has caused centuries of extreme mental gymnastics.' "

The statement was a direct quote, levelled at me some years before during the defence of a paper by none other than Professor Clarissa Ledger.

She remembered, and laughed. "I believe that was the only time I heard you apply volume over logic."

"Around you, only the once. But I think the author of *Testimony* never had you as a teacher."

"Pray God, no." The idea was, clearly, repugnant.

"Does the book suggest anything else about the man?" I asked her.

"He has a particular fascination for Scandinavian mythology, which I should suppose ties in with his interest in light—how the soul craves sunlight in the depths of a northern winter! I don't suppose you found any of the bodies hanging from trees?"

I glanced involuntarily around, but for once, there were no innocents in earshot. "Sorry, no."

"So he is not specifically fixed on Woden."

"No, but Norse myth, yes. He served a gathering of his closest followers a drink based on mead, which I think of as very Norse."

"Just mead?"

"It was drugged as well, with hashish and some kind of toadstool."

"Oh! Oh dear, that is not at all good."

"Er, why?"

She looked up, surprise battling the fatigue in her wrinkled features. "Ragnarok, of course. The final battle between chaos and order, the end of times and the beginning of a new age. I should say that, considering the impetus towards synthesis evinced by *Testimony*'s author, the deluded soul that wrote these words sincerely believes that by committing sacrifice under the influence of the 'Lights,' he can bring about the end of the world."

Chapter Thirty-seven

Great Work (2): The thrice-born man shapes the world
by learning to focus his will and the will of his community.
He uses the Tool to cut through empty pretence and loose
the contents of a vessel. He calculates the hour and
place to align the Universe with his act. This together
makes his Great Work.
Testimony, IV:1

RMAGEDDON?" HOLMES STARED AS IF I WERE THE
one about to initiate the events of Ragnarok.

"Not precisely, but essentially, yes."

He had been at Mycroft's flat when I returned at five-thirty and
found him disgruntled at failing to locate a seller of illicit drugs on a
Sunday afternoon. My own return—glowing with sun, exercise, and
information—did not make matters smoother.

"We're not after a gibbering idiot ripe for Bedlam, Russell."

"No, we're after a very clever fanatic obsessed with dark religion. A
man practical enough to use Millicent Dunworthy as a keystone to
his church, and at the same time, mad enough to believe in human

sacrifice. Holmes, the man makes careful annotations in his books with blood, he doesn't splash it across people in his meeting hall."

"Not yet," he retorted grimly.

Mycroft came in then from his daily perambulation, jauntily tipping his cane into the stand and tossing his hat onto the table. He rubbed his hands together, an anticipatory gesture, and went to survey the bottles of wine awaiting his attention.

Holmes glowered at the broad back of this second self-satisfied member of his immediate family, and demanded, "I don't suppose you made any progress in locating the so-called Reverend?"

Mycroft spoke over his shoulder, his hands pulling out one bottle, pushing it back, then sliding out the next. "My dear Sherlock, it is Sunday; my men may work, but the rest of the world is, I fear, enjoying what may be the last sunshine of the summer."

With an oath, Holmes seized his hat and flung himself down the hallway towards the study's hidden exit. Mycroft looked around, then raised his eyebrows at me. "What did I say?"

Holmes returned late, radiating failure. The next morning found him staring gloomily into his coffee; when I left, he was heaping an armful of cushions into a corner of Mycroft's study, making himself a nest in which to smoke and think. I was just as happy to make my escape before the reek of tobacco settled in.

Yesterday's warmth was indeed looking to be the last of the summer, and the dull sky suggested the rain would return, in earnest, before long. I took an umbrella with me as I set off with my copy of *Testimony* and my photograph of the Shanghai Reverend, to explore the possibilities of the book-binding trade.

I had a list—Mycroft might not be much for active footwork, but he was a magnificent source of lists—and started with the printers and binders nearest the meeting hall. There were a lot of names on the page, five of them in a circle around the Museum of Natural History. The morning wore on, one printer after another taking *Testimony* in his ink-stained hand, paging through it with a professional eye, then shaking his head and handing it back to me. I drank a cup of tea in the Cromwell Road, a glass of lemonade with a sliver of rapidly melting ice near the Brompton Hospital, and a cup of coffee on Sloane Street. The photograph grew worn. My right heel developed a blister. At two o'clock I had covered less than a third of Mycroft's list, and I was sick of the smell of paper and ink.

The bell in my next shop tinkled, and I had to stifle an impulse to rip it from its bracket. The shopkeeper was finishing with a customer, a woman with a particularly irritating whine in her voice and an even more irritating inability to make up her mind. I squelched the urge to elbow her to the side, and eventually she dithered her way into an order and left. I marched up to the man and thrust the book out at him.

"Do you know who printed this?"

He raised an eyebrow at the book under his nose, then turned the raised eyebrow on me. I shut my eyes for a moment. "I beg your pardon. It's been a hot and tiresome morning, but that's no excuse. Do you by any chance know who might have printed this book?"

Mollified, he took the thing and opened it, as twenty-one men already had that day. He, too, ran an interested professional eye across it; he, as the other twenty had, paused to study the illustrations; then he, as they had, swung his heavy head to one side.

"I can't be certain, but it might be Marcus Tolliver's work."

I stood motionless, my hand half-extended to receive the book. "What? Where?"

"Tolliver? Not sure. Somewhere up near Lord's."

"St John's Wood?"

"Or Maida Vale, perhaps."

My hand completed the gesture and returned the book to the carry-bag. I gave him my best smile, and said, "Sir, you don't know how close you came to being kissed."

He was imperturbable. "Next time you have a print job, madam, just keep us in mind."

A casual stroll past Tolliver's bindery told me that this establishment did not do much of its business printing menus and playbills. Two small windows faced the street. One of them had neat black-and-gilt letters across it:

Tolliver
BOOKS BOUND

The other window looked more like the display of a jeweller than a printer, with two small volumes nestled into folds of deep green velvet. One book stood, showing a cover of bleached deerskin that invited touch. The leather was graced with a delicate vine curling around letters that said, with an incongruous lack of originality, ALBUM. The vine had three blue-green fruits, round turquoise beads set into the embossing.

The other book lay open, and showed a page from what looked like the diary of a very gifted amateur watercolourist, with a shadowy sketch of a Venice canal surrounded by handwritten commentary.

I had found the shop twenty minutes earlier, passing on the opposite side of the busy street, then making a circle around its block of shops and flats. Unfortunately, there was no access to the back of the shop, as there might have been for a printer that used greater quantities of ink and paper. If I wanted to break in, I should have to do so through the front door.

I tore my gaze away from the pair of books and went through that front door now. The air bore a rich amalgam of expensive paper, leather, ink, machine oil, and dye-stuffs, with a trace of cigar smoke underneath. A bell rang, somewhere in the back, but the man himself was already there, bent and balding although he moved like a man in his thirties. He greeted me with an encouraging smile.

I laid my prepared tale before him: aged uncle with an interesting life; upcoming birthday; big family; multiple copies needed of his

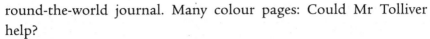

round-the-world journal. Many colour pages: Could Mr Tolliver help?

Mr Tolliver could help.

I then drew out the copy of *Testimony* and placed it on the counter. "I rather liked what you did with the sketches in this, and the paper—what's wrong?"

He had taken an almost imperceptible step away from the book; his smile had disappeared. "Is this your book?" he asked.

"No, I borrowed it from a friend." His expression remained closed, so I changed my answer. "Well, not so much a friend, just someone I know." Still no response. "And not so much borrowed. I sort of took it."

"You *stole* this?"

An effective witness interview is dependent on tiny hints and clues, reading from words, gestures, and the shift of muscles beneath skin, just what the person is thinking, and what he wants to hear. It happens so swiftly it seems intuitive, although in fact it is simply fast. Here, Tolliver was disapproving of the theft, but also, faintly, reassured.

"No no, I didn't steal anything, I borrowed it. But I didn't give my friend too much of a choice in the matter, short of snatching it out of my hands. I will return it, honest, I merely wanted to look at it more closely. Apart from the words, it is very beautiful."

I hoped he might relent a shade at the compliment, but if anything, he appeared less forthcoming than before.

And sometimes, an effective witness interview is dependent on techniques one finds distasteful. Such as telling the truth.

I sighed. "I am not actually in need of a printer. A friend's wife was murdered. I believe the police are looking in the wrong direction. I think the man who had this made knows something that might help. I need to find him."

He studied me for a long time, until I began to feel nervous: He had no reason to know that I was avoiding the police—my image was not yet posted across the news—but it was possible he knew of Damian

Adler's connexion with this book. At last, he reached out to caress one leather edge with his thick finger. He looked regretful, like a father whose son had committed a shameful crime.

"Twice in my career I have turned down commissions for reasons other than practical ones," he said. "The first was early, just my second year, when I was asked to bind a photograph collection of young girls that I found—well, intrusive. The second was to be a privately issued novel built around a series of police photographs of murder victims. Again, the salacious overtones were repugnant.

"In neither case, you understand, was it the display of flesh that made me say no. Why, just this past autumn, I bound a collection of, shall we say, personal drawings and poems as a gift from a wife to her husband. It turned out very pretty indeed.

"Those other two projects I rejected because I didn't like the thought of my work around that content. Do you understand?"

"I believe so."

"This book," he said, laying his hand flat on the cover, "made me wonder if I shouldn't regretfully decline it as well."

"But you did not."

"I did not. I read it, before I started on the plates, which I do not always do. I found it odd, but not overtly offensive."

"So why were you tempted to reject it?"

He tapped the cover thoughtfully with his fingertips: *one, two, three, four.* "It might have been the attitude of the man himself. Somehow he reminded me of the two men who brought me their little prizes to beautify. A trace of defiance, as if daring me to find fault with requests they knew to be unsavoury."

"But in this case, you could not."

"The sketches alone justified the project. In fact, I suggested to him that he might like to do a second version with just the artwork."

"What did he say to that?"

Tolliver's eyes twinkled. "He wasn't entirely pleased—the words, I understood, were his. He did say that he was working on a simpler version of the text, to be used with those same illustrations, a book intended for higher numbers. But I had to tell him that on my equipment, I should not be able to do a large print run." Tolliver did not sound regretful about the refusal.

"When was this?"

"January," he said promptly. "I generally take two weeks' holiday the beginning of the year—I'm always rushed off my feet December, and seldom finish the last-minute commissions until after Christmas—and he was one of the first customers to come through the door after that. Which may explain my inclination to take on his job."

"What—" I started to ask, but he had not finished his thought.

"Although the sketches would probably have decided me even if he'd come in during December, because Damian Adler was a client I wished to keep."

My heart gave a thump; it was all I could do to keep from looking over my shoulder to see if the police lurked outside of the door: The wry tone to his words told me he knew that Damian as a long-term customer was no longer a sure thing.

"Damian Adler is a client?"

"This is the friend whom the police are mistakenly looking for? I do read the newspapers. I thought him a most personable young man, with the kind of talent one does not see every day. He was one of the few new clients I undertook in December—he had a portfolio of prints and sketches that he wished me to mount and bind as a present. For his father, I believe it was, although he called by a few days later to tell me that there was no longer any urgency."

"I've seen that book," I interrupted—why hadn't I realised this earlier? "It's stunning."

Tolliver dipped his head at the statement, but did not disagree. "However, I stayed up late for several nights to finish it before my holiday, both for the sheer pleasure of the thing, and to encourage Mr Adler to bring me other commissions. When I saw these drawings, I recognised them as being his, and I understood that Mr Adler had recommended me to Reverend Harris."

Harris—yet another name to the man's armoury.

"This is a man in his forties? With a scar next to his left eye?"

"That is right."

"Do you know where he lives?"

He idly opened *Testimony*, paging through the text until he came to one of the ink drawings: the moon, in sharp black and white, centred on the page. He studied the drawing as if consulting it, then abruptly stepped away and bent, knees cracking, to draw a heavy leather-bound order-book from beneath the counter.

He flipped back through the pages, then turned the ledger around on the counter for me to read.

The address, I thought, would be phoney—Bedford Gardens was a street in Kensington, but I didn't think the numbers went that high. However, written beside it was a telephone number. If Smythe-Hayden-Harris-Brothers valued *Testimony* as highly as I thought, he might have been unable to bring himself to give a fake telephone number. Capping my pen, I ran my eyes across the ledger page, blinking involuntarily as I noted the sums involved. Then I looked more closely, and saw that this was for nine books.

"I see you made him nine copies?"

"Eight, actually. I offered to make fifteen or twenty—it's the plates that cost the money, you see, the actual materials are, well, not negligible, but the lesser of the whole. But he wanted precisely eight, and ordered the plates of the text destroyed."

"Really?"

"Yes. He even insisted on seeing the destroyed plates—not those of the drawings, those he asked me to save for the simpler edition of the book.

"The ninth book consisted of blank sheets of very high quality paper interspersed with the original drawings. That one was called *The Book of Truth*—inside, not on the cover. The cover had the same design I put on *Testimony*."

"I see. Well, thank you, Mr Tolliver. You've been a considerable help."

"I hope you find what you are looking for," he replied. Then, as I turned for the door, his voice stopped me. "Just, take care."

I studied his face, seeing more than mere politeness there. "Why do you say that?"

He was regretting it, this revelation about a customer, but he an-

swered anyway. "I don't know that Reverend Harris is the most whole-some of individuals. He did not strike me as altogether . . . balanced."

"I'll watch myself," I assured him, and went to find a public tele-phone, to set Mycroft onto the telephone number. I then took shelter in a café, drinking tea in a back corner well away from any constabu-lary eyes, until it was nearer to dusk.

When I rang Mycroft again, he had an address for me.

The address was one of a street of sturdy, proud, brick-and-stone ter-race houses that rose three stories above the street. Its stone steps were scrubbed, its trim freshly painted. Unlike its neighbours the cur-tains were tightly drawn—because the master of the house was ex-pected back after dark, or because he was not expected back at all? I strolled slowly past, taking in what details I could from a house with no eyes, then turned right and right again, down the service lane of dustbins and delivery vans.

And stopped dead.

A man was coming down the alley from the other end, a dapper fig-ure in a crisp linen suit, a neck-tie of a blue that glowed even in the crepuscular light, and a straw hat. He was swinging an ebony cane. He wore a black ribbon around his neck, which disappeared behind the bright blue silk scrap inhabiting his breast pocket: a monocle. Seeing my approach, he doffed his hat-brim half an inch above his sleeked-down hair.

Holmes.

Chapter Thirty-eight

Will: When a group of people are devoted to a goal, when they are consecrated into a way of living and dedicated to a Great Work, their communal Will glows and pulses like a small sun, providing energy for the Practitioner's Work.
Testimony, IV:2

WELL MET, HUSBAND," I SAID WHEN HE HAD CLOSED the distance between us.

He tipped his hat, then tucked my arm through his and propelled me back the way I had come, for all the world as if we were two residents whose afternoon stroll had brought them down an unexpected path.

Which was, one might say, nothing less than the truth.

"Did you find a drugs seller who knew the good Reverend's home address?" I asked him.

"Indirectly, yes."

"Am I to understand your nicotinic meditations were effective?"

"They generally are. Although it wasn't until the third pipe that it occurred to me that a man who attracts legal secretaries, titled young women, and Oxbridge undergraduates need not skulk through the dark and criminous parts of town to buy his drugs."

"A drawing-room drugs seller?"

"A doctor with a taste for the better things in life. A doctor with a remarkable number of neurasthenics in his practice, poor souls who require the assistance of chemical substances to make each day bearable."

"It makes sense."

"Shocking, that it took me so long to put it together. I have moved too long among the frankly criminal classes, that I overlook those on the upper tier."

"Still," I said, "no doubt there are any number of doctors who supplement their income by accepting payment for a little something extra. How did you find this particular one?"

"I recalled a certain Lady—literally, the second daughter of a duke—who holds an open house once a week attended by precisely that class of bored neurasthenics. So I decided to drop in on her and put to her a few questions."

"Hence the stylish suiting."

"It distracted her long enough to get me in the door. And as you know, I am a difficult person to evict, once I have settled in." He reached down to pluck a fragment of lint from his sleeve.

"Threatening a lady, Holmes?"

"Oh, my remarks were so delicate, they could scarcely bear the name of threat. Still, Her Ladyship's sense of vulnerability is painfully acute. One need only mention a name here, drop a hint there. The doctor she directed me to was of sterner stuff, but even he held out for very few minutes before identifying the man in the photograph, and admitted to having delivered a quantity of liquid Veronal once to the man's house. He insists on house calls, you see, both to provide a hold over his clientèle, and to get the stuff off of his premises, in case of a police raid."

I shook my head. "There is no loyalty among the criminal classes."

"Sad, but true. And you? You found the man who made *Testimony*?"

"And I didn't even have to lie to him," I said. "Well, I started off lying, but the truth became the simpler proposition. It seemed he didn't care much for the unwholesome atmosphere that surrounded Reverend Harris, as our man called himself."

I told him about my conversation with the book binder as we strolled the edges of Regent's Park and waited for dark. When the world had settled itself behind the dinner table, we returned to the house with the neat trim, and broke in.

A generation earlier, Brothers would have had a maid and even a valet in residence, but times had changed, and at half past eight on a Sunday night, his day help was gone.

By the stuffiness of the air and the lack of cooking odours, so was Brothers. There had been no lights visible through the curtains when we made our second pass by the front, but we stood motionless inside the dark kitchen for twenty minutes, listening to the emptiness. When we moved into the house, our soft soles made no impact on the silence.

The curtains at the back of the house were as tightly drawn as those in the front. There was no milk in the ice-box, no bread in the bin, and several advertising flyers on the floor inside the mail flap.

We started with a cursory, scullery-to-attic survey, our hand-torches confirming that the place was empty apart from a startled mouse—confirming, too, that this was the house we wanted: Two large and three small Adlers hung on its walls.

One of those, a fanciful portrait of Brothers in a cloak and wide-brimmed hat, solved the question that had niggled at me since Saturday night: The reason Lofte's photograph had seemed familiar was that Damian had used a segment of "Hayden's" face for the painting of *Woden in the World Tree* that I had seen a week before, although he had exaggerated the damage to Brothers' eye.

Studying this version of the face, I had a strong impression that Damian had enjoyed putting Hayden on the tree more than he had showing him as Woden the wanderer.

For a man of God, the Reverend enjoyed his luxuries: expensive drink in the cabinet, bespoke suits in the wardrobe, half a dozen pair of hand-crafted shoes, a set of silver-handled brushes for hair and clothing, and an ornate, high-poster bed that must have been two hundred years old. The coverlet was brocade with gold thread, and on the foot of the bed was folded a sumptuous blanket too soft for mere wool. I left the room, then on second thought returned, to pull back the brocade cover.

The bed's pillows and feather mattress were bare.

I found Holmes in the study. He had propped a heavy book against the wall, trapping the crack in the curtains to ensure the centre would remain closed, then switched on the desk lamp. He was not, I noticed, wearing gloves.

"The maid has stripped the linen from the bed," I told him from the doorway.

"Then we shall have plenty of time."

"His shoes match the size of the boot-prints you found. And I'd say he took with him a pair of rough foot-wear—there are signs of dirt-clots, but no soles to match."

He grunted, concentrating on the shelves, and I reluctantly stepped inside. The room smelt of incense, but under the sweetness lay an unpleasant air, as if some small carrion-eater had taken up residence under the settee. I ran my eyes over the spines of those books shelved nearest the lamp: a pamphlet on "Blood Cults of Kerala"; a Sixteenth-Century Inquisitor's manifesto on witchcraft; several books with Chinese writing on the spines. On the next shelf up resided a family of skulls, four of them, in descending height, elaborately engraved with designs.

Holmes came to the desk with an armload of books.

"What have you found?" I asked.

What he had found were three copies of *Testimony*. He dropped them onto the desk litter and opened the first to the frontispiece: the usual figure, followed by a numeral written in a dry brown ink, its rough outlines suggesting a nib other than metal:

"Six? Oh, sweet God, *six*? Is that—" My head filled with a rushing noise. I sat down.

"Blood," he said. "Yes. Although it may as well be that of a sheep rather than a human being." The words were dispassionate, almost academic: The iron control in his voice said something else entirely.

"Still." I realised that I was sitting in Brothers' chair and stood up hastily, while Holmes opened the other two copies. One had a *7*, although its brown colour was nearly obscured by the blotting sand stuck to it; the next, with an *8*, looked like the others I had seen.

"The Adlers' copy," I said abruptly. "That smear on its title page is actually the numeral one."

Holmes left the three books open under the desk lamp and went back to the shelf. "The binder told you he made eight?"

I forced my mind to his question. "Brothers seems to like the number eight—eight books, eight sections in each of the four chapters of the book. It would suggest that he has given away three others." Millicent Dunworthy possessed number two, but I thought I could identify the other Inner Circle members who had received three, four, and five: the nurse, her brother, and the sharp-nosed woman.

"It would also suggest that he took his *Book of Truth* with him," Holmes said. "Here's his blotting sand." He pulled the top off of a surprisingly large decorative tin, and picked up a pencil to stir its contents.

"What a lot," I said—there must have been a pound of the stuff, easily. I had seen blotting sand used at a solicitor's office, but it was generally a small sifting, easily dusted away. I reached out and took a pinch from the tin, rubbing it through my fingers. Blotting sand. And all those blank pages that wanted filling.

"Holmes—the sand. You found too much. Far more than he would need for just one numeral. And the repeated quill-sharpenings. *The Book of Truth* is his journal. He's setting down an account of the killings, then and there."

Holmes looked at the sand, and murmured, " 'It will have blood, they say; blood will have blood.' "

The power of the stuff in our veins: Professor Ledger had told me, and I had not taken it far enough. I had failed to imagine how full-blown the man's madness might be.

At least, I thought, grasping for some relief—at least this was not Damian Adler's madness. Although, even now I had to admit there was nothing to guarantee that Damian was not one of Brothers' acolytes. Nothing, that is, but the impossibility of his participation in the murder of Yolanda Adler, beloved wife, mother of his child.

"However," Holmes said, bent over the books with his strong glass, "I should have said this number seven has used some material other than blotting sand."

I took a look, and agreed: The material used to blot this number was fine enough that much of it had stuck. What that meant, if anything, there was no telling.

We replaced the copies of *Testimony* on the shelf, and while Holmes turned his attention to the walls, I settled to the desk (carrying over a stool, rather than sit again in Brothers' chair). The surface was covered in notes, books, pamphlets, and well-marked guidebooks to Scandinavia, Germany, and Great Britain. I found a desk-diary, which told us that Brothers had been away for the first three weeks of May, and a pamphlet extolling the charms of Bergen, Norway.

His current project, *Text of Lights,* took up most of the desk, in the form of notes made by a tight hand in a pen that leaked, typescript pages with cross-hatchings and notes, and the occasional torn-out page of a book or magazine with a paragraph circled. This would be *Testimony* for the masses, with simpler language, lots of Biblical references, astrological details, and concrete examples of the miraculous side-effects of becoming a Child of Lights.

I fished three crumpled sheets from the waste-paper basket, ironing them out with the side of my hand, but found they were only notes he had transferred to the typescript, and in one case, a fresh note spoilt by a gout of ink. I studied the smear, then searched through the debris for the pen that I had spotted, finding it under a discussion of astrological birth-charts. It was an ornate instrument with a twenty-four-karat gold nib, but ink clotted the lower edge of its barrel.

I said to Holmes, "Did you agree that the stain on Yolanda Adler's fingers looked like ink?"

"I did."

"Because it's possible she wrote that final letter to Damian at this desk, with this pen." I showed him; he said nothing, just turned his attention to the wall safe that he had found beneath a painting of Stonehenge under a full moon (amateurish and melodramatic and markedly not by Damian Adler).

I opened the desk's upper drawers and found, among the discarded pens, stationery, and paper clips, a wooden box containing half a dozen of the heavy, crude gold rings worn by the Inner Circle, in various sizes. Despite their solid appearance, they felt like gold plate. The next drawer down held maps of England, Scotland, Iceland, Germany, and all of the Scandinavian countries.

The bottom drawer held an assortment of rubbish, including a dog's collar that had clearly been buried for years, a pair of new-looking leather bedroom slippers, and a pretty little dollies' tea-cup.

I did not find a master journal filled with bloody writing, nor did Holmes.

He did, however, find something nearly as obscene.

Holmes finally gave a grunt of satisfaction, and the safe door came open. I went to look over his shoulder.

There was money, quite a bit of money, in the currencies of several countries. Two passports, one well-used British document under the name of Harris, the other for a resident of Shanghai named Hawthorn. A velvet pouch containing a palmful of diamonds, cut and polished and splashing a startling brilliance across the dim-lit room. A bottle holding several ounces of unidentified liquid, with three small glass phials waiting to be filled. And seven envelopes of heavy white paper, folded shut but not sealed.

On each was written a number; in each was a sample of hair. As Holmes had anticipated, several were from animals—envelopes one and two had tufts of sheep's wool, while number four had three tail-feathers from a rooster. Number three, however, was definitely human, grey and about eight inches long. Number five was from a man, brown with a few grey hairs, its pomade staining the envelope. Number six held half a dozen strands of a horse's tail. And number seven: heavy black hair four inches long, one end neatly bound with white silk thread, attaching it to a beautifully worked gold wedding ring, a delicate version of the one I had seen on Damian's hand.

Yolanda.

Holmes took a clean handkerchief from his breast pocket and spread it on the desk, tipping the black lock and ring into its centre. The empty envelope went back into the safe; the handkerchief he folded over and tucked into his pocket. I did not object: Its incriminating value in Brothers' possession was not worth the revulsion of leaving it here. He shut the safe, and came back to where I sat.

"Anything of interest?"

I pointed out several oddities that I had come across in the drawers but took care to leave in place. Now, Holmes pulled each out, tossing them onto the blotting-paper: Clearly, he cared no more for alerting Brothers to the search than he did about leaving finger-prints. "The blade is the wrong shape," he said of the stiletto I had found in the top drawer. He glanced through the pamphlet on Norse gods published by the United Kingdom Associated Sons of Scandinavia, but the rest—the monographs on Stonehenge and Hadrian's Wall, a *Times* article on a hoard uncovered in Devon, a booklet about the northern constellations, the dollies' tea-cup—those he flicked over with a dismissive finger before returning to the shelves, to pull down and shake out each book, one after another.

I fitted the tiny porcelain cup onto the end of my little finger. It was an odd thing to find in the possession of this man. And exactly a week before, I had seen a set the precise match of this one, three cups on a diminutive enamel-ware tray. Had we found this missing cup with the other trophies in the safe, it would have had a very different meaning, but dropped with other things into a drawer . . . ?

And now, the object started off a series of thoughts that I had tried to keep at the back of my mind. However, it had to be brought to light, and when, if not now?

"Holmes, do three-year-olds play dollies' tea-party?"

"My experience with three-year-olds is limited," he replied.

"The Adlers' neighbours, at number eleven, have a daughter of eight or nine. She plays dollies' tea-party. I did myself when I was her age. And she is in the habit of playing with Estelle Adler when they meet in the park. She made reference to books as well. Although some children do read at a young age. I did, myself."

"Does this fascinating narrative have a direction?"

I took a bracing breath. "All along, Holmes, Damian has been . . . less than completely forthcoming with us."

"He has lied?" Holmes said bluntly. "People generally do, although I have told you his reasons."

"But, about the child."

He stopped what he was doing. "What about her?"

I spun the tea-cup around the end of my finger, so as not to meet his eyes. "That photograph, of the Adlers. It looked out of date."

"How do you mean?"

"Yolanda's dress and hair. Fashion changes rapidly these days, particularly skirt lengths. The dresses in her house reflected current tastes— even those that were not new had had their hems adjusted. I noticed, because it struck me as incongruous, a Bohemian so attentive to fashion." I lifted my gaze from the cup on my finger. "I'd have said the skirt in that photograph is three or four years old. And the hair-cut."

"The photograph was taken in Shanghai," he pointed out.

"Where, I agree, styles may be behind the times. It is equally possible that Yolanda only discovered a sense of fashion after she came to London. But—"

"You are suggesting that the picture was taken some years ago? Why should Damian—"

He stopped.

I finished the thought. "If the photograph was in fact taken some years ago, then the child is older than Damian permitted us to believe. Would the neighbour's girl be as interested in exchanging books, were Estelle three and a half years old?"

"This could not be the child born in 1913," he declared.

"Dorothy Hayden? No, I agree, not unless this photograph is a re-markably good fake. But even if Yolanda and Brothers—Hayden—this man has entirely too many names! Even if they separated in 1917, a child could have been born after that, and been small when Damian arrived in 1920."

"You are proposing that, were Damian concerned that I would not search for his wife once I knew her history, it would apply doubly were I to suspect the child was not even his. And it would," he conceded, "further explain Yolanda's continued contact with her former hus-band, were he the father of the child."

He turned back to the shelves, but I thought his mind was not on his actions. Nor, in truth, was mine.

We found nothing of further interest, although I was grateful Brothers had been here for less than a year, and had not filled the house with a lifetime of macabre treasures.

When we had finished, Holmes wrapped a sheet of paper around a glass paperweight from the desk, for the finger-prints, and slid it into his pocket, along with a phial of the unidentified liquid from the safe and a sample of the blotting sand. He stood looking down at the desk with its litter of pamphlets and objects—not the tea-cup, which lay in my pocket—and then picked up the stiletto. He considered it with his thumb for a moment, then raised it high and drove it viciously down: through a postcard photograph of an Irish stone cross; through the train time-table below that; through the cheaply printed pamphlet of Norse churches in Britain and the almanac page showing the phases of the moon for 1924 and the stained green blotter, deep into the wood of the desk itself.

We left it there, a declaration of war.

———

Back at Mycroft's flat, which was silent but for the snores rumbling down the hallway, we assembled a dinner of bread and cheese, drank some tea, and took ourselves to bed.

Most unusually, it was Holmes who fell asleep and I who lay, gazing at the patterns of street-lights on the ceiling. After an hour, shortly after four a.m., I slipped out into the sitting room and settled with a rug over my legs and another pot of tea at my side, reading Monday's newspapers.

Something was stirring in my mind, and I did not know what it was. It was in part the awareness of tension: Yes, I was relieved that Damian seemed to be in the clear, but that had been replaced by the growing conviction that he and the child had driven away into mortal danger.

More than that, some combination of events, or of objects witnessed, prowled in the back of my mind; some alarming shape was growing in the darkness, and the only way of encouraging it to emerge into the light of consciousness was to ignore it. I turned resolutely to the news, important and trivial, and drank my tea until it was cold and bitter. Finally, I switched off the light and sat in the gathering dawn.

Today I should have to have another conversation with the Adlers' maid, Sally. Nothing she had said gave a shape to the child's age, but surely if I asked, she would be able to tell me just how old Estelle was. Other than size, what were the determining differences between an ordinary eight-year-old and a precocious four-year-old? Teeth, perhaps? I should have to find out first. And why hadn't I thought to confirm her age with that neighbour?

(Something I had read, days ago, teased at the back of my mind. That heap of papers in Sussex, it must have been, month after month of news items that blurred into one another. A murder here, a drugs raid there, given equal weight with a photograph of a hunt breakfast and a June excursion to the seaside . . . I firmly withdraw my mind from the direct approach.)

Also today, we should have to find the owner of that trim terrace house a short walk from three train stations. Whether Brothers

owned it or let it, there would be paperwork—which could be why he had taken such care to keep Gunderson from knowing about it.

(An excursion to the seaside. But, not the seaside . . .)

Should I ask Holmes to review with Mycroft the crimes of the full moons? Perhaps the two brothers together would see a pattern I had missed.

(She died on a full moon, and I'd been reading the newspapers that week and come across something. . . .)

My days in Sussex had, actually, been a lovely holiday, four entire days of solitude and bees, brought together, now that I thought of it, in Holmes' book. A man who retired at a remarkably early age from the busy hive of humanity that was London, resigning himself to the conviction that the person he called "The Woman" was lost to him, that his life was—for all he knew—sterile. He had disappeared, freeing me to enjoy the peace and the book and the skies—first the meteors, then that remarkable eclipse of the moon. What a pity he had been in the city, where the skies were no doubt too light—

(An advert! For a Thomas Cook tour, to the eclipse—but not to the lunar eclipse; why run a tour to something visible from one's back garden? That meant—)

I threw off the rug and padded down the hallway to Mycroft's study, impatiently running my grit-filled eyes across the shelves until I spotted his 1924 almanac.

I found the page, read it, and looked up to see Holmes in the door-way, summoned by my footsteps, or by my brain's turmoil.

"What have you found?"

"It may be nothing."

"Tell me," he demanded.

"Thomas Cook was advertising an expedition to Scandinavia—well, that's not important." I tried to order my thoughts. "Holmes, it may not be the September full moon that Brothers is waiting for. Full moons enter into it, but I think he's picking off celestial events. The ram at Long Meg died on the first of May, the Celtic festival of Beltane. Albert Seaforth died on the night of the Perseids. Brothers may be aiming for the solar eclipse."

"An eclipse? In England?"

"No, it's mostly Arctic. Parts of northern Scandinavia will see it, although it looks as if Bergen, Norway, might be on the very edge. However, Holmes, I—"

"When?"

I looked back at the page, hoping I had read it wrong, but I had not. "August the thirtieth."

Four days away.

Chapter Thirty-nine

*The Tool: A Tool must incorporate all four Elements.
Beyond that, the Tool must be shaped by the Practitioner
to have a life of its own, both to draw in and to give out
Power. The Tool must move the hand even as the
hand moves it.*
Testimony, IV:3

EAVY SILENCE PRESSED ON US. HOLMES STARED
at me for the longest time before his eyes flicked down to
the almanac, and he drew a ragged breath. His mouth was coming
open as he turned to the door.

"Mycroft!" he shouted.

With a crash of feet on the floor, Mycroft Holmes woke to his
brother's need. Within minutes, the telephone was summoning help
from near and far. The voices of the Holmes brothers were soon
joined by others, and I listened through the open study door as the
complex machinery of Mycroft's department was seized and turned
towards finding a pair of men, the younger of whom could possibly
appear ill or intoxicated, with a child, age three to eight. Borders;

ferries; telegrams: By seven-thirty, the sitting room sounded like a general headquarters on the eve of battle.

All the while, I sat at Mycroft's oversized desk, trying to order my thoughts. A part of my mind was occupied with drawing up a list of possible sites Brothers might choose that were within striking distance of Bergen: Viking country, whence the raiders had set off to conquer the British Isles; home of Woden, the Viking's chief god and a figure who occupied much of Brothers' image of himself.

But when I had made the list, I then pulled out a small-scale map of the United Kingdom and studied that, chin on hands. After a while, I put on some proper clothes and went down to ask the building's concierge for his copy of *Bradshaw's* time-table. I came back up and passed through the room, unnoticed by nine urgently occupied men, to settle again at the desk.

An hour later, I saw Mycroft, still in his dressing-gown, go into his room. Holmes was speaking on the sitting room telephone, but a minute later, silence fell for the first time since he had called his brother out of sleep. I heard the click of his cigarette lighter, and the puffing noise of pillows being arranged on the divan.

I went out and found Holmes sitting before the fireplace, staring intently at the cold stones. While the water was boiling for coffee, I went through the sitting room and gathered half a dozen empty cups, piling them up for washing. Absently, I toasted bread, and had managed to scrape half their burnt substance into the sink when Mrs Cowper arrived for the day. She looked in astonishment at the signs of turmoil and dishevelment where normally she would find a cup and one sullied ash-tray, then snatched open the oven door, releasing yet another cloud of smoke. I hastily retreated with my own ravaged toast to where Holmes sat.

He looked startled when I held a cup under his nose, and the long ash from his forgotten cigarette dropped to the carpet. "Russell, there you are. Ah, coffee, good. Did you see your letter?"

The morning post lay on the table near the door. A cream-coloured envelope bore my name, in an antique and slightly shaky hand. I carried it back to the divan and thumbed it open. It was from Professor Ledger, to whom I had given my address in London.

"Mycroft has arranged that all border crossings be watched," Holmes was saying. "All international ferries and steamers will be searched, and all ports in northern Europe sent photographs of the two men, in case they've already crossed over. The same with aeroplanes—and harbour masters, in case he tries to hire a small boat. I fear we are closing the stable door on the horse's tail, and that they left the country immediately you saw them drive away from the walled house, but perhaps we can at least track where he has broken out."

The housekeeper came in with a more recognisable breakfast tray, moving a table in front of Holmes' eccentric choice of seating. "Have something to eat, Holmes," I urged.

He seemed not to hear me, so I took a slice of pristine toast, smeared it with butter and marmalade, and folded it in two, placing it into his hand. Absently, he took a bite, but kept talking.

"Steamers to Bergen leave from Hull, and Mycroft has two men on their way, with photographs. It shouldn't require delaying the boat, which is scheduled—"

"Holmes, may I say something?"

His grey eyes came up, and he looked at me for the first time. "Of course, Russell. What is it?" He took a bite of the toast, his body feeding itself while his mind was elsewhere.

"We may be on the wrong track."

He swallowed impatiently, dropping the remains of his breakfast in the ash-tray. "Explain."

"When we believed Estelle to be three years old, you thought it unlikely that a solitary man—Brothers—would risk burdening himself with an infant. And as you said, disposing of a small body is lamentably easy. However, we know that the child was alive as of Wednesday night. Which makes this important." I handed him the letter.

Monday, 25 August

Dear Miss Russell,

The infirmities of age are sufficiently vexing upon one's body, but the effects on the mind I find particularly troublesome. This note is by way of being a second thought, which in better times would have come to me while you were still in my presence. I can only trust that there is an element of truth in the saying, better late than never.

As I thought over the situation with which you presented me yesterday, I came to realise that I had neglected to mention one aspect of necromancy, perhaps because it is one of the things so abhorrent, it causes the healthy mind to shudder away. I speak of the relative potency of the blood of an innocent.

Throughout the ages and across the world, the sacrifice of a virgin is regarded as being the most efficacious. When I lay down to sleep last night, I found my rest disturbed by the thought that your suspected necromancer might be in the vicinity of young innocents.

If there are young women near him, or a child of either sex, warn them away, I beg you.

Yours,
Clarissa Ledger

When his eyes had reached the bottom of the page, I asked, "What if his intended sacrificial victim isn't Damian? What if it's the child? Who could be his own child. As he sacrificed his own wife?"

Hope and horror warred in his face, but without a word he carried the letter out of the room. Two minutes later, Mycroft came in, his braces down and dots of shaving cream under his chin, and picked up the telephone. When he had reached his second in command, he said, "Morton? We need to change the search description. The two men and a child may be one man and a child. Yes."

In twenty minutes, the orders made previously had been amended, and the phone was set back into its hooks. Mycroft left us, and came back clean of shaving cream, tie knotted, waistcoat buttoned. We moved to the dining table, where Mrs Cowper set a bowl of freshly boiled eggs in a napkin before Mycroft. Holmes and I had coffee; he supplemented his beverage with another cigarette. A number of times over the years, I had cause to regret that I did not use tobacco: This was one of those. Instead, I dropped my head in my hands and rubbed my scalp, as if to massage my thoughts into order.

"It would help," I complained, "if we knew just what Brothers had in mind. His is not a random striking-out. He has a plan. What is it?"

"Human sacrifice at a point of solar eclipse to bring about the end of times?" Holmes asked. It sounded truly mad, when put that way. I scratched my head some more, and a thought surfaced.

"Why kill Yolanda? Was it entirely in service of the ritual, and she was convenient? Or was it revenge, that she left him and married Damian?"

"We don't know that *she* left *him*," Mycroft objected. "Granted, she brought proceedings against him, but that is the way of amicable divorces."

"*Testimony* reveals Brothers to be a man eager to embrace coincidence," Holmes remarked. "He could have seen the two impulses as driving him to the same point."

"And a third," I added as something came back to me. "Remember Damian told us that Yolanda was troubled about something in the middle of June? What if she found out that her former husband and head of her church had killed Fiona Cartwright at Cerne Abbas? If Brothers thought she was about to turn him in, that would have been a further reason."

Mycroft shifted in his chair. "Still, I should have said the ritual element was particularly strong, if he went to the trouble of dressing her in new clothing."

"Were any of the others wearing new clothes?" I asked, but that question had not been addressed on the police reports.

"We may have to wait until we give what we have to Lestrade," Holmes said, "before we can answer that."

"In any case," I decided, "we may not be certain what he wants with the child, but I should say his goal with Damian is twofold: revenge over Yolanda, and doing what *Testimony* calls 'loosing' Damian's power."

" 'He has the Tool,' " Mycroft recited, " 'to cut through empty pretence and loose the contents of a vessel.' "

"He would consider the 'contents' of Damian's 'vessel' to be considerable."

"As for the child," Holmes said, " 'The greater the sacrifice, the greater the energies loosed.' "

" 'The world lies primed,' " I said quietly, " 'for a transformative spark.' "

The morning that had begun in a storm of activity dragged slowly. Holmes paced and smoked, frustrated by the difficulties of leaving this place while Lestrade's arrest warrants waited for us outside. I retreated to Mycroft's study with the list of livestock deaths that I had begun to incorporate on Friday evening, and Mycroft picked up a novel by G. K. Chesterton, to all appearances completely undistracted.

Two hours later, I heard the two men talking; a short time later, Holmes put his head through the study doorway.

"I'm going to Norway," he said abruptly. "They may need me in Bergen."

I did not know if *they* meant Damian and Estelle or Mycroft's men, but it hardly mattered. "All right."

His look on me sharpened. "You don't agree?"

"How the hell should I know?"

"Russell, this questioning of your abilities must stop. If you have something to contribute, speak up."

"Patterns," I said helplessly. "He *has* to have a pattern, and the only one I can find makes little sense."

"Show me."

So I showed him. And Mycroft, who had abandoned Chesterton to help Holmes assemble a kit for Scandinavia, and heard us talking.

I had been unable to shake the idea that my path over the past two weeks was littered with crumbs of evidence, like the trail left through the woods in the fairy-tale. But, just as a random scattering of crumbs can be connected into lines, so will random evidence appear to coincide.

And I was not sure enough of myself to be certain that the patterns I saw were real.

"One might think that if a sacrifice draws on and reflects the power of an eclipse, the performer would move heaven and earth to be standing in a place of greatest darkness. But I'm not sure that is of paramount importance to the author of *Testimony*. The book is full of minor inconsistencies; symbolic truth is far more important to him than mere fact."

Most men, launched on a desperate search for a son or nephew, would be impatient with this excursion into academic theory; these two men were not.

"So, two small pieces of evidence bother me. First, one of the books on Brothers' desk was a guide to Great Britain. He'd made marks on the entries for London and Manchester, and had dog-eared, then smoothed out, several other pages, including the one describing the Wilmington Giant. There were two slips of paper in the guide-book. One marked the beginning of the London section, the other was for the Scottish Isles.

"Second. In Millicent Dunworthy's desk was a folder pertaining to the Children of Lights. A ledger recorded costs—hiring the hall, building cabinets, candles, tea—but there were also other notes. One concerned the cost of placing an advertisement in various newspapers; there were several estate agent listings for halls for hire, larger than the room they're using now. And there was a page in Miss Dunworthy's handwriting with times and prices. The sort of thing you'd jot down without needing to write the details, because you knew what they referred to.

"I did not write those down, but to the best of my recollection, those times and prices match your concierge's *Bradshaw's* for trains from London to Scotland."

I reached for the small map I'd been studying, then rejected it in favour of a proper one from Mycroft's map drawer. Elbowing aside the accumulated notes and books, I laid the map on the blotter, then found a yard-stick in the corner and a rusty protractor probably not used since Mycroft was a school-boy.

"Now, this part I'm not sure about, since I was working on a smaller scale, but let's see how it transfers to this one." I made a small X halfway up the left side of Britain. "Four sites in England, beginning with May Day, or Beltane, when a ram was slaughtered in a stone circle in Cumbria. The second, on the seventeenth of June—a full moon—was Fiona Cartwright, at the carving of a male figure in the hillside in Dorset." I put a second *x* on the map, over Cerne Abbas, then a third in the upper right, the emptiness of the Yorkshire Downs. "On the twelfth of August, the night of the Perseids meteor shower, Albert Seaforth was killed at a stone circle in Yorkshire. And three days later, on the second night of the full moon, Yolanda Adler died at another male hill carving, in Sussex." I put an *x* for Yolanda at the map's lower right.

"The male victims—the ram and Albert Seaforth—were found at the circles: Long Meg and her Daughters, and the High Bridestones, both female places. The two women were found at the male figures."

Four marks on a map; two pairs of balanced masculine-feminine energies. I laid the straight-edge across the marks and connected them, making a shape that was not quite trapezoidal, since the upper corners were slightly higher on the left.

"A quadrilateral polygon," Holmes noted, his voice unimpressed.

But I was not finished. "I asked Mycroft about events occurring around full moons. Among those he recalled were a sheep with its throat savaged in a Neolithic tomb in Orkney, on the eighteenth of May, and an odd splash of blood on the altar of the cathedral in Kirkwall, also in Orkney, on July the sixteenth: Both of those dates were full moons."

They watched as I laid the yard-stick along the two side lines of the shape and extended them up to form a long, narrow triangle stretching the entire length of Britain, and more.

The meeting point was in the sea north of the Orkney Islands. I tapped my front teeth with the pencil, dissatisfied. "On the other map, they came together in the middle of the Orkney group. Here—"

I duplicated the lines on the smaller map, then set the point of the protractor at the triangle's tip, describing a circle that encompassed the islands. When I took my hands away, this was the shape that remained:

"However, the four points could as easily signify this," Holmes objected, taking the pencil and yard-stick to connect the corners of the polygon, determining its centre point. We bent to look at an area north of Nottingham and Derby.

"Ripley?" I said. "Sutton? There's nothing Neolithic there, that I can see."

"There's nothing Neolithic at the meeting place of the triangle, either, unless it's under the North Sea."

"You're right." I took off my spectacles and rubbed my tired eyes. "I told you it made little sense. Although it did look better on the smaller map."

"It is but a matter of three or four degrees," Mycroft said in a soothing voice, and stood up. "In any case, perhaps I had better widen the recipients of the watch order to include domestic steamers."

"And trains," I said.

Holmes said nothing, just studied the map as if hoping for the appearance of glowing runes in the vicinity of Nottingham. Then his gaze shifted north, to the spatter of islands off the end of Scotland.

I knew what he was thinking, as surely as if he were muttering his thoughts aloud. He was weighing how certain I was, how carefully I had gathered those snippets of evidence, if his eyes might not have caught something mine missed. After all, in both cases—the time-table and the dog-eared guide-book—the information was caught on the run, as it were, noted in passing while I was closely focused on something that appeared more important. Had I been actively looking for train tables at the time, then he could have counted on my memory of some scribbled notes as being rock-hard and dependable. But numbers seen and half-noted while my mind was elsewhere?

He had, before this, trusted his life to my hands. Now he was contemplating putting the lives of his son and the child in those same hands. I did not know if he would. Frankly, I hoped he would not.

"We have noted that the man is willing to sacrifice chronological and geographic precision for the sake of symbolic truth," he mused.

"Fifty miles is a lot of imprecision," I argued.

"Yes, but two degrees is not, Russell. If his map told him that the High Bridestones were one or two miles to the west, or the Giant the same distance to the east, then your lines would meet in Orkney."

"But we don't know his map, and we do know where the eclipse will be." I really did not want to wrestle him for the responsibility of saving those two lives.

"If he were going to Orkney for this . . . event, where would you imagine?"

"Stenness," I answered. "Two stone circles, several free-standing stones, and a causeway. The tomb where the sheep was found back in May is a part of the same complex."

The piece of paper on which I had noted likely sites near Bergen lay on the corner of the desk. He looked from the inaccurate map to the list, and then scrubbed his face with both hands, pausing for several breaths with his fingertips resting against his eyelids. "As I remember, Sir Walter Scott fancied the centre stone at Stenness as an altar for human sacrifices," he commented idly. Then he dropped his hands and met my eyes.

"I shall go to Bergen. You'll need warm clothing for Scotland. And, Russell? Take a revolver."

Chapter Forty

*Time: As the workings of a clock must align before the
hour strikes, so must the stars and planets align before a
Great Work is done.
Time is round and repeating as a clock face; time is
straight and never-duplicated as a calendar. Only at
midnight—the witching hour—does time suspend between
one day and the next.
Opposite concepts, only brought together in a Work.*
Testimony, IV:4

OLMES TUNNELLED INTO MYCROFT'S STORAGE
room, creating a storm of wool and waterproofs, while I
addressed myself to the *Bradshaw's* and the problem of getting from
London to Orkney. St Pancras to Edinburgh: nine to twelve hours;
Edinburgh to Inverness: another six or eight; Inverness to Thurso, at
the northern tip of Scotland—trains twice daily: six or seven hours.
Unless I caught the Friday express . . . but no, leaving it to Friday was
not a good idea, since there appeared to be only one steamer a day
from Thurso to Orkney.

What if I took to the water before I ran out of Scotland? There were sure to be regular sailings from Inverness or Aberdeen, although those wouldn't be in *Bradshaw's*.

Mycroft came into the study and found me searching his shelves.

"I don't suppose you have a time-table for the steamers into Orkney?" I asked him, although I was more thinking aloud than putting a question to him. "I'll ask your concierge—I need to see if it would be better to work my way north by train, or to take a steamer along the way. Of course, if the weather is bad there, I'm a bit caught. Although I suppose there's always some mad Scotsman willing to put out in a typhoon if I offered him enough money."

"Or held a gun to his head," Mycroft said. Before I could decide if this was his peculiar sense of humour or a serious proposal, the telephone rang. He reached past me for the instrument on the desk, and I went back to my *Bradshaw's*.

His half of the conversation consisted mostly of disapproving grunts, as he received what was clearly a negative report from one of the men dispatched earlier that morning. He placed the earpiece in its hooks with a precision that indicated he was not much removed from throwing the instrument across the room.

"No luck?"

"Nothing," he said.

"I'll catch the night express for Scotland," I told him. "It'll be tight, but I should make it north in time for the Thursday steamer." I shook my head. "Ridiculous, to think your man Lofte could come halfway around the world in a week when it's going to take me three days to get seven hundred miles."

"Why not employ an aeroplane?"

I stared at him. "What?"

"An aeroplane. Heavier-than-air fixed-wing contraption? Been around since two brothers in America persuaded a propeller and some canvas to go airborne? You have been up in one, I believe?"

"Memorably," I said, with feeling.

"Well?"

For thrilling entertainments, darting air battles, or emergency exits from sticky situations, aeroplanes were ideal; for transporting human beings over long stretches of countryside, I was none too certain. Yes, Lofte could throw himself headlong on a dare; yes, the mail now flew daily across America; still, there was a great deal of difference between sacks of mail and human beings when it came to surviving mechanical difficulties a thousand feet in the air.

I had to clear my throat before I could say mildly, "They're hardly dependable."

"Imperial Airways has been in existence since March," he pointed out. "Not all that many flights, to be sure, but air travel is the way of the future."

"You're not saying that there is commercial aeroplane travel from London to Orkney?" I demanded.

"No," he admitted. "I should have to arrange something more private."

I had a brief vision of Lofte's bedraggled condition on Saturday night, but told myself that had been the result of six thousand miles; this would be a mere tenth the bedragglement.

As if following my thoughts, Mycroft said, "If I can find you a 'plane, you could be there in a day, Thursday at the latest."

"You needn't make this sound like some treat you're offering a child, Mycroft."

"What is this you're offering Russell, Mycroft?" Holmes had come into the room at the last phrase, to fetch the stack of photographs showing the Adlers and Reverend "Hayden."

"Aeroplane travel," I said bluntly. "And do leave us some of those."

He concentrated on setting aside a few of each photograph, but emotions played over his face: surprise giving way to a queasy apprehension, then serious consideration, finally settling into wonderment.

"One forgets," he reflected, "that in half a year's absence, technological advances will have been made."

"It's been an entire year since Kelly and Macready crossed America without stopping," Mycroft said, stretching out an arm for the telephone. "And the American Army round-the-world team has reached Iceland with two of its original three machines."

"Yes, and the *Boston* wrecked off Orkney, didn't it?"

"Is that your answer, Mary?"

"No, I suppose I could think—"

But Mycroft's hand was already on the instrument. "Sherlock, if you are looking for the folded maps, I've moved them to the escritoire. Hello, is that Carver? Can you find Lofte and send him to me?"

Holmes pawed through the maps and removed several, then noticed me. "Need you stand there gawping, Russell? Don't you have things to do? I recommend you begin with locating a pilot who has taken a pledge."

"Thank you, Holmes, for offering me up to the gods of technology." It appeared that I was to become a barn-stormer.

Holmes' driver rang the bell a few minutes later, and the two men left through the hidden doorway. Ten minutes later, the bell rang again, this time for me.

Mr Lofte's appearance had improved out of all recognition in the three days since I had seen him. His face was shaved, his suit so new it still bore traces of tailor's chalk, and the only odour about him was the faint aura of shaving soap.

Mycroft greeted him by saying, "My brother's wife needs to be in Orkney immediately. I wish you to assist her."

The unflappable modern-day Phileas Fogg merely asked, "Will you need both the 'plane and the pilot?"

"I can requisition the machine, if need be."

"When you say 'immediately,' do you wish to undertake a night landing?" I hastened to assure him that my need for speed was merely desperate, not suicidal. He nodded.

"In that case, let me see what I can scare up at the Society."

"I'll come with you, if I may," I said, thinking: my life, my choice of pilots. Then Mycroft gently cleared his throat. I looked over. He was simply reading the paper, but after a moment, I saw the source of his objection.

"Actually," I told Lofte, "I have a few things I must do. How about if I meet you down the road a piece? In, say, twenty minutes?"

"I don't mind wait—"

"No no, it's a lovely day out there." I plucked his shiny new Panama hat from the side-table and thrust it back into his hands. "Where are we headed?"

"Albemarle Street," he answered.

"The Burlington Arcade, then. Twenty minutes. See you there."

Obedient, if uncomprehending, he stepped out of Mycroft's front door. Three minutes later, I stepped through Mycroft's private back exit.

What happened next is no-one's fault but my own. Leaving the dim tunnel near Angel Court with my mind on aeroplanes, I came face to face with a man I had last seen in the corridors of Scotland Yard. Worse, his reactions were quick.

Leaving behind the light cardigan I wore seemed preferable to assaulting one of Lestrade's men, but it was training, not speed, that wrenched my arm free from his hard fingers. Speed did make it possible to draw away from him on the street, as I led him on a circuit of St James's Palace and up to the mid-afternoon crowds along Piccadilly.

He was persistent, give him that. I didn't shake him off until I dodged in and out of the Dorchester, and even then, I took care to work my way back through the by-ways of Mayfair. All in all, it was a full half hour before I spotted Lofte, browsing a display of silk kerchiefs in the Burlington Arcade.

"Good," I said nonchalantly, my eyes everywhere but on him. "Shall we go?"

He took in my breathless condition and proved his worth by whipping the hat from his head and popping it on mine, then did the same with his jacket, which fit my arms rather less completely than it had his. He smoothed his hair with both hands and followed me back up the Arcade, removing his neck-tie and rolling up his sleeves to make for a more complete change of image. From a distance, the two men who left the Arcade, one of them regrettably *en dishabille,* bore little resemblance to the young woman who had sprinted away from an officer of the law.

Lofte's "Society" was, it transpired, the Aeronautical Society of

Great Britain. And Mr Lofte himself, I found as we strolled up Old
Bond Street with watchful eyes, had been Captain Lofte of the RAF,
beginning in the early days of the War when, if memory served me, the
average life span of an active fighter pilot had been three weeks. Even
after several years in the Far East, he still knew half the world's air-
men, and those he didn't, had at least heard of him. It explained how
he had been able to thumb rides across two continents at the drop of
a hat.

The Aeronautical Society wore the face of science over the heart
of madcap undergraduates. We walked past a dignified sign and
through a polished front door into a minor riot that would not have
been tolerated at that bastion of Bohemian excess, the Café Royal.
Five boisterous young men were racing—literally—down a long staircase while a sixth flung his legs over the banister and leapt to the
floor below, staggering into a scramble as he hit the carpet ahead of
the pack that rounded the newel and circled towards whatever rooms
lay behind. Voices raised from the depths of the building indicated
disputed results and an accusation of cheating; the dignified Swiss
man at my side looked only marginally discomfited.

"We shall wait for them in here," he suggested, leading me to a
sitting room too tidy to be used for anything but the occasional entertainment of guests and ladies. He pressed into my hand an unasked-
for glass of sherry, and slipped out. I set the glass on the table, and
looked around me.

The quiet room was decorated primarily with photographs: Blériot
after crossing the Channel in 1909; the Wrights' first flyer, wings
drooping alarmingly but its wheels clear of the ground; an aerial dog-
fight over English fields; Alcock and Brown standing next to the bi-
plane they crossed the Atlantic in. I lingered over this last—surely
immeasurably harder than a jaunt to Scotland, and that was five
whole years ago. I puzzled over the next photograph, of a curious
looking aeroplane with an enormous set of propellers misplaced to its
roof. It resembled some unlikely insect.

"That's an autogiro," said an American voice from behind me.

I had not known there was anyone else in the room, but the man had been sitting in a high-backed chair in a dim corner. I smiled vaguely in his direction, and returned to the photo. "It looks like the result of two aeroplanes flying into each other," I commented. Then, realising that a jest about mid-air collisions might not be in the best of taste here, I amended it to, "—or a piece of very Modernist sculpture. Does it actually function?"

"They go up," he said laconically. "Something I could help you with?"

"No, I'm here with Mr—Captain—Lofte. I think he's gone to find someone."

"Probably me." The man peeled himself out of the chair and started in my direction. Watching the unevenness of his progress, I thought at first that he had been injured, then decided he was intoxicated. When he stood before me, I saw it was both.

He'd been burned. Shiny scar tissue spread up his neck to his jaw-line, the skin on his left hand was taut enough to affect mobility, and the stiffness of his gait suggested further damage. He held his drink in his right hand, and watched my reaction to his appearance.

It must be hard, to have to wait for every new acquaintance to absorb the implications of scars. Particularly when the new acquaintance was a not entirely unattractive young woman.

"I'm Mary Russell," I said, and hesitated about whether or not to put out my hand.

He decided for me, moving his glass over to his left hand, concentrating for a moment until the fingers grasped it, then putting his right hand out for me to shake. "Pleased to meet you. The name's Cash Javitz."

I narrowed my eyes. "Detroit?"

He transferred the glass back to the more secure grasp. " 'Bout fifty miles away. How'd you guess?"

"Accents are one of my husband's . . . hobbies, you might say. I pick things up from him."

"I been here so long, some Yanks think I'm a Brit."

"Me, too. Mother was English, I'm from California, my father from Boston."

"So, what's Lofty want?"

"I need to get to Scotland in a hurry. Mr Lofte seemed to think this was the place to start looking."

He lifted the glass to his face and drank, watching me over it. "Where in Scotland?"

"Well, actually, the Orkneys. Those are the islands—"

"I know where Orkney is. Don't I, you snake?"

I was taken aback until Lofte's voice answered; I hadn't heard him come in.

"Don't be rude to the lady, Cash. A simple no will suffice."

"How much?" Javitz said instead.

"Do you have a 'plane?"

"Wait a minute," I interrupted. "Not to offend, Mr Javitz, but my husband suggested I find a pilot who had taken the pledge. Considering the distance, I'd say that was a good idea."

"He'll be sober," Lofte assured me.

"Mostly," Javitz muttered under his breath.

Lofte frowned at the American, than said, "Cash knows the terrain like no other. When the RAF wouldn't let him fly any more, he joined the Navy, and spent so much time around Scapa Bay they've made him an honorary Orcadian. The islands are tricky, the winds can be difficult. I'd trust my mother to Cash."

"This mother of yours: Is she still alive?"

"My sister, then."

"I've seen a picture of his sister," the American commented. "She'd be safe from me, no question."

I eyed him. This was adding up to one of those situations whose details Holmes did not need to know.

"To answer your question, Cash," Lofte said, "we will have a 'plane by evening. I'll ring here as soon as we know what kind and where it is. We can discuss then your fees."

"By which time you'll be sober," I added firmly.

Javitz laughed and swigged down the last of his drink. "If I'm not, what will you do? Fly her yourself?"

"I'll fly her," Lofte said.

"To Orkney?"

The question was close to being a jeer, but Lofte held the American's gaze. "Innocent lives are at stake, Cash. A man and a child. Miss Russell has to reach the Orkneys no later than Friday."

"Right. Okay. 'Phone me, when you know. But if it's some piece of rubbish held together by chewing gum and baling wire, you can take it yourself. I'm going to go find me some lunch."

He stalked out, putting his empty glass on a polished table as he went by. I watched him leave.

"Can he fly, with that hand?" I asked my companion.

"He flies with his will, not his flesh. He will get you there."

With a final glance at the doorway the American had gone through, I thought it a pity that we could not take Lofte with us. A man that experienced at conjuring transportation from thin air might be useful if we ran out of fuel halfway over the Cairngorms.

Chapter Forty-one

*Place (1): As celestial bodies work their influence, so do
historical bodies shape one another. Britain is the sum of
its peoples: the ancients; the Romans; the Angles and
Saxons; the North Peoples; the Norman French.
All built their roads, raised their children, and left their
names, their Gods, and their Powers.*
Testimony, IV:6

I REACHED HENDON AIR FIELD JUST BEFORE DAWN
on Wednesday. The aeroplanes that greeted my eyes were reassuringly solid, gleaming new, proud, broad-chested harbingers of the
muscular future of flight.

Unfortunately, they were not the aeroplane we had been given.

Mycroft's car drove me farther into the field, where I saw Lofte and
Javitz hanging from the wing of a machine that even in the half-light
appeared worn. The two men wielded spanners, and a third man
stood on the ground with an electric torch. They had been at the field
for hours, judging by the state of their clothing and the greasy hand-
prints that covered the fuselage from propeller to rudder.

Mycroft's assistant, a fifty-year-old Cockney by the name of Carver, would have driven off once I was out of the car, but I stopped him.

"These men need coffee and something to eat. You have twenty minutes."

"Twenty—do you know what time it is?"

"I do. Consider this one of Mr Holmes' . . . requests."

Carver threw up his hands and drove away with a squeal of tyres. I went over to the men, who had their back ends pointed at me and were arguing.

"Is there a problem?" I asked loudly.

"No," Lofte said.

At the same instant, Javitz answered, "Not if you are wanting to fall out of the sky."

"There is no problem," Lofte repeated. "My friend is merely scrupulous about his machinery."

" 'Scrupulous' is a good thing to be," I said encouragingly.

The machine was reassuringly large, with nearly forty feet of wing, towering over me at a height of ten feet. Lofte came to stand next to me and told me rather more about it than I needed to know: made by the Bristol company four years before, cruising speed of eighty-five miles per hour, a 230 horsepower Siddeley Puma engine, 405 square feet of wing surface. I nodded my head at the right places, and wondered who owned the thing, and why he might be letting us remove it.

"The best thing about it, from your point of view," he said, "is that it has a range of five hundred miles."

"You mean we can fly to Orkney with only one stop?" I asked in astonishment.

"Well," he said, "theoretically, perhaps. In practice it's not the best idea to push matters. He'll put down in York first, just to look things over."

There was something ominous about the way he suggested that. "What sorts of things?"

"It's an unfamiliar machine, he'll be . . . conservative."

"There's something you're not telling me."

"Nothing important. Well, just, the last time she was up, she came down a little hard. He's now making certain that—"

"This machine crashed?"

"Not so much crashed as . . . well, I suppose yes, it crashed."

Javitz finally spoke up; I rather wished he hadn't. "It's a piece of crap machine that's been driven into the ground, literally. If I had three days to pull it apart I'd be happier. But I'll get you there, in one piece, if it's the last thing I do."

"That's not exactly encouraging, Mr—"

"Joke," he said, baring his teeth at me in a grin. "She'll be fine."

It was surely not too late to catch the train to Edinburgh. And I might have, if Javitz hadn't chosen that moment to throw his spanner into the nearest tool-bag with a grunt signifying satisfaction, if not actual happiness. He scrubbed his hands on a grease-coloured rag, and picked up my bag to stow it inside the side compartment. Carver came back with the food and drink, and Javitz helped himself to a fried-eggs-on-toast sandwich and a cup of coffee. Carver also handed him a piece of paper.

"Bloke waved me down and asked me to give you this," he said.

Javitz took the page in the hand that held the cup; whatever he read made the look on his face go grim again.

"What is that?" I asked.

He stuffed it into a pocket, and said, "Weather conditions. We'll have some wind, nothing to worry about."

"I think—"

He turned on his heel and fixed me with an evil gaze. "I don't fly dual controls. You want to drive the thing? Go right ahead, it's your machine. If you want me to take you north, you're gonna have to let me do the worrying."

Twice in a year I had climbed into an aeroplane under the control of someone in whom I had less than complete confidence. I must learn how to drive one myself, and soon.

I nodded, and let Lofte show me how to climb up the ladder. He followed me to demonstrate the special hinged cover that transformed the passenger seat into an enclosed box. I eyed the glass on all sides, wondering how hard a landing would be required to turn the windows into flying daggers.

I had brought my heaviest fur-lined coat, which I now wrapped around me. Javitz shook Lofte's hand and leapt into the pilot's open compartment in front while Lofte walked forward and waited for the signal to work the prop. Javitz fiddled with the controls in front of him, pulled on his goggles, then stuck up his thumb; Lofte vanished, the propeller kicked a few times before the engine caught, sputtered, then thundered into life. The fragile construction around me jerked and drifted forward. Lofte reappeared off the port side and waved at me with an air of confidence neither of us altogether believed. The sound of the big engine built, the seat pressed itself into my back, and with no ceremony at all we leapt once, twice, and the ground dropped away.

The compartment was freezing until the sun came up, then I sat in my mile-high conservatory and roasted. I tore the end off of my handkerchief and pushed little screws of the cotton into my ears against the unremitting bellow of the engine and the scream of wind. My bones rattled, my teeth threatened to crack unless I kept my jaws clamped shut, and the ground was a long, long way down. Tiny dollhouses grew among picturesque fields; miniature trains rode pencil-drawing tracks and emitted diminutive puffs of smoke: England was translated into an Ordnance Survey portrait, as real as a coloured moving-picture projected beneath our feet.

It was—if one didn't stop to consider the consequences—really quite thrilling.

We flew on through the morning. From time to time, Javitz craned to look over his shoulder at me, and once shouted a question. I shrugged; he laughed, and turned again so I could continue my study of the back of his coat, scarf, and leather cap.

Two and a half hours later, the engine sound changed and the ground began to grow nearer—slowly, which was a comfort. We had skirted several towns on the way up, and now I could make out the distinctive outline of York with its Minster off to the northeast. There was an air field here—*field* being the operative term—that Javitz seemed to know, because he made for it and took us down on the hard-packed grass. He shut off the engine, and I pulled the twists of cotton from my ears. They rang anyway. I let Javitz hand me down from my perch; on *terra firma,* I could feel my bones sway as if I'd been on a long sea voyage. I said, "It's hard to believe we left London at dawn and we're already in York."

"You needn't shout, Miss Russell."

"Sorry," I said. "My ears are ringing."

"But it's true, this is the next revolution in travel."

Emergency speed was one thing, but I did not imagine the world was full of people eager to be cramped into place, shaken about, deafened, frozen, boiled, and frightened silly for the sake of a few hours saved. "I don't believe I'll invest in Imperial Airways quite yet, thank you."

"You're losing an opportunity," he said, and went off to poke gingerly inside the hot engine. A short time later, a laconic individual motored up with tins of petrol in the back of his Model T, and Javitz topped up the tank. He came back before my legs had altogether regained their normal sensation.

"Ready?" he asked. "Next stop, Edinburgh—we should be there in no time at all."

In fact, however, five hours later Javitz and I were barely twenty miles away, in a pasture heavy with cow droppings, working on the engine while two young cow-herds watched us from their perch atop a barred gate.

Half a mile away, train after train steamed imperturbably northwards.

We had come down briskly. One minute we were flying merrily northwards, the next, moving air was the loudest thing around us, and through the glass, I could hear Javitz cursing under his breath. Fortunately, it would seem that rebellious engines were commonplace to him, because after an alarmingly long time spent fiddling with the controls and slapping instruments, he stood up in his seat to peer around, found a likely field, and aimed us in that direction.

After one hour, he'd found a number of problems that it was not. I now had as much grease on me as Javitz did, since his scarred hand could not manage the more demanding manipulations of the tools. Under his direction, I pulled one piece after another out of the engine, waited as he debated its qualities, and saw him lay it to one side before turning to the extrication of the next one. After an hour and a half, one of the cow-herds had taken pity on us and fetched up a pot of tea.

After two hours, I wiped the perspiration from my forehead and said, "Mr Javitz, if we continue with the process of elimination, we'll soon reach the rudder."

"It's hard to think with you wittering at me."

I looked at the sturdy spanner in my hand, dropped it, and walked away.

Two fields over, a pair of huge mares were pulling a combine harvester, inexorably up and down. Had they been cart horses, I might have stolen one and pointed its nose towards the nearest train station, but between the entangling harness and their placid gait, it would be faster to walk.

Another train flew past, an express by the looks of it. Perhaps I could climb up the telegraph pole and fashion an impromptu Morse generator, asking Mycroft to work his magic over the trains. No doubt I could find tools in the repair kit. Or I could be more straightforward and just build a fire over the tracks, commandeering the thing by gunpoint when it stopped.

Walking back to our makeshift aerodrome, I saw Javitz in conversation with the two boys. They trotted away, chattering avidly. When I got back to the 'plane, I saw that he had restored a fair number of the parts to their places.

"Have you fixed it?"

"The problem's with the petrol. I was hoping to find garbage in the carburettor, or in the fuel line, but it's in the petrol itself. The filter's a mess."

"Can you fix it?"

"Sure, just drain the petrol and replace it."

We surveyed the countryside, which had a singular lack of petrol stations.

"You've sent the boys for petrol?"

"I've sent them for clean, empty containers. If I drain it through a chamois, it'll be fine."

"How many containers are we talking about?"

"Lots," he said.

The tank, it turned out, contained seventy gallons of petrol when full, which it had been when we left the York field. When the two boys returned, an hour later, they were loaded down with a mad variety of vessels, from chipped tea-pot to tin bath. My job was to check each container, rinsing it if necessary in petrol, before handing it to Javitz. He would then position his chamois rag under the stream of petrol dribbling from the tank, and let the bowl, or coffee-pot, or tin bath fill up.

We ran out of containers before the machine ran out of petrol, so the four of us wrestled the machine forward, clear of the tin bath, for Javitz to open the plug, draining the remainder on the ground. I kept an eye on the growing puddle, to make sure our assistants didn't go near it with a lit cigarette, but he finished without mishap, cleared the lines, scrubbed the filter, and put everything back in place.

The petrol took a long time to replace, and even with the care we took, it splashed around and had us reeking and light-headed. At last, when the sun was well down in the afternoon sky, Javitz tossed down the coffee-pot he had been using to transfer the liquid, and we were ready.

He spent some time warning the boys about the danger of the fumes and traces that remained on their utensils, and more time explaining to the larger boy, in painful detail, how to work the prop and exactly what the consequences would be if the boy did it wrong.

He climbed back, I dropped my cover down, and we crossed our fingers. When he shouted his command, the lad yanked hard on the propeller. The engine sputtered and died, and Javitz shouted for him to do it again. On the fourth try, the engine cleared its throat and came to life.

When the boys were well clear of the wings, Javitz aimed our nose down the mild slope we had landed on, and opened the throttle.

Hard.

The engine noise built as 230 horses stirred themselves to life. We rattled and rumbled over the field, bouncing and nearly flipping over. My teeth felt loose in my jaw, and each bounce left us only slightly closer to air-bound.

There was a rock wall at the far end of the field, and we were coming at it fast.

Too fast. It looked as high as a building and was certainly solid enough to smash us to pieces. I caught only glimpses past my pilot's shoulders, but I was in no doubt that the rocks were there, greedy for our fragility, vanishing with each bounce, only to reappear closer and higher than before. Three times this happened, and I closed my eyes and drew down my head, because when we descended again, we should be on top of it.

But we did not descend. The wings clawed at air, and the wheels kissed the stones in passing, then before us was only the violet expanse of the heavens.

Exultation lasted perhaps thirty seconds, before it penetrated my mind that the lighter portion of sky was to our right. I rapped on the glass, then unlatched it and wrestled it up a crack to shout, "Mr Javitz, why are we going south?"

There was no response; between the noise and the partition, communication threatened to be a one-way event. I drew breath and shouted more loudly: "We're going south!"

I thought he had still not heard me—either that, or was refusing to acknowledge it. Then I saw that he was bent over something held near his lap. After a minute, he held up a note-pad on which he had printed:

BE NIGHT IN EDINBURGH.

I protested, loudly, cursing that my revolver was in the storage locker, but before I could excavate through my layers of clothing for the knife, I realised he was right: I had to trust his decisions. If we could get safely to Edinburgh, we would be going there.

We made it back to the air field near York well before dark. Fortunately for the laconic individual who had sold us the petrol earlier, Javitz did not find him, and when he laboriously filtered the new petrol through his cloth, not a trace of foreign matter showed up. We spent the night in a nearby farmhouse that let rooms, and before it was truly light, the farmer motored us back to the air field and swung the prop for us. In minutes, the clamour drew us forward and into the sky.

I had, I need hardly mention, given up any real expectation that this northward journey would be anything but a wild-goose chase. I was by now quite certain that Holmes would be closing in on Bergen, and he and Mycroft's men would be baying on the trail of Brothers and his captives.

For me, onward motion was merely a thing to cling to until someone told me to stop.

Chapter Forty-two

*Place (2): All these are considerations in choosing the site
for a Work: Central and apart, it must draw from the ages
yet be ageless, between the worlds yet of the world,
recognised as holy yet wholly secular.
A man may search his whole life, for such a place.*
Testimony, IV:6

WE COVERED THE TWO HUNDRED MILES TO
Edinburgh in no time at all, the machine demurely slipping northwards as if in all the days since it had rolled out of the
shop, it had never so much as hesitated.

This time, the problem lay not in the engine, but outside: As we
flew north, the clouds tumbled down to meet us.

Fifty miles south of Edinburgh, the wind began—and not just
wind, but rain. One moment we were grumbling along in the nice
firm air, and the next the bottom dropped out of the world. It seemed
eerily quiet as I rose out of my seat, stomach clenched and my skin
shuddering into ice—until the machine slammed into air again and I
was suddenly heavy as the propellers bit in and pulled us forward
once more. It had happened so quickly, Javitz had not even shifted his

hands on the controls. He glanced over his shoulder and laughed, more in relief than amusement. We climbed, I breathed, deliberately, and unclenched my rigid fingers from the seat. Two minutes later it happened again, only this time when the hole ended and we were buoyed and beginning to climb, a sudden gust from the side nearly slapped us over. Javitz fought the controls, raised our nose, and held on.

Then drops began sporadically to spatter my glass cage. Most of it blew past Javitz, but his hand came up several times, wiping his face.

It made for a long fifty miles, tumbling and tossing in the clouds. We came out of the mid-day murk alarmingly close to the ground, and Javitz corrected our course to point us at the aerodrome. A gust hit us just short of the ground and we hit the grass with a terrifying crack from below.

The American gingerly slowed the machine, and I waited for him to turn us about and head back to the hangers we had flashed past. Instead, he throttled down the motor, then stood to look back at the buildings: It seemed that we were to walk back to the aerodrome. I popped up the cover and started to rise, but he stopped me.

"Stay right there. We need your weight."

"Sorry?"

"If you get out," he explained impatiently, "we'll shuttlecock. Flip over."

"I see." I sat firmly in my seat, thinking heavy thoughts, until I heard voices from outside.

Two large men clung to the wings, the wind bullying us back and forth, while we came about and made our way back to the aerodrome. Only then was I permitted to climb down. I felt like going down on quivering knees to kiss the earth.

One of the men directed me to a café adjoining the air field, where I went in a wobbly scurry while the rain spat down and Javitz tied down the machine and contemplated the wounded undercarriage.

In the shelter of a room with a baking coal stove, I peered through the window and amended my thought: It appeared we would be making arrangements for repairs as well. Javitz and a man in a waterproof were squatting on either side of the right wheel, peering at where the struts connected with the body.

I closed my eyes for a moment, then turned and looked at the waitress. "Would it be possible to have something hot to eat? It looks as though I shall be here for a while."

She was a maternal sort, and ticked her tongue at my state. "We'll get you something nice and warming," she said, beginning with drink both hot and stout. I allowed her to slip a hefty and illicit dollop of whisky into the cup of tea before me, and downed the tepid atrocity in one draught. It hit me like a swung punching bag, but when the top of my head had settled back into place, I found that the impulse to pull out my revolver and begin shooting had subsided as well.

I placed the cup gently back into its saucer, took a couple of breaths, and decided that the day was not altogether lost. The men would fix the strut, the wind would die down, we would be in Orkney by nightfall.

And when we found that, in fact, Brothers had opted for Norway?

I would not think about that at the moment.

I reached for the tea-pot, and my eyes were filled with tweed: a man, beside the table; a small, round man in need of a shave, wearing a freckled brown suit and rather rumpled shirt.

"Miss Russell?" His accent was as Scots as his suit.

"Yes?"

"M' name's MacDougall. Ah've a message for yeh."

"From?"

"Mr Mycroft Holmes."

"Sit. Please. Tea?" For some reason, my tongue seemed limited to one-word sentences. But he sat, and the arrival of a second cup saved me the difficult decision of how to carry out my offer, so that was good. I watched him slip in and out of clear focus, and summoned my thoughts.

"He sent me a wire, askin' me t'watch for an aeroplane. Wi' the weather as it is, I'd gone home, but the man here rang me."

"Mycroft. Yes. Good."

"Er, are you altogether well, mum?"

My gaze slid towards the window, where the machine that had tried so hard to kill us sat, wet and complacent as men addressed themselves to its undercarriage. "It was a dilli—a difficult flight."

The man's gaze followed mine. "Ah can imagine. Ah know three men who've bein kilt flyin'—ye'll never get me up in one a'them infernal machines."

"Thank you," I said coolly.

His eyes came back to mine. "Sorry. I'm sure they're ever so much safer now, and your pilot's sure ta—"

"You were saying," I interrupted. "About Mycroft."

"Yes. Well, Ah was the one took his orders Tuesday, to be looking for one and possibly two men and a bairn—and sorry to say we've seen nothing of them, although it was nobbut an hour after receivin' the first wire that Ah had men at Waverley, Princes Street, and Haymarket—for the trains, yeh know—and at Leith for the steamers."

So it is Bergen after all, I thought, that mad-man with his knife at the throat of—

"But while they were watching, Ah myself made the roonds of the restaurants in the toon. And Ah found they may have been here on Monday."

"No! Really?" I said, frankly astonished. "But you're not certain?"

"Not without a photograph. But two Englishmen took luncheon at the hotel near Waverley Station on Monday, and the younger was tall and had a beard. And they had a bairn with them."

"The child is with them?"

"So the waiter said."

I felt like weeping with relief. "Waverley Station—where do trains from there go?"

"London, Glasgow, and the north of Scotland. But if you're going to ask me to question the ticket-sellers, there's little point, without a pho—"

I stood up fast, then grabbed at the table to keep from sprawling on my face. While the room spun around me, I said through gritted teeth, "Take me to that hotel."

"Mum, I dinna think—"

"Do you have a motor?" I demanded.

"Yes, but—"

"I have photographs," I told him, and began to hunt them out of my pocket when my eye was caught by a figure trotting across the tarmac towards us. I left my hand where it was; Javitz opened the door and stuck his head inside. Rain dripped from his hat.

"Miss Russell? We're set to go, as soon as she's fuelled up."

I stood motionless, caught by indecision: I deeply mistrusted leaving a vital interrogation to others, even if the other was one of Mycroft's. . . . The tableau might have lasted forever—one dripping, one with her hand in her pocket, one waiting in apprehension—had the waitress not decided this was a good time to present me with my meal.

The aroma of meat and roast potatoes reached me where the motion did not. I pulled my hand from my pocket, then looked at the plate, and at her.

"I don't think I'm going to have time to eat that. But if your cook could make me half a dozen bacon butties or fried-egg sandwiches to take with me, there'll be a gold guinea if it's here in four minutes. Mr Javitz, do you plan to stop again short of Thurso?"

"Inverness."

"I'll be with you as soon as the food is ready." The two left, in opposite directions. I turned to Mycroft's tweed-suited agent. "Mr. . . . ?"

"MacDougall," he provided.

"Yes. Did you question the waiter about . . . anything?"

"Just if those men had been here."

"Not about their behaviour, their temper?"

"Mr Holmes didna' ask for that."

"Well, I am asking. I need you to go back to the hotel with these photographs, and confirm that this was the older man, this the younger, and this the child—he has a fuller beard now, and she's a bit older. I also need you to ask about the behaviour of the men—were they amiable or angry, did one of them seem drunk or drugged? Did they seem to be working in harness, or was one of them in charge and the other fearful, or resentful, or . . . You see what I'm asking?"

"Ah do."

"Can you then find a way to get me that information at either Inverness or Thurso?"

"Ah've a colleague in Inverness, although Ah dunno if Ah'll have the information by the time you reach there."

"We shall probably be forced to spend the night at Inverness," I told him. "Have your colleague there ask for us at the air field. And lacking Inverness, send a wire to the telegraph office in Thurso."

A large, warm parcel was thrust into my arms by the breathless waitress, and I duly dug out the cost of the luncheon, laying one of the gold guineas on top. She wandered off, transfixed by the gleam in her palm. I thanked MacDougall and trotted back to the aeroplane, to share out the meal with Javitz and eye the repair on the undercarriage. It looked like a splint held in place with baling wire and sticking plasters; I opened my mouth, closed it, and climbed into my seat. We made it down the field and into the air without it breaking, so that was good.

The fur coat and rugs around my shoulders were almost adequate. The knowledge that the child was alive warmed my thoughts, but made little inroad on my icy toes.

Chapter Forty-three

The Stars (1): The man was but a child when he heard the message of the stars, seeing the precision of the link between their paths and those of human beings.
Testimony, IV:7

A HUNDRED TWENTY MILES FROM EDINBURGH TO Inverness, and we fought the wind and rain every inch of the way. We followed the railway lines, which added miles but gave us sure guidance. As the clouds dropped ever lower, we did as well, until I feared we might meet an engine head-on. Javitz hunched over the controls, the juddering of the stick knocking through his body like a blow. Every so often, I saw him peer forward at the instruments, and I could tell when he braced his knees around the control stick to reach out and tap at the instruments.

The wind howled, the rain beat us sideways, the 'plane groaned and cracked, and even the wind clawing at the cover could not take away the stink of fear in my boxed-in space.

On a good day, we might have covered the distance in ninety minutes, but between the head-wind and being continually blown off course, it was twice that by the time we saw signs of a city below. The number of times Javitz leant forward to rap at the gauges did not make my stomach any easier around the stony eggs and sloshing coffee.

We came down ominously close to dusk, slowing, dropping, teetering on the gusts. Javitz chose what appeared to be a mowed hayfield, although as we descended I noticed a faded red length of cloth nailed to a high post at the far end, tugged back and forth, tautly horizontal to the ground. He slowed us further, rising into a half-stand so he could see past the nose. No aerodrome here: If his undercarriage repairs failed, we would be grounded.

Then again, if the repairs failed on landing, further transportation might be the least of our worries.

Clearly, the danger was foremost on the pilot's mind, as well. Javitz fought the machine for control, our low tanks and the 405 square feet of wing threatening to upend us before we touched down. When he did tap the wheels to the ground—gently, cautiously—the wind perversely refused to let us go, lifting and playing us on the razor's edge of flipping over all the way down the field.

We came to a halt, wings still quivering, ten feet from the hedgerow at the field's end.

Javitz peeled one hand off the control stick and cut the fuel.

Silence pounded at our eardrums. In a calm voice that sounded very far away, Javitz said, "I'm going to go get drunk now, if you don't mind. I'll meet you back here at dawn."

"What—" I strangled on the word, cleared my throat and tried again. "What about the machine?"

"I'll make arrangements."

The arrangements came from the nearby house to meet us, in the form of a grizzled farmer and his strapping young son, the latter of whom was clearly the enthusiast. The lad stared from the aeroplane to the pilot in open admiration, while his disapproving father moved to tie our eager machine down to earth. I half-fell down the ladder, accepted the valise that Javitz thrust into my arms, and watched him march away down the field with the young man trailing behind, pelting him with unanswered questions.

After a minute, I realized an older man was standing at my side, and had asked me something. "Terribly sorry," I said. "I could rather use a Ladies', if you might direct me?"

I felt his hand on my elbow, propelling me in the direction of the building he'd come out of. He led me through a kitchen, showed me a door, and went away. I put down the valise, closed the door, and knelt to vomit into the tidy enamel lavatory.

When the spasm had passed, I stayed where I was for a time, shuddering with a combination of cold and reaction, emitting a noise that was part groan and part cry. Not unlike the noise the wind had made all afternoon around my head.

All right, I said after a minute. Enough. I got to my feet, washed my hands, splashed water on my face, and even went into my valise for a comb to restore my hair to order. When I came out, I felt approximately halfway to human.

Which was just as well: The man standing in the farmer's kitchen was so out of place, he could only be Mycroft's Inverness contact, colleague to Mr MacDougall.

"Mungo Clarty, at your service," he declared. His name and speech patterns were Scots, although the accent originated two hundred miles to the south. He marched across the room with his hand extended, pumping my arm as if trying to draw water. "I've been instructed to make you welcome and get whatever you might want. And if you're fretting over your pilot, I've sent a friend to look after him, in case he decides to get a bit the worse for wear. I've telephoned to a dear friend of mine, runs a lovely boarding-house in the town with more hot water than you could ask for, beds fit for a queen and a cellar second to none. Does that sound like what you'll be needing?"

Had he remained where he was, I might have draped myself around him in gratitude and wept on his shoulder, but he had let go of my hand and picked up my valise, and was already taking our leave from the farmer, leading me from the warm kitchen to his waiting motor, talking over his shoulder all the time.

"You haven't had any information from MacDougall?" I asked when he paused for breath. His motorcar was not as warm as the farmer's kitchen, but it was blessedly out of the wind, and the travel-ling rug he tucked over my knees was thick.

"He said to tell you the waiter had gone to see his mother, whatever that means, but that he's going after him."

I took a breath, and pushed away temptation. "Good man. I need to visit all the hotels and restaurants in town."

"All the—that'll take most of the night!"

"What, in a town this size?"

"Inverness is the door to the north," he said, sounding reproachful. "Anyone going to northern Scotland passes through here."

"Superb," I muttered. "Perhaps we should begin with any ticket agencies that may be open."

It was, as Clarty had warned me, many hours before I took to that bed fit for a queen. Even when I did, so cold through that I gasped with relief at the hot-water bottle against my feet, the physical warmth had no chance against the turmoil of my thoughts.

We had found no trace of them. I had looked at my last pair of the photographs Holmes had left me, loath to let go of them, but in the end decided that, from here on, the places I would be asking were so remote, any three strangers would attract notice: descriptions would suffice. I left the photographs with Clarty, so he could repeat the cir-cuit of ticket agents and hotels during the daylight hours.

Friday morning, at dawn, I returned to the air field to do it all again.

If Inverness was a tenth the size of Edinburgh, Thurso would have a tenth the population of Inverness, too small a setting for Mycroft to have any sort of an agent: From here on, I was on my own. I had asked for a car to pick me up well before dawn, not wanting to rob Clarty of his already short sleep, and I could hear its engine chuckling on the street outside when I walked down the stairs of the boarding-house, so ill-slept I felt hung over.

The owner was there, looking fresh as a terrier, and greeted me a good morning.

"I don't suppose you had any messages during the night, for me?" I asked her.

But she had not had a message to assure me that Holmes had re-solved the issue on his own. Nothing to transform my Valkyrie ride through hell into a placid, unadventurous, puffing, ground-based train-ride back to the warm, dry, August-kissed South Downs. I would even process the honey from the other hives, I pledged, were it to absolve me from climbing back into that aeroplane.

But, no message, telegraphic, telephonic, or even telepathic.

I followed the obscenely cheerful driver out onto the rain-shined street, and he drove me to the hay-field.

Javitz was there before me, his young admirer lingering at a dis-tance. My pilot looked no better than I felt. Still, his hands were steady as he poured me a cup from a thermal flask filled with scalding coffee.

He walked away and finished his check of our various levels by torch-light. I cradled the coffee to its dregs, and dropped the cup back onto the flask. When he came back, I handed it to him, and glanced up at the glass-wrapped passenger chamber with loathing.

Instead of offering me a hand, as he had before, he leant back against the wing and lit a cigarette. "It's ninety miles, more or less, to Thurso," he began. "That weather report you saw me with, back in London, warned me that the wind was building, and it's out of the north-east. That's why we came across the mountains from Edinburgh instead of following the coast-line.

"But from here on, we don't have a choice. Even if we keep inland, we'll get the wind. The weather's going to be bad," he said bluntly. "It's expected to blow itself out by tomorrow, but today's going to be rough. And when we leave Thurso, it'll be worse." He studied me in the half-light. "This could kill us."

Since I had come to work with Holmes, I had spent rather more time than most women my age in contemplating my imminent death. Gun, knife, bomb—I had faced all those and survived. Death by fire would be terrible, and drowning awful, but relatively quick. Falling from a great height, however, with no control, no hope, no avoiding

the knowledge of a terrible meeting with the earth: That would be forever.

I swallowed: It would be easier, if I only *knew*. If I were certain that
we were on the right track, that my presence in Orkney was the only
hope for Damian and his Estelle, I would not hesitate to risk my life,
or that of this brave man who had blindly done all I asked, and more.
If I were sure . . .

I met his eyes. "I can't lie to you. There is a good chance that we are
chasing a wild goose. We may get to Orkney and find our quarry has
never been there, never had any intention of going there. And before
you ask, yes, I knew it before we left London. My partner and his
brother both disagree with me, and are hunting elsewhere.

"Two things I am certain about: One, that I *could* be right. And two,
we only have today. Right or wrong, tomorrow will be too late for two
lives, one of those a child. If I could fly this machine myself, I would.
If your professional judgment decides that it is insane to go into the
air today, I'll see what I can do by train."

Javitz tossed away his cigarette end and said merely, "Okay. Let's
see how things look in Thurso. Lad," he called. "Help us get the machine turned around."

When the 'plane was facing the other way, he handed me up, then
scrambled past me into his own seat. Our eager helper took up his position at the front, and when Javitz gave him a shout, he yanked the
prop with all his young strength and passion. Instantly, the roar of
the engine assaulted our ears. The boy whipped away the chocks, and
we bumped down the deserted field before the sun cleared the horizon. The head-lamps of an arriving motor-car sought us out, but we
were already throwing ourselves at the clouds.

The furs and rugs were cold and damp; they never did actually
warm up.

They say that a woman in labour enters a state in which time is suspended and the sensations she is undergoing become dream-like.
Men attacked by ferocious beasts claim to enter a similar other-

worldly state of grace, when their horror and pain become distant, and oddly unreal. I know, having flown that day from Inverness to Thurso, that a person can only hold so much sheer terror before the mind folds itself away.

We were shaken by giant hands every one of those 150 miles, tossed about and batted up and down. Sometimes we flew above unyielding ground; other times we were suspended above cold, white-licked sea; once we flattened ourselves against a young mountain that loomed abruptly out of the clouds. That time, Javitz emitted a string of distracted curses, and I curled over with my hands wrapped around my head, whimpering and waiting for a ripping impact and nothingness.

The engine roared on.

I retreated into myself and wrapped the world around my head like the travelling rugs. We bounced and rattled and I felt nothing—not until the unending noise suddenly halted and the 'plane ceased its inexorable press against my spine. We both came bolt upright, flooded with panic for three interminable seconds of silence before the engine caught again and the propellers resumed. The shoulders before me were bent over the controls so tightly I thought the stick was in danger of shearing off; my throat felt peculiar, until I found I was keening with the wind.

We followed railroad tracks along the coast, up a river, and through mountains to another river. The ground below settled somewhat, although the wind relented not a whit, and I eyed the green fields and the river with love, knowing that they would be marginally softer than the mountains and warmer than the sea.

Finally, a gap in the clouds permitted us a glimpse of open water with a small town at its edge.

Then the clouds obscured it; at the same moment, the engine spluttered into silence for a terrifying count of four, then caught again.

It did it once more when the town was directly to our right. This time the silence held long enough that the machine grew heavy and tilted, eager to embrace gravity. Javitz cursed; I made a little squeak of a noise; with a sputtering sound, the propeller found purpose again.

If Thurso was too small for an agent of Mycroft Holmes, it was also too small for an air field. However, it did have an apparently smooth and not entirely under-water pasture free of boulders, cattle, and rock walls—Javitz seemed to know it, or else he spotted it and was too desperate to survey the ground for other options. The house beside it had sheets hanging out to dry; as we aimed our descent at the field, I noted numbly that, in the space of a few seconds, the laundry flipped around to cover roughly 200 of a circle's 360 degrees.

We splashed down, skidded and slewed around, and came to rest facing the way we had come. Javitz shut down the motor and we sat, incapable of either speech or movement, until we became aware of shouting. I raised the cover, and a red-faced farmer pulled himself up. "Wha' the bliudy 'ell're yeh playing at, yeh blooten' idjit?" the man shouted. "Ye think p'raps we enjoy scrapin' you lot off'n our walls? May waif thought he'd be comin' threw the sittin' room winda— c'mere and A'll kick yer— Captain Javitz? Is that you?" His hard Scots suddenly lost a great degree of its regionality.

"Hello there, Magnuson. Sorry to give your wife a fright, it wasn't half what we gave ourselves."

"Jaysus be damned, Javitz, I'd not have thought it even of you. Oh, miss, pardon me, I didn't see you."

"Quite all right," I said. One might have thought I would be growing accustomed to life in a state of fear and trembling, but my voice wasn't altogether steady. Nor were my legs, when I made to stand.

Javitz and I staggered into open air. The rain had stopped, but the sea-scented wind beat at us and made the aeroplane twitch like a fractious horse. The farmer, Magnuson, eyed it as if it were about to take to the air on its own—not, in fact, an impossibility.

"Come inside and we'll see about finding you rooms until this blows over."

Javitz shook his head. "We'll tie her down and find some petrol. As soon as I've cleared the fuel line, we'll be away."

"Never!" the other man roared. "My wife would have my guts for garters if I let Cash Javitz take off into this hurricane."

"No choice, I'm afraid."

I interrupted. "Mr Magnuson? I'm Mary Russell, pleased to meet you. Pardon me for a moment. Captain Javitz, what the devil made it do that?"

"Probably a scrap of the same rubbish we picked up on that load of fuel in York."

"But that time the motor just stopped, not stopped and started."

"This'll just be something that worked itself down to the fuel line."

"How long will it take you to clear it?"

"An hour at the most. We should pick up petrol, too, while we're here."

"And you honestly feel we can resume after that?"

"Don't see why not."

"You're certain?"

"Yes! For Chr—for heaven's sake, it's just the fuel line." *Just* the fuel line.

"Very well. Mr Magnuson, can you tell me, is this wind apt to be worse, or better, later in the day?"

"I can't imagine it getting worse."

"Would you agree, Captain Javitz?"

He studied the sky, sniffed the air, and said, "It should settle a little by nightfall."

"We can't wait that long, but I believe we can afford to spend a few hours here. I pray you can fix that sputter before we set off over water. You do that, I'll go into town and see if there's a telegram waiting."

"If you say so," Javitz said, but the relief was clear despite the words.

"I shall be back by noon, one o'clock at the latest. Will we still reach Kirkwall by mid-afternoon?"

"If we don't, neither of us will be in any condition to worry about it," he said.

"Er, right. Mr Magnuson, could I trouble you to direct me to the general post office?"

Magnuson did better than that; he summoned a friend, who motored me there.

Thurso was more a village than a town, some four thousand

inhabitants looking across fifteen miles of strait at the Orkney Islands. The harbour was small, which explained why the larger boats I had glimpsed earlier were slightly north of the town itself. Despite its size, Thurso appeared busy and polished, possibly because the fleet had not that long ago moved its training exercises into Scapa Bay in the Orkneys, spilling a degree of prosperity onto this, the nearest mainland town.

The neighbour with the motor-car was happy to act as my taxi for a couple of hours. We started at the post and telegraph office, where a harried gentleman informed me that no, there was nothing for me, however, a tree had taken out the telegraph line somewhere to the south, and service had only just been restored. Could I try again in an hour?

I climbed back inside the motor-car, and asked the driver if the day's steamer to Orkney had left.

"Might not, considering this wind," he answered, and put the motor-car into gear for the short drive along the water.

There, at last, I caught scent of my quarry. My description of Brothers had the ticket-seller shaking his head, and mention of a child the same, but when I asked about a tall bearded individual with an English accent, his face brightened.

"Ach, yais, him. Peculiar feller. He was here airlier."

"Just him? Not another man and a child?"

"No, just the one."

I did not know what to make of that. Had Brothers gone ahead? Had he taken the child instead of Damian, leaving Damian trailing desperately behind? Or was Damian operating independently, for some unknown reason?

"Which day was that?"

"Airlier," he repeated, as if I were hard of hearing.

"What, you mean *today*?"

"That's right."

"Good heavens. Has the steamer for Orkney left yet?"

"That's her there," he said, pointing.

The first good news since we'd left York. I threw a thanks over my shoulder, touching the pocket that held my revolver as I moved in the direction of the waiting boat. Then I heard the man's voice tossed about on the wind.

I turned around and called, "Sorry?"

He raised his voice. "He's not on it, if tha's what ye're wanting."

I retraced my steps. "Why not?"

"I told him she wouldna'be leavin' fer hours yet, what with the wind wanting to blow her halfway to Denmark."

"Did he buy any tickets?"

"No. Last I saw'im, he was heading back t'toon."

Town. Surely not to take a room, not if the solar eclipse was to take place tomorrow. Did they have another—

Town: The harbour was in Thurso itself; only large boats put in here at Scrabster.

I trotted back to my unofficial taxi and directed him to the harbour.

The harbour master's office was empty. All the boats I could see were lying at anchor, not setting out into the gale. I studied the buildings along the shore until I spotted a likely one.

The air inside the pub was thick with the smells of beer, wet wool, and fish. It was also warm and damp, which made my spectacles go opaque, but not before I had seen the universal outrage on the faces of every man in the place. I removed my glasses and, as long as I had their attention, spoke clearly into the silence.

"Pardon me, gentlemen, but I'm looking for a man who may have tried to hire a boat earlier today. Tall, thin, Englishman with a beard. Has anyone seen him?"

If anything, the hostility thickened. I cleaned my glasses and threaded them back over my ears, then dug into my pocket for one of the two remaining gold coins. I held it up. "He's trying to get over to the islands. I'd really appreciate it, if anyone has news of him."

There was a general shifting in the room, and someone cleared his throat. After a minute, a chair scraped. A man in the back rose and threaded his way forward.

"Keep your coin, mum," he said. "Let's step into the saloon bar and Ah'll tell yeh what yeh want to know."

I followed him into the adjoining empty room, a bare closet of a space that might have been designed to discourage any lady who might have mistaken permission for approval. One could just imagine a daring local feminist bravely venturing inside, ordering a sherry, and forcing it quickly down.

However, I did not intend to drink.

"When was he here?" I asked the man. A fisherman, by the looks of him, waiting out the wind.

"Who's he to yeh?"

"My husband's son," I said.

He looked startled.

"My husband's quite a bit older than I," I told him impatiently. Asymmetrical marriages were commonplace, in the wake of a devastating war. Perhaps here in the North fewer men had died? Perhaps women were more resigned to their solitary lot? Perhaps it was none of his business. "What does it matter? Have you seen my step-son?"

He surprised me by grinning.

"If that was the step-son, Ah'd laik t'meet the father. He was a stubborn one, that. Up and down the boats, not about t'take no for an answer. Started out askin' ta be taken o'er t'Mainland, and—"

"He wanted to go to the mainland?" I interrupted. Weren't we on the mainland?

"Mainland's the big island. Kirkwall's the town."

"I see. Go on."

"Laik Ah say, he wanted to go to Mainlan', and when we all looked at 'im laik he was ravin', he then offered t'buy a boat outright."

"Oh, Lord. I hope no-one sold him one?"

"Nah. You'll find few here willin' t'send a man t'his death for money."

I was aware of a hollow feeling within. "You think the wind is that bad?"

"D'ye think we're in the habit of taking a holiday every time there's a wee breeze?"

"I see. So, where did he go?"

"He's on a boat."

"But—"

"You're willin' to pay enough, there'll be a man desperate enough for yer gelt." The heavy disapproval in his voice gave a different cast to the thick silence in the next room: This Englishman's need threatened to take one of their own.

"Just him, or another man and a child?"

"Just the one." Although Brothers could have been waiting along the coast, with E'stelle.

"When did they leave?"

"Two hours. Maybe more."

"They should be there by now, then."

"If they're not at the bottom, or in Stavanger."

Norway? I hoped he was making a grim joke.

"I am sorry. It's . . . I'm sorry."

"It was a lot of money." He made no attempt to hide his bitterness. "Enough to keep a family a year or more. A young man'd be tempted. Young men always think they'll come back safe, don't they? E'en when they have two wee bairns at home. Ach, at least he had the sense to leave the purse with us, in case he's not around to bring it home."

I thanked him and went back out into the wind. What more was there to say?

We were halfway to Magnuson's farm when I remembered the telegraph office. Should I bother to go back, on the chance something had come through? I already knew where my quarry was.

But Mycroft didn't. So I had the driver turn back into the town, and went into the office to compose a telegram. When I had it written down, I took it to the window. The man recognised me.

"Miss Russell, was it? There's two come through for you. Shall I send this for you as well?"

"Wait, there might be an answer for one of these."

I carried the flimsies to one side. The first was from MacDougall:

IDENTITY OF TRIO CONFIRMED STOP ATTITUDE
QUOTE FRIENDLY ENOUGH BUT SOME

ARGUMENT AND YOUNGER MAN SEEMED
IMPATIENT STOP MESSAGE FROM LONDON
QUOTE TWO PIECES ORKNEY NEWS FIRST
CATHEDRAL STAIN TREATED WITH QUERY
SODIUM CITRATE TO STAY LIQUID AND SECOND
CREMATED REMAINS ARRIVED STENNESS HOTEL
WITH REQUEST TO SCATTER THEM AT BRODGAR
RING ON FOURTEEN AUGUST STOP

The other message came from Mungo Clarty in Inverness:

TWO ADULT ONE CHILD STEAMER TICKETS
PURCHASED TUESDAY MORNING ABERDEEN STOP
SELF WENT ABERDEEN FOUND TRIO BOUGHT
TICKETS TO KIRKWALL STOPPING WICK FIRST
STOP FOUR PIECES NEWS FROM LONDON STOP
ONE CATHEDRAL STAIN TREATED TO STAY LIQUID
TWO CREMATED REMAINS SCATTERED BRODGAR
RING FOURTEEN AUGUST THREE GUNDERSON
RELEASED FOUR PALL MALL FLAT RAIDED NO
ARREST STOP GOOD HUNTING STOP

Raided? Mycroft's flat? Had Lestrade completely lost his mind? I did not even want to think of Mycroft Holmes in a rage. Or was something else going on in London, something larger and darker than my current hunt for a religious nut-job?

I tore my eyes away from that part of the telegram, and tried to concentrate on the rest.

The fourteenth of August was the day of the lunar eclipse, the day before Yolanda had died. The news must have come out of London Thursday night—why hadn't Clarty learned of it earlier? Then I remembered the head-lamps racing towards the air field as we took off, and thought that perhaps he had received his wire at dawn that day.

I realised someone was addressing me, and raised my head to see the telegraph gentleman gesture at the form on which I'd written to

Mycroft. I shook my head and tore the page across: Anything I sent to Mycroft now would be intercepted by Lestrade.

"No," I said. "There won't be a reply." I went slowly back to the car. The idea of Scotland Yard raiding the flat of Mycroft Holmes was as puzzling as it was alarming, but I found it difficult to take it as a serious threat. Would Lestrade be walking a beat when we returned, or just fired outright?

And Brothers: Why had he moved about the countryside so much? Was he afraid they would be spotted if they sat in one place too long? Did he fear that Damian would see a newspaper, and finally learn of Yolanda's death? Had he perhaps felt someone on his tail and hoped to shake them off?

Or—what if the person he had been shaking off had been Damian? What if Brothers had taken Estelle and deliberately slipped away from Damian in Aberdeen, after buying tickets for Orkney but before boarding the ship? That would explain why Damian was here in Thurso by himself, a frantic father who had spent the past three days searching the northern tip of Scotland for his daughter and Brothers. And if Damian knew that something was going to happen tomorrow in Orkney, it would explain why he had been desperate enough to buy the services of a young fisherman to take him across.

Back at Magnuson's farm, I paid off the pleased driver and walked to the door, which opened before I could knock. The odour of roast lamb and potatoes swept over me, poles apart from my bleak mood; it was not made any easier by the cheeriness of the woman who urged me inside, tempting me with a hot meal.

"Thank you," I said. "Mrs Magnuson, is it? I'm not actually hungry, so I won't join you. Can I just ask you for a bit of writing paper and an envelope?"

"Are yeh sure yeh won't have a wee bite?"

"It smells delicious, but no." Actually, the rich aroma was making me queasy, and I wanted to be alone. She showed me into the cold, disused parlour, lit the fire, and left me with stationery and pen. I warmed my hands in front of the flames, and eventually removed my coat and hat, taking up the pen.

Dear Holmes,

I write from Thurso, about to set off for Orkney. Something must have delayed Brothers on the way—they were seen in Edinburgh on Monday, yet Damian was here just this morning, hiring a local fisherman to cross them over. The wind is powerful, unusually so, and the reproving locals were not sanguine about their chances of success. If I do not make it home, would you be so good as to locate the family of the man whose boat Damian hired, and see that they are recompensed?

R

I looked at the inadequacy of that ending, and added:

P.S.: I do not know if Damian is acting alone and against Brothers, or if he was under duress as the man's agent. If the latter, I can only believe he had good reason.

Again I hesitated, tempted to black the postscript out, or change it for something more affectionate, less bleak, but in the end I sealed the flap and wrote the Sussex address, leaving it with a coin for the stamp and a note instructing Mrs Magnuson not to post it until the end of September. It felt like one of those letters soldiers were encouraged to write before a battle. I regretted the melodrama, but I did not wish to take chances with the young fisherman's family.

I sat in the slowly warming room until I heard voices in the hallway, then went to join Captain Javitz for the final assault north.

Chapter Forty-four

*The Stars (2): It is no secret that the stars note greatness:
A star drew the sages to the infant Jesus, as the sun went
dark at His death. A comet brought William the
Conqueror to the throne. The sun lingered to give Joshua
time to complete his conquest.*
Testimony, IV:7

JAVITZ AND MAGNUSON HAD CLEARED THE FUEL LINE,
the culprit in our faltering engine, and used the farmer's horse to
drag the aeroplane back to the start of the rough field. The laundry
was still veering wildly back and forth, but I thought it was not quite
so rigid in its pull.

Perhaps that was self-delusion: I decided not to ask.

Once airborne, we turned east, so as to be over land as long as possible, and battled the wind until we ran out of mainland. When there
was nothing before us but sea until Scandinavia, Javitz turned due
north across the Pentland Firth, and the wind seized us, shaking us in
its teeth like a dog with a rat.

I do not think there were ten feet on the five miles between John
o'Groat's and the first island when we were flying still and steady.

When Javitz turned to study the rudder, his face had a greenish tint. I found after a while that I was reciting, over and over again, a passage from Job that I hadn't thought about since my mother died. Clouds scudded across our windows, pushing us lower and tempting us off-course until Javitz returned to the compass and corrected our line of flight. Glimpses of land teased at us, seeming no closer, although the white wave-caps grew ever nearer. Then suddenly with a moment of clarity, land lay below us again.

Javitz dropped further, seeking protection from the wind, and followed the little island's eastern coast. At the end of it, we passed over a brief stretch of sea to another, even smaller, island, then a landscape that indeed resembled mainland came up underneath us. He directed the nose west again, skimming above countryside that looked surprisingly like England—I don't know what I expected of an island nation ruled by Vikings for seven hundred years, but placid green fields bordered by hedgerows was not it.

In a few miles, a dark steeple rose up in the distance: the cathedral in the centre of Kirkwall, on whose altar chemically liquefied blood had been splashed on the July full moon. Javitz began to examine the passing fields, in an expectant manner I had seen before. Soon, on the outskirts of the town, a length of pasture beckoned. He aimed at it, but it seemed to me he was high—too high, I started to exclaim, then realised that he was making a deliberate pass over it. It was as well he did: Three shaggy cattle grazed in the intended landing strip, solid as a dry-stone wall. As we roared forty feet away from the adjoining stone house, a small boy came running out. Javitz raised the nose and wrestled the 'plane back in a wide circle; when we aimed again at the field, the boy was driving the cows through a gap in a wall.

We hit the ground, rose up, then settled down into a landing as smooth as could be had on uneven terrain. Javitz ran the plane into a wide place at the end of the field, made a wide circle, and shut down the motor.

With quivering fingertips, I uncovered my watch: a quarter past two on Friday, 29 August.

The day before the sun would darken in the north.

"Captain Javitz," I said, my voice loud in the echoing silence, "I am immensely grateful and in your considerable debt. But I hope to God I never have to fly with you again."

He laughed, with more than a touch of manly hysteria in his voice.

And only then—because experience had taught me that some things are best done without permitting discussion—did I tell him what I wanted to do.

"This machine will attract a great deal of attention, I should imagine?"

"It's sure to."

"Our story is, you are offering joy-rides, and I took you up on one out of Wick. You must stay with the machine, talk to people about joy-riding, maybe even offer to take one or two up with you when the wind drops. Can you do that?"

"What about you?"

"I shall slip away, as I could not if you were with me."

"You can't go alone."

"Yes, I can."

"I'm not going to let you go by yourself," he insisted.

I sighed: Sometimes I think I married the world's only sensible male. Anticipating this, I had given my pilot the barest details of why I was here. "Captain Javitz, please don't flex your chivalrous muscles at me. I assure you, I can do what needs to be done. I will go now, while you distract these people. I will come back for you tonight. Shall we meet here?"

That last was an outright lie: I had no intention of bringing him any further into danger. He, on the other hand, had no reason to think a young woman might prefer to face an enemy on her own. And the first curious residents were beginning to gather—constable and local newsman would not be far behind. Grudgingly, he agreed.

We climbed out, and I prepared to chatter like a brainless maniac about the thrill of flying, the speed and noise, the loops and dead-falls, how it was worth every ha'penny. But there was a slight hitch in the plans: It appeared that Cash Javitz was not a stranger here.

I heard him call a cheerful greeting—not to the boy, but to a buxom, red-cheeked woman who came out of the kitchen door behind us.

"Hello, sweetheart," he boomed, nearly knocking me over in surprise.

"Captain Javitz! I might have known it was you, dropping out of the mist and frightening the cows." What she said was more like, *Ca'n Yavitz, Ah mait've knawn it war thee, drawpin' fra' the muggry an' fleggin' tha caws;* however, such dialect is as tiresome to write as it is to decipher. Still, the sound of it was a delight, a lilt more like a Scandinavian tongue than anything I'd heard in Britain, and impossible to duplicate on the page without musical notations.

"I knew you didn't believe me, that I was a fly-boy, so I thought I'd drop in and prove it."

"What, after five years you just drop in?"

"I was pining, couldn't keep away from you any longer."

"Don't let my husband hear you," she warned playfully.

"Plenty to go around," he replied, and she crowed in delight. "Brigid Ross, meet Mary Russell. Miss Russell is my excuse for crossing the Strait."

She came down the steps and took my hand, eyeing me sharply before deciding that the gold ring I wore indicated that I was no rival for the good Captain's bantering affections.

I realised I was neither dressed nor wearing sufficient make-up to present myself as a Bright Young Thing out for a day's lark, so instead I merely asked Mrs Ross where I might find a cup of tea.

She told me that the kettle was on, and although I demurred, I did not demur all that much. She and I went inside, leaving Javitz to his gathering crowd of would-be customers.

The tea was supplemented by thick slices of a chewy, slightly sweet soda bread slathered with fresh-churned butter, and my stomach, after a moment's hesitation, woke to the aroma and savour. I ate three slabs, and only stopped there because the boy appeared at the door, panting slightly but beaming with excitement.

"May I have a ride in the Captain's aeroplane?" he begged.

"Certainly not," she replied. "But if you wash your hands, you can have your tea. Will you two be stopping the night in Kirkwall?" she asked me as I rose and picked up my coat.

"We may, especially if the wind gets worse," I said. "In any event, I think I'll take a turn through the town. I've never been in Orkney before."

"If you do get caught here and have trouble finding rooms, let me know," she said, showing me to the door. "It's the height of the season, and rooms were tight even before the hotel at the Stones burned down."

I turned. "Do you mean at Stenness?"

"That's the one."

"When did this happen?"

"Two days past? No, I'm a liar, it was on Tuesday, so three days. Booked to the rafters with anglers, it was, and everything a smoky mess. The owner was a day in hospital, they're staying with his wife's family in St Mary's for at least a fortnight."

"But the place didn't actually burn down?"

"Not down, no, just left a terrible stinking mess. They boarded over the windows and everyone's moved into town until the floors dry and the roof is patched."

"I see. Well, I certainly shan't plan on staying there," I told her with a smile, and set off towards Kirkwall, deep in thought. If Brothers and the child boarded a steamer in Aberdeen on Tuesday, how could he be in place to set a fire by the evening? But it could not be coincidence— no, he had help on Orkney, the same assistant who'd scattered cock's blood in the cathedral whose spire I could see rising ahead of me.

As Mrs Ross had said, it being August, the facilities for tourist entertainment were laid on in strength. Shops sold knitted wear or cheese made from local cows, tea houses posted banners advertising their authentic Orcadian cakes, and coaches waited to transport visitors to the sites of Orkney.

One of these caught my ear, an enterprising coach driver trying to turn the waning day into a bonus rather than a disadvantage. "See the Ring of Brodgar in the rich light of evening, when the sun throws shadows far across the loch," he was calling in a stentorian voice.

One glance at the sky drew his thrown shadows into question, but in fact, an evening trip was precisely what I required. An added benefit was the handful of tourists he had already attracted, three earnest Dutch couples and an adolescent belonging to one of them. I gave the man my coin, took my seat, and we were soon away.

The benefits of concealment in numbers had been suggested by my first look at the Ordnance Survey map, and was the reason I had carried a pair of field glasses in my bag all the way. As we approached, with our driver cheerfully shouting over his shoulder all sorts of misinformation about Vikings, Celts, and Druids, it became ever more apparent that my only options for concealment in daylight were to hide in plain sight among a group, or to dig a hole in the turf and pull it over my head.

From the hills down, the land was bare as an egg.

I could see at a glance why this remote site had been marked as holy by the early Orcadians. It was a between-place: neither sea nor land, neither Britain nor Europe, a stretch of solid ground between two wide lochs, one salt, the other fresh. For four thousand years, the residents had built temples in this low and brooding marshland, from the giant stone ring that capped a rise at one end of the causeway separating the lochs to the smaller but more dramatic circle nearer the road. Christianity, too, had a toehold, with a small church and cemetery laying claim to its ground in the midst of burial mounds and standing stones.

Even modern-day religion was represented, in the person of devoted anglers, scattered along the shores of the lochs.

The driver-guide pulled his coach over to a wide place near the smaller stone circle, whose dark granite slabs resembled shards of broken window-pane dropped by the gods, and informed us that these were the Stones of Stenness. On a low hill to the north-west, across the causeway, rode the Ring of Brodgar (where, he did not tell us but my telegram had informed me, cremated remains had been recently scattered). To the north-east, beyond the church, was the pregnant belly-mound of Maeshowe, where a slaughtered sheep had been found on the May full moon.

The Dutch contingent were kept occupied translating and commenting upon what the guide had to say about the artefacts we walked past: first the Stones of Stenness, then a couple of pencil-thin pillars jabbed into the ground, and the now-destroyed Odin Stone (which had been one of those venerable objects that inspire courting couples, entertain amateur antiquarians, and infuriate the farmer on whose land they lie—hence this stone's demolition). We crossed the causeway, passing farm buildings and more standing stones, until the ground began to rise, revealing the size of the lochs on either side. Ahead of us lay the wide, low Ring of Brodgar.

I left the others to their misinformed lecture and circumnavigated the ring on my own, feeling the press of ground beneath me. Many of the stones were fallen or missing entirely; those that remained were cracked and uneven; nonetheless, the original Ring had been perfectly round. Perhaps that was why, despite its wear, it retained the feel of a precise mechanism, a circle tightly calibrated to enclose and concentrate any worship carried out on this barren and wind-swept hillock. It reminded me of an ancient brass-work device in a museum, whose function remained unimpaired by the surface ravages of time.

Standing in the centre, I looked down to see traces of ash among the grass.

From the Ring's heather-grown perimeter, which had once been ditched and banked to form a henge, I studied the countryside. Water stretched out before me and at my back; to my right, the peninsula between the lochs was littered with standing stones, brochs, and earthen mounds. To my left, peninsula narrowed into causeway before joining the road; on one side were the Stones of Stenness and Maeshowe; on the other lay the burnt-out anglers' hotel. A brief spill of sun showed boards across its windows.

The Dutch were being led away by the guide, tempted after his conversational carrots that seemed to link Vikings and Druids—although

I might have been mistaken, I was not listening very closely. I dawdled among the stones, allowing the others to pull ahead, before following them down the causeway towards the Stones of Stenness.

Perhaps it was the approaching dusk coupled with the racing clouds and biting wind. Perhaps it was the knowledge that, somewhere near, a man with a knife waited to loose blood on the earth. In any event, I was aware of an atmosphere here such as I had seldom felt before: not at Stonehenge, a gloomy and isolated huddle of stones, nor even Avebury—what metaphysical authority it once possessed had long since been overbuilt by barns and homely cottages. This place held another kind of aura entirely: One could feel it brooding.

The Stenness stones had been a henge as well, although this site's ditch and bank were more elliptical than the Ring, and what had once been a stone circle was little more than a collection of slabs. They were tall, one of them nearing twenty feet, and unbelievably thin—it seemed impossible that they had stood here for millennia without snapping off in the wind. One of them jutted out of the ground at an angle, then turned sharply back on itself, like a directional arrow for giants.

In their centre was the restored altar. According to a guide-book in Mycroft's study, some twenty years ago a well-meaning enthusiast had decided that the half-buried stone in the middle of the circle had originally been an altar-stone, and had raised it, stretching it between a stone that lay to one side and a pair of stones that had been cracked and mounted upright with a gap between the halves.

Although the position of the cracked stone seemed to have a significance beyond that of a support—the gap between its halves would frame the mound of Maeshowe—the massive three-legged table was, nonetheless, most impressive. It did not require the imagination of a Sir Walter Scott to picture it as a sacrificial altar, longer than any man, fenced in by the towering grey granite shards.

My tour companions had been marched away to Maeshowe, our guide having clearly decided that I was unappreciative of his expertise. Alone, I made a slow circuit of the Stones, memorising the arrangement of the upright rocks, letting my feet learn the low depression of the ditch-works and the ground-level bridge that had once passed through ditch and bank.

Under the guise of studying waterfowl, I took out my glasses and aimed them at the saltwater loch to the south. Three swans stretched their wings and thought about dinner; seagulls darted and cried on the wind. A pair of fishermen occupying the shallows between me and the hotel had begun to work their way back to the shore, no doubt with dinner on their minds as well; behind them, I could see where the flames had been doused before they ate into the fabric of the hotel. The windows on this side of the building showed the backs of curtains—the fire must have started at night.

Its inner rooms, while not cosy, would be liveable.

Snatches of voice warned me of my companions' return, and I let the glasses wander along the shore-line for a minute before packing them away. I turned for a last look at the nearby proto-circle.

There was an intensity, almost a violence, to these Stones that the Ring on the hill did not have. I had fancied them earlier as having been dropped by the gods, but that was too passive. Rather, they looked as if the gods had seized each sharp-edged slab to drive it savagely into the turf, pulling away a blood-smeared hand.

I caught myself: I'd been away from Holmes for too long, and my imagination was running away with me.

Still, when I looked at that stone altar, I shivered.

I returned to the coach and rode unprotesting to the island's second town of Stromness, but when the others were shepherded in the direction of a restaurant, I slipped away. I walked back the way we had come, taking my time with the four miles so it would be deep dusk for the last mile; three motor-cars passed; each time, I dropped into the grassy verge away from their head-lamps.

The sky was moonless; the hotel was a faint outline against a marginally lighter expanse of clouds. I crept towards the smell of smoke and pressed myself into the wall between the first two windows, trying to hear above the perpetual sough of the wind. In the absence of a stethoscope, I pulled the knife from my boot-sheath and rested its point against the stones, setting the handle in back of my ear. Nothing.

Moving down the wall to the next windows, I tried again, and again heard only the sounds of the night and the thud of my own heart. Around the corner, the wind was loud enough to obscure anything less than a shout, so I kept circling to the side facing away from the loch. Again I listened, again—wait. Not voices, but a rhythmic thump, thump, thump, that then quickened in pace for a dozen or so beats. Feet, coming down stairs?

I moved to the boarded-up back of the hotel, and there I glimpsed motion. A light flickered, danced, and steadied: a candle, half-visible through the boards. A figure moved around the room; I heard the sound of water flowing into a vessel, saw a flare of light as a gas cooker lit beneath the kettle. The shadowy figure pulled open drawers, coming out from the third one with a long knife. He took it to a shapeless lump on the table beside the tea-pot, and began sawing: bread.

All this was with his back to me, so he was nothing but an indistinct shape in a dim room. I considered moving around to the boarded-up door and seeing if I could find a crack, but before I could move, he turned, and the unruly hair and beard identified him: Damian Adler.

If prisoner he was, then a very blasé prisoner indeed, making tea and sandwiches as if living in a burnt-out building with a religious fanatic was the humdrum stuff of everyday Bohemian life.

He turned away to the tea-pot, and I pressed my face closer against the glass, trying to get some sense of the man. Did he, too, burn with the fanaticism of *Testimony*? Had this rumpled figure participated in the ritual murder of his wife? Was he about to join in the similar slaughter of an innocent step-daughter?

My nose hovered near the glass, my spectacles dangerously close to tapping its hard surface; without warning, a hand came down on my shoulder.

Chapter Forty-five

*The Sacrifice of Setting Loose (1): As we have seen,
the greater the sacrifice, the greater the energies loosed.
This is an age of War, when the earth has drunk the
sacrificial blood of millions. The world lies primed,
for a transformative spark.*

Testimony, IV:8

THE SCREAM THAT CAME FROM MY THROAT WAS instantly stifled, emerging as a strangled death-rattle. Before Damian could turn I was already gone, attacking my attacker.

My muscles responded automatically to the hand on my shoulder, but as instantly lost all strength at the hasty whisper, "Russell!"

"Holmes? Holmes! What the hell are you— Quick, away from the window."

I pushed him away, to the corner and beyond, then eased my head back: A shadow pressed against the window, looking for the sound; after a minute, it retreated. I turned and punched Holmes on the chest.

"Damn it, Holmes, what are you *doing* here? You were on your way to Norway, for God's sake."

"You did not receive my message?"

"No—how would I receive a message? I haven't heard a word from you since you left London."

"Interesting. I'd have thought Mycroft . . ."

"Holmes."

"I rethought my plans."

"Obviously."

" 'Many things having full reference to one consent, may work contrariously; as many arrows, loosed several ways, fly to one mark.' "

"Holmes!"

"Shakespeare, on bees. *Henry the Fifth,*" he added.

"Damn it, Holmes!"

"I decided you were right."

"You decided—? Good heavens. Well, sweet bloody hell, I wish you'd let me know earlier, I nearly jumped through the window when you grabbed me."

"That would have been unfortunate."

I hit him again, for good measure, and felt somewhat better. Felt considerably better, in fact, with him at my side. I threw my arms around him and hugged him, hard, then stood back and explored his face with my hands.

"You haven't shaved in days," I exclaimed, "and why are you so damp? You're freezing."

"I have spent most of the past three days at sea," he answered, which explained both the difficulty of shaving and the permeating moisture.

"We need to get you out of the cold."

"That is of secondary importance."

"They're brewing tea, they won't be going anywhere for a time. Let me just check—" I tip-toed back to the window, and glimpsed Damian unconcernedly pouring water into the tea-pot. I retrieved Holmes and led him towards the hotel's out-buildings.

These were securely locked, but the padlock on the biggest one would not have challenged a child. The interior stank of fish and contained a lot of nets, poles, gum boots, and paddles, but in a window-less corner room I found a store of elderly bed-clothes and parapher-nalia for the guests, from water carafes to expensive fly-fishing rods. A wicker picnic basket contained a filled paraffin burner, a packet of tea leaves, and even a tin of slightly crumbled biscuits. When I lit the burner, a remarkably bearded husband came into view, tugging a blanket around his shoulders.

I was startled, then began to laugh. "*You* were the bearded Englishman!"

"I did not know you found facial hair so amusing," he grumbled.

"Not on its own—but when I was asking after Damian and Brothers in Thurso, I described him as a 'bearded Englishman.' I didn't think to add, 'of thirty.' So when a man said he'd seen such a person and I told him the Englishman was my step-son, the poor fel-low was taken aback, that my husband should be so . . ."

"Truly ancient."

"I thought his astonishment odd, at the time, but I never consid-ered . . . Holmes, what are you *doing* here?"

"When did you last hear from Mycroft?" he asked.

"Not directly since I left, but I had two telegrams in Thurso at mid-day today. They were from Mycroft's men, passing on the information that the blood found in the Kirkwall cathedral had been analysed and found to have been kept liquefied by chemicals, and that ashes had been found in the Ring of Brodgar, but then—"

"Those pieces of news were what turned me from my path."

"I see. So perhaps you didn't hear that Mycroft's flat had been raided?"

"Lestrade?" Holmes' incredulity matched my own, when I had heard.

"So it would appear." I told him what little I knew, but he could find no sense in Lestrade's imprudent assault on Mycroft's home, ei-ther.

"That does explain why I haven't heard further from my brother, and why he did not pass on to you my change in plans."

"How far had you got?"

"Well into the North Sea, I fear, when one of the officers brought me a cable from Mycroft with the information about the blood in the cathedral."

"Oh, Holmes, you didn't make them turn back to Hull?"

"I attempted to, but failed. I did, however, convince them that an aquatic transfer exercise would be in order, as soon as he could raise a boat headed the opposite direction. I left the packet of photographs for Mycroft's men in Norway, and succeeded in transferring onto a boat bound for Newcastle without more than a mild wetting."

"I'm astonished you don't have pneumonia. But if your wire reached his place after the raid, Lestrade may know we're here."

"The Chief Inspector won't be able to organise anything tonight, I don't think."

"Probably not. So, ashes and sodium citrate changed your mind?"

He fixed me with a look. "The dates and the impossibility of co-incidence changed my mind. Eight events, eight sites."

I recited the deaths: "Beltane at Long Meg; the May full moon at Maeshowe; Fiona Cartwright during the June full moon at Cerne Abbas; the July full moon at Kirkwall—"

"That last was a cock, according to the envelope in Brothers' safe, although he did not himself sprinkle the blood in the cathedral—he was in London."

"I wonder if Kirkwall has an employment agency—or he could have made arrangements when he was here in May, to kill the sheep at Maeshowe."

Holmes picked up the list where I had left off. "Then came Albert Seaforth in Yorkshire, during the Perseids. Two days later, on the night of the lunar eclipse, an hotel employee in Stenness dutifully scattered the ashes of some unknown person—"

"Which was, in fact, a horse, if those envelopes are to be believed."

"A portion of a horse, I should say, considering that the employee believed it to be the ashes of a human being. And the following night, the August full moon, Yolanda Adler."

"Dorset, Orkney, Cumbria, Orkney, York, Orkney, Sussex, and back to Orkney for the end. But whose blood was used to mark the *Testimony* he gave Yolanda?" I wondered. "Millicent Dunworthy received hers on the fourteenth of May and it had the numeral two. Did we miss one earlier?"

"Not necessarily. He may have simply pricked his own finger, to start the process. Certainly he used his own for number seven, to adhere the horse's ashes to the page."

"How would one find a crematorium willing to dispose of a horse?" I wondered.

"A haunch already in a coffin would be unremarkable. In any case, the pattern was clear, so I caught a boat north along the coast of Britain instead of the coast of Europe. Several boats, working their way against a hurricane. The last one cost me a prince's ransom."

"I know. The fellow's friends are planning his funeral."

"He was hale and more or less dry when I rowed away in his dinghy. He dropped anchor near Stromness, said he would stay there until the wind dies."

I gave him an equally laconic description of my own hair-raising journey, and poured us both tea, filtering it through a sterling tea-strainer.

"What, no milk?" Holmes asked.

"Pretend you're Chinese," I said. The little cook stove was taking the edge off the bitter cold of the room; Holmes had energy for a joke, and was no longer the colour of chalk.

I cradled my hands around the steaming cup. "How much detail was in the wire you sent Mycroft?"

"Knowing that police eyes were on him, very little. However, I said I was joining you, and if either of his men were less cautious in their information—"

"Then we'll find Orkney's finest waiting for us. Holmes, you don't imagine anything has happened to Mycroft? Another heart attack, brought on by outrage?"

"I think it more likely we'll find him arrested for assaulting a police officer," he replied. "Mycroft takes the authority of his position seriously."

I suddenly thought of something. "Good heavens. I wonder if the local forces have arrested poor Captain Javitz?"

"Your pilot? Would you anticipate he might tell the police all?"

"He's as gallant as they come, and in any event, he doesn't know my plans. Speaking of which, Holmes, what are our plans? I had intended to wait until Brothers came out and pull a gun on him. Would you prefer to storm the house?"

He shook his head. "The chances of breaking in without noise are slim, and I fear the child would have a knife at her throat before we reached the stairs."

"So we wait until they come out?"

"We wait until the child is clear of danger."

I took a breath. "Holmes, have you—"

"Yes," he said. "I know. The question of Damian. Russell, I may be a fool, but I'm not blind. Despite the improbability of my son's ignorance, I do not believe he is fully *au fait* with what Brothers intends. However, I was wrong about his mother from the moment I laid eyes on her, and I could be wrong about him."

"I agree, that he does not know," I said, to his surprise. "In fact, he may still not know of Yolanda's death." I explained my reasoning: the largely amiable relationship between the two men; Brothers' odd disinclination to keep to one place.

"So why the devil does Damian remain with Brothers, if he is neither prisoner nor true believer?" Holmes fretted.

"Wouldn't he stay with Brothers if he thought it was what his wife wanted? If Brothers has convinced him that they're to meet Yolanda in this strange place, because she's utterly determined to carry out a ritual?"

"My son is not blind, either."

"No, but his wife was notoriously unpredictable. Remember that letter she wrote, telling Damian that she was in the country with friends? What if there was a second letter, that Brothers gave him when he got to the walled house, explaining that she was going off on one of her dotty adventures, and pleading with him to join her?"

Holmes shook his head unhappily. "I see no alternative to letting the play work itself out until the final act, and determine the villains then. All I ask is that you refrain from using your gun on my son unless you are absolutely certain." He drained his tea and dropped the blanket, turning off the small stove. The light died with it.

I turned on the small torch and followed Holmes out of the storage room, bringing with me two of the dark grey woollen blankets. Outside of the shed, it was nearly as dark as it had been inside, but at least the stiff breeze had subsided a bit. It was the first time in what seemed like weeks that I had not felt battered by wind; it was a pleasure to stand in the lee of the building while our eyes adjusted to the darkness, listening to the whisper of loch-waves licking the shore.

Slowly, stars appeared overhead; the faintest trace of light still marked the western sky. Holmes, who possessed the night-vision of a cat, moved in the direction of the Stones, while I followed more slowly, going by memory of the terrain rather than sight. An instant before I stumbled against the rise of the ditch-works, Holmes murmured, "Watch your step."

I grumbled and picked my way, and when we had negotiated the ditch itself, I said softly, "I suggest we wait on the far side of the ditch-work. That will be beyond the reach of any lights they may bring."

"And also beyond reach of providing assistance. No, let us make use of this altar-stone. Even if they have a torch, it should be simple enough to keep away from its beam."

"You want to sit under that massive slab of rock?" I said, my voice climbing.

"It's been there forever, Russell, it's not about to flatten us."

"Holmes, a bunch of amateur archaeologists hoiked it up barely twenty years ago," I protested.

"You don't say? Well, it hasn't fallen yet," he noted serenely, and ducked underneath.

It would be an irony if I had survived numerous opportunities to plummet from the sky only to be squashed by a boulder. All in all, I thought as I inserted myself beneath the precarious dolmen, I'd rather be harvesting honey in Sussex, where the greatest risk was being stung to death.

I draped us in the blankets, which would not only keep our muscles from freezing stiff but might help us blend into the shadows underneath the rocks. Hunched together, shoulder to shoulder, we waited for Ragnarok, the end of the world.

Chapter Forty-six

*The Sacrifice of Setting Loose (2): This is when the
Practitioner knows that the Work is ready: when his Focus
is absolute. When the Will of his community is behind him.
When the Tool is in his hand and his hand is in the Tool.
When the Place is understood, and arranged, and reached.
When the stars are aligned, and he can feel the quiver as
Time's mechanism prepares to strike.*
Testimony, IV: 8

D O YOU SUPPOSE THEY'LL WAIT UNTIL MIDNIGHT?"
I asked, after what seemed a long time.

"*Testimony* refers to it as the 'witching hour.' "

"Can he actually believe that human sacrifice 'looses powers'?" I
wondered.

"Russell, you are the expert in religion, I merely pursue crime."

"This is neither. It's madness."

"Yes. But madness has method."

We were gambling a life—possibly a child's life—on the demands of
that method. That the man—the men?—in the abandoned hotel
would place ritual above the practical. That a man—or men—who

would dismiss as unimportant the fact that an eclipse did not actually touch the chosen site, would nonetheless preserve the details of the act as if it did. That an ordinary midnight would take precedence over the actual hour of fullest eclipse.

"One of us should go back to the hotel," I told Holmes.

"They will be on guard there; here, they will be preoccupied." The decisive words were belied by the tightness in his voice, but I did not argue, because he was right.

We huddled together, a terrible weight over our heads, and our doubts grew along with the cold.

"I have my pick-locks," I said forty minutes later. "If we let ourselves in the front door—"

His body rather than words cut me off, as he went from tense to taut. I stared in the direction of the hotel, seeing nothing.

"Did you—" I began.

He hissed me to silence, and a moment later, I saw it too: a brief play of light defining the corner of the building, there and gone again.

Several minutes passed before it came back, but when it did, the light was steady and general, not the darting beam of a torch. Good: A lamp made it less likely they would spot us.

With a single movement, Holmes and I drew our revolvers from our pockets and held them to our chests beneath the concealing wool. The approaching group was at first a confusion of legs, dancing in and out of the light; then it resolved itself into two men.

They paused at the encircling ditch-works, and we heard voices, but not the words. When they moved again, it was around the Stones, following the raised earthen mound in a clockwise direction. We watched, shifting to keep well back from their side of the altar stone: One man, wearing dark trousers, held the lamp, and moved slightly to the fore; the other was dressed in corduroy trousers. They marched in a circle, and when they were back where they had started, walked down the earthen bridge towards us.

Snatches of conversation reached our ears:

"—really don't think she's at all (something)." Damian's voice.

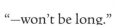

"—won't be long."

"(something something) morning to see a doctor."

"Yolanda asked (something)."

Then they either cleared an obstruction or turned towards us, because Damian's voice came loud and clear, and high like Holmes' when he is angry or on edge. "You know, Hayden, I've never played the pompous husband rôle and told Yolanda that she couldn't participate in your church, but this really has taken the cake. It's two weeks now—I've a one-man show I should be working on, Estelle has a cold, and here we are out in the middle of a piss-freezing night because Yolanda has a bee in her bonnet. I think she must have gone mad, truly I—"

As his voice came clearer, I realised that he sounded more than a little drunk. By contrast, when Brothers—Hayden—interrupted, his voice, which I had last heard at the walled house, was calm, soothing, and reasonable.

"I know, Damian, I know. Your wife is a passionate woman, and when she gets her mind set on a thing, nothing will turn her."

"But wha' does she imagine, having me follow around in her wake for two weeks and then . . . follow around after her and then get up on a rock in the middle of the night . . . up on a rock to pray . . . oops."

His last sound was accompanied by a jerk of the approaching lamp-light; around the stones I saw that Brothers was now supporting him, and I breathed in Holmes' ear, "That's drugs, not drink."

I felt him nod.

The two men came to a halt at the edge of the stone, their shoes at arm's reach from where we crouched. Light danced and receded as Brothers put the lamp on top of the stone, then took a step back.

"Get up on top, Damian," he said.

"It's bloody cold. Juss say your prayers and less go."

If Brothers had maintained his reasonable attitude, he might well have cajoled Damian into obedience, but the effort of control was too much, and his voice went tight and hard. "Get up, Damian," he ordered the younger man and took another step back. "Now."

"What the bloody hell—?" Damian staggered a couple of steps before he caught himself, leaving Brothers on a direct line between us and him. It was too dangerous to risk our guns; the night was too silent to permit our movement.

"Sorry old man," Brothers said. "I don't wish to use this on you, but it's important, really it is. I just need you to get up on the rock, now."

Damian faced him for several seconds, swaying, then answered. "Oh, very well," he grumbled, sounding eerily like his father.

He wove his way to the stone: It took him three tries to get his body onto it. His boots swung free for a moment, then his legs followed him up. For the first time we now had a clear view of Brothers, while we remained hidden in shadow. However, neither Holmes nor I doubted that the gun in his hand rested steady on Damian.

Holmes' hand was on my arm, gripping hard, warning me against premature movement. We had both stopped breathing as we waited for Brothers to put away the gun and take out his Tool, the sacrificial knife that had "moved" his hand too many times.

"That's good, Damian. Yolanda would be happy."

His response was a wordless mutter, trailing off to nothing.

"Can you stretch out on your back?" Brothers asked, drawing again on the voice of reason. "Damian? Stretch out, please. Damian!"

We heard the sound of clothing against stone, but no words.

Still, Brothers was cautious. When he approached, he kept the gun on Damian until he was standing at the edge of the stone. Holmes' hand stayed steady on me, although he too had to be doubting himself, asking if Brothers wouldn't choose the sure way over the ritual purity of the knife. We hunched like wound springs, eyes fastened on the coat-tails that would move when Brothers put away his gun and reached for his knife—

One forgot that Damian Adler was a soldier. I know I did, and certainly Brothers had. But beneath the sedative, hidden under the persona of a long-haired Bohemian painter, waited a soldier's instinct for survival. That Damian Adler now acted, using the only weapon available to him: the lamp.

Our first warning was a simultaneous shout and gunshot, followed in an instant by a crisp sound of breaking glass. A stream of fire poured itself down the supporting stones and across the ground.

Holmes launched himself through the edge of the flames at Brothers' legs, but the blanket he threw back tangled across my feet. It cost me two seconds to fight clear of the encumbering wool, by which time the flame had spread into a crackling sheet the length of the altar stone. I shoved away from the igniting paraffin, cracking my head painfully on stone as I scrambled to my feet on the opposite side of the altar.

My eyes were met by a nightmare scene worthy of Hieronymus Bosch. A confusion of leaping flames and shadows was punctuated by yells and curses, then another shot, but when my eyes cleared from the blow, they were drawn to the fire that licked down the top of the stone towards the man who lay there.

My gun flew into the night as both hands reached out to drag Damian's uncontrolled body away from the flames. I dumped him on the ground and slapped at the burning shoulder of his overcoat. Once it was out—a matter of seconds—I sprinted, still crouched, to the prow of the altar-stone, where two men wrestled for control of a gun.

I jumped to hit the weapon hard with my fist, knocking it onto the altar stone, but Brothers' elbow slammed hard into my chest and sent me flying. I rolled and regained my feet, and saw Holmes stretched over the stone for the gun.

But Brothers was not interested in the revolver. His arm was moving and he took two quick steps forward, holding in the air a knife with a curved blade, gleaming and vicious in the leaping fire-light. I opened my mouth to scream a warning as I gathered myself to jump, but I knew I would be too late, long seconds too late, because the arm was flashing down towards Holmes' exposed back.

A third shot smashed the night. The descending arm lost its aim; metal sparked against stone. The knife made a skittering noise as it flew down the altar, followed by a coughing sound and the slump of a heavy body.

The flames were already beginning to die, and I drew my torch to shine it on Holmes: He had a cut, bloody but shallow, on the side of his face. Then I turned it on Brothers, and saw the bullet hole directly over his heart, and blood staining his thick overcoat near the hole.

With one motion, Holmes and I stepped clear of the altar, and saw Damian, lying where I had left him, gazing with surprise at the gun in his hand—my gun, I saw, flown from my grasp as I jerked him from the flames, fallen to the ground where he lay. His hand drooped, recovered, then sank to the ground, followed by his chin.

Holmes rolled Damian onto his back, and pulled his son's overcoat away: blood on the right side of Damian's chest, a hand's width and growing. Holmes ripped away the shirt, and exhaled in relief: The bullet had missed the lungs, and might, if we were lucky, have avoided the major organs as well.

"He needs a doctor," I said.

"Estelle," Damian muttered through clenched teeth.

Holmes didn't answer me.

"Holmes, we have to get him to a doctor."

"If we do, he'll be arrested."

I met his eyes, aghast. "You don't intend . . ."

"Let's at least take him to the hotel where we can see the extent of the injury. We can decide after that."

"Holmes, no. I'll go to that farm and see if they have a telephone—see, there's already a light on upstairs, they'll have heard all this—"

He reached for the pile of blankets. "We can use one of these as a stretcher."

"You'll kill him, Holmes!"

"Being locked up in gaol will kill him." Holmes stared at me in the dying light of the flames; I had never seen such desperation in his face. "Are you going to help me, Russell, or do I have to carry him?"

We worked the blanket under Damian's limp weight and dragged him free, then Holmes stuffed the other blanket around him. "We don't want to leave a trail," he said.

Damian groaned at the motion, then fell silent.

Holmes gathered up the three guns, handing me one, slipping the second into his pocket, and laying the third near the dead man's hand. Then he wrapped two corners of the blanket around his fists, and waited for me to do the same.

We dropped our burden once, and a second time, I fell. Damian cried out that time, but we were far enough from the lamp bobbing in our direction from the nearby farmhouse that the farmer wouldn't hear.

And, thank God, the man had no dogs.

Chapter Forty-seven

*The End and the Beginning: When the stars are in
alignment, and the ages look down in approval.
When his masculinity prepares to act, and his feminine
nature is ready to receive. At that moment,
the Work is ready for consummation.
Thus Testifies a man.*
Testimony: Part the Greatest

W E MADE IT TO THE HOTEL. WHILE HOLMES STOOD
winded just inside the back door, I tucked my agonised
hands under my arms and conducted a quick survey of the ground
floor, finding an inner storage room in which a light would not show
outside. I hauled the brooms and buckets out and replaced them with
cushions, and we staggered through the dark hotel with our half-
conscious burden. While Holmes was undressing his son, I went in
search of the hotel medical kit.

I came back to find Holmes standing above the sprawled figure,
frowning at the wound. It looked terrible, but Damian was breathing
cleanly, which meant no broken rib had entered a lung, and the seep-
ing blood indicated that no major blood vessel had been severed.

"Is the bullet still in there?" I asked.

"It's travelled along the ribs, probably broken a couple of them, and lodged around the back, under his arm."

"You're not going to perform surgery, Holmes," I warned.

"It's buried fairly deep in the muscle," he more or less agreed. "I shouldn't want to be responsible for having damaged the use of his right arm."

As if hearing the threat to his painter's hand, Damian stirred, then gasped.

"He doesn't seem very heavily drugged," I said.

"He's a big man, and Brothers may not have wanted to risk knocking him out too early. He might have carried an unconscious Yolanda, but not Damian."

"Bugger, that hurts," Damian said in surprise then went slack again.

"I'm going to find the child," I told Holmes. "Should we try and get some coffee into him?"

"It might be simpler to transport him unconscious."

I ignored the proposal. Instead, I passed through the kitchen to set a kettle on the gas cooker.

I found Estelle in an upstairs room that was dimly lit by a burning candle. Her small body lay in a tangle of bed-clothes. She was not moving.

In an agony of trepidation, I crossed the floor to bend over her still figure. Seconds passed, and my heart failed at the thought of telling Damian—but then she made a tiny sound in the back of her throat and followed it by a childish snore.

My legs gave out and I had to sit down on the unmade bed beside hers. Slightly dizzy, I dropped my head in my hands and sat listening to her breathe, hearing the precious air go in and out of her throat. I didn't know if this was Holmes' granddaughter or not, but in truth, it no longer mattered: Damian loved her, therefore she was ours.

It took some time to recall the heating kettle and the waiting men. I sat up, studying the tiny, limp form. I shouldn't be surprised if Brothers hadn't given her a dose of the Veronal as well.

The thought of the dead man finally roused me to my feet. I left the sleeping child and went to the next room, where I found signs of Brothers. Unlike Damian, whose clothes were scattered about the room he shared with his daughter, Brothers had packed his bag, ready to leave.

When I opened the bag, I saw two passports. I picked them up, checked again to make sure Estelle was still sleeping, and went downstairs.

I made coffee and took it to the inner room, where Holmes had managed to sit Damian up and rouse him into a state of groggy semi-consciousness. The coffee was thick enough to stimulate the dead, much less the merely sedated. I pressed a cup into Damian's good hand, waited to see that he was not about to drop it, then pulled the passports out of my pocket and handed them to Holmes.

One was for a British citizen named Jonas Algier; the other was for the same person, but included his young daughter Estelle.

The distaste on Holmes' face matched my own; when he laid the passports to one side, his fingers surreptitiously wiped themselves on his trouser-leg before he reached out to shake his son's shoulder.

"Damian," he said forcefully. "I need you sensible. Can you talk?"

"Where's Estelle?" came the reply, slurred but coherent.

"She's fine," I assured him. "Sleeping."

"God, what the hell happened?"

"Brothers tried to kill you."

"Don't be 'diculous."

"He shot you."

"That's what . . . ? Ah. Hurts like the devil."

"You shot him back, if it makes you feel any better. He's dead."

"Dead? I killed Hayden? Oh Christ—"

"Damian!" Holmes said sharply, and waited for his son's eyes to focus on his. "We need to get you away from here, now. Can you move?"

"Hayden's dead. Can't just walk away from a dead man. The police'll be after us."

"The police are already after us."

"Why?"

Holmes looked at me, then returned his gaze to his son. "Yolanda was killed. Scotland Yard—"

"No," Damian said. "Not possible. She's on one of her religious adventures."

"Your wife died," Holmes said gently. "Two weeks ago, at the Wilmington Giant. I saw her, Damian. The Sunday after you left me, three days before you and Hayden left London, I saw her. In a morgue. She'd been drugged, as you were, and then sacrificed, as you would have been. She felt nothing."

"No," Damian repeated. "There was a letter. Hayden—Brothers, he changed his name—left me a message on how to meet him."

By way of answer, Holmes took something from his pocket and pressed it into Damian's palm.

Damian opened his hand and stared at the gold band we had found in Brothers' safe. Still, he kept talking, low and fast, as if words might push back the testimony of his eyes. "We met at Piccadilly Circus, and he gave me a letter she'd written. On the Friday. That's why I came away. I wrote to you, to tell you what I was doing. I did write to you."

"We received it," Holmes said. "What did Yolanda's letter say?"

"It was just one of Yolanda's . . ." But with the voicing of her name, the truth hit him. He clenched his hand around the ring. "She was always going on about spiritual experiments, always wanting to drag me in on them. And I did. I never minded, it kept her happy. She was always so happy, those times. Oh, God. So when she wrote that she had a really vital adventure—that's what she called them, *adventures*— and that she knew it was asking a lot of me, but that she wanted me to go with Hayden and Estelle for a few days while she was getting ready, and then Hayden would bring us together and this would be the very last one." He was weeping now, choking on his words. "She said that it would be a lot of bother for me, and that she was sorry, but that it would be worth it and if I wanted her never to do it again, she wouldn't, after this one."

He couldn't talk any more, just dropped his head back against the wall and wept. Holmes eased him gently onto the cushions, then pulled me out into the hotel bar.

By the trickle of lamp-light from the half-open door, Holmes searched around behind the smoke-covered bar. He found a bottle, threw the first glass down his throat and poured a second; I took a generous swallow of mine.

"The boat will be there until the tide changes in the morning," he said.

"The trip might kill him."

"And it might not."

"Holmes, it's four miles to Stromness. It would take the both of us to carry him, and what would we do with the child?"

"We could drape her on top of him."

"And when she wakes up from this drug, in a dark place, cold air, strange movement? You think she'll be silent?"

"What about a motor-car—there must be one here?"

"An old lorry, yes. And there's a cart, if we want to borrow a horse from the paddock across the way. But don't you suppose that farmer with the lamp has already rung the police?"

I saw his dim shape walk over to the window, and manoeuvre his way down until he located a viewing hole between the boards. By the way he came back, I knew what he had seen.

"They're already here, aren't they?" I asked. "They'd catch you up long before you got Damian on board."

"We could give the child another dose of—"

"Absolutely not. I won't be party to drugging a child."

"Then you propose we leave her here?"

We looked at each other for a moment, and I gave in. "She was very limp. I'd expect she'll sleep until dawn. Plenty of time for me to help you get Damian to the boat, and get back before she wakes."

"Are you sure?" He was not asking about the timing.

"No," I said. "But I saw a stretcher in the shed."

So we carried him.

He nearly refused to go without his child. Only when I promised to guard her with my life did he agree, and even then he demanded to see her himself first. It took both of us to convince him that waking the child by moving her downstairs to say good-bye would put her in danger.

"Almost as much danger as the delay you're causing puts her in," Holmes finally pointed out. We carried him. Two and a half miles to the end of the bay near Stromness; only once did we have to flatten ourselves to the verge to avoid head-lamps. The dinghy was there, hidden among reeds, and was big enough for two. Holmes and I got Damian upright, and Holmes started to lead him to the small boat.

Damian shook him off and grabbed my hand. "You promise you'll protect my Estelle? Tell her that her mother and I have to be away, but we'll be together very soon? You promise?"

"I promise to do everything I can to make her safe and comfortable."

"And loved?"

"Yes. And loved."

Holmes helped him into the boat, wrapping the blankets around him. Then he came to stand beside me. The water surged and ebbed gently at our boots; the few lights of Stromness sparkled across the ever-shifting surface.

"Thank you," he said.

"You're going to find my services as nanny come expensive," I told him, the threat both playful and real. But baby-sitting was not what he had in mind.

"I knew you would persist," he said abruptly. "I knew that, were there evidence against Damian, you would find it."

"Holmes," I said, startled.

"Thank you for not forcing me to investigate my son."

"I . . . yes. Get him to a doctor."

"Soon."

"And stay in touch—through Mycroft."

"If he isn't also under arrest," he said wryly, climbing into the dinghy.

"I'd almost forgot. You don't suppose he is?"

"If he is, you can always reach me through *The Times* agony column." He sounded unworried about his brother's fate, and I agreed: Mycroft Holmes could look after himself.

"Holmes, don't—" I caught myself, and changed it to, "Just, take care." Too melodramatic, to say, *Don't make me tell the bees that their keeper has gone.*

And so it ended as it had begun: Holmes vanished into the night with his son, leaving me with his other responsibilities.

I waited on the shore until he had reached the off-lying fishing boat and raised its captain. I heard the sounds as they pulled Damian on board, and the noise of the engine reached me half a mile down the road; after that I moved at a fast jog, all the way to the burnt-out hotel. I could see lights at the Stones, as the police puzzled out what had taken place there, but they did not seem to have discovered the violated hotel.

I let myself in and went upstairs. The candle was burning low in its saucer. Estelle was still asleep, although I thought the sound of her breathing was less profoundly drugged. I crept forward and eased my arms into the warm bed-clothes, moving so cautiously one might have thought I was handling nitro-glycerine. She smelt of milk and almonds, and as I pulled the tangle of cotton and wool towards me, her breath caught. I froze. After a moment, she sighed, then nestled into my chest like a kitten in the sun.

An extraordinary sensation.

I stood slowly, and with exquisite care picked my way down the stairs to the inner room. There I reversed the process, letting her weight settle onto the pads where her father had rested earlier. Cautiously, I slipped my hands out from under her: Her breathing continued, uninterrupted, and I felt as if I had won some sort of a trophy.

I left the lamp burning, in case she woke, and returned upstairs to see what had been left behind.

I took anything that would identify Damian or Brothers, including Damian's sketch-book and passport. I put a few of Estelle's warm garments and an old doll into a pillow-case, then shut everything else that might shout *Child!* into her small hard-sided suitcase. I carried it out of the back door, weighted it with rocks, and hurled it far into the loch.

The night was clearing, the wind gentle: Holmes and his Thurso fisherman would have no problems crossing the strait. I walked to where I could see the Stones, and found them dark, which seemed odd. Perhaps rural police were less equipped with search-lights? Or less concerned about the dead, and satisfied with taking the body away and delaying an examination of the site until daylight?

I went inside, took some food from the hotel's pantries, and returned to where my young charge gently snored.

I chewed on dry biscuits and drank a bottled beer, studying her. She was, I saw, the three-and-a-half-year-old Damian had led us to believe, not the eight- or nine-year-old I had hypothesised: Reading or not, friends with an older child or not, that sleeping face had the soft and unformed features of a near-infant.

So it was no surprise, when she stirred and woke half an hour later, to feel myself looked upon by a pair of eerily familiar grey eyes, imperious as a newly hatched hawk.

They were Holmes' eyes. Estelle was Damian's child.

The grey gaze travelled around the room, registering the absence of her father and the man she knew as Hayden. Unafraid, she sat upright.

"Who are you?" Her voice that of a small child: The intelligence behind it was something more.

"I'm . . ." I smiled at the thought, and at her. "I suppose you could say that I'm your grandmother."

"Where's my Papa?"

"I'm afraid your Papa's hurt, Estelle. His own Papa came to help him, and is taking him to a doctor."

"My Mama hasn't come yet, has she?"

"I . . . no."

"Are you a friend of Mr Brothers?"

"No, I'm not."

"I don't like him very much."

"I can see why."

"His other name is Mr Hayden. He got angry, when I tried to colour in his book."

"Did he?"

"I thought it was a book for colouring," she explained. "My Papa has books for his colouring, and my Mama has books for her writing, and they don't mind when I colour in theirs, but Mr Brothers didn't want me to use his."

"It sounds reasonable—" I stopped, feeling a cold trickle up my spine. My God, how could I have overlooked it? "This book of Mr Brothers'. It had blank pages?"

"Some. It had writing, too, but I couldn't read it. I don't read cursive yet. And it had some of Papa's drawings."

The Book of Truth, Tolliver's other binding project. It hadn't been in London, it wasn't in his room here. Which could only mean that Brothers had it with him—but of course he did, along with the quill and the blotting sand. And even if he hadn't dared risk writing then and there, and been forced to bring some of the blood away in a flask, the book was the culmination of his ritual. He would carry it with him.

He would carry it always . . .

There had been blood, on Brothers' overcoat, where Damian shot him: That I had seen. Granted, the blood had been slightly to one side of the hole—surely that was because the garments shifted when he fell? And the relatively small amount of bleeding was because he'd died immediately the bullet entered his heart. Wasn't it?

Fifty blank pages, six drawings, two covers—heavy covers, knowing Tolliver's work. If his Book of Truth had been in Brothers' inner breast pocket—worn over his heart, as it were—when the bullet hit him, would it have been heavy enough to deflect a bullet upward, so it lodged in a shoulder rather than the heart?

I was on my feet before I realised I had moved. The child drew back in alarm; I tried to think. My impulse was to snatch her and sprint for the door, but I told myself that, if Brothers hadn't found her in the three hours since we had left him for dead, the chances were that I had a few more minutes. And I did have a gun.

"Honey, we have to leave," I told her. "Can you get dressed for me, and put on your shoes and your coat?"

I helped her slow fingers, stuffed the remaining biscuits in my pocket and turned off the light. I took her hand in my free one, and whispered, "We have to be very quiet. We're going out of this place and down the road a little, and after that we can talk again. All right?"

She said nothing, and it took me a moment to realise that she had responded by nodding: No, not older, just preternaturally clever. I squeezed her hand, and opened the door.

The hotel was nothing but shadow. Estelle tried her best, but her shoes made noise against the grit on the floor, and in a few steps I bent and picked her up. Which was better, but now she was breathing in my ear and I could hear nothing else.

I crept with her across the room. Brothers had used the back door, so I went to the front, putting her down to work the lock.

Once the door was open, I caught her up and ran: no following footsteps, no shout or motion behind us.

We made it to the road, and across, then up a small lane to a barn before at last I accepted that we were safe. I put the child down and sat beside her, my head dropping onto my knees as I caught my relieved breath.

After a minute, I felt a small hand touch my leg, and I wrapped my own around it.

"Shall I call you my Grandmama?" she asked.

I choked down a laugh. "Maybe you ought to just call me Mary, until we decide."

"Very well," she said, which made me laugh again.

"Mary?" she asked. "Where are we going?"

I lifted my head to the sky, and saw the stars.

The sensible thing would be to go to the police and trust them to accept my explanation. True, they would take Estelle away, and in the lack of other family they would put her into care, but they were not ogres. Surely they would return her to me, or to her father, as soon as things were settled. The sensible thing would be to send Mycroft a wire and hope that he was in a position to get me out of this.

But then, were I a sensible person, would I have been sitting on an Orcadian hillside at five in the morning with an unknown step-granddaughter's hand in mine? I looked at her, and squeezed her tiny, trusting hand.

"Estelle, how would you like to go up in an aeroplane?"

Post Script

Many days later, lodged in the hidden depths of Scotland, I read an out-of-date newspaper article concerning a farmer who lived beside the Stones of Stenness, wakened that Friday night by gunshots and the sight of flames amidst the stones. When he reached the spot, with shotgun and paraffin lamp to hand, he found only a broken lamp, the burnt edge of a blanket, and signs of a bloody struggle.

No sign of a hand-bound book written in blood; no knife crafted from a meteor's iron.

Police investigations the following day turned up no body, and no injured person had been seen by the doctor's surgery. The police were puzzled, and suggested that a youthful prank at the Stones had gone awry.

Some of us knew otherwise.

. . . to be continued.

Acknowledgments

This book owes much to the extraordinary willingness of a lot of people to put up with peculiar questions and offer expertise in exchange.

Anthony and Anna Tomasso, Clare Claydon and Win Westerhof, and Susan Rice, ASH, BSI, all tried to educate me about bees; where I resisted their tutoring, I apologize for the demands of the fictional process. Zoe Elkaim brought me books and researched a myriad of weird factoids. Glen Miranker, a most dependable gentleman, traded a donation to the Baker Street Irregulars for the chance to be turned into a broken reed of a Sussex beekeeper. Alice Wright did the same, permitting herself to be re-shaped into a Soho sculptress of questionable virtue in exchange for a donation to the Enoch Pratt library and Viva House.

John Mallinson, North West, and Burt Gabriel at the Hiller Air Museum; Francis King and Keith Jillings helped me get a 1924 Bristol Tourer into the air, on paper anyway. Cara Black nudged my French, Doug P. Lyle, MD gave me all kinds of problems when he corrected my forensic history, and Vicki Van Valkenburgh and Kathy Long helped keep my electronic identity in order.

As always, I owe the librarians of UCSC's McHenry Library a hive's-worth of blessings, for their boundless energy and creativity.

A portion of the proceeds from this book go to the beehive project of Heifer International. For details, see my website at www.LaurieRKing.com.

About the Author

Laurie R. King is the *New York Times* bestselling author of nine Mary Russell mysteries, five contemporary novels featuring Kate Martinelli, and the acclaimed novels *A Darker Place, Folly, Keeping Watch,* and *Touchstone*. She is one of only two novelists to win the Best First Crime Novel awards on both sides of the Atlantic, from MWA and CWA. She lives in northern California where she is at work on her next Russell and Holmes mystery.